The Citadel
of the Autarch

The Citadel
of the Autarch

VOLUME FOUR OF
THE BOOK OF THE NEW SUN

Gene Wolfe

Timescape Books
DISTRIBUTED BY SIMON AND SCHUSTER
NEW YORK

Copyright © 1983 by Gene Wolfe
A Timescape Book
Published by Pocket Books, a Simon & Schuster
Division of Gulf & Western Corporation
Simon & Schuster Building
Rockefeller Center
1230 Avenue of the Americas
New York, New York 10020
Use of the trademark TIMESCAPE is by exclusive license from Gregory
Benford, the trademark owner
Manufactured in the United States of America
10 9 8 7 6 5 4 3 2 1
Library of Congress Cataloging in Publication Data

Wolfe, Gene.
    The Citadel of the Autarch.

    (The Book of the new Sun ; v. 4)
    I. Title. II. Series: Wolfe, Gene.   Book of the
new Sun ; v. 4.
PS3573.052C5 1982   813'.54   82-5964
                                    AACR2

ISBN 0-671-45251-7

At two o'clock in the morning, if you open your window and listen,
You will hear the feet of the Wind that is going to call the sun.
And the trees in the shadow rustle and the trees in the moonlight glisten,
And though it is deep, dark night, you feel that the night is done.
        —Rudyard Kipling

The Citadel
of the Autarch

I

The Dead Soldier

I HAD NEVER seen war, or even talked of it at length with someone who had, but I was young and knew something of violence, and so believed that war would be no more than a new experience for me, as other things—the possession of authority in Thrax, say, or my escape from the House Absolute—had been new experiences.

War is not a new experience; it is a new world. Its inhabitants are more different from human beings than Famulimus and her friends. Its laws are new, and even its geography is new, because it is a geography in which insignificant hills and hollows are lifted to the importance of cities. Just as our familiar Urth holds such monstrosities as Erebus, Abaia, and Arioch, so the world of war is stalked by the monsters called battles, whose cells are individuals but who have a life and intelligence of their own, and whom one approaches through an ever-thickening array of portents.

One night I woke long before dawn. Everything seemed still, and I was afraid some enemy had come near, so that my mind had stirred at his malignancy. I rose and looked about. The hills were lost in the darkness. I was in a nest of long grass, a nest I had trampled flat for myself. Crickets sang.

Something caught my eye far to the north: a flash, I thought, of violet just on the horizon. I stared at the point from which it seemed to have come. Just as I had convinced myself that what I believed I had seen was no more than a fault of vision, perhaps some lingering effect of the drug I had been given in the hetman's house, there was a flare of magenta a trifle to the left of the point I had been staring at.

I continued to stand there for a watch or more, rewarded from time to time with these mysteries of light. At last, having satisfied myself that they were a great way off and came no nearer, and that they did not appear to change in frequency, coming on the average with each five hundredth beat of my heart, I lay down again. And because I was then thoroughly awake, I became aware that the ground was shaking, very slightly, beneath me.

When I woke again in the morning it had stopped. I watched the horizon diligently for some time as I walked along, but saw nothing disturbing.

It had been two days since I had eaten, and I was no longer hungry, though I was aware that I did not have my normal strength. Twice that day I came upon little houses falling to ruin, and I entered each to look for food. If anything had been left, it had been taken long before; even the rats were gone. The second house had a well, but some dead thing had been thrown down it long ago, and in any case there was no way to reach the stinking water. I went on, wishing for something to drink and also for a better staff than the succession of rotten sticks I had been using. I had learned when I had used *Terminus Est* as a staff in the mountains how much easier it is to walk with one.

About noon I came upon a path and followed it, and a short time afterward heard the sound of hoofs. I hid where I could look down the road; a moment later a rider crested the next hill and flashed past me. From the glimpse I had of him, he wore armor somewhat in the fashion of the commanders of Abdiesus's dimarchi, but his wind-stiffened cape was green instead of red and his helmet seemed to have a visor like the bill of a cap. Whoever he was, he was magnificently mounted: His destrier's mouth was bearded with foam and its sides drenched, yet it flew by as though the racing signal had dropped only an instant before.

Having encountered one rider on the path, I expected others. There were none. For a long while I walked in tranquillity, hearing the calls of birds and seeing many signs of game. Then (to my inexpressible delight) the path forded a young stream. I walked up a dozen strides to a spot where deeper, quieter water flowed over a bed of white gravel. Minnows skittered away from my boots—always a sign of good water—and it was still cold from the mountain peaks and sweet with the memory of snow. I drank and drank again, and then again, until I could hold no more, then took off my clothes and washed myself, cold though it was. When I had finished my bath and dressed and returned to the place where the path crossed the stream, I saw two pug marks on the other side, daintily close together, where the animal had crouched to drink. They overlay the hoofprints of the officer's mount, and each was as big as a dinner plate, with no claws showing beyond the soft pads of the toes. Old Midan, who had been my uncle's huntsman when I was the girl-child Thecla, had told me once that smilodons drink only after they have gorged themselves, and that when they have gorged and drunk they are not dangerous unless molested. I went on.

The path wound through a wooded valley, then up into a saddle between hills. When I was near the highest point, I noticed a tree two spans in diameter that had been torn in half (as it appeared) at about the height of my eyes. The ends of both the standing stump and the felled trunk were ragged, not at all like the smooth chipping of an ax. In the next two or three leagues I walked, there were several score like it. Judging from the lack of leaves, and in some cases of bark, on‹

the fallen parts, and the new shoots the stumps had put
forth, the damage had been done at least a year ago, and
perhaps longer.

At last the path joined a true road, something I had heard
of often, but never trodden except in decay. It was much like
the old road the uhlans had been blocking when I had become separated from Dr. Talos, Baldanders, Jolenta, and
Dorcas when we left Nessus, but I was unprepared for the
cloud of dust that hung about it. No grass grew upon it,
though it was wider than most city streets.

I had no choice except to follow it; the trees about it were
thick set, and the spaces between them choked with brush.
At first I was afraid, remembering the burning lances of the
uhlans; still, it seemed probable that the law that prohibited
the use of roads no longer had force here, or this one would
not have seen as much traffic as it clearly had; and when, a
short time later, I heard voices and the sound of many marching feet behind me, I only moved a pace or two into the trees
and watched openly while the column passed.

An officer came first, riding a fine, champing blue whose
fangs had been left long and set with turquoise to match his
bardings and the hilt of his owner's estoc. The men who
followed him on foot were antepilani of the heavy infantry, big shouldered and narrow waisted, with sun-bronzed,
expressionless faces. They carried three-pointed korsekes,
demilunes, and heavy-headed voulges. This mixture of arma-
ments, as well as certain discrepancies among their badges
and accouterments, led me to believe that their mora was
made up of the remains of earlier formations. If that were so,
the fighting they must have seen had left them phlegmatic.
They swung along, four thousand or so in all, without excitement, reluctance, or any sign of fatigue, careless in their bearing but not slovenly, and seemed to keep step without
thought or effort.

Wagons drawn by grunting, trumpeting trilophodons followed. I edged nearer the road as they came, for much of

the baggage they carried was clearly food; but there were mounted men among the wagons, and one called to me, asking what unit I belonged to, then ordering me to him. I fled instead, and though I was fairly sure he could not ride among the trees and would not abandon his destrier to pursue me on foot, I ran until I was winded.

When I stopped at last, it was in a silent glade where greenish sunlight filtered through the leaves of spindly trees. Moss covered the ground so thickly that I felt as if I walked upon the dense carpet of the hidden picture-room where I had encountered the Master of the House Absolute. For a while I rested my back against one of the thin trunks, listening. There came no sound but the gasping of my own breath and the tidal roar of my blood in my ears.

In time I became aware of a third note: the faint buzzing of a fly. I wiped my streaming face with the edge of my guild cloak. That cloak was sadly worn and faded now, and I was suddenly conscious that it was the same one Master Gurloes had draped about my shoulders when I became a journeyman, and that I was likely to die in it. The sweat it had absorbed felt cold as dew, and the air was heavy with the odor of damp earth.

The buzzing of the fly ceased, then resumed—perhaps a trifle more insistently, perhaps merely seeming so because I had my breath again. Absently, I looked for it and saw it dart through a shaft of sunlight a few paces off, then settle on a brown object projecting from behind one of the thronging trees.

A boot.

I had no weapon whatsoever. Ordinarily I would not have been much afraid of confronting a single man with my hands alone, especially in such a place, where it would have been impossible to swing a sword; but I knew much of my strength was gone, and I was discovering that fasting destroys a part of one's courage as well—or perhaps it is only that it consumes a part of it, leaving less for other exigencies.

However that might be, I walked warily, sidelong and silently, until I saw him. He layed sprawled, with one leg crumpled under him and the other extended. A falchion had fallen near his right hand, its leather lanyard still about his wrist. His simple barbute had dropped from his head and rolled a step away. The fly crawled up his boot until it reached the bare flesh just below the knee, then flew again, with the noise of a tiny saw.

I knew, of course, that he was dead, and even as I felt relief my sense of isolation came rushing back, though I had not realized that it had departed. Taking him by the shoulder, I turned him over. His body had not yet swelled, but the smell of death had come, however faint. His face had softened like a mask of wax set before a fire; there was no telling now with what expression he had died. He had been young and blond—one of those handsome, square faces. I looked for a wound but found none.

The straps of his pack had been drawn so tight that I could neither pull it off nor even loosen the fastenings. In the end I took the coutel from his belt and cut them, then drove the point into a tree. A blanket, a scrap of paper, a fire-blackened pan with a socket handle, two pairs of rough stockings (very welcome), and, best of all, an onion and a half loaf of dark bread wrapped in a clean rag, and five strips of dried meat and a lump of cheese wrapped in another.

I ate the bread and cheese first, forcing myself, when I found I could not eat slowly, to rise after every third bite and walk up and down. The bread helped by requiring a great deal of chewing; it tasted precisely like the hard bread we used to feed our clients in the Matachin Tower, bread I had stolen, more from mischief than from hunger, once or twice. The cheese was dry and smelly and salty, but excellent all the same; I thought that I had never tasted such cheese before, and I know I have never tasted any since. I might have been eating life. It made me thirsty, and I learned how well an onion quenches thirst by stimulating the salivary glands.

By the time I reached the meat, which was heavily salted too, I was satiated enough to begin debating whether I should reserve it against the night, and I decided to eat one piece and save the other four.

The air had been still since early that morning, but now a faint breeze blew, cooling my cheeks, stirring the leaves, and catching the paper I had pulled from the dead soldier's pack and sending it rattling across the moss to lodge against a tree. Still chewing and swallowing, I pursued it and picked it up. It was a letter—I assume one he had not had the opportunity to send, or perhaps to complete. His hand had been angular, and smaller than I would have anticipated, though it may be that its smallness only resulted from his wish to crowd many words onto the small sheet, which appeared to have been the last he possessed.

O my beloved, we are a hundred leagues north of the place from which I last wrote you, having come by hard marches. We have enough to eat and are warm by day, though sometimes cold at night. Makar, of whom I told you, has fallen sick and was permitted to remain behind. A great many others claimed then to be ill and were made to march before us without weapons and carrying double packs and under guard. In all this time we have seen no sign of the Ascians, and we are told by the lochage that they are still several days' march off. The seditionists killed sentries for three nights, until we put three men on each post and kept patrols moving outside our perimeter. I was assigned to one of these patrols on the first night and found it very discomforting, since I feared one of my comrades would cut me down in the dark. My time was spent tripping over roots and listening to the singing at the fire—

> *"Tomorrow night's sleep*
> *Will be on stained ground,*
> *So tonight all drink deep,*
> *Let the friend-cup go round.*
> *Friend, I hope when they shoot,*

Every shot will fly wide,
And I wish you good loot,
And myself at your side.
Let the friend-cup go round,
For we'll sleep on stained ground."

Naturally, we saw no one. The seditionists call themselves the Vodalarii after their leader and are said to be picked fighters. And well paid, receiving support from the Ascians. . . .

The Living Soldier

I PUT ASIDE the half-read letter and stared at the man who had written it. Death's shot had not flown wide for him; now he stared at the sun with lusterless blue eyes, one nearly winking, the other fully open.

Long before that moment I should have recalled the Claw, but I had not. Or perhaps I had only suppressed the thought in my eagerness to steal the rations in the dead man's pack, never reasoning that I might have trusted him to share his food with the rescuer who had recalled him from death. Now, at the mention of Vodalus and his followers (who I felt would surely assist me if only I were able to find them), I remembered it at once and took it out. It seemed to sparkle in the summer sunlight, brighter indeed than I had ever seen it without its sapphire case. I touched him with it, then, urged by I cannot say what impulse, put it into his mouth.

When this, too, effected nothing, I took it between my thumb and first finger and pushed its point into the soft skin of his forehead. He did not move or breathe, but a drop of blood, fresh and sticky as that of a living man, welled forth and stained my fingers.

I withdrew them, wiped my hand with some leaves, and

would have gone back to his letter if I had not thought I heard a stick snap some distance away. For a moment I could not choose among hiding, fleeing, and fighting; but there was little chance of successfully doing the first, and I had already had enough of the second. I picked up the dead man's falchion, wrapped myself in my cloak, and stood waiting.

No one came—or at least, no one visible to me. The wind made a slight sighing among the treetops. The fly seemed to have gone. Perhaps I had heard nothing more than a deer bounding through the shadows. I had traveled so far without any weapon that would permit me to hunt that I had almost forgotten the possibility. Now I examined the falchion and found myself wishing it had been a bow.

Something behind me stirred, and I turned to look.

It was the soldier. A tremor seemed to have seized him—if I had not seen his corpse, I would have thought him dying. His hands shook, and there was a rattling in his throat. I bent and touched his face; it was as cold as ever, and I had the impulsive need to kindle a fire.

There had been no fire-making gear in his pack, but I knew every soldier must carry such things. I searched his pockets and found a few aes, a hanging dial with which to tell time, and a flint and striking bar. Tinder lay in plenty under the trees—the danger was that I might set fire to all of it. I swept a space clear with my hands, piling the sweepings in the center, set them ablaze, then gathered a few rotten boughs, broke them, and laid them on the fire.

Its light was brighter than I had expected—day was almost done, and it would soon be dark. I looked at the dead man. His hands no longer shook; he was silent. The flesh of his face seemed warmer. But that was, no doubt, no more than the heat of the fire. The spot of blood on his forehead had nearly dried, yet it seemed to catch the light of the dying sun, shining as some crimson gem might, some pigeon's blood ruby spilled from a treasure hoard. Though our fire gave little smoke, what there was seemed to me fragrant as incense, and like incense it rose straight until it was lost in the gathering dark, suggesting something I could not quite recall. I shook myself and found more wood, breaking and stacking it until I had a pile I thought large enough to last the night.

Evenings were not nearly so cold here in Orithyia as they had been in the mountains, or even in the region about Lake Diuturna, so that although I recalled the blanket I had found in the dead man's pack, I felt no need of it. My task had warmed me, the food I had eaten had invigorated me, and for a time I strode up and down in the twilight, brandishing the falchion when such warlike gestures accorded with my thoughts but taking care to keep the fire between the dead man and myself.

My memories have always appeared with the intensity, almost, of hallucinations, as I have said often in this chronicle. That night I felt I might lose myself forever in them, making of my life a loop instead of a line; and for once I did not resist the temptation but reveled in it. Everything I have described to you came crowding back to me, and a thousand things more. I saw Eata's face and his freckled hand when he sought to slip between the bars of the gate of the necropolis, and the storm I had once watched impaled on the towers of the Citadel, writhing and lashing out with its lightnings; I felt its rain, colder and fresher far than the morning cup in our refectory, trickle down my face. Dorcas's voice whispered in my ears: "Sitting in a window . . . trays and a rood. What will you do, summon up some Erinys to destroy me?"

Yes. Yes, indeed, I would have if I could. If I had been Hethor, I would have drawn them from some horror behind the world, birds with the heads of hags and the tongues of vipers. At my order they would have threshed the forests like wheat and beaten cities flat with their great wings . . . and yet, if I could, I would have appeared at the final moment to save her—not walking coldly off afterward in the way we all wish to do when, as children, we imagine ourselves rescuing and humiliating the loved one who has given us some supposed slight, but raising her in my arms.

Then for the first time, I think, I knew how terrible it must have been for her, who had been hardly more than a child when death had come, and who had been dead so long, to have been called back.

And thinking of that, I remembered the dead soldier whose food I had eaten and whose sword I held, and I paused and listened to hear if he drew breath or stirred. Yet I was so lost in the worlds of memory that it seemed to me the soft forest earth under my feet had come from the grave Hildegrin the Badger had despoiled for Vodalus, and the whisper of the leaves was the soughing of the cypresses in our necropolis and the rustle of the purple-flowered roses, and that I listened, listened in vain for breath from the dead woman Vodalus had lifted with the rope beneath her arms, lifted in her white shroud.

At last, the croaking of a nightjar brought me to myself. I seemed to see the soldier's white face staring at me, and went around the fire and searched until I found the blanket, and draped his corpse with it.

Dorcas belonged, as I now realized, to that vast group of women (which may, indeed, include all women) who betray us—and to that special type who betray us not for some present rival but for their own pasts. Just as Morwenna, whom I had executed at Saltus, must have poisoned her husband and her child because she recalled a time in which she was free and, perhaps, virginal, so Dorcas had left me because I had not existed (had, as she must unconsciously have seen it, failed to exist) in that time before her doom fell upon her.

(For me, also, that is the golden time. I think I must have treasured the memory of the crude, kindly boy who fetched books and blossoms to my cell largely because I knew him to be the last love before the doom, the doom that was not, as I learned in that prison, the moment at which the tapestry was cast over me to muffle my outcry, nor my arrival at the Old Citadel in Nessus, nor the slam of the cell door behind me, nor even the moment when, bathed in such a light as never shines on Urth, I felt my body rise in rebellion against me—but that instant in which I drew the blade of the greasy paring knife he had brought, cold and mercifully sharp, across my own neck. Possibly we all come to such a time, and it is the will of the Caitanya that each damn herself for what she has done. Yet can we be hated so much? Can we be hated at all? Not when I can still remember his kisses on my breasts, given, not breathing to taste the perfume of my flesh—as Aphrodisius's were, and that young man's, the nephew of the chiliarch of the Companions—but as though he were truly hungry for my flesh. Was something watching us? He has eaten of me now. Awakened by the memory, I lift my hand and run fingers through his hair.)

I slept late, wrapped in my cloak. There is a payment made by Nature to those who undergo hardships; it is that the lesser ones, at which people whose lives have been easier would complain, seem almost comfortable. Several times before I actually rose, I woke and congratulated myself to think how easily I had spent this night compared to those I had endured in the mountains.

At last the sunlight and the singing birds brought me to myself. On the other side of our dead fire, the soldier shifted and, I think, murmured something. I sat up. He had thrown the blanket aside and lay with his face to the sky. It was a pale face with sunken cheeks; there were dark shadows beneath the eyes and deeply cut lines running from the mouth; but it was a living face. The eyes were truly closed, and breath sighed in the nostrils.

For a moment I was tempted to run before he woke. I had his falchion still—I started to replace it, then took it back for fear he would attack me with it. His coutel still protruded from the tree, making me think of Agia's crooked dagger in the shutter of Casdoe's house. I thrust it back into the sheath at his belt, mostly because I was ashamed to think that I, armed with a sword, should fear any man with a knife.

His eyelids fluttered, and I drew away, remembering a time when Dorcas had been frightened to find me bending over her when she woke. So that I should not appear a dark figure, I pushed back my cloak to show my bare arms and chest, browned now by so many days' suns. I could hear the sighing of his breath; and when it changed from sleep to waking, it seemed to me a thing almost as miraculous as the passage from death to life.

Empty-eyed as a child, he sat up and looked about him. His lips moved, but only sound without sense came forth. I spoke to him, trying to make my tone friendly. He listened but did not seem to understand, and I recalled how dazed the uhlan had been, whom I had revived on the road to the House Absolute.

I wished that I had water to offer him, but I had none. I drew out a piece of the salt meat I had taken from his pack, broke it into two, and shared that with him instead.

He chewed and seemed to feel a little better. "Stand up," I said. "We must find something to drink." He took my hand and allowed me to pull him erect, but he could hardly stand. His eyes, which had been so calm at first, grew wilder as they became more alert. I had the feeling that he feared the trees might rush upon us like a pride of lions, yet he did not draw his coutel or attempt to reclaim the falchion.

When we had taken three or four steps, he tottered and nearly fell. I let him lean upon my arm, and together we made our way through the wood to the road.

III

Through Dust

I DID NOT KNOW whether we should turn north or south. Somewhere to the north lay the Ascian army, and it was possible that if we came too near the lines we would be caught up in some swift maneuver. Yet the farther south we went, the less likely we were to find anyone who would help us, and the more probable it became that we would be arrested as deserters. In the end I turned northward; no doubt I acted largely from habit, and I am still not sure if I did well or ill.

The dew had already dried upon the road, and its dusty surface showed no footprints. To either side, for three paces or more, the vegetation was a uniform gray. We soon passed out of the forest. The road wound down a hill and over a bridge that vaulted a small river at the bottom of a rock-strewn valley.

We left it there and went down to the water to drink and bathe our faces. I had not shaved since I had turned my back on Lake Diuturna, and though I had noticed none when I took the flint and striker from the soldier's pocket, I ventured to ask him if he carried a razor.

I mention this trifling incident because it was the first

thing I said to him that he seemed to comprehend. He nodded, then reaching under his hauberk produced one of those little blades that country people use, razors their smiths grind from the halves of worn oxshoes. I touched it up on the broken whetstone I still carried and stropped it on the leg of my boot, then asked if he had soap. If he did, he failed to understand me, and after a moment he seated himself on a rock from which he could stare into the water, reminding me very much of Dorcas. I longed to question him about the fields of Death, to learn all that he remembered of that time that is, perhaps, dark only to us. Instead, I washed my face in the cold river water and scraped my cheeks and chin as well as I could. When I sheathed his razor and tried to return it to him, he did not seem to know what to do with it, so I kept it.

For most of the rest of that day we walked. Several times we were stopped and questioned; more often we stopped others and questioned them. Gradually I developed an elaborate lie: I was the lictor of a civil judge who accompanied the Autarch; we had encountered this soldier on the road, and my master had ordered me to see that he was cared for; he could not speak, and so I did not know what unit he was from. That last was true enough.

We crossed other roads and sometimes followed them. Twice we reached great camps where tens of thousands of soldiers lived in cities of tents. At each, those who tended the sick told me that though they would have bandaged my companion's wounds had he been bleeding, they could not take responsibility for him as he was. By the time I spoke to the second, I no longer asked the location of the Pelerines but only to be directed to a place where we might find shelter. It was nearly night.

"There is a lazaret three leagues from here that may take you in." My informant looked from one of us to the other, and seemed to have almost as much sympathy for me as for the soldier, who stood mute and dazed. "Go west and north until you see a road to the right that passes between two big trees. It is about half as wide as the one you will have been following. Go down that. Are you armed?"

I shook my head; I had put the soldier's falchion back in his scabbard. "I was forced to leave my sword behind with my master's servants—I couldn't have carried it and managed this man too."

"Then you must beware of beasts. It would be better if you had something that would shoot, but I can't give you anything."

I turned to go, but he stopped me with a hand on my shoulder.

"Leave him if you're attacked," he said. "And if you're forced to leave him, don't feel too badly about it. I've seen cases like his before. He's not likely to recover."

"He has already recovered," I told him.

Although this man would not allow us to stay or lend me a weapon, he did provide us with something to eat; and I departed with more cheerfulness than I had felt for some time. We were in a valley where the western hills had risen to obscure the sun a watch or more before. As I walked along beside the soldier, I discovered that it was no longer necessary for me to hold his arm. I could release it, and he continued to walk at my side like any friend. His face was not really like Jonas's, which had been long and narrow, but once when I saw it sidelong I caught something there so reminiscent of Jonas that I felt almost that I had seen a ghost.

The gray road was greenish-white in the moonlight; the trees and brush to either side looked black. As we strode along I began to talk. Partially, I admit, it was from sheer loneliness; yet I had other reasons as well. Unquestionably there are beasts, like the alzabo, who attack men as foxes do fowls, but I have been told that there are many others who will flee if they are warned in time of human presence. Then too, I thought that if I spoke to the soldier as I might have to any other man, any ill-intentioned persons who heard us would be less apt to guess how unlikely he was to resist them.

"Do you recall last night?" I began. "You slept very heavily."

There was no reply.

"Perhaps I never told you this, but I have the facility of recalling everything. I can't always lay hands on it when I want, but it is always there; some memories, you know, are like escaped clients wandering through the oubliette. One may not be able to produce them on demand, but they are always there, they cannot get away.

"Although, come to think of it, that isn't entirely true. The fourth and lowest level of our oubliette has been abandoned—there are never enough clients to fill the topmost three anyway, and perhaps eventually Master Gurloes will give up the third. We only keep it open now for the mad ones that no official ever comes to see. If they were in one of the higher levels, their noise would disturb the others. Not all of them are noisy, of course. Some are as quiet as yourself."

Again there was no reply. In the moonlight I could not tell if he was paying attention to me, but remembering the razor I persevered.

"I went that way myself once. Through the fourth level, I mean. I used to have a dog, and I kept him there, but he ran away. I went after him and found a tunnel that left our oubliette. Eventually I crawled out of a broken pedestal in a place called the Atrium of Time. It was full of sundials. I met a young woman there who was really more beautiful than anyone I've ever seen since—more lovely even than Jolenta, I think, though not in the same way."

The soldier said nothing, yet now something told me he heard me; perhaps it was no more than a slight movement of his head seen from a corner of my eye.

"Her name was Valeria, and I think she was younger than I, although she seemed older. She had dark, curling hair, like

Thecla's, but her eyes were dark too. Thecla's were violet. She had the finest skin I have ever seen, like rich milk mixed with the juice of pomegranates and strawberries.

"But I didn't set out to talk about Valeria, but about Dorcas. Dorcas is lovely too, though she is very thin, almost like a child. Her face is a peri's, and her complexion is flecked with freckles like bits of gold. Her hair was long before she cut it; she always wore flowers there."

I paused again. I had continued to talk of women because that seemed to have caught his attention. Now I could not say if he were still listening or not.

"Before I left Thrax I went to see Dorcas. It was in her room, in an inn called the Duck's Nest. She was in bed and naked, but she kept the sheet over herself, just as if we had never slept together—we who had walked and ridden so far, camping in places where no voice had been heard since the land was called up from the sea, and climbing hills where no feet had ever walked but the sun's. She was leaving me and I her, and neither of us really wished it otherwise, though at the last she was afraid and asked me to come with her after all.

"She said she thought the Claw had the same power over time that Father Inire's mirrors are said to have over distance. I didn't think much of the remark then—I'm not really a very intelligent man, I suppose, not a philosopher at all—but now I find it interesting. She told me, 'When you brought the uhlan back to life it was because the Claw twisted time for him to the point at which he still lived. When you half-healed your friend's wounds, it was because it bent the moment to one when they would be nearly healed.' Don't you think that's interesting? A little while after I pricked your forehead with the Claw, you made a strange sound. I think it may have been your death rattle."

I waited. The soldier did not speak, but quite unexpectedly I felt his hand on my shoulder. I had been talking almost flippantly; his touch brought home to me the seriousness of what I had been saying. If it were true—or even some trifling approximation to the truth—then I had toyed with powers I understood no better than Casdoe's son, whom I had tried to make my own, would have understood the giant ring that took his life.

"No wonder then that you're dazed. It must be a terrible thing to move backward in time, and still more terrible to pass backward through death. I was about to say that it would be like being born again; but it would be much worse than that, I think, because an infant lives already in his mother's womb." I hesitated. "I . . . Thecla, I mean . . . never bore a child."

Perhaps only because I had been thinking of his confusion, I found I was confused myself, so that I scarcely knew who I was. At last I said lamely, "You must excuse me. When I'm tired, and sometimes when I'm near sleep, I come near to becoming someone else." (For whatever reason, his grip on my shoulder tightened when I said that.) "It's a long story that has nothing to do with you. I wanted to say that in the Atrium of Time, the breaking of the pedestal had tilted the dials so their gnomons no longer pointed true, and I have heard that when that happens, the watches of day stop, or run backward for some part of each day. You carry a pocket dial, so you know that for it to tell time truly you must direct its gnomon toward the sun. The sun remains stationary while Urth dances about him, and it is by her dancing that we know the time, just as a deaf man might still beat out the rhythm of a tarantella by observing the swaying of the dancers. But what if the sun himself were to dance? Then, too, the march of the moments might become a retreat.

"I don't know if you believe in the New Sun—I'm not sure I ever have. But if he will exist, he will be the Conciliator come again, and thus *Conciliator* and *New Sun* are only two names for the same individual, and we may ask why that individual should be called the New Sun. What do you think? Might it not be for this power to move time?"

Now I felt indeed that time itself had stopped. Around us the trees rose dark and silent; night had freshened the air. I could think of nothing more to say, and I was ashamed to talk nonsense, because I felt somehow that the soldier had been listening attentively to all I had said. Before us I saw two pines far thicker through their trunks than the others lining the road, and a pale path of white and green that threaded its way between them. "There!" I exclaimed.

But when we reached them, I had to halt the soldier with my hands and turn him by the shoulders before he followed me. I noticed a dark splatter in the dust and bent to touch it.

It was clotted blood. "We are on the right road," I told him. "They have been bringing the wounded here."

Fever

I CANNOT SAY how far we walked, or how far worn the night was before we reached our destination. I know that I began to stumble some time after we turned aside from the main road, and that it became a sort of disease to me; just as some sick men cannot stop coughing and others cannot keep their hands from shaking, so I tripped, and a few steps farther on tripped again, and then again. Unless I thought of nothing else, the toe of my left boot caught at my right heel, and I could not concentrate my mind—my thoughts ran off with every step I took.

Fireflies glimmered in the trees to either side of the path, and for a long time I supposed that the lights ahead of us were only more such insects and did not hurry my pace. Then, very suddenly as it seemed to me, we were beneath some shadowy roof where men and women with yellow lamps moved up and down between long rows of shrouded cots. A woman in clothes I supposed were black took charge of us and led us to another place where there were chairs of leather and horn, and a fire burned in a brazier. There I saw that her gown was scarlet, and she wore a scarlet hood, and for a moment I thought that she was Cyriaca.

"Your friend is very ill, isn't he?" she said. "Do you know what is the matter with him?"

And the soldier shook his head and answered, "No. I'm not even sure who he is."

I was too stunned to speak. She took my hand, then released it and took the soldier's. "He has a fever. So do you. Now that the heat of summer is come, we see more disease each day. You should have boiled your water and kept yourselves as clean of lice as you could."

She turned to me. "You have a great many shallow cuts too, and some them are infected. Rock shards?"

I managed to say, "I'm not the one who is ill. I brought my friend here."

"You are both ill, and I suspect you brought each other. I doubt that either of you would have reached us without the other. Was it rock shards? Some weapon of the enemy's?"

"Rock shards, yes. A weapon of a friend's."

"That is the worst thing, I am told—to be fired upon by your own side. But the fever is the chief concern." She hesitated, looking from the soldier to me and back. "I'd like to put you both in bed now, but you'll have to go to the bath first."

She clapped her hands to summon a burly man with a shaven head. He took our arms and began to lead us away, then stopped and picked me up, carrying me as I had once carried little Severian. In a few moments we were naked and sitting in a pool of water heated by stones. The burly man splashed more water over us, then made us get out one at a time so he could crop our hair with a pair of shears. After that we were left to soak awhile.

"You can speak now," I said to the soldier.

I saw him nod in the lamplight.

"Why didn't you, then, when we were coming here?"

He hesitated, and his shoulders moved a trifle. "I was thinking of many things, and you didn't talk yourself. You seemed so tired. Once I asked if we shouldn't stop, but you didn't answer."

I said, "It seemed to me otherwise, but perhaps we are both correct. Do you recall what happened to you before you met me?"

Again there was a pause. "I don't even remember meeting you. We were walking down a dark path, and you were beside me."

"And before that?"

"I don't know. Music, perhaps, and walking a long way. In sunshine at first but later through the dark."

"That walking was while you were with me," I said. "Don't you recall anything else?"

"Flying through the dark. Yes, I was with you, and we came to a place where the sun hung just above our heads. There was a light before us, but when I stepped into it, it became a kind of darkness."

I nodded. "You weren't wholly rational, you see. On a warm day it can seem that the sun's just overhead, and when it is down behind the mountains it seems the light becomes darkness. Do you recall your name?"

At that he thought for several moments, and at last smiled ruefully. "I lost it somewhere along the way. That's what the jaguar said, who had promised to guide the goat."

The burly man with the shaven head had come back without either of us noticing. He helped me out of the pool and gave me a towel with which to dry myself, a robe to wear, and a canvas sack containing my possessions, which now smelled strongly of the smoke of fumigation. A day earlier it would have tormented me nearly to frenzy to have the Claw out of my possession for an instant. That night I had hardly realized it was gone until it was returned to me, and I did not verify that it had indeed been returned until I lay on one of the cots under a veil of netting. The Claw shone in my hand

then, softly as the moon; and it was shaped as the moon
sometimes is. I smiled to think that its flooding light of pale
green is the reflection of the sun.

On the first night I slept in Saltus, I had awakened thinking I was in the apprentices' dormitory in our tower. Now I
had the same experience in reverse: I slept and found in sleep
that the shadowy lazaret with its silent figures and moving
lamps had been no more than a hallucination of the day.

I sat up and looked around. I felt well—better, in fact, than
I had ever felt before; but I was warm. I seemed to glow from
within. Roche was sleeping on his side, his red hair tousled
and his mouth slightly open, his face relaxed and boyish without the energy of his mind behind it. Through the port I
could see snow drifts in the Old Court, new-fallen snow that
showed no tracks of men or their animals; but it occurred to
me that in the necropolis there would be hundreds of footprints already as the small creatures who found shelter there,
the pets and the playmates of the dead, came out to search
for food and to disport themselves in the new landscape Nature had bestowed on them. I dressed quickly and silently,
holding my finger to my own lips when one of the other
apprentices stirred, and hurried down the steep stair that
wound through the center of the tower.

It seemed longer than usual, and I found I had difficulty in
going from step to step. We are always aware of the hin-
drance of gravity when we climb stairs, but we take for
granted the assistance it gives us when we descend. Now that
assistance had been withdrawn, or nearly so. I had to force
each foot down, but do it in a way that prevented it from
sending me shooting up when it struck the step, as it would
have if I had stamped. In that uncanny way we know things
in dreams, I understood that all the towers of the Citadel
had risen at last and were on their voyage beyond the circle
of Dis. I felt happy in the knowledge, but I still desired to go
into the necropolis and track the coatis and foxes. I was

hurrying down as fast as I could when I heard a groan. The stairway no longer descended as it should but led into a cabin, just as the stairs in Baldanders's castle had stretched down the walls of its chambers.

This was Master Malrubius's sickroom. Masters are entitled to spacious quarters; still, this was larger by far than the actual cabin had been. There were two ports just as I remembered, but they were enormous—the eyes of Mount Typhon. Master Malrubius's bed was very large, yet it seemed lost in the immensity of the room. Two figures bent over him. Though their clothing was dark, it struck me that it was not the fuligin of the guild. I went to them, and when I was so near I could hear the sick man's labored breathing, they straightened up and turned to look at me. They were the Cumaean and her acolyte Merryn, the witches we had met atop the tomb in the ruined stone town.

"Ah, sister, you have come at last," Merryn said.

As she spoke, I realized that I was not, as I had thought, the apprentice Severian. I was Thecla as she had been when she was his height, which is to say at about the age of thirteen or fourteen. I felt an intense embarrassment—not because of my girl's body or because I was wearing masculine clothes (which indeed I rather enjoyed) but because I had been unaware of it previously. I also felt that Merryn's words had been an act of magic—that both Severian and I had been present before, and that she had by some means driven him into the background. The Cumaean kissed me on the forehead, and when the kiss was over wiped blood from her lips. Although she did not speak, I knew this was a signal that I had in some sense become the soldier too.

"When we sleep," Merryn told me, "we move from temporality to eternity."

"When we wake," the Cumaean whispered, "we lose the facility to see beyond the present moment."

"She never wakes," Merryn boasted.

Master Malrubius stirred and groaned, and the Cumaean

took a carafe of water from the table by his bed and poured a little into a tumbler. When she set down the carafe again, something living stirred in it. I, for some reason, thought it the undine; I drew back, but it was Hethor, no higher than my hand, his gray, stubbled face pressed against the glass.

I heard his voice as one might hear the squeaking of mice: "Sometimes driven aground by the photon storms, by the swirling of the galaxies, clockwise and counterclockwise, ticking with light down the dark sea-corridors lined with our silver sails, our demon-haunted mirror sails, our hundred-league masts as fine as threads, as fine as silver needles sewing the threads of starlight, embroidering the stars on black velvet, wet with the winds of Time that goes racing by. The bone in her teeth! The spume, the flying spume of Time, cast up on these beaches where old sailors can no longer keep their bones from the restless, the unwearied universe. Where has she gone? My lady, the mate of my soul? Gone across the running tides of Aquarius, of Pisces, of Aries. Gone. Gone in her little boat, her nipples pressed against the black velvet lid, gone, sailing away forever from the star-washed shores, the dry shoals of the habitable worlds. She is her own ship, she is the figurehead of her own ship, and the captain. Bosun, Bosun, put out the launch! Sailmaker, make a sail! She has left us behind. We have left her behind. She is in the past we never knew and the future we will not see. Put out more sail, Captain, for the universe is leaving us behind. . . ."

There was a bell on the table beside the carafe. Merryn rang it as though to overpower Hethor's voice, and when Master Malrubius had moistened his lips with the tumbler, she took it from the Cumaean, flung what remained of its water on the floor, and inverted it over the neck of the carafe. Hethor was silenced, but the water spread over the floor, bubbling as though fed by a hidden spring. It was icy cold. I thought vaguely that my governess would be angry because my shoes were wet.

A maid was coming in answer to the ring—Thecla's maid,

whose flayed leg I had inspected the day after I had saved
Vodalus. She was younger, as young as she must have been
when Thecla was actually a girl, but her leg had been flayed
already and ran with blood. "I am so sorry," I said. "I am so
sorry, Hunna. I didn't do it—it was Master Gurloes, and some
journeymen."

Master Malrubius sat up in bed, and for the first time I
observed that his bed was in actuality a woman's hand, with
fingers longer than my arm and nails like talons. "You're
well!" he said, as though I were the one who had been dying.
"Or nearly well, at least." The fingers of the hand began to
close upon him, but he leaped from the bed and into water
that was now knee high to stand beside me.

A dog—my old dog Triskele—had apparently been hiding
beneath the bed, or perhaps only lying on the farther side of
it, out of sight. Now he came to us, splashing the water with
his single forepaw as he drove his broad chest through it and
barking joyously. Master Malrubius took my right hand and
the Cumaean my left; together they led me to one of the
great eyes of the mountain.

I saw the view I had seen when Typhon had led me there:
The world rolled out like a carpet and visible in its entirety.
This time it was more magnificent by far. The sun was behind us; its beams seemed to have multiplied their strength.
Shadows were alchemized to gold, and every green thing grew
darker and stronger as I looked. I could see the grain ripening
in the fields and even the myriad fish of the sea doubling and
redoubling with the increase of the tiny surface plants that
sustained them. Water from the room behind us poured
from the eye and, catching the light, fell in a rainbow.

Then I woke.

While I slept, someone had wrapped me in sheets packed
with snow. (I learned later that it was brought down from the
mountaintops by sure-footed sumpters.) Shivering, I longed
to return to my dream, though I was already half-aware of

the immense distance that separated us. The bitter taste of medicine was in my mouth, the stretched canvas felt as hard as a floor beneath me, and scarlet-clad Pelerines with lamps moved to and fro, tending men and women who groaned in the dark.

V

The Lazaret

I DO NOT BELIEVE I really slept again that night, though I may have dozed. When dawn came, the snow had melted. Two Pelerines took the sheets away, gave me a towel with which to dry myself, and brought dry bedding. I wanted to give the Claw to them then—my possessions were in the bag under my cot—but the moment seemed inappropriate. I lay down instead, and now that it was daylight, slept.

I woke again about noon. The lazaret was as quiet as it ever became; somewhere far off two men were talking and another cried out, but their voices only emphasized the stillness. I sat up and looked around, hoping to see the soldier. On my right lay a man whose close-cropped scalp made me think at first that he was one of the slaves of the Pelerines. I called to him, but when he turned his head to look at me, I saw I had been mistaken.

His eyes were emptier than any human eyes I had ever seen, and they seemed to watch spirits invisible to me. "Glory to the Group of Seventeen," he said.

"Good morning. Do you know anything about the way this place is run?"

A shadow appeared to cross his face, and I sensed that my

question had somehow made him suspicious. He answered, "All endeavors are conducted well or ill precisely in so far as they conform to Correct Thought."

"Another man was brought in at the same time I was. I'd like to talk to him. He's a friend of mine, more or less."

"Those who do the will of the populace are friends, though we have never spoken to them. Those who do not do the will of the populace are enemies, though we learned together as children."

The man on my left called, "You won't get anything out of him. He's a prisoner."

I turned to look at him. His face, though wasted nearly to a skull, retained something of humor. His stiff, black hair looked as though it had not seen a comb for months.

"He talks like that all the time. Never any other way. *Hey, you!* We're going to beat you!"

The other answered, "For the Armies of the Populace, defeat is the springboard of victory, and victory the ladder to further victory."

"He makes a lot more sense than most of them, though," the man on my left told me.

"You say he's a prisoner. What did he do?"

"Do? Why, he didn't die."

"I'm afraid I don't understand. Was he selected for some kind of suicide mission?"

The patient beyond the man on my left sat up—a young woman with a thin but lovely face. "They all are," she said. "At least, they can't go home until the war is won, and they know, really, that it will never be won."

"External battles are already won when internal struggles are conducted with Correct Thought."

I said, "He's an Ascian, then. That's what you meant. I've never seen one before."

"Most of them die," the black-haired man told me. "That's what I said."

"I didn't know they spoke our language."

"They don't. Some officers who came here to talk to him said they thought he'd been an interpreter. Probably he questioned our soldiers when they were captured. Only he did something wrong and had to go back to the ranks."

The young woman said, "I don't think he's really mad. Most of them are. What's your name?"

"I'm sorry, I should have introduced myself. I'm Severian." I almost added that I was a lictor, but I knew neither of them would talk to me if I told them that.

"I'm Foila, and this is Melito. I was of the Blue Huzzars, he a hoplite."

"You shouldn't talk nonsense," Melito growled. "I am a hoplite. You are a huzzar."

I thought he appeared much nearer death than she.

"I'm only hoping we will be discharged when we're well enough to leave this place," Foila said.

"And what will we do then? Milk somebody else's cow and herd his pigs?" Melito turned to me. "Don't let her talk deceive you—we were volunteers, both of us. I was about to be promoted when I was wounded, and when I'm promoted I'll be able to support a wife."

Foila called, "I haven't promised to marry you!"

Several beds away, someone said loudly, "Take her so she'll shut up about it!"

At that, the patient in the bed beyond Foila's sat up. "She will marry me." He was big, fair skinned, and pale haired, and he spoke with the deliberation characteristic of the icy isles of the south. "I am Hallvard."

Surprising me, the Ascian prisoner announced, "United, men and women are stronger; but a brave woman desires children, and not husbands."

Foila said, "They fight even when they're pregnant—I've seen them dead on the battlefield."

"The roots of the tree are the populace. The leaves fall, but the tree remains."

I asked Melito and Foila if the Ascian were composing his

remarks or quoting some literary source with which I was
unfamiliar.

"Just making it up, you mean?" Foila asked. "No. They
never do that. Everything they say has to be taken from an
approved text. Some of them don't talk at all. The rest have
thousands—I suppose actually tens or hundreds of thousands—of those tags memorized."

"That's impossible," I said.

Melito shrugged. He had managed to prop himself up on
one elbow. "They do it, though. At least, that's what every-
body says. Foila knows more about them than I do."

Foila nodded. "In the light cavalry, we do a lot of scouting,
and sometimes we're sent out specifically to take prisoners.
You don't learn anything from talking to most of them, but
just the same the General Staff can tell a good deal from
their equipment and physical condition. On the northern
continent, where they come from, only the smallest children
ever talk the way we do."

I thought of Master Gurloes conducting the business of
our guild. "How could they possibly say something like 'Take
three apprentices and unload that wagon'?"

"They wouldn't *say* that at all—just grab people by the
shoulder, point to the wagon, and give them a push. If they
went to work, fine. If they didn't, then the leader would
quote something about the need for labor to ensure victory,
with several witnesses present. If the person he was talking to
still wouldn't work after that, then he would have him
killed—probably just by pointing to him and quoting something about the need to eliminate the enemies of the populace."

The Ascian said, "The cries of the children are the cries of
victory. Still, victory must learn wisdom."

Foila interpreted for him. "That means that although children are needed, what they say is meaningless. Most Ascians
would consider us mute even if we learned their tongue,
because groups of words that are not approved texts are with-

out meaning for them. If they admitted—even to them-selves—that such talk meant something, then it would be possible for them to hear disloyal remarks, and even to make them. That would be extremely dangerous. As long as they only understand and quote approved texts, no one can accuse them."

I turned my head to look at the Ascian. It was clear that he had been listening attentively, but I could not be certain of what his expression meant beyond that. "Those who write the approved texts," I told him, "cannot themselves be quot-ing from approved texts as they write. Therefore even an approved text may contain elements of disloyalty."

"Correct Thought is the thought of the populace. The populace cannot betray the populace or the Group of Sev-enteen."

Foila called, "Don't insult the populace or the Group of Seventeen. He might try to kill himself. Sometimes they do."

"Will he ever be normal?"

"I've heard that some of them eventually come to talk more or less the way we do, if that's what you mean."

I could think of nothing to say to that, and for some time we were quiet. There are long periods of silence, I found, in such a place, where almost everyone is ill. We knew that we had watch after watch to occupy; that if we did not say what we wished to say that afternoon there would be another op-portunity that evening and another again the next morning. Indeed, anyone who talked as healthy people normally do—after a meal, for example—would have been intolerable.

But what had been said had set me thinking of the north, and I found I knew next to nothing about it. When I had been a boy, scrubbing floors and running errands in the Cit-adel, the war itself had seemed almost infinitely remote. I knew that most of the matrosses who manned the major bat-teries had taken part in it, but I knew it just as I knew that the sunlight that fell upon my hand had been to the sun. I would be a torturer, and as a torturer I would have no reason to enter the army and no reason to fear that I would be impressed into it. I never expected to see the war at the gates of Nessus (in fact, those gates themselves were hardly more than legends to me), and I never expected to leave the city, or even to leave that quarter of the city that held the Citadel.

The north, Ascia, was then inconceivably remote, a place as distant as the most distant galaxy, since both were forever out of reach. Mentally, I confused it with the dying belt of tropical vegetation that lay between our own land and theirs, although I would have distinguished the two without difficulty if Master Palaemon had asked me to in the classroom.

But of Ascia itself I had no idea. I did not know if it had great cities or none. I did not know if it was mountainous like the northern and eastern parts of our Commonwealth or as level as our pampas. I did have the impression (though I could not be sure it was correct) that it was a single land mass, and not a chain of islands like our south; and most distinct of all, I had the impression of an innumerable people—our Ascian's populace—an inexhaustible swarm that almost became a creature in itself, as a colony of ants does. To think of those millions upon millions without speech, or confined to parroting proverbial phrases that must surely have long ago lost most of their meaning, was nearly more than the mind could bear. Speaking almost to myself, I said, "It must surely be a trick, or a lie, or a mistake. Such a nation could not exist."

And the Ascian, his voice no louder than my own had been, and perhaps even softer, answered, "How shall the state be most vigorous? It shall be most vigorous when it is without conflict. How shall it be without conflict? When it is without disagreement. How shall disagreement be banished? By banishing the four causes of disagreement: lies, foolish talk, boastful talk, and talk which serves only to incite quarrels. How shall the four causes be banished? By speaking only Correct Thought. Then shall the state be without disagreement. Being without disagreement it shall be without conflict. Being without conflict it shall be vigorous, strong, and secure."

I had been answered, and doubly.

Miles, Foila, Melito, and Hallvard

THAT EVENING I fell prey to a fear I had been trying to put from my mind for some time. Although I had seen nothing of the monsters Hethor had brought from beyond the stars since little Severian and I had escaped from the village of the sorcerers, I had not forgotten that he was searching for me. While I traveled in the wilderness or upon the waters of Lake Diuturna, I had not been much afraid he would over-take me. Now I was traveling no longer, and I could feel the weakness in my limbs, for despite the food I had eaten I was weaker than I had ever been while starving in the mountains.

Then too, I feared Agia almost more than Hethor's notules, his salamanders and slugs. I knew her courage, her cleverness, and her malice. Any one of the scarlet-clad priest-esses of the Pelerines moving between the cots might easily be she, with a poisoned stiletto beneath her gown. I slept badly that night; but though I dreamed much, my dreams were indistinct, and I will not attempt to relate them here.

I woke feeling less than rested. My fever, of which I had hardly been conscious when I came to the lazaret, and which had seemed to subside on the day previous, returned. I felt its heat in every limb—it seemed to me that I must glow, that the very glaciers of the south would melt if I came among them. I took out the Claw and clasped it to me, and for a time even held it in my mouth. My fever sank again, but left me weak and dizzied.

That morning the soldier came to see me. He wore a white gown the Pelerines had given him in place of his armor, but he appeared wholly recovered, and told me he hoped to leave the next day. I said I would like to introduce him to the acquaintances I had made in this part of the lazaret and asked if he now recalled his name.

He shook his head. "I can remember very little. I am hoping that when I go among the units of the army I will find someone there who knows me."

I introduced him anyway, calling him Miles since I could think of nothing better. I did not know the Ascian's name either and discovered that no one did, not even Foila. When we asked him what it was, he only said, "I am Loyal to the Group of Seventeen."

For a time Foila, Melito, the soldier, and I chatted among ourselves. Melito seemed to like him very well, though perhaps only because of the similarity of the name I had given him to his own. Then the soldier helped me into a sitting posture, lowered his voice, and said, "Now I have to talk to you privately. As I said, I think I will leave here in the morning. From what I have seen of you, you won't be getting out for several days—maybe not for a couple of weeks. I may never see you again."

"Let us hope that isn't so."

"I hope not either. But if I can find my legion, I may be killed by the time you're well. And if I can't find it, I'll probably go into another to keep from being arrested as a deserter." He paused.

I smiled. "And I may die here, of the fever. You didn't want to say that. Do I look as bad as poor Melito?"

He shook his head. "Not as bad, no. I think you'll make it—"

"That's what the thrush sang while the lynx chased the hare around the bay tree."

Now it was his turn to smile. "You're right; I was about to say that."

"Is it a common expression in that part of the Commonwealth where you were brought up?"

The smile vanished. "I don't know. I can't remember where my home is, and that's part of the reason I have to talk to you now. I remember walking down a road with you at night—that's the only thing I *do* remember, before I came here. Where did you find me?"

"In a wood, I suppose about five or ten leagues south of here. Do you recall what I told you about the Claw as we walked?"

He shook his head. "I think I remember you mentioning such a thing, but not what you said."

"What do you remember? Tell me all of it, and I'll tell you what I know, and what I can guess."

"Walking with you. A lot of darkness . . . I fell, or maybe flew through it. Seeing my own face, multiplied again and again. A girl with hair like red gold and enormous eyes."

"A beautiful woman?"

He nodded. "The most beautiful in the world."

Raising my voice, I asked if anyone had a mirror he would lend us for a moment. Foila produced one from the possessions beneath her cot, and I held it up for the soldier. "Is this the face?"

He hesitated. "I think so."

"Blue eyes?"

". . . I can't be sure."

I returned the mirror to Foila. "I will tell you again what I told you on the road, and I wish we had a more private place in which to do it. Some time ago a talisman came into my hands. It came innocently, but it does not belong to me, and it is very valuable—sometimes, not always, but sometimes—it has the power to heal the sick, and even to revive the dead.

Two days ago, as I was traveling north, I came across the body of a dead soldier. It was in a forest, away from the road. He had been dead less than a day; I would say it's likely he had died sometime during the preceding night. I was very hungry then, and I cut his pack straps and ate most of the food he had been carrying with him. Then I felt guilty about doing that and got out the talisman and tried to restore him to life. It has failed often before, and this time I thought for a while it was going to fail again. It didn't, although he returned to life slowly and for a long time did not seem to know where he was or what was happening to him."

"And I was that soldier?"

I nodded, looking into his honest blue eyes.

"May I see the talisman?"

I took it out and held it in the palm of my hand. He took it from me, examined both sides carefully, and tested the point against the ball of his finger. "It doesn't look magical," he said.

"I'm not sure *magical* is the right term for it. I've met magicians, and nothing they did reminded me of this or the way it acts. Sometimes it glows with light—it's very faint now, and I doubt if you can see it."

"I can't. There doesn't seem to be any writing on it."

"You mean spells or prayers. No, I've never noticed any, and I've carried it a long way. I don't really know anything about it except that it acts at times; but I think it is probably the kind of thing spells and prayers are made with, and not the kind that is made with them."

"You said it didn't belong to you."

I nodded again. "It belongs to the priestesses here, the Pelerines."

"You just came here. Two nights ago, when I did."

"I came looking for them, to give it back. It was taken from them—not by me—some time ago, in Nessus."

"And you're going to return it?" He looked at me as though he somehow doubted it.

"Yes, eventually."

He stood up, smoothing his robe with his hands.

I said, "You don't believe me, do you? Not about any of it."

"When I came here, you introduced me to the others nearby, the ones you'd talked with while you lay here on your cot." He spoke slowly, seeming to ponder every word. "Of course I've met some people too, where they put me. There's one who isn't really wounded very badly. He's just a boy, a youngster off some small holding a long way from here, and he mostly sits on his cot and looks at the floor."

"Homesick?" I asked.

The soldier shook his head. "He had an energy weapon. A korseke—that's what somebody told me. Are you familiar with them?"

"Not very."

"They project a beam straight forward, and at the same time two quartering beams, forward left and forward right. Their range isn't great, but they say they're very good for dealing with mass attacks, and I suppose they are."

He looked about for a moment to see if anyone was listening, but it is a point of honor in the lazaret to disregard completely any conversation not intended for oneself. If it were not so, the patients would soon be at each other's throats.

"His hundred was the target of one of those attacks. Most of the others broke and ran. He didn't, and they didn't get him. Another man told me there were three walls of bodies in front of him. He had dropped them until the Ascians were climbing up to the top and jumping down at him. Then he had backed away and piled them up again."

I said, "I suppose he got a medal and a promotion." I could not be sure if it was my fever returning or merely the heat of the day, but I felt sticky and somehow suffocated.

"No, they sent him here. I told you he was only a boy from the country. He had killed more people that day than he had ever seen up to the time a few months before when he went into the army. He still hasn't gotten over it, and maybe he never will."

"Yes?"

"It seems to me you might be like that."

"I don't understand you," I said.

"You talk as if you've just come here from the south, and I suppose that if you've left your legion that's the safest way to talk. Just the same, anybody can see it isn't true—people don't get cut up the way you are except where the fighting is. You were hit by rock splinters. That's what happened to you, and the Pelerine who spoke to us the first night we were here saw that right away. So I think you've been north longer than you'll admit, and maybe longer than you think yourself. If you've killed a lot of people, it might be nice for you to believe you have a way to bring them back."

I tried to grin at him. "And where does that leave you?"

"Where I am now. I'm not trying to say I owe you nothing. I had fever, and you found me. Maybe I was delirious. I think it's more likely I was unconscious, and that let you think I was dead. If you hadn't brought me here, I probably would have died."

He started to stand up; I stopped him with a hand on his arm. "There are some things I should tell you before you go," I said. "About yourself."

"You said you didn't know who I was."

I shook my head. "I didn't say that, not really. I said I found you in a wood two days ago. In the sense you mean, I *don't* know who you are—but in another sense I think I may. I think you're two people, and that I know one of them."

"Nobody is two people."

"I am. I'm two people already. Perhaps more people are two than we know. The first thing I want to tell you is much simpler, though. Now listen." I gave him detailed directions for finding the wood again, and when I was certain he understood them, I said, "Your pack is probably still there, with the straps cut, so if you find the place you won't mistake it. There was a letter in your pack. I pulled it out and read a part of it. It didn't carry the name of the person you were writing to, but if you had finished it and were just waiting for a chance to send it off, it should have at least a part of your name at the end. I put it on the ground and it blew a little and caught against a tree. It may still be possible for you to find it."

His face had tightened. "You shouldn't have read it, and you shouldn't have thrown it away."

"I thought you were dead, remember? Anyway, a good deal was going on at the time, mostly inside my head. Perhaps I was getting feverish—I don't know. Now here's the other part. You won't believe me, but it may be important that you listen. Will you hear me out?"

He nodded.

"Good. Have you heard of the mirrors of Father Inire? Do you know how they work?"

"I've heard of Father Inire's Mirror, but I couldn't tell you where I heard about it. You're supposed to be able to step into it, like you'd step into a doorway, and step out on a star. I don't think it's real."

"The mirrors are real. I've seen them. Up until now I always thought of them in much the same way you did—as if they were a ship, but much faster. Now I'm not nearly so sure. Anyway, a certain friend of mine stepped between those mirrors and vanished. I was watching him. It was no trick and no superstition; he went wherever the mirrors take you. He went because he loved a certain woman, and he wasn't a whole man. Do you understand?"

"He'd had an accident?"

"An accident had had him, but never mind that. He told me he would come back. He said, 'I will come back for her when I have been repaired, when I am sane and whole.' I didn't quite know what to think when he said that, but now I believe he has come. It was I who revived you, and I had been wishing for his return—perhaps that had something to do with it."

There was a pause. The soldier looked down at the trampled soil on which the cots had been set, then up again at me. "Possibly whenever a man loses his friend and gets another, he feels the old friend is with him again."

"Jonas—that was his name—had a habit of speech. Whenever he had to say something unpleasant, he softened it, made a joke of it, by attributing what he said to some comic situation. The first night we were here, when I asked you your name, you said, 'I lost it somewhere along the way. That's what the jaguar said, who had promised to guide the goat.' Do you recall that?"

He shook his head. "I say a lot of foolish things."

"It struck me as strange; because it was the kind of thing Jonas said, but he wouldn't have said it in that way unless he meant more by it than you seemed to. I think he would have said, 'That was the basket's story, that had been filled with water.' Something like that."

I waited for him to speak, but he did not.

"The jaguar ate the goat, of course. Swallowed its flesh and cracked its bones, somewhere along the way."

"Haven't you ever thought that it might be just the peculiarity of some town? Your friend might have come from the same place I do."

I said, "It was a time, I think, and not a place. Long ago, someone had to disarm fear—the fear that men of flesh and blood might feel when looking into a face of steel and glass. Jonas, I know you're listening. I don't blame you. The man was dead, and you still alive. I understand that. But Jonas, Jolenta is gone—I watched her die, and I tried to bring her back with the Claw, but I failed. Perhaps she was too artificial, I don't know. You will have to find someone else."

The soldier rose. His face was no longer angry, but empty as a somnambulist's. He turned and left without another word.

· · ·

For perhaps a watch I lay on my cot with my hands behind my head, thinking of many things. Hallvard, Melito, and Foila were talking among themselves, but I did not attend to what they said. When one of the Pelerines brought the noon meal, Melito got my ear by rapping his platter with a fork and announced, "Severian, we have a favor to ask of you."

I was eager to put my speculations behind me, and told him I would help them in any way I could.

Foila, who had one of those radiant smiles Nature grants to some women, smiled at me now. "It's like this. These two have been bickering over me all morning. If they were well they could fight it out, but it will be a long time before they are, and I don't think I could stand it so long. Today I was thinking of my mother and father, and how they used to sit before the fire on long winter nights. If Hallvard and I marry, or Melito and I, someday we'll be doing that too. So I have decided to marry the best storyteller. Don't look at me as if I were mad—it's the only sensible thing I've done in my life. Both of them want me, both are very handsome, neither has any property, and if we don't settle this they'll kill each other or I'll kill them both. You're an educated man—we can tell by the way you talk. You listen and judge. Hallvard first, and the stories have to be original, not out of books."

Hallvard, who could walk a little, got up from his cot and came to sit on the foot of Melito's.

Hallvard's Story—The Two Sealers

"THIS IS A true story. I know many stories. Some are made up, though perhaps the made up ones were true in times everyone has forgotten. I also know many true ones, because many strange things happen in the isles of the south that you northern people never dream of. I chose this one because I was there myself and saw and heard as much of it as anyone did.

"I come from the easternmost of the southern isles, which is called Glacies. On our isle lived a man and a woman, my grandparents, who had three sons. Their names were Anskar, Hallvard, and Gundulf. Hallvard was my father, and when I grew large enough to help him on his boat, he no longer hunted and fished with his brothers. Instead, we two went out so that all we caught could be brought home to my mother, and my sisters and younger brother.

"My uncles never married, and so they continued to share a boat. What they caught they ate themselves or gave to my grandparents, who were no longer strong. In the summer they farmed my grandfather's land. He had the best on our isle, the only valley that never felt the ice wind. You could grow things there that would not ripen anywhere else on Glacies, because the growing season in this valley was two weeks longer.

"When my beard was starting to sprout, my grandfather called all the men of our family together—that was my father, my two uncles, and myself. When we got to his house, my grandmother was dead, and the priest from the big isle was there to lay out her body. Her sons wept, as I did myself.

"That night, when we sat at my grandfather's table, with him at one end and the priest at the other, he said, 'Now it is time that I dispose of my property. Bega is gone. Her family has no more claim on it, and I shall follow her shortly. Hallvard is married and has the portion that came to him from his wife. With that he provides for his family, and though they have little to spare, they do not go hungry. You, Anskar. And you, Gundulf. Will you ever marry?'

"Both my uncles shook their heads.

" 'Then this is my will. I call upon the Omnipotent to hear, and I call upon the servants of the Omnipotent also. When I die, all that I have shall go to Anskar and Gundulf. If one die, it shall go to the other. When both are dead, it shall go to Hallvard, or if Hallvard is dead, it shall be divided among his sons. You four—if you do not agree my will is just, speak now.'

"No one spoke, and thus it was decided.

"A year passed. A ship of Erebus came raiding out of the mists, and two ships put in for hides, sea ivory, and salt fish. My grandfather died, and my sister Fausta bore her girl. When the harvest was in, my uncles fished with the other men.

"When spring comes in the south, it is still too early to plant, for there will be many freezing nights to come. But when men see that the days are lengthening fast, they seek out the rookeries where the seals breed. These are on rocks far from any shore, there is much fog, and though they are growing longer, the days are still short. Often it is the men who die and not the seals.

"And so it was with my Uncle Anskar, for my Uncle Gundulf returned in their boat without him.

"Now you must know that when our men go sealing, or
fishing, or hunting any other kind of sea game, they tie themselves to their boats. The rope is of braided walrus hide, and
it is long enough to let the man move about in the boat as
much as is needful, but not longer. The sea water is very cold
and soon kills whoever remains in it, but our men dress in
sealskin tight-sewn, and often a man's boat-mate can pull
him back and in that way save his life.

"This is the tale my Uncle Gundulf told. They had gone
far, seeking a rookery others had not visited, when Anskar
saw a bull seal swimming in the water. He cast his harpoon;
and when the seal sounded, a loop of the harpoon line had
caught his ankle, so that he was dragged into the sea. He,
Gundulf, had tried to pull him out, for he was a very strong
man. But his pulling and the pulling of the seal on the harpoon line, which was tied to the base of the mast, had capsized their boat. Gundulf had saved himself by pulling
himself hand over hand back to it and cutting the harpoon
line with his knife. When the boat was righted he had tried
to haul in Anskar, but the life rope had broken. He showed
the frayed rope end. My Uncle Anskar was dead.

"Among my people, women die on land but men at sea,
and therefore we call the kind of grave you make 'a woman's
boat.' When a man dies as Uncle Anskar did, a hide is
stretched and painted for him and hung in the house where
the men meet to talk. It is never taken down until no man
living can recall the man who was honored so. A hide like
that was prepared for Anskar, and the painters began their
work.

"Then one bright morning when my father and I were
readying the tools to break ground for the new year's crop—
well I remember it!—some children who had been sent to
gather birds' eggs came running into the village. A seal, they
said, lay on the shingle of the south bay. As everyone knows,

no seal comes to land where men are. But it sometimes happens that a seal will die at sea or be injured in some fashion. Thinking of that, my father and I and many others ran to the beach, for the seal would belong to the first whose weapon pierced it.

"I was the swiftest of all, and I provided myself with an earth-fork. Such a thing does not throw well, but several other young men were at my heels, so when I was a hundred strides away I cast it. Straight and true it flew and buried its tines in the thing's back. Then followed such a moment as I hope never to see again. The weight of the fork's long handle overbalanced it, and it rolled until the handle rested on the ground.

"I saw the face of my Uncle Anskar, preserved by the cold sea brine. His beard was tangled with the dark green kelp, and his life rope of stout walrus hide had been cut only a few spans from his body.

"My Uncle Gundulf had not seen him, for he was gone to the big isle. My father took Anskar up, and I helped him, and we carried him to Gundulf's house and put the end of the rope upon his chest where Gundulf would see it, and with some other men of Glacies sat down to wait for him.

"He shouted when he saw his brother. It was not such a cry as a woman makes, but a bellow like the bull seal gives when he warns the other bulls from his herd. He ran in the dark. We set a guard on the boats and hunted him that night across the isle. The lights that spirits make in the ultimate south flamed all night, so we knew Anskar hunted with us. Brightest they flashed before they faded, when we found him among the rocks at Radbod's End."

Hallvard fell silent. Indeed, silence lay about us everywhere. All the sick within hearing had been listening to him. At last Melito said, "Did you kill him?"

"No. In the old days it was so, and a bad thing. Now the mainland law avenges bloodguilt, which is better. We bound his arms and legs and laid him in his house, and I sat with him while the older men readied the boats. He told me he had loved a woman on the big isle. I never saw her, but he said her name was Nennoc, and she was fair, and younger than he, but no man would have her because she had borne a child by a man who had died the winter before. In the boat, he had told Anskar he would carry Nennoc home, and Anskar called him *oath-breaker*. My Uncle Gundulf was strong. He seized Anskar and threw him out of the boat, then wrapped the life rope about his hands and snapped it as a woman who sews breaks her thread.

"He had stood then, he said, with one hand on the mast, as men do, and watched his brother in the water. He had seen the flash of the knife, but he thought only that Anskar sought to threaten him with it or to throw it."

Hallvard was silent again, and when I saw he would not speak, I said, "I don't understand. What did Anskar do?"

A smile, the very smallest smile, tugged at Hallvard's lips under his blond mustache. When I saw it, I felt I had seen the ice isles of the south, blue and bitterly cold. "He cut his life rope, the rope Gundulf had already broken. In that way, men who found his body would know that he had been murdered. Do you see?"

I saw, and for a while I said nothing more.

"So," Melito grunted to Foila, "the wonderful valley land went to Hallvard's father, and by this story he has managed to tell you that though he has no property, he has prospects of inheriting some. He has also told you, of course, that he comes of a murderous family."

"Melito believes me much cleverer than I am," the blond man rumbled. "I had no such thoughts. What matters now is not land or skins or gold, but who tells the best tale. And I, who know many, have told the best I know. It is true as he says that I might share my family's property when my father dies. But my unmarried sisters will have some part too for their marriage portions, and only what remained would be divided between my brother and myself. All that matters nothing, because I would not take Foila to the south, where life is so hard. Since I have carried a lance I have seen many better places."

Foila said, "I think your Uncle Gundulf must have loved Nennoc very much."

Hallvard nodded. "He said that too while he lay bound. But all the men of the south love their women. It is for them that they face the sea in winter, the storms and the freezing fogs. It is said that as a man pushes his boat out over the shingle, the sound the bottom makes grating on the stones is *my wife, my children, my children, my wife.*"

I asked Melito if he wanted to begin his story then; but he shook his head and said that we were all full of Hallvard's, so he would wait and begin next day. Everyone then asked Hallvard questions about life in the south and compared what they had learned to the way their own people lived. Only the Ascian was silent. I was reminded of the floating islands of Lake Diuturna and told Hallvard and the others about them, though I did not describe the fight at Baldanders's castle. We talked in this way until it was time for the evening meal.

The Pelerine

BY THE TIME we had finished eating, it was beginning to get dark. We were always quieter then, not only because we lacked strength, but because we knew that those wounded who would die were more liable to do so after the sun set, and particularly in the deep of the night. It was the time when past battles called home their debts.

In other ways too, the night made us more aware of the war. Sometimes—and on that night I remember them particularly—the discharges of the great energy weapons blazed across the sky like heat lightning. One heard the sentries marching to their posts, so that the word *watch*, which we so often used with no meaning beyond that of a tenth part of the night, became an audible reality, an actuality of tramping feet and unintelligible commands.

There came a moment when no one spoke, that lengthened and lengthened, interrupted only by the murmurings of the well—the Pelerines and their male slaves—who came to ask the condition of this patient or that. One of the scarlet-clad priestesses came and sat by my cot, and my mind was so slow, so nearly sleeping, that it was some time before I realized that she must have carried a stool with her.

"You are Severian," she said, "the friend of Miles?"

"Yes."

"He has recalled his name. I thought you would like to know."

I asked her what it was.

"Why, Miles, of course. I told you."

"He will recall more than that, I think, as time goes by."

She nodded. She seemed to be a woman past middle age, with a kindly, austere face. "I am sure he will. His home and family."

"If he has them."

"Yes, some do not. Some lack even the ability to make a home."

"You're referring to me."

"No, not at all. Anyway, that lack is not something the person can do something about. But it is much better, particularly for men, if they have a home. Like the man your friend talked about, most men think they make their homes for their families, but the fact is that they make both homes and families for themselves."

"You were listening to Hallvard, then."

"Several of us were. It was a good story. A sister came and got me at the place where the patient's grandfather made his will. I heard all the rest. Do you know what the trouble was with the bad uncle? With Gundulf?"

"I suppose that he was in love."

"No, that was what was right with him. Every person, you see, is like a plant. There is a beautiful green part, often with flowers or fruit, that grows upward toward the sun, toward the Increate. There is also a dark part that grows away from it, tunneling where no light comes."

I said, "I have never studied the writings of the initiates, but even I am aware of the existence of good and evil in everyone."

"Was I speaking of good and evil? It is the roots that give the plant the strength to climb toward the sun, though they know nothing of it. Suppose that some scythe, whistling along the ground, should sever the stalk from its roots. The stalk would fall and die, but the roots might put up a new stalk."

"You are saying that evil is good."

"No. I am saying that the things we love in others and admire in ourselves spring from things we do not see and seldom think about. Gundulf, like other men, had the instinct to exercise authority. Its proper growth is the founding of a family—and women, too, have a similar instinct. In Gundulf that instinct had long been frustrated, as it is in so many of the soldiers we see here. The officers have their commands, but the soldiers who have no command suffer and do not know why they suffer. Some, of course, form bonds with others in the ranks. Sometimes several share a single woman, or a man who is like a woman. Some make pets of animals, and some befriend children left homeless by the struggle."

Remembering Casdoe's son, I said, "I can see why you object to that."

"We do not object—most certainly not to that, and not to things vastly less natural. I am only speaking of the instinct to exercise authority. In the bad uncle it made him love a woman, and specifically one who already possessed a child, so there would be a larger family for him as soon as there was a family for him at all. In that way, you see, he would have regained some part of the time he had lost."

She paused, and I nodded.

"Too much time, however, had been lost already; the instinct broke out in another way. He saw himself as the rightful master of lands he only held in trust for one brother, and the master of the life of the other. That vision was delusive, was it not?"

"I suppose so."

"Others can have visions equally deluding, though less dangerous." She smiled at me. "Do you regard yourself as possessing any special authority?"

"I am a journeyman of the Seekers for Truth and Penitence, but that position carries no authority. We of the guild only do the will of judges."

"I thought the torturers' guild abolished long ago. Has it become, then, a species of brotherhood for lictors?"

"It still exists," I told her.

"No doubt, but some centuries ago it was a true guild, like that of the silversmiths. At least so I have read in certain histories preserved by our order."

As I heard her, I felt a moment of wild elation. It was not that I supposed her to be somehow correct. I am, perhaps, mad in certain respects, but I know what those respects are, and such self-deceptions are no part of them. Nevertheless, it seemed wonderful to me—if only for that moment—to exist in a world where such a belief was possible. I realized then, really for the first time, that there were millions of people in the Commonwealth who knew nothing of the higher forms of judicial punishment and nothing of the circles within circles of intrigue that ring the Autarch; and it was wine to me, or brandy rather, and left me reeling with giddy joy.

The Pelerine, seeing nothing of all this, said, "Is there no other form of special authority that you believe yourself to possess?"

I shook my head.

"Miles told me that you believe yourself to possess the Claw of the Conciliator, and that you showed him a small black claw, such as might perhaps have come from an ocelot or a caracara, and that you told him you have raised many from the dead by means of it."

The time had come then; the time when I would have to give it up. Ever since we had reached the lazaret, I had known it must come soon, but I had hoped to delay it until I was ready to depart. Now I took out the Claw, for the last time as I thought, and pressed it into the Pelerine's hand, saying, "With this you can save many. I did not steal it, and I have sought always to return it to your order."

"And with it," she asked gently, "you have revived numbers of the dead?"

"I myself would have died months ago without it," I told her, and I began to recount the story of my duel with Agilus.

"Wait," she said. "You must keep it." And she returned the Claw to me. "I am not a young woman any longer, as you see. Next year I will celebrate my thirtieth anniversary as a full member of our order. At each of the five superior feasts of the year, until this past spring, I saw the Claw of the Conciliator when it was elevated for our adoration. It was a great sapphire, as big around as an orichalk. It must have been worth more than many villas, and no doubt it was for that reason that the thieves took it."

I tried to interrupt her, but she silenced me with a gesture.

"As for its working miraculous cures and even restoring life to the dead, do you think our order would have any sick among us if it were so? We are few—far too few for the work we have to do. But if none of us had died before last spring, we would be much more numerous. Many whom I loved, my teachers and my friends, would be among us still. Ignorant people must have their wonders, even if they must scrape the mud from some epopt's boots to swallow. If, as we hope, it still exists and has not been cut to make smaller gems, the Claw of the Conciliator is the last relic we possess of the greatest of good men, and we treasured it because we still treasure his memory. If it had been the sort of thing you believe yourself to have, it would have been precious to everyone, and the autarchs would have wrested it from us long ago."

"It *is* a claw—" I began.

"That was only a flaw at the heart of the jewel. The Conciliator was a man, Severian the Lictor, and not a cat or a bird." She stood up.

"It was dashed against the rocks when the giant threw it from the parapet—"

"I had hoped to calm you, but I see that I am only exciting

you," she said. Quite unexpectedly she smiled, leaned forward, and kissed me. "We meet many here who believe things that are not so. Not many have beliefs that do them as much credit as yours do you. You and I shall talk of this again some other time."

I watched her small, scarlet-clad figure until it was lost from sight in the darkness and silence of the rows of cots. While we talked, most of the sick had fallen asleep. A few groaned. Three slaves entered, two carrying a wounded man on a litter while the third held up a lamp so they could see their way. The light gleamed on their shaven heads, which were covered with sweat. They put the wounded man on a cot, arranged his limbs as though he were dead, and went away.

I looked at the Claw. It had been lifelessly black when the Pelerine saw it, but now muted sparks of white fire ran from its base to its point. I felt well—indeed, I found myself wondering how I had endured lying all day upon the narrow mattress; but when I tried to stand my legs would hardly hold me. Afraid at every moment that I would fall on one of the wounded, I staggered the twenty paces or so to the man I had just seen carried in.

It was Emilian, whom I had known as a gallant at the Autarch's court. I was so startled to see him here that I called him by name.

"Thecla," he murmured. "Thecla . . ."

"Yes. Thecla. You remember me, Emilian. Now be well." I touched him with the Claw.

He opened his eyes and screamed.

I fled, but fell when I was halfway to my own cot. I was so weak I don't believe I could have crawled the remaining distance then, but I managed to put away the Claw and roll beneath Hallvard's cot and so out of sight.

When the slaves came back, Emilian was sitting up and able to speak—though they could not, I think, make much sense of what he said. They gave him herbs, and one of them remained with him while he chewed them, then left silently.

I rolled from under the cot, and by holding on to the edge was able to pull myself erect. All was still again, but I knew that many of the wounded must have seen me before I had fallen. Emilian was not asleep, as I had supposed he would be, but he seemed dazed. "Thecla," he murmured. "I heard Thecla. They said she was dead. What voices are here from the lands of the dead?"

"None now," I told him. "You've been ill, but you'll be well soon."

I held the Claw overhead and tried to focus my thoughts on Melito and Foila as well as Emilian—on all the sick in the lazaret. It flickered and was dark.

Melito's Story—The Cock, the Angel, and the Eagle

"ONCE NOT VERY long ago and not very far from the place where I was born, there was a fine farm. It was especially noted for its poultry: flocks of ducks white as snow, geese nearly as large as swans and so fat they could scarcely walk, and chickens that were as colorful as parrots. The farmer who had built up this place had a great many strange ideas about farming, but he had succeeded so much better with his strange ideas than any of his neighbors with their sensible ones, that few had the courage to tell him what a fool he was.

"One of his queer notions concerned the management of his chickens. Everyone knows that when chicks are observed to be little cocks they must be caponized. Only one cock is required in the barnyard, and two will fight.

"But this farmer saved himself all that trouble. 'Let them grow up,' he said. 'Let them fight, and let me tell you something, neighbor. The best and cockiest cock will win, and he is the one who will sire many more chicks to swell my flock. What's more, his chicks will be the hardiest, and the best suited to throwing off every disease—when your chickens are wiped out, you can come to me and I'll sell you some breeding stock at my own price. As for the beaten cocks, my family and I can eat them. There's no capon so tender as a cock that has been fought to death, just as the best beef comes from a bull that has died in the bull ring and the best venison from a stag the hounds have run all day. Besides, eating capons saps a man's virility.'

"This odd farmer also believed that it was his duty to select the worst bird from his flock whenever he wanted one for dinner. 'It is impious,' he said, 'for anyone to take the best. They should be left to prosper under the eye of the Pancreator, who made cocks and hens as well as men and women.' Perhaps because he felt as he did, his flock was so good that it seemed sometimes there was no worst among it.

"From all I have said, it will be clear that the cock of this flock was a very fine one. He was young, strong, and brave. His tail was as fine as the tails of many sorts of pheasants, and no doubt his comb would have been fine too, save that it had been torn to ribbons in the many desperate combats that had won him his place. His breast was of glowing scarlet—like the Pelerines' robes here—but the geese said it had been white before it was dyed in his own blood. His wings were so strong that he was a better flier than any of the white ducks, his spurs were longer than a man's middle finger, and his bill was as sharp as my sword.

"This fine cock had a thousand wives, but the darling of his heart was a hen as fine as he, the daughter of a noble race and the acknowledged queen of all the chickens for leagues around. How proudly they walked between the corner of the barn and the water of the duck pond! You could not hope to see anything finer, no, not if you saw the Autarch himself showing off his favorite at the Well of Orchids—the more so since the Autarch is a capon, as I hear it.

"Everything was bugs for breakfast for this happy pair until one night the cock was wakened by a terrible row. A great, eared owl had broken into the barn where the chickens roosted and was making his way among them as he sought for his dinner. Of course he seized upon the hen who was the particular favorite of the cock; and with her in his claws, he spread his wide, silent wings to sail away. Owls can see marvelously well in the dark, and so he must have seen the cock flying at him like a feathered fury. Who has ever seen an amazed expression on the face of an owl? Yet surely there was one on that owl in the barn that night. The cock's spurs shuffled faster than the feet of any dancer, and his bill struck for those round and shining eyes as the bill of a woodpecker hammers the trunk of a tree. The owl dropped the hen, flew from the barn, and was never seen again.

"No doubt the cock had a right to be proud, but he became too proud. Having defeated an owl in the dark, he felt he could defeat any bird, anywhere. He began to talk of rescuing the prey of hawks and bullying the teratornis, the largest and most terrible bird that flies. If he had surrounded himself with wise counselors, particularly the llama and the pig, those whom most princes choose to help guide their affairs, I feel sure his extravagances would soon have been effectively though courteously checked. Alas, he did not do so. He listened only to the hens, who were all infatuated with him, and to the geese and ducks, who felt that as his fellow barnyard fowl they shared to some extent in whatever glory he won. At last the day came, as it always does for those who show too much pride, when he went too far.

"It was sunrise, ever the most dangerous time for those who do not do well. The cock flew up and up and up, until he seemed about to pierce the sky, and at last, at the very apogee of his flight, perched himself atop the weathervane on the loftiest gable of the barn—the highest point in the entire farmyard. There as the sun drove out the shadows with lashes of crimson and gold, he screamed again and again that he was lord of all feathered things. Seven times he crowed so, and he might have got away with it, for seven is a lucky number. But he could not be content with that. An eighth time he made the same boast, and then flew down.

"He had not yet landed among his flock when there began a most marvelous phenomenon high in the air, directly above the barn. A hundred rays of sunlight seemed to tangle themselves as a kitten snarls a ball of wool, and to roll themselves together as a woman rolls up dough in a kneading pan. This collection of glorious light then put out legs, arms, a head, and at last wings, and swooped down upon the barnyard. It was an angel with wings of red and blue and green and gold, and though it seemed no bigger than the cock, he knew as soon as he had looked into its eyes that it was far larger on the inside than he.

" 'Now,' said the angel, 'hear justice. You claim that no feathered thing can stand against you. Here am I, plainly a feathered thing. All the mighty weapons of the armies of light I have left behind, and we will wrestle, we two.'

"At that the cock spread his wings and bowed so low that his tattered comb scraped the dust. 'I shall be honored to the end of my days to have been thought worthy of such a challenge,' he said, 'which no other bird has ever received before. It is with the most profound regret that I must tell you I cannot accept, and that for three reasons, the first of which is that though you have feathers on your wings, as you say, it is not against your wings that I would fight but against your head and breast. Thus you are not a feathered creature for the purposes of combat.'

"The angel closed his eyes and touched his hands to his own body, and when he drew them away the hair of his head had become feathers brighter than the feathers of the finest canary, and the linen of his robe had become feathers whiter than the feathers of the most brilliant dove.

" 'The second of which,' continued the cock, nothing daunted, 'is that you, having, as you so clearly do, the power to transform yourself, might choose during the course of our combat to change yourself into some creature that does not possess feathers—for example, a large snake. Thus if I were to fight you, I should have no guarantee of fair play.'

"At that, the angel tore open his breast, and displaying all the qualities therein to the assembled poultry, took out his ability to alter his shape. He handed it to the fattest goose to hold for the duration of the match, and the goose at once transformed himself, becoming a gray salt goose, such as stream from pole to pole. But he did not fly off, and he kept the angel's ability safe.

" 'The third of which,' continued the cock in desperation, 'is that you are clearly an officer in the Pancreator's service, and in prosecuting the cause of justice, as you do, are doing your duty. If I were to fight you as you ask, I should be committing a grave crime against the only ruler brave chickens acknowledge.'

" 'Very well,' said the angel. 'It is a strong legal position, and I suppose you think you've won your way free. The truth is that you have argued your way to your own death. I was only going to twist your wings back a bit and pull out your tail feathers.' Then he lifted his head and gave a strange, wild cry. Immediately an eagle dove from the sky and dropped like a thunderbolt into the barnyard.

"All around the barn they fought, and beside the duck pond, and across the pasture and back, for the eagle was very strong, but the cock was quick and brave. There was an old cart with a broken wheel leaning against one wall of the barn, and under it, where the eagle could not fly at him from above and he could cool himself somewhat in the shadow, the cock sought to make his final stand. He was bleeding so much, however, that before the eagle, who was almost as bloodied as he, could come at him there, he tottered, fell, tried to rise, and fell again.

" 'Now,' said the angel, addressing all the assembled birds, 'you have seen justice done. Be not proud! Be not boastful, for surely retribution will be visited upon you. You thought your champion invincible. There he lies, the victim not of this eagle but of pride, beaten and destroyed.'

"Then the cock, whom they had all thought dead, lifted

his head. 'You are doubtless very wise, Angel,' he said. 'But you know nothing of the ways of cocks. A cock is not beaten until he turns tail and shows the white feather that lies beneath his tail feathers. My strength, which I made myself by flying and running, and in many battles, has failed me. My spirit, which I received from the hand of your master the Pancreator, has not failed me. Eagle, I ask no quarter from you. Come here and kill me now. But as you value your honor, never say that you have beaten me.'

"The eagle looked at the angel when he heard what the cock said, and the angel looked at the eagle. 'The Pancreator is infinitely far from us,' the angel said. 'And thus infinitely far from me, though I fly so much higher than you. I guess at his desires—no one can do otherwise.'

He opened his chest once more and replaced the ability he had for a time surrendered. Then he and the eagle flew away, and for a time the salt goose followed them. That is the end of the story."

Melito had lain upon his back as he spoke, looking up at the canvas stretched overhead. I had the feeling he was too weak even to raise himself on one elbow. The rest of the wounded had been as quiet for his story as for Hallvard's.

At last I said, "That is a fine tale. It will be very hard for me to judge between the two, and if it is agreeable to you and Hallvard, and to Foila, I would like to give myself time to think about them both."

Foila, who was sitting up with her knees drawn under her chin, called, "Don't judge at all. The contest isn't over yet."

Everyone looked at her.

"I'll explain tomorrow," she said. "Just don't judge, Severian. But what did you think of that story?"

Hallvard rumbled, "I will tell you what I think. I think Melito is clever the way he claimed I was. He is not so well as I am, not so strong, and in this way he has drawn a woman's sympathy to himself. It was cunningly done, little cock."

Melito's voice seemed weaker than it had while he was recounting the battle of the birds. "It is the worst story I know."

"The worst?" I asked. We were all surprised.

"Yes, the worst. It is a foolish tale we tell our little children, who know nothing but the dust and the farm animals and the sky they see above them. Surely every word of it must make that clear."

Hallvard asked, "Don't you want to win, Melito?"

"Certainly I do. You don't love Foila as I love her. I would die to possess her, but I would sooner die than disappoint her. If the story I have just told can win, then I shall never disappoint her, at least with my stories. I have a thousand that are better than that."

Hallvard got up and came to sit on my cot as he had the day before, and I swung my legs over the edge to sit beside him. To me he said, "What Melito says is very clever. Everything he says is very clever. Still, you must judge us by the tales we told, and not by the ones we say we know but did not tell. I, too, know many other stories. Our winter nights are the longest in the Commonwealth."

I answered that according to Foila, who had originally thought of the contest and who was herself the prize, I was not yet to judge at all.

The Ascian said, "All who speak Correct Thought speak well. Where then is the superiority of some students to others? It is in the speaking. Intelligent students speak Correct Thought intelligently. The hearer knows by the intonation of their voices that they understand. By this superior speaking of intelligent students, Correct Thought is passed, like fire, from one to another."

I think that none of us had realized he was listening. We were all a trifle startled to hear him speak now. After a moment, Foila said, "He means you should not judge by the content of the stories, but by how well each was told. I'm not sure I agree with that—still, there may be something in it."

"I do not agree," Hallvard grumbled. "Those who listen soon tire of storyteller tricks. The best telling is the plainest."

Others joined in the argument, and we talked about it and about the little cock for a long time.

X

Ava

WHILE I WAS ILL I had never paid much attention to the people who brought our food, though when I reflected on it I was able to recall them clearly, as I recall everything. Once our server had been a Pelerine—she who had talked to me the night before. At other times they had been the shaven-headed male slaves, or postulants in brown. This evening, the evening of the day on which Melito had told his story, our suppers were carried in by a postulant I had not seen before, a slender, gray-eyed girl. I got up and helped her to pass around the trays.

When we were finished, she thanked me and said, "You will not be here much longer."

I told her I had something to do here, and nowhere else to go.

"You have your legion. If it has been destroyed, you will be assigned to a new one."

"I am not a soldier. I came north with some thought of enlisting, but I fell sick before I got the opportunity."

"You could have waited in your native town. I'm told that recruiting parties go to all the towns, twice a year at least."

"My native town is Nessus, I'm afraid." I saw her smile.

"But I left it some time ago, and I wouldn't have wanted to sit around someplace else for half a year waiting. Anyway, I never thought of it. Are you from Nessus too?"

"You're having trouble standing up."

"No, I'm fine."

She touched my arm, a timid gesture that somehow reminded me of the tame deer in the Autarch's garden. "You're swaying. Even if your fever is gone, you're no longer used to being on your feet. You have to realize that. You've been abed for several days. I want you to lie down again now."

"If I do that, there'll be no one to talk to except the people I've been talking with all day. The man on my right is an Ascian prisoner, and the man on my left comes from some village neither you nor I ever heard of."

"All right, if you'll lie down I'll sit and talk to you for a while. I've nothing more to do until the nocturne must be played anyway. What quarter of Nessus do you come from?"

As she escorted me to my cot, I told her that I did not want to talk, but to listen; and I asked her what quarter she herself called home.

"When you're with the Pelerines, that's your home—wherever the tents are set up. The order becomes your family and your friends, just as if all your friends had suddenly become your sisters too. But before I came here, I lived in the far northwestern part of the city, within easy sight of the Wall."

"Near the Sanguinary Field?"

"Yes, very near it. Do you know the place?"

"I fought there once."

Her eyes widened. "Did you, really? We used to go there and watch. We weren't supposed to, but we did anyway. Did you win?"

I had never thought about that and had to consider it. "No," I said after a moment. "I lost."

"But you lived. It's better, surely, to lose and live than to take another man's life."

I opened my robe and showed her the scar on my chest that Agilus's avern leaf had made.

"You were very lucky. Often they bring in soldiers with chest wounds like that, but we are seldom able to save them." Hesitantly she touched my chest. There was a sweetness in her face that I have not seen in the faces of other women. For a moment she stroked my skin, then she jerked her hand away. "It could not have been very deep."

"It wasn't," I told her.

"Once I saw a combat between an officer and an exultant in masquerade. They used poisoned plants for weapons—I suppose because the officer would have had an unfair advantage with the sword. The exultant was killed and I left, but afterward there was a great hullabaloo because the officer had run amok. He came dashing by me, striking out with his plant, but someone threw a cudgel at his legs and knocked him down. I think that was the most exciting fight I ever saw."

"Did they fight bravely?"

"Not really. There was a lot of argument about legalities—you know how men do when they don't want to begin."

" 'I shall be honored to the end of my days to have been thought worthy of such a challenge, which no other bird has ever received before. It is with the most profound regret that I must tell you I cannot accept, and that for three reasons, the first of which is that though you have feathers on your wings, as you say, it is not against your wings that I would fight.' Do you know that story?"

Smiling, she shook her head.

"It's a good one. I'll tell it to you some time. If you lived so near the Sanguinary Field, your family must have been an important one. Are you an armigette?"

"Practically all of us are armigettes or exultants. It's a rather aristocratic order, I'm afraid. Occasionally an optimate's daughter like me is admitted, when the optimate has been a longtime friend of the order, but there are only three of us. I'm told some optimates think all they have to do is make a large gift and their girls will be accepted, but it really isn't so—they have to help out in various ways, not just with money, and they have to have done it for a long time. The world, you see, is not really as corrupt as people like to believe."

I asked, "Do you think it is right to limit your order in that way? You serve the Conciliator. Did he ask the people he lifted out of death if they were armigers or exultants?"

She smiled again. "That's a question that has been debated many times in the order. But there are other orders that are quite open to optimates, and to the lower classes too, and by remaining as we are we get a great deal of money to use in our work and have a great deal of influence. If we nursed and fed only certain kinds of people, I would say you were right. But we don't; we even help animals when we can. Conexa Epicharis used to say we stopped at insects, but then she found one of us—I mean a postulant—trying to mend a butterfly's wing."

"Doesn't it bother you that these soldiers have been doing their best to kill Ascians?"

Her answer was very far from what I had expected. "Ascians are not human."

"I've already told you that the patient next to me is an Ascian. You're taking care of him, and as well as you take care of us, from what I've seen."

"And I've already told *you* that we take in animals when we can. Don't you know that human beings can lose their humanity?"

"You mean the zoanthropes. I've met some."

"Them, of course. They give up their humanity deliberately. There are others who lose theirs without intending to, often when they think they are enhancing it, or rising to some state higher than that to which we are born. Still others, like the Ascians, have it stripped from them."

I thought of Baldanders, plunging from his castle wall into

Lake Diuturna. "Surely these . . . things deserve our sympathy."

"Animals deserve our sympathy. That is why we of the order care for them. But it isn't murder for a man to kill one."

I sat up and gripped her arm, feeling an excitement I could scarcely contain. "Do you think that if something—some arm of the Conciliator, let us say—could cure human beings, it might nevertheless fail with those who are not human?"

"You mean the Claw. Close your mouth, please—you make me want to laugh when you leave it open like that, and we're not supposed to when people outside the order are around."

"You know!"

"Your nurse told me. She said you were mad, but in a nice way, and that she didn't think you would ever hurt anyone. Then I asked her about it, and she told. You have the Claw, and sometimes you can cure the sick and even raise the dead."

"Do you believe I'm mad?"

Still smiling, she nodded.

"Why? Never mind what the Pelerine told you. Have I said anything to you tonight to make you think so?"

"Or spellbound, perhaps. It isn't anything you've said at all. Or at least, not much. But you are not just one man."

She paused after saying that. I think she was waiting for me to deny it, but I said nothing.

"It is in your face and the way you move—do you know that I don't even know your name? She didn't tell me."

"Severian."

"I'm Ava. Severian is one of those brother—sister names, isn't it? Severian and Severa. Do you have a sister?"

"I don't know. If I do, she's a witch."

Ava let that pass. "The other one. Does she have a name?"

"You know she's a woman then."

"Uh huh. When I was serving the food, I thought for a moment that one of the exultant sisters had come to help me. Then I looked around and it was you. At first it seemed that it was just when I saw you from the corner of my eye, but sometimes, while we've been sitting here, I see her even when I'm looking right at you. When you glance to one side sometimes you vanish, and there's a tall, pale woman using your face. Please don't tell me I fast overmuch. That's what they all tell me, and it isn't true, and even if it were, this isn't that."

"Her name is Thecla. Do you remember what you were just saying about losing humanity? Were you trying to tell me about her?"

Ava shook her head. "I don't think so. But I wanted to ask you something. There was another patient here like you, and they told me he came with you."

"Miles, you mean. No, my case and his are quite different. I won't tell you about him. He should do it himself, or no one should. But I will tell you about myself. Do you know of the corpse-eaters?"

"You're not one of them. A few weeks ago we had three insurgent captives. I know what they're like."

"How do we differ?"

"With them . . ." She groped for words. "With them it's out of control. They talk to themselves—of course a lot of people do—and they look at things that aren't there. There's something lonely about it, and something selfish. You aren't one of them."

"But I am," I said. And I told her, without going into much detail, of Vodalus's banquet.

"They made you," she said when I was through. "If you had shown what you felt, they would have killed you."

"That doesn't matter. I drank the alzabo. I ate her flesh. And at first it was filthy, as you say, though I had loved her. She was in me, and I shared the life that had been hers, and yet she was dead. I could feel her rotting there. I had a wonderful dream of her on the first night; when I go back among my memories it is one the things I treasure most. Afterward, there was something horrible, and sometimes I seemed to be dreaming while I was awake—that was the talking and staring you mentioned, I think. Now, and for a long time, she seems alive again, but inside me."

"I don't think the others are like that."

"I don't either," I said. "At least, not from what I've heard of them. There are a great many things I do not understand. What I have told you is one of the chief ones."

Ava was quiet for the space of two or three breaths, then her eyes opened wide. "The Claw, the thing you believe in. Did you have it then?"

"Yes, but I didn't know what it could do. It had not acted—or rather, it had acted, it had raised a woman called Dorcas, but I didn't know what had happened, where she had come from. If I had known, I might have saved Thecla, brought her back."

"But you had it? You had it with you?"

I nodded.

"Then don't you see? It *did* bring her back. You just said it could act without your even knowing it. You had it, and you had her, rotting, as you say, inside you."

"Without the body . . ."

"You're a materialist, like all ignorant people. But your materialism doesn't make materialism true. Don't you know that? In the final summing up, it is spirit and dream, thought and love and act that matter."

I was so stunned by the ideas that had come crowding in on me that I did not speak again for some time, but sat wrapped in my own speculations. When I came to myself again at last, I was surprised that Ava had not gone and tried to thank her.

"It was peaceful, sitting here with you, and if one of the sisters had come, I could have said I was waiting in case one of the sick should cry out."

"I haven't decided yet about what you said about Thecla. I'll have to think about it a long time, probably for many days. People tell me I am a rather stupid man."

She smiled, and the truth was that I had said what I had (though it was true) at least in part to make her smile. "I don't think so. A thorough man, rather."

"Anyway, I have another question. Often when I tried to sleep, or when I woke in the night, I have tried to connect my failures and my successes. I mean the times when I used the Claw and revived someone, and the times when I tried to but life did not return. It seems to me that it should be more than mere chance, though perhaps the link is something I cannot know."

"Do you think you've found it now?"

"What you said about people losing their humanity—that might be a part of it. There was a woman . . . I think she may have been like that, though she was very beautiful. And a man, my friend, who was only partly cured, only helped. If it's possible for someone to lose his humanity, surely it must be possible for something that once had none to find it. What one loses another finds, everywhere. He, I think, was like that. Then too, the effect always seems less when the deaths come by violence. . . ."

"I would expect that," Ava said softly.

"It cured the man-ape whose hand I had cut away. Perhaps that was because I had done it myself. And it helped Jonas, but I—Thecla—had used those whips."

"The powers of healing protect us from Nature. Why should the Increate protect us from ourselves? We might protect ourselves from ourselves. It may be that he will help us only when we come to regret what we have done."

Still thinking, I nodded.

"I am going to the chapel now. You're well enough to walk a short distance. Will you come with me?"

While I had been beneath that wide canvas roof, it had seemed the whole of the lazaret to me. Now I saw, though

only dimly and by night, that there were many tents and
pavilions. Most, like ours, had their walls gathered up for
coolness, furled like the sails of a ship at anchor. We entered
none of them but walked between them by winding paths
that seemed long to me, until we reached one whose walls
were down. It was of silk, not canvas, and shone scarlet because of the lights within.

"Once," Ava told me, "we had a great cathedral. It could
hold ten thousand, yet be packed into a single wagon. Our
Domnicellae had it burned just before I came to the order."

"I know," I said. "I saw it."

Inside the silken tent, we knelt before a simple altar
heaped with flowers. Ava prayed. I, knowing no prayers,
spoke without sound to someone who seemed at times within
me and at times, as the angel had said, infinitely remote.

Loyal to the Group of Seventeen's Story—The Just Man

THE NEXT MORNING, when we had eaten and everyone was awake, I ventured to ask Foila if it was now time for me to judge between Melito and Hallvard. She shook her head, but before she could speak, the Ascian announced, "All must do their share in the service of the populace. The bullock draws the plow and the dog herds the sheep, but the cat catches mice in the granary. Thus men, women, and even children can serve the populace."

Foila flashed that dazzling smile. "Our friend wants to tell a story too."

"What!" For a moment I thought Melito was actually going to sit up. "Are you going to let him—let one of them—consider—"

She gestured, and he sputtered to silence. "Why yes." Something tugged at the corners of her lips. "Yes, I think I shall. I'll have to interpret for the rest of you, of course. Will that be all right, Severian?"

"If you wish it," I said.

Hallvard rumbled, "This was not in the original agreement. I recall each word."

"So do I," Foila said. "It isn't against it either, and in fact it's in accordance with the *spirit* of the agreement, which was that the rivals for my hand—neither very soft nor very fair now, I'm afraid, though it's becoming more so since I've been confined in this place—would compete. The Ascian would be my suitor if he thought he could; haven't you seen the way he looks at me?"

The Ascian recited, "United, men and women are stronger; but a brave woman desires children, and not husbands."

"He means that he would like to marry me, but he doesn't think his attentions would be acceptable. He's wrong." Foila looked from Melito to Hallvard, and her smile had become a grin. "Are you two really so frightened of him in a storytelling contest? You must have run like rabbits when you saw an Ascian on the battlefield."

Neither of them answered, and after a time, the Ascian began to speak: "In times past, loyalty to the cause of the populace was to be found everywhere. The will of the Group of Seventeen was the will of everyone."

Foila interpreted: *"Once upon a time . . ."*

"Let no one be idle. If one is idle, let him band together with others who are idle too, and let them look for idle land. Let everyone they meet direct them. It is better to walk a thousand leagues than to sit in the House of Starvation."

"There was a remote farm worked in partnership by people who were not related."

"One is strong, another beautiful, a third a cunning artificer. Which is best? He who serves the populace."

"On this farm lived a good man."

"Let the work be divided by a wise divider of work. Let the food be divided by a just divider of food. Let the pigs grow fat. Let rats starve."

"The others cheated him of his share."

"The people meeting in counsel may judge, but no one is to receive more than a hundred blows."

"He complained, and they beat him."

"How are the hands nourished? By the blood. How does

the blood reach the hands? By the veins. If the veins are closed, the hands will rot away."

"He left that farm and took to the roads."

"Where the Group of Seventeen sit, there final justice is done."

"He went to the capital and complained of the way he had been treated."

"Let there be clean water for those who toil. Let there be hot food for them and a clean bed."

"He came back to the farm, tired and hungry after his journey."

"No one is to receive more than a hundred blows."

"They beat him again."

"Behind everything some further thing is found, forever; thus the tree behind the bird, stone beneath soil, the sun behind Urth. Behind our efforts, let there be found our efforts."

"The just man did not give up. He left the farm again to walk to the capital."

"Can all petitioners be heard? No, for all cry together. Who, then, shall be heard—is it those who cry loudest? No, for all cry loudly. Those who cry longest shall be heard, and justice shall be done to them."

"Arriving at the capital, he camped upon the very door-step of the Group of Seventeen and begged all who passed to listen to him. After a long time he was admitted to the palace, where those in authority heard his complaints with sympathy."

"So say the Group of Seventeen: From those who steal, take all they have, for nothing that they have is their own."

"They told him to go back to the farm and tell the bad men—in their name—that they must leave."

"As a good child to its mother, so is the citizen to the Group of Seventeen."

"He did just as they had said."

"What is foolish speech? It is wind. It has come in at the ears and goes out of the mouth. No one is to receive more than a hundred blows."

"*They mocked him and beat him.*"

"Behind our efforts, let there be found our efforts."

"*The just man did not give up. He returned to the capital once more.*"

"The citizen renders to the populace what is due to the populace. What is due to the populace? Everything."

"*He was very tired. His clothes were in rags and his shoes worn out. He had no food and nothing to trade.*"

"It is better to be just than to be kind, but only good judges can be just; let those who cannot be just be kind."

"*In the capital he lived by begging.*"

At this point I could not help but interrupt. I told Foila that I thought it was wonderful that she understood so well what each of the stock phrases the Ascian used meant in the context of his story, but that I could not understand how she did it—how she knew, for example, that the phrase about kindness and justice meant that the hero had become a beggar.

"Well, suppose that someone else—Melito, perhaps—were telling a story, and at some point in it he thrust out his hand and began to ask for alms. You'd know what that meant, wouldn't you?"

I agreed that I would.

"It's just the same here. Sometimes we find Ascian soldiers who are too hungry or too sick to keep up with the rest, and after they understand we aren't going to kill them, that business about kindness and justice is what they say. In Ascian, of course. It's what beggars say in Ascia."

"Those who cry longest shall be heard, and justice shall be done to them."

"This time he had to wait a long while before he was admitted to the palace, but at last they let him in and heard what he had to say."

"Those who will not serve the populace shall serve the populace."

"They said they would put the bad men in prison."

"Let there be clean water for those who toil. Let there be hot food for them, and a clean bed."

"He went back home."

"No one is to receive more than a hundred blows."

"He was beaten again."

"Behind our efforts, let there be found our efforts."

"But he did not give up. Once more he set off for the capital to complain."

"Those who fight for the populace fight with a thousand hearts. Those who fight against them with none."

"Now the bad men were afraid."

"Let no one oppose the decisions of the Group of Seventeen."

"They said to themselves, 'He has gone to the palace again and again, and each time he must have told the rulers there that we did not obey their earlier commands. Surely, this time they will send soldiers to kill us."

"If their wounds are in their backs, who shall stanch their blood?"

"The bad men ran away."

"Where are those who in times past have opposed the decisions of the Group of Seventeen?"

"They were never seen again."

"Let there be clean water for those who toil. Let there be hot food for them, and a clean bed. Then they will sing at their work, and their work will be light to them. Then they will sing at the harvest, and the harvest will be heavy."

"The just man returned home and lived happily ever after."

. . .

Everyone applauded this story, moved by the story itself, by the ingenuity of the Ascian prisoner, by the glimpse it had afforded us of life in Ascia, and most of all, I think, by the graciousness and wit Foila had brought to her translation.

I have no way of knowing whether you, who eventually will read this record, like stories or not. If you do not, no doubt you have turned these pages without attention. I confess that I love them. Indeed, it often seems to me that of all the good things in the world, the only ones humanity can claim for itself are stories and music; the rest, mercy, beauty, sleep, clean water and hot food (as the Ascian would have said) are all the work of the Increate. Thus, stories are small things indeed in the scheme of the universe, but it is hard not to love best what is our own—hard for me, at least.

From this story, though it was the shortest and the most simple too of all those I have recorded in this book, I feel that I learned several things of some importance. First of all, how much of our speech, which we think freshly minted in our own mouths, consists of set locutions. The Ascian seemed to speak only in sentences he had learned by rote, though until he used each for the first time we had never heard them. Foila seemed to speak as women commonly do, and if I had been asked whether she employed such tags, I would have said that she did not—but how often one might have predicted the ends of her sentences from their beginnings.

Second, I learned how difficult it is to eliminate the urge for expression. The people of Ascia were reduced to speaking only with their masters' voice; but they had made of it a new tongue, and I had no doubt, after hearing the Ascian, that by it he could express whatever thought he wished.

And third, I learned once again what a many-sided thing is the telling of any tale. None, surely, could be plainer than the Ascian's, yet what did it mean? Was it intended to praise the Group of Seventeen? The mere terror of their name had routed the evildoers. Was it intended to condemn them?

They had heard the complaints of the just man, and yet they had done nothing for him beyond giving him their verbal support. There had been no indication they would ever do more.

But I had not learned those things I had most wished to learn as I listened to the Ascian and to Foila. What had been her motive in agreeing to allow the Ascian to compete? Mere mischief? From her laughing eyes I could easily believe it. Was she perhaps in truth attracted to him? I found that more difficult to credit, but it was surely not impossible. Who has not seen women attracted to men lacking every attractive quality? She had clearly had much to do with Ascians, and he was clearly no ordinary soldier, since he had been taught our language. Did she hope to wring some secret from him?

And what of him? Melito and Hallvard had accused each other of telling tales with an ulterior purpose. Had he done so as well? If he had, it had surely been to tell Foila—and the rest of us too—that he would never give up.

Winnoc

THAT EVENING I had yet another visitor: one of the shaven-headed male slaves. I had been sitting up and attempting to talk with the Ascian, and he seated himself beside me. "Do you remember me, Lictor?" he asked. "My name is Winnoc."

I shook my head.

"It was I who bathed you and cared for you on the night you arrived," he told me. "I have been waiting until you were well enough to speak. I would have come last night, but you were deep in talk already with one of our postulants."

I asked what he wished to speak to me about.

"A moment ago I called you Lictor, and you did not deny it. Are you indeed a lictor? You were dressed as one that night."

"I have been a lictor," I said. "Those are the only clothes I own."

"But you are a lictor no longer?"

I shook my head. "I came north to enter the army."

"Ah," he said. For a moment he looked away.

"Surely others do the same."

"A few, yes. Most join in the south, or are made to join. A

few come north like you, because they want some special unit where a friend or relation is already. A soldier's life . . ."

I waited for him to continue.

"It's a lot like a slave's, I think. I've never been a soldier myself, but I've talked to a lot of them."

"Is your life so miserable? I would have thought the Pelerines kind mistresses. Do they beat you?"

He smiled at that and turned until I could see his back. "You've been a lictor. What do you think of my scars?"

In the fading light I could scarcely make them out. I ran my fingers across them. "Only that they are very old and were made with the lash," I said.

"I got them before I was twenty, and I'm nearly fifty now. A man with black clothes like yours made them. Were you a lictor for long?"

"No, not long."

"Then you don't know much of the business?"

"Enough to practice it."

"And that's all? The man who whipped me told me he was from the guild of torturers. I thought maybe you might have heard of them."

"I have."

"Are they real? Some people have told me they died out a long time ago, but that isn't what the man who whipped me said."

I told him, "They still exist, so far as I'm aware. Do you happen to recall the name of the torturer who scourged you?"

"He called himself Journeyman Palaemon—ah, you know him!"

"Yes. He was my teacher for a time. He's an old man now."

"He's still alive, then? Will you ever see him again?"

"I don't think so."

"I'd like to see him myself. Maybe sometime I will. The

Increate, after all, orders all things. You young men, you live wild lives—I know I did, at your age. Do you know yet that he shapes everything we do?"

"Perhaps."

"Believe me, it's so. I've seen much more than you. Since it is so, it may be that I'll never see Journeyman Palaemon again, and you've been brought here to be my messenger."

Just at that point, when I expected him to convey to me whatever message he had, he fell silent. The patients who had listened so attentively to the Ascian's story were talking among themselves now; but somewhere in the stack of soiled dishes the old slave had collected, one shifted its position with a faint clink, and I heard it.

"What do you know of the laws of slavery?" he asked me at last. "I mean, of the ways a man or a woman can become a slave under the law?"

"Very little," I said. "A certain friend of mine" (I was thinking of the green man) "was called a slave, but he was only an unlucky foreigner who'd been seized by some unscrupulous people. I knew that wasn't legal."

He nodded agreement. "Was he dark of skin?"

"You might say that, yes."

"In the olden times, or so I've heard, slavery was by skin color. The darker a man was, the more a slave they made him. That's hard to believe, I know. But we used to have a chatelaine in the order who knew a lot about history, and she told me. She was a truthful woman."

"No doubt it originated because slaves must often toil in the sun," I observed. "Many of the usages of the past now seem merely capricious to us."

At that he became a trifle angry. "Believe me, young man, I've lived in the old days and I've lived now, and I know a lot better than you which was the best."

"So Master Palaemon used to say."

As I had hoped it would, that restored him to the principal

topic of his thought. "There's only three ways a man can be a slave," he said. "Though for a woman it's different, what with marriage and the like.

"If a man's brought—him being a slave—into the Commonwealth from foreign parts, a slave he remains, and the master that brought him here can sell him if he wants. That's one. Prisoners of war—like this Ascian here—are the slaves of the Autarch, the Master of Masters and the Slave of Slaves. The Autarch can sell them if he wants to. Often he does, and because most of these Ascians aren't much use except for tedious work, you often find them rowing on the upper rivers. That's two.

"Number three is that a man can sell himself into somebody's service, because a free man is the master of his own body—he's his own slave already, as it were."

"Slaves," I remarked, "are seldom beaten by torturers. What need of it, when they can be beaten by their own masters?"

"I wasn't a slave then. That's part of what I wanted to ask Journeyman Palaemon about. I was just a young fellow that had been caught stealing. Journeyman Palaemon came in to talk to me on the morning I was going to get my whipping. I thought it was a kindly thing for him to do, although it was then that he told me he was from the guild of torturers."

"We always prepare a client, if we can," I said.

"He told me not to try to keep from yelling—it doesn't hurt quite so bad, is what he told me, if you yell out just as the whip comes down. He promised me there wouldn't be any hitting more than the number the judge said, so I could count them if I wanted to, and that way I'd know when it was about over. And he said he wouldn't hit harder than he had to, to cut the skin, and he wouldn't break any bones."

I nodded.

"I asked him then if he'd do me a favor, and he said he would if he could. I wanted for him to come back afterward and talk to me again, and he said he would try to when I was a little recovered. Then a caloyer came in to read the prayer.

"They tied me to a post, with my hands over my head and the indictment tacked up above my hands. Probably you've done it yourself many times."

"Often enough," I told him.

"I doubt the way they did me was any different. I've got the scars of it still, but they've faded, just like you say. I've seen many a man with worse ones. The jailers, they dragged me back to my cell as the custom is, but I think I could have walked. It didn't hurt as much as losing an arm or a leg. Here I've helped the surgeons take off a good many."

"Were you thin in those days?" I asked him.

"Very thin. I think you could have counted every rib I had."

"That was much to your advantage, then. The lash cuts deep in a fat man's back, and he bleeds like a pig. People say the traders aren't punished enough for short weighing and the like, but those who speak so don't know how they suffer when they are."

Winnoc nodded to that. "The next day I felt almost as strong as ever, and Journeyman Palaemon came like he'd promised. I told him how it was with me—how I lived and all—and asked him a bit about himself. I guess it seems queer to you that I'd talk so to a man that had whipped me?"

"No. I've heard of similar things many times."

"He told me he'd done something against his guild. He wouldn't tell me what it was, but because of it he was exiled for a while. He told me how he felt about it and how lonesome he was. He said he'd tried to feel better by thinking how other people lived, by knowing they had no more guild than he did. But he could only feel sorry for them, and pretty soon he felt sorry for himself too. He told me that if I wanted to be happy, and not go through this kind of thing again, to find some sort of brotherhood for myself and join."

"Yes?" I asked.

"And I decided to do what he's said. When I was let out, I spoke to the masters of a lot of guilds, picking and choosing them at first, then talking to any I thought might take me, like the butchers and the candlemakers. None of them would take on an apprentice as old as I was, or somebody that didn't have the fee, or somebody with a bad character—they looked at my back, you see, and decided I was a trouble-maker.

"I thought about signing on a ship or joining the army, and since then I've often wished I'd gone ahead with one or the other, although maybe if I had I'd wish now I hadn't, or maybe not be living to wish at all. Then I got the notion of joining some religious order, I don't know why. I talked to a bunch of them, and two offered to take me, even when I told them I didn't have any money and showed them my back. But the more I heard about the way they were supposed to live in there, the less I felt like I could do it. I had been drunk a lot, and I liked the girls, and I didn't really want to change.

"Then one day when I was standing around on a corner I saw a man I took to belong to some order I hadn't talked to yet. By that time I was planning to sign aboard a certain ship, but it wasn't going to sail for almost a week, and a sailor had told me a lot of the hardest work came while they were getting ready, and I'd miss it if I waited until they were about to get up the anchor. That was all a lie, but I didn't know it then.

"Anyway, I followed this man I'd seen, and when he stopped—he'd been sent to buy vegetables, you see—I went up to him and asked him about his order. He told me he was a slave of the Pelerines and it was about the same as being in an order, but better. A man could have a drink or two and nobody'd object so long as he was sober when he came to his work. He could lie with the girls too, and there were good chances for that because the girls thought they were holy men, more or less, and they traveled all around.

"I asked if he thought they'd take me, and I said I couldn't believe the life was as good as he made it out to be. He said he was sure they would, and although he couldn't prove what he'd said about the girls right then and there, he'd prove what he'd said about drinking by splitting a bottle of red with me.

"We went to a tavern by the market and sat down, and he was as good as his word. He told me the life was a lot like a sailor's, because the best part of being a sailor was seeing various places, and they did that. It was like being a soldier too, because they carried weapons when the order journeyed in wild parts. Besides all of that, they paid you to sign. In an order, the order gets an offering from every man who takes their vow. If he decides to leave later, he gets some of it back, depending on how long he's been in. For us slaves, as he explained to me, all that went the other way. A slave got paid when he signed. If he left later he'd have to buy his way out, but if he stayed he could keep all the money.

"I had a mother, and even though I never went to see her I knew she didn't have an aes. While I was thinking about the religious orders, I'd got to be more religious myself, and I didn't see how I was going to minister to the Increate with her on my mind. I signed the paper—naturally Goslin, the slave who'd brought me in, got a reward for it—and I took the money to my mother."

I said, "That made her happy, I'm sure, and you too."

"She thought it was some kind of trick, but I left it with her anyhow. I had to go back to the order right away, naturally, and they'd sent somebody with me. Now I've been here thirty years."

"You're to be congratulated, I hope."

"I don't know. It's been a hard life, but then all lives are hard, from what I've seen of them."

"I too," I said. To tell the truth, I was becoming sleepy and wished that he would go. "Thank you for telling me your story. I found it very interesting."

"I want to ask you something," he said, "and I want you to ask Journeyman Palaemon for me if you see him again."

I nodded, waiting.

"You said you thought the Pelerines would be kind mistresses, and I suppose you're right. I've had a lot of kindness from some of them, and I've never been whipped here—nothing worse than a few slaps. But you ought to know how they do it. Slaves that don't behave themselves get sold, that's all. Maybe you don't follow me."

"I don't think I do."

"A lot of men sell themselves to the order, thinking like I did that it'll be an easy life and an adventure. So it is, mostly, and it's a good feeling to help cure the sick and the wounded. But those who don't suit the Pelerines are sold off, and they get a lot more for them than they paid them. Do you see how it is now? This way, they don't have to beat anybody. About the worst punishment you get is scrubbing out the jakes. Only if you don't please them, you can find yourself getting driven down into a mine.

"What I've wanted to ask Journeyman Palaemon all these years . . ." Winnoc paused, gnawing at his lower lip. "He was a torturer, wasn't he? He said so, and so did you."

"Yes, he was. He still is."

"Then what I want to know is whether he told me what he did to torment me. Or was he giving me the best advice he could?" He looked away so that I would not see his expression. "Will you ask him that for me? Then maybe sometime I'll see you again."

I said, "He advised you as well as he could, I'm certain. If you'd stayed as you were, you might have been executed by him or another torturer long ago. Have you ever seen a man executed? But torturers don't know everything."

Winnoc stood up. "Neither do slaves. Thank you, young man."

I touched his arm to detain him for a moment. "May I ask you something now? I myself have been a torturer. If you've feared for so many years that Master Palaemon had said what he did only to give you pain, how do you know that I haven't done the same just now?"

"Because you would have said the other," he told me. "Good night, young man."

I thought for a time about what Winnoc had said, and about what Master Palaemon had said to him so long ago. He too had been a wanderer, then, perhaps ten years before I was born. And yet he had returned to the Citadel to become a master of the guild. I recalled the way Abdiesus (whom I had betrayed) had wished to have me made a Master. Surely, whatever crime Master Palaemon had committed had been hidden later by all the brothers of the guild. Now he was a master, though as I had seen all my life, being too accustomed to it to wonder at it, it was Master Gurloes who directed the guild's affairs despite his being so much younger. Outside the warm winds of the northern summer played among the tent ropes; but it seemed to me that I climbed the steep steps of the Matachin Tower again and heard the cold winds sing among the keeps of the Citadel.

At last, hoping to turn my mind to less painful matters, I stood and stretched and strolled to Foila's cot. She was awake, and I talked with her for a time, then asked if I might judge the stories now; but she said I would have to wait one more day at least.

Foila's Story—The Armiger's Daughter

"HALLVARD AND MELITO and even the Ascian have had their chances. Don't you think I'm entitled to one too? Even a man who courts a maid thinking he has no rivals has one, and that one is herself. She may give herself to him, but she may also choose to keep herself for herself. He has to convince her that she will be happier with him than by herself, and though men convince maids of that often, it isn't often true. In this competition I will make my own entry, and win myself for myself if I can. If I marry for tales, should I marry someone who's a worse teller of them than I am myself?"

"Each of the men has told a story of his own country. I will do the same. My land is the land of the far horizons, of the wide sky. It is the land of grass and wind and galloping hoofs. In summer the wind can be as hot as the breath of an oven, and when the pampas take fire, the line of smoke stretches a hundred leagues and the lions ride our cattle to escape it, looking like devils. The men of my country are brave as bulls and the women are fierce as hawks.

"When my grandmother was young, there was a villa in my country so remote that no one ever came there. It belonged to an armiger, a feudatory of the Liege of Pascua. The lands were rich, and it was a fine house, though the roof beams had been dragged by oxen all one summer to get them to the site. The walls were of earth, as the walls of all the houses in my country are, and they were three paces thick. People who live in woodlands scoff at such walls, but they are cool and make a fine appearance whitewashed and will not burn. There was a tower and a wide banqueting hall, and a contrivance of ropes and wheels and buckets by which two merychips, walking in a circle, watered the garden on the roof.

"The armiger was a gallant man and his wife a lovely woman, but of all their children only one lived beyond the first year. She was tall, brown as leather yet smooth as oil, with hair the color of the palest wine and eyes dark as thunderheads. Still, the villa where they dwelt was so remote that no one knew and no one came to seek her. Often she rode all day alone, hunting with her peregrine or dashing after her spotted hunting cats when they had started an antelope. Often too she sat alone in her bedchamber all the day, hearing the song of her lark in its cage and turning the pages of old books her mother had carried from her own home.

"At last her father determined that she must wed, for she was near the twentieth year, after which few would want her. Then he sent his servants everywhere for three hundred leagues around, crying her beauty and promising that on his death her husband should hold all that was his. Many fine riders came, with silver-mounted saddles and coral on the pommels of their swords. He entertained them all, and his daughter, with her hair in a man's hat and a long knife in a man's sash, mingled with them, feigning to be one of them, so that she might hear who boasted of many women and see who stole when he thought himself unobserved. Each night she went to her father and told him their names, and when she had gone he called them to him and told them of the stakes where no one goes, where men bound in rawhide die in the sun; and the next morning they saddled their mounts and rode away.

"Soon there remained but three. Then the armiger's daughter could go among them no more, for with so few she feared they would surely know her. She went to her bed-chamber and let down her hair and brushed it, and took off her hunting clothes and bathed in scented water. She put rings on her fingers and bracelets on her arms and wide hoops of gold in her ears, and on her head that thin circlet of fine gold that an armiger's daughter is entitled to wear. In short, she did all she knew to make herself beautiful, and because her heart was brave, perhaps there was no maid anywhere more beautiful than she.

"When she was dressed as she wished, she sent her servant to call her father and the three suitors to her. 'Now behold me,' she said. 'You see a ring of gold about my brow, and smaller rings suspended from my ears. The arms that will embrace one of you are themselves embraced by rings smaller still, and rings yet smaller are on my fingers. My chest of jewels lies open before you, and there are no more rings to be found in it; but there is another ring still in this room—a ring I do not wear. Can one of you discover it and bring it to me?'

"The three suitors looked up and down, behind the arras, and beneath the bed. At last the youngest took the lark's cage from its hook and carried it to the armiger's daughter; and there, about the lark's right leg, was a tiny ring of gold. 'Now hear me,' she said. 'My husband shall be the man who shows me this little brown bird again.'

"And with that she opened the cage and thrust in her hand, then carrying the lark upon her finger took it to the window and tossed it in the air. For a moment the three suitors saw the gold ring glint in the sun. The lark rose until it was no more than a dot against the sky.

"Then the suitors rushed down the stair and out the door, calling for their mounts, the swift-footed friends that had carried them already so many leagues across the empty pampas. Their silver-mounted saddles they threw upon their backs, and in less than a moment all three were gone from the sight of the armiger and the armiger's daughter, and from each other's as well, for one rode north toward the jungles, and one east toward the mountains, and the youngest west toward the restless sea.

"When he who went north had ridden for some days, he came to a river too swift for swimming and rode along its bank, ever harkening to the songs of the birds who dwelt there, until he reached a ford. In that ford a rider in brown sat a brown destrier. His face was masked with a brown neck-cloth, his cloak, his hat, and all his clothing were of brown, and about the ankle of his brown right boot was a ring of gold.

" 'Who are you?' " called the suitor.

The figure in brown answered not a word.

" 'There was among us at the armiger's house a certain young man who vanished on the day before the last day,' said the suitor, 'and I think that you are he. In some way you have learned of my quest, and now you seek to prevent me. Well, stand clear of my road, or die where you stand.'

"And with that he drew sword and spurred his destrier into the water. For some time they fought as the men of my country fight, with the sword in the right hand and the long knife in the left, for the suitor was strong and brave, and the rider in brown was quick and blade-crafty. But at last the latter fell, and his blood stained the water.

" 'I leave you your mount,' the suitor called, 'if your strength is sufficient to get you into the saddle again. For I am a merciful man.' And he rode away.

"When he who had ridden toward the mountains had ridden for some days also, he came to such a bridge as the mountain people build, a narrow affair of rope and bamboo, stretched across a chasm like the web of a spider. No man but a fool attempts to ride across such a contrivance, and so he dismounted and led his mount by the reins.

"When he began to cross it seemed to him that the bridge was all empty before him, but he had not come a quarter of the way when a figure appeared in the center. In form it was much like a man, but it was all of brown save for one flash of white, and it seemed to fold brown wings about itself. When the second suitor was closer still he saw that it wore a ring of gold about the ankle of one boot, and the brown wings now seemed no more than a cloak of that color.

"Then he traced a Sign in the air before him to protect him from those spirits that have forgotten their creator, and he called, 'Who are you? Name yourself!'

" 'You see me,' the figure answered him. 'Name me true, and your wish is my wish.'

" 'You are the spirit of the lark sent forth by the armiger's daughter,' said the second suitor. 'Your form you may change, but the ring marks you.'

"At that, the figure in brown drew sword and presented it hilt foremost to the second suitor. 'You have named me rightly,' it said. 'What would you have me do?'

" 'Return with me to the armiger's house,' said the suitor, 'so that I may show you to the armiger's daughter and so win her.'

" 'I will return with you gladly, if that is what you wish,' said the figure in brown. 'But I warn you now that if she sees me, she will not see in me what you see.'

" 'Nevertheless, come with me,' answered the suitor, for he did not know what else to say.

"On such a bridge as the mountain people build, a man may turn about without much difficulty, but a four-legged beast finds it nearly impossible to do so. Therefore, they were forced to.continue to the farther side in order that the second suitor might face his mount toward the armiger's house once more. 'How tedious this is,' he thought as he walked the great catenary of the bridge, 'and yet, how difficult and dangerous. Cannot that be used to my benefit?' At last he called to the figure in brown, 'I must walk this bridge, and then walk it again. But must you do so as well? Why don't you fly to the other side and wait there for me?'

"At that, the figure in brown laughed, a wondrous trilling. 'Did you not see that one of my wings is bandaged? I fluttered too near one of your rivals, and he slashed at me with his sword.'

" 'Then you cannot fly far?' asked the second suitor.

" 'No indeed. As you approached this bridge I was perched on the brown walkway resting, and when I heard your tread I had scarcely strength to flutter up.'

" 'I see,' said the second suitor, and no more. But to himself he thought: 'If I were to cut this bridge, the lark would be forced to take bird-form again—yet it could not fly far, and I should surely kill it. Then I could carry it back, and the armiger's daughter would know it.' "

"When they reached the farther side, he patted the neck of his mount and turned it about, thinking that it would die, but that the best such animal was a small price to set against the ownership of great herds. 'Follow us,' he said to the figure in brown, and led his mount onto the bridge again, so that over that windy and aching chasm he went first, and the destrier behind him, and the figure in brown last of all. 'The beast will rear as the bridge falls,' he thought, 'and the spirit of the lark will not be able to dash past, so it must resume its bird shape or perish.' His plans, you see, were themselves shaped by the beliefs of my land, where those who set store in shape-changers will tell you that like thoughts they will not change once they have been made prisoner.

"Down the long curve of the bridge again walked the three, and up the side from which the second suitor had come, and as soon as he set foot on the rock, he drew his sword, sharp as his labor could make it. Two handrails of rope the bridge had, and two cables of hemp to support the roadway. He ought to have cut those first, but he wasted a moment on the handrails, and the figure in brown sprang from behind into the destrier's saddle, drove spur to its flanks, and rode him down. Thus he died under the hoofs of his own mount.

"When the youngest suitor, who had gone toward the sea, had ridden some days as well, he reached its marge. There on the beach beside the unquiet sea he met someone cloaked in brown, with a brown hat, and a brown cloth across nose and mouth, and a gold ring about the ankle of a brown boot.

" 'You see me,' the person in brown called. 'Name me true, and your wish shall be my wish.'

" 'You are an angel,' replied the youngest suitor, 'sent to guide me to the lark I seek.'

"At that the brown angel drew a sword and presented it, hilt foremost, to the youngest suitor, saying, 'You have named me rightly. What would you have me do?'

" 'Never will I attempt to thwart the will of the Liege of Angels,' answered the youngest suitor. 'Since you are sent to guide me to the lark, my only wish is that you shall do so.'

" 'And so I shall,' said the angel. 'But would you go by the shortest road? Or the best?'

"At that the youngest suitor thought to himself, 'Here surely is some trick. Ever the empyrean powers rebuke the impatience of men, which they, being immortal, can easily afford to do. Doubtless the shortest way lies through the horrors of caverns underground, or something like.' Therefore he answered the angel, 'By the best. Would not it dishonor her whom I shall wed to travel any other?'

" 'Some say one thing and some another,' replied the angel. 'Now let me mount up behind you. Not far from here there is a goodly port, and there I have just sold two destriers as good as yours or better. We shall sell yours as well, and the gold ring that circles my boot.'

"In the port they did as the angel had indicated, and with their money purchased a ship, not large but swift and sound, and hired three knowing seamen to work her.

"On the third day out from port, the youngest suitor had

such a dream by night as young men have. When he woke he touched the pillow near his head and found it warm, and when he lay down to sleep again, he winded some delicate perfume—the odor, it might have been, of the flowering grasses the women of my land dry in spring to braid in their hair.

"An isle they reached where no men come, and the youngest suitor went ashore to search for the lark. He found it not, but at the dying of the day stripped off his garments to cool himself in the surging sea. There, when the stars had brightened, another joined him. Together they swam, and together lay telling tales on the beach.

"One day while they were peering over the prow of their ship for another (for they traded at times and at times fought also) a great gust of wind came and the angel's hat was blown into the all-devouring sea, and soon the brown cloth that had covered her face went to join it.

"At last they grew weary of the unresting sea and thought of my land, where the lions ride our cattle in autumn when the grass burns, and the men are brave as bulls and the women fierce as hawks. Their ship they had called the *Lark*, and now the *Lark* flew across blue waters, each morn impaling the red sun upon her bowsprit. In the port where they had bought her they sold her and received three times the price, for she had become a famous vessel, renowned in song and story; and indeed, all who came to the port wondered at how small she was, a trim, brown craft hardly a score of paces from stem to rudderpost. Their loot they sold also, and the goods they had gained by trading. The people of my land keep the best destriers they breed for themselves, but it is to this port that they bring the best of those they sell, and there the youngest suitor and the angel bought good mounts and filled their saddlebags with gems and gold, and set out for the armiger's house that is so remote that no one ever comes there.

"Many a scrape did they have upon the way, and many a

time bloody the swords that had been washed so often in the cleansing sea and wiped on sailcloth or sand. Yet at last come they did. There the angel was welcomed by the armiger, shouting, and by his wife, weeping, and by all the servants, talking. And there she doffed her brown clothing and became the armiger's daughter of old once more.

"A great wedding was planned. In my land such things take many days, for there are roasting pits to be dug anew, and cattle to be slaughtered, and messengers who must ride for days to fetch guests who must ride for days also. On the third day, as they waited, the armiger's daughter sent her servant to the youngest suitor, saying, "My mistress will not hunt today. Rather, she invites you to her bedchamber, to talk of times past upon sea and land."

"The youngest suitor dressed himself in the finest of the clothes he had bought when they had returned to port, and soon was at the door of the armiger's daughter.

"He found her sitting on a window seat, turning the pages of one of the old books her mother had carried from her own home and listening to the singing of a lark in a cage. To that cage he went, and saw that the lark had a ring of gold about one leg. Then he looked at the armiger's daughter, wondering.

" 'Did the angel you met upon the strand not promise you should be guided to this lark?' she said. 'And by the best road? Each morning I open his cage and cast him out upon the wind to exercise his wings. Soon he returns to it again, where there is food for him, clean water, and safety.'

"Some say the wedding of the youngest suitor and the armiger's daughter was the finest ever seen in my land."

Mannea

THAT NIGHT THERE WAS much talk of Foila's story, and this time it was I who postponed making any judgment among the tales. Indeed, I had formed a sort of horror of judging, the residue, perhaps, of my education among the torturers, who teach their apprentices from boyhood to execute the instructions of the judges appointed (as they themselves are not) by the officials of our Commonwealth.

In addition, I had something more pressing on my mind. I had hoped that our evening meal would be served by Ava, but when it was not, I rose anyway, dressed myself in my own clothes, and slipped off in the gathering dark.

It was a surprise—a very pleasant one—to find that my legs were strong again. I had been free of fever for several days, yet I had grown accustomed to thinking myself ill (just as I had earlier been accustomed to thinking myself well) and had lain in my cot without complaint. No doubt many a man who walks about and does his work is dying and ignorant of it, and many who lie abed all day are healthier than those who bring their food and wash them.

I tried to recall, as I followed the winding paths between

the tents, when I had felt so well before. Not in the mountains or upon the lake—the hardships I had suffered there had gradually reduced my vitality until I fell prey to the fever. Not when I fled Thrax, for I was already worn out from my duties as lictor. Not when I had arrived at Thrax; Dorcas and I had undergone privations in the roadless country nearly as severe as I was to bear alone in the mountains. Not even when I had been at the House Absolute (a period that now seemed as remote as the reign of Ymar), because I had still been suffering the aftereffects of the alzabo and my ingestion of Thecla's dead memories.

At last it came to me: I felt now as I had on that memorable morning when Agia and I had set out for the Botanic Gardens, the first morning after I had left the Citadel. That morning, though I had not known it, I had acquired the Claw. For the first time I wondered if it had not been cursed as well as blessed. Or perhaps it was only that all the past months had been needed for me to recover fully from the leaf of the avern that had pierced me that same evening. I took out the Claw and stared at its silvery gleam, and when I raised my eyes, I saw the glowing scarlet of the Pelerines' chapel.

I could hear the chanting, and I knew it would be some time before the chapel would be empty, but I proceeded anyway, and at last slipped through the door and took a place in the back. Of the liturgy of the Pelerines, I will say nothing. Such things cannot always be well described, and even when they can, it is less than proper to do so. The guild called the Seekers for Truth and Penitence, to which I at one time belonged, has its own ceremonies, one of which I have described in some detail in another place. Certainly those ceremonies are peculiar to it, and perhaps those of the Pelerines were peculiar to them as well, though they may once have been universal.

Speaking in so far as I can as an unprejudiced observer, I

would say that they were more beautiful than ours but less theatrical, and thus in the long run perhaps less moving. The costumes of the participants were ancient, I am sure, and striking. The chants possessed a queer attraction I have not encountered in other music. Our ceremonies were intended chiefly to impress the role of the guild upon the minds of our younger members. Possibly those of the Pelerines had a similar function. If not, then they were designed to engage the particular attention of the All-Seeing, and whether they did so I cannot say. In the event, the order received no special protection.

When the ceremony was over and the scarlet-clad priestesses filed out, I bowed my head and feigned to be deep in prayer. Very readily, I found, the pretense became the thing itself. I remained conscious of my kneeling body, but only as a peripheral burden. My mind was among the starry wastes, far from Urth and indeed far from Urth's archipelago of island worlds, and it seemed to me that that to which I spoke was farther still—I had come, as it were, to the walls of the universe, and now shouted through the walls to one who waited outside.

"Shouted," I said, but perhaps that is the wrong word. Rather I whispered, as Barnoch, perhaps, walled up in his house, might have whispered through some chink to a sympathetic passerby. I spoke of what I had been when I wore a ragged shirt and watched the beasts and birds through the narrow window of the mausoleum, and what I had become. I spoke too, not of Vodalus and his struggle against the Autarch, but of the motives I had once foolishly attributed to him. I did not deceive myself with the thought that I had it in me to lead millions. I asked only that I might lead myself; and as I did so, I seemed to see, with a vision increasingly clear, through the chink in the universe to a new universe bathed in golden light, where my listener knelt to hear me. What had seemed a crevice in the world had expanded until

I could see a face and folded hands, and the opening, like a tunnel, running deep into a human head that for a time seemed larger than the head of Typhon carved upon the mountain. I was whispering into my own ear, and when I realized it I flew into it like a bee and stood up.

Everyone was gone, and a silence as profound as any I have ever heard seemed to hang in the air with the incense. The altar rose before me, humble in comparison to that Agia and I had destroyed, yet beautiful with its lights and purity of line and panels of sunstone and lapis lazuli.

Now I came forward and knelt before it. I needed no scholar to tell me the Theologoumenon was no nearer now. Yet he seemed nearer, and I was able—for the final time—to take out the Claw, something I had feared I could not do. Forming the syllables only in my mind, I said, "I have carried you over many mountains, across rivers, and across the pampas. You have given Thecla life in me. You have given me Dorcas, and you have restored Jonas to this world. Surely I have no complaint of you, though you must have many of me. One I shall not deserve. It shall not be said that I did not do what I might to undo the harm I have done."

I knew the Claw would be swept away if I were to leave it openly on the altar. Mounting the dais, I searched among its furnishings for a place of concealment that should be secure and permanent, and at last noticed that the altar-stone itself was held from below with four clamps that had surely never been loosed since the altar was constructed, and seemed likely to remain in place so long as it stood. I have strong hands, and I was able to free them, though I do not think most men could. Beneath the stone some wood had been chiseled away so that it should be supported at the edges only and would not rock—it was more than I had dared to hope for. With Jonas's razor I cut a small square of cloth from the edge of my now-tattered guild cloak. In it I wrapped the Claw, then I laid it under the stone and retightened the clamps, bloodying my fingers in my effort to make sure they would not come loose by accident.

As I stepped away from the altar I felt a profound sorrow, but I had not gone halfway to the door of the chapel before I was seized with wild joy. The burden of life and death had been lifted from me. Now I was only a man again, and I was delirious with delight. I felt as I had felt as a child when the long lessons with Master Malrubius were over and I was free to play in the Old Yard or clamber across the broken curtain wall to run among the trees and mausoleums of our necropolis. I was disgraced and outcast and homeless, without friend and without money, and I had just given up the most valuable object in the world, which was, perhaps, in the end the only valuable object in the world. And yet I knew that all would be well. I had climbed to the bottom of existence and felt it with my hands, and I knew that there *was* a bottom, and that from this point onward I could only rise. I swirled my cloak about me as I had when I was an actor, for I knew that I was an actor and no torturer, though I had been a torturer. I leaped into the air and capered as the goats do on the mountainside, for I knew that I was a child, and that no man can be a man who is not.

Outside, the cool air seemed expressly made for me, a new creation and not the ancient atmosphere of Urth. I bathed in it, first spreading my cloak then raising my arms to the stars, filled my lungs as does one who has just escaped drowning in the fluids of birth.

All this took less time than it has required to describe it, and I was about to start back to the lazaret tent from which I had come when I became aware of a motionless figure watching me from the shadows of another tent some distance off. Ever since the boy and I had escaped the blindly questing creature that had destroyed the village of the magicians, I had been afraid that some of Hethor's servants might search me out again. I was about to flee when the figure stepped into the moonlight, and I saw it was only a Pelerine.

"Wait," she called. Then, coming nearer, "I am afraid I frightened you."

Her face was a smooth oval that seemed almost sexless. She was young, I thought, though not so young as Ava and a good two heads taller—a true exultant, as tall as Thecla had been.

I said, "When one has lived long with danger . . ."

"I understand. I know nothing of war, but much of the men and women who have seen it."

"And now how may I serve you, Chatelaine?"

"First I must know if you are well. Are you?"

"Yes," I said. "I will leave this place tomorrow."

"You were in the chapel giving thanks, then, for your recovery."

I hesitated. "I had much to say, Chatelaine. That was a part of it, yes."

"May I walk with you?"

"Of course, Chatelaine."

I have heard it said that a tall woman seems taller than any man, and perhaps it is true. This woman was far less in stature than Baldanders had been, yet walking beside her made me feel almost dwarfish. I recalled too how Thecla had bent over me when we embraced, and how I had kissed her breasts.

When we had taken two score steps or so, the Pelerine said, "You walk well. Your legs are long, and I think they have covered many leagues. You are not a cavalry trooper?"

"I have ridden a bit, but not with the cavalry. I came through the mountains on foot, if that's what you mean, Chatelaine."

"That is well, for I have no mount for you. But I do not believe I have told you my name. I am Mannea, mistress of the postulants of our order. Our Domnicellae is away, and so for the moment I am in charge of our people here."

"I am Severian of Nessus, a wanderer. I wish that I could give you a thousand chrisos to help carry out your good work, but I can only thank you for the kindness I have received here."

"When I spoke of a mount, Severian of Nessus, I was neither offering to sell you one nor offering to give you one in the hope of thus earning your gratitude. If we do not have your gratitude now, we shall not get it."

"You have it," I told her, "as I've said. As I've also said, I will not linger here presuming on your kindness."

Mannea looked down at me. "I did not think you would. This morning a postulant told me how one of the sick had gone to the chapel with her two nights ago and described him. This evening, when you remained behind after the rest left, I knew you were he. I have a task, you see, and no one to perform it. In calmer days I would send a party of our slaves, but they are trained in the care of the sick, and we have need of every one of them and more. Yet it is said, 'He sends the beggar a stick and to the hunter a spear.' "

"I have no wish to insult you, Chatelaine, but I think that if you trust me because I went to your chapel you trust me for a bad reason. For all you know, I could have been stealing gems from the altar."

"You mean that thieves and liars often come to pray. By the blessing of the Conciliator they do. Believe me, Severian, wanderer from Nessus, no one else does—in the order or out of it. But you molested nothing. We have not half the power ignorant people suppose—nevertheless, those who think us without power are more ignorant still. Will you go on an errand for me? I'll give you a safe-conduct so you will not be taken up as a deserter."

"If the errand is within my powers, Chatelaine."

She put her hand on my shoulder. It was the first time she had touched me, and I felt a slight shock, as though I had been brushed unexpectedly by the wing of a bird.

"About twenty leagues from here," she said, "is the hermitage of a certain wise and holy anchorite. Until now he has been safe, but all this summer the Autarch has been driven back, and soon the fury of the war will roll over that place. Someone must go to him and persuade him to come to us—or if he cannot be persuaded, force him to come. I believe the Conciliator has indicated that you are to be the messenger. Can you do it?"

"I'm no diplomatist," I told her. "But for the other business, I can honestly say I have received long training."

The Last House

MANNEA HAD GIVEN me a rough map showing the location of
the anchorite's retreat, emphasizing that if I failed to follow
the course indicated on it precisely, I would almost certainly
be unable to locate it.

In what direction that house lay from the lazaret I cannot
say. The distances shown on the map were in proportion to
their difficulty, and turnings were adjusted to suit the dimen-
sions of the paper. I began by walking east, but soon found
that the route I followed had turned north, then west
through a narrow canyon threaded by a rushing stream, and
at last south.

On the earliest leg of my journey, I saw a great many soldiers—once a double column lining both sides of the road
while mules carried back the wounded down the center.
Twice I was stopped, but each time the display of my safe-
conduct permitted me to proceed. It was written on cream-
colored parchment, the finest I had then seen, and bore the
narthex sigil of the order stamped in gold. It read:

To Those Who Serve—
    The letter you read shall identify our servant Severian of
Nessus, a young man dark of hair and eye, pale of face, thin,

and well above the middle height. As you honor the memory we guard, and yourselves may wish in time for succor and if need be an honorable interment, we beg you not hinder this Severian as he prosecutes the business we have entrusted to him, but rather provide him such aid as he may require and you can supply.

For the Order of the Journeying Monials of the Conciliator, called *Pelerines,* I am

> The Chatelaine Mannea
> Instructress and
> Directress

Once I had entered the narrow canyon, however, all the armies of the world seemed to vanish. I saw no more soldiers, and the rushing water drowned the distant thundering of the Autarch's sacars and culverins—if indeed they could have been heard in that place at all.

The anchorite's house had been described to me and the description augmented by a sketch on the map I carried; moreover, I had been told that two days would be required for me to reach it. I was considerably surprised, therefore, when, at sunset, I looked up and saw it perched atop the cliff looming over me.

There was no mistaking it. Mannea's sketch had captured perfectly that high, peaked gable with its air of lightness and strength. Already a lamp shone in one small window.

In the mountains I had climbed many cliffs; some had been much higher than this one, and some—at least in appearance—more sheer. I had by no means been looking forward to camping among the rocks, and as soon as I saw the anchorite's house, I decided I would sleep in it that night.

The first third of the climb was easy. I scaled the rock face like a cat and was more than halfway up the whole of it before the fading of the light.

I have always had good night vision; I told myself the moon would soon be out and continued. In that I was wrong. The old moon had died while I lay in the lazaret, and the new would not be born for several days. The stars shed some light, though they were crossed and recrossed by bands of hurrying clouds; but it was a deceptive light that seemed worse than none, save when I did not have it. I found myself recalling then how Agia had waited with her assassins for me to emerge from the underground realm of the man-apes. The skin of my back crawled as though in anticipation of the arbalests' blazing bolts.

Soon a worse difficulty overtook me: I lost my sense of balance. I do not mean that I was entirely at the mercy of vertigo. I knew, in a general way, that *down* was in the direction of my feet and *up* in the direction of the stars; but I could be no more precise than that, and because I could not, I could judge only poorly how far I might lean out to search for each new handhold.

Just when this feeling was at its worst, the hurrying clouds closed their ranks, and I was left in total darkness. Sometimes it seemed to me that the cliff face had assumed a more gentle slope, so that I might almost have stood erect and walked up it. Sometimes I felt that it was beetling out—I must cling to the underside or fall. Often I felt certain I had not been climbing at all, but edging long distances to the left or right. Once I found myself almost head downward.

At last I reached a ledge, and there I determined to stay until the light came again. I wrapped myself in my cloak, lay down, and shifted my body to bring my back firmly against the rock. No resistance met it. I shifted once more and still felt nothing. I grew afraid that my sense of direction had deserted me even as my sense of balance had, and that I had somehow turned myself about and was edging toward the drop. After feeling the rock to either side, I rolled on my back and extended my arms.

At that moment there came a flash of sulfurous light that dyed the belly of every cloud. Not far off, some great bombard had loosed its cargo of death, and in that hectic illumination I saw that I had gained the top of the cliff, and that the house I had seen there was nowhere to be found. I lay upon an empty expanse of rock and felt the first drops of the coming rain patter against my face.

Next morning, cold and miserable, I ate some of the food I had carried from the lazaret and made my way down the farther side of the high hill of which the cliff had formed a part. The slope there was easier, and it was my intention to double about the shoulder of the hill until I again reached the narrow valley indicated on my map.

I could not do so. It was not that my way was blocked, but rather that when, after long walking, I arrived at what should have been the location I sought, I found an entirely different place, a shallower valley and a broader stream. After several watches wasted searching there, I discovered the spot from which (as it seemed to me) I had seen the anchorite's house perched upon the cliff top. Needless to say, it was not there now, nor was the cliff so high nor so steep as I recalled it.

It was there that I took out the map again, and studying it noticed that Mannea had written, in a hand so fine that I could scarcely believe it had been done with the pen I had seen her use, the words *THE LAST HOUSE* beneath the image of the anchorite's dwelling. For some reason those words and the picture of the house itself atop its rock recalled to me the house Agia and I had seen in the Jungle Garden, where husband and wife had sat listening to the naked man called Isangoma. Agia, who had been wise in the ways of all the Botanic Gardens, had told me there that if I turned on the path and attempted to go back to the hut I should not find it. Reflecting upon that incident, I discovered that I did not now believe her, but that I had believed her at the time. It might be, of course, that my loss of credulity was only a reaction to her treachery, of which I had by now had a sufficient sample. Or it might merely be that I was far more ingenuous then, when I was less than a day gone from the Citadel and the nurturing of the guild. But it was also possible—so it seemed to me now—that I had believed then because I had just seen the thing for myself, and that the sight of it, and the knowledge of those people, had carried its own conviction.

Father Inire was alleged to have built the Botanic Gardens. Might it not be that some part of the knowledge he commanded was shared by the anchorite? Father Inire, too, had built the secret room in the House Absolute that had appeared to be a painting. I had discovered it by accident but only because I had followed the instructions of the old picture cleaner, who had meant that I should. Now I was no longer following the instructions of Mannea.

I retraced my way around the shoulder of the hill and up the easy slope. The steep cliff I recalled dropped before me, and at its base rushed a narrow stream whose song filled all the strait valley. The position of the sun indicated that I had at most two watches of light remaining, but by that light the cliff was far easier to descend than it had been to climb by night. In less than a watch I was down, standing in the narrow valley I had left the evening before. I could see no lamp at any window, but the Last House stood where it had been, founded upon stone over which my boots had walked that day. I shook my head, turned away from it, and used the dying light to read the map Mannea had drawn for me.

Before I go further, I wish to make it clear that I am by no means certain there was anything preternatural in all that I have described. I saw the Last House thus twice, but on both occasions under similar lighting, the first time being by late twilight and the second by early twilight. It is surely possible that what I saw was no more than a creation of rocks and shadows, the illuminated window a star.

As to the vanishing of the narrow valley when I tried to come upon it from the other direction, there is no geographical feature more prone to disappear from sight than such a narrow declivity. The slightest unevenness in the ground conceals it. To protect themselves from marauders, some of the autochthonous peoples of the pampas go so far as to build their villages in that form, first digging a pit whose bottom can be reached by a ramp, then excavating houses and stables from the sides of it. As soon as the grass has covered the cast-out earth, which occurs very rapidly after the winter rains, one may ride to within half a chain of such a place without realizing it exists.

But though I may have been such a fool, I do not believe I was. Master Palaemon used to say that the supernatural exists in order that we may not be humiliated at being frightened by the night wind; but I prefer to believe that there was some element truly uncanny surrounding that house. I believe it now more firmly than I did then.

However it may be, I followed the map I had been given from that time forward, and before the night was more than two watches old, found myself climbing a path that led to the door of the Last House, which stood at the edge of just such a cliff as I remembered. As Mannea had said, the trip had taken just two days.

The Anchorite

THERE WAS A PORCH. It was hardly higher than the stone upon which it stood, but it ran to either side of the house and around the corners, like those long porches one sometimes sees on the better sort of country houses, where there is little to fear and the owners like to sit in the cool of the evening and watch Urth fall below Lune. I rapped at the door, and then, when no one answered, walked around this porch, first right, then left, peering in the windows.

It was too dark inside for me to see anything, but I found that the porch circled the house as far as the edge of the cliff, and there ended without a railing. I knocked again as fruitlessly as before and had laid myself on the porch to sleep (for having a roof over it, it was a better place than any I was likely to find among the rocks) when I heard faint footsteps.

Somewhere high in that high house, a man was walking. His steps were but slow at first, so that I thought he must be an old man or a sick one. As they came nearer, however, they became firmer and more swift, until as they neared the door they seemed the regular tread of a man of purpose, such a one as might, perhaps, command a maniple, or an ile of cavalry.

I had stood again by then and dusted my cloak and made myself as presentable as I could, yet I was only poorly prepared for him I saw when the door swung back. He carried a candle as thick as my wrist, and by its light I beheld a face that was like the faces of the Hierodules I had met in Baldanders's castle, save that it was a human face—indeed, I felt that as the faces of the statues in the gardens of the House Absolute had imitated the faces of such beings as Famulimus, Barbatus, and Ossipago, so their faces were only imitations, in some alien medium, of such faces as the one I saw now. I have said often in this account that I remember everything, and so I do; but when I try to sketch that face beside these words of mine I find I cannot do so. No drawing that I make resembles it in the least. I can only say that the brows were heavy and straight, the eyes deep-set and deep blue, as Thecla's were. This man's skin was fine as a woman's too, but there was nothing womanish about him, and the beard that flowed to his waist was of darkest black. His robe seemed white, but there was a rainbow shimmering where it caught the candlelight.

I bowed as I had been taught in the Matachin Tower and told him my name and who had sent me. Then I said, "And are you, sieur, the anchorite of the Last House?"

He nodded. "I am the last man here. You may call me Ash."

He stood to one side, indicating that I should enter, then led me to a room at the rear of the house, where a wide window overlooked the valley from which I had climbed the night before. There were wooden chairs there and a wooden table. Metal chests, dully gleaming in the candlelight, rested in the corners and in the angles between floor and walls.

"You must pardon the poor appearance of this place," he said. "It is here that I receive company, but I have so little company that I have begun to use it as a storeroom."

"When one lives alone in such a lonely spot, it is well to seem poor, Master Ash. This room, however, does not."

I had not thought that face capable of smiling, yet he smiled. "You wish to see my treasures? Look." He rose and opened a chest, holding the candle so that it lit the interior. There were square loaves of hard bread and packages of pressed figs. Seeing my expression he asked, "Are you hungry? There is no spell upon this food, if you are fearful of such things."

I was ashamed, because I had carried food for the journey and still had some left for the return; but I said, "I would like some of that bread, if you can spare it."

He gave me half a loaf already cut (and with a very sharp knife), cheese wrapped in silver paper, and dry yellow wine.

"Mannea is a good woman," he told me. "And you, I think, are a good man of the kind who does not know himself to be one—some say that is the only kind. Does she think I can help you?"

"Rather she believes that I can help you, Master Ash. The armies of the Commonwealth are in retreat, and soon the battle will overwhelm all this part of the country, and after the battle, the Ascians."

He smiled again. "The men without shadows. It is one of those names, of which there are many, that are in error and yet perfectly correct. What would you think if an Ascian told you he really cast no shadow?"

"I don't know," I said. "I never heard of such a thing."

"It is an old story. Do you like old stories? Ah, I see a light in your eyes, and I wish I could tell it better. You call your enemies Ascians, which of course is not what they call themselves, because your fathers believed they came from the waist of Urth, where the sun is precisely overhead at noon. The truth is that their home is much farther north. Yet Ascians they are. In a fable made in the earliest morning of our race, a man sold his shadow and found himself driven out everywhere he went. No one would believe that he was human."

Sipping wine, I thought of the Ascian prisoner whose cot

had stood beside my own. "Did this man ever regain his shadow, Master Ash?"

"No. But for a time he traveled with a man who had no reflection."

Master Ash fell silent. Then he said, "Mannea is a good woman; I wish that I could oblige you. But I cannot go, and the war will never reach me here, no matter how its columns march."

I said, "Perhaps it would be possible for you to come with me and reassure the Chatelaine."

"That I cannot do either."

I saw then that I would have to force him to accompany me, but there seemed to be no reason to resort to duress now; there would be plenty of opportunity in the morning. I shrugged my shoulders as though in resignation and asked, "May I then at least sleep here tonight? I will have to return and report your decision, but the distance is fifteen leagues or more, and I could not walk much farther now."

Again I saw his faint smile, just such a smile as a carving of ivory might make when the motion of a torch altered the shadow of its lips. "I had hoped to have some news of the world from you," he said. "But I see that you are weary. Come with me when you have finished eating. I will show you to your bed."

"I have no courtly manners, Master, but I am not so ill-bred as to sleep when my host still desires my conversation—though I'm afraid I have little enough news to give. From what I've learned from my fellow sufferers in the lazaret, the war proceeds and waxes hotter each day. We are reinforced with legions and half legions, they by whole armies sent down from the north. They have much artillery too, and therefore we must rely more upon our mounted lances, who can charge swiftly and engage the enemy closely before his heavy pieces can be pointed. They have more fliers also than they boasted last year, although we have destroyed many. The Autarch himself has come to command, bringing many of his household troops from the House Absolute. But . . ." Shrugging again, I paused to take a bite of bread and cheese.

"The study of war has always seemed to me the least interesting part of history. Even so, there are certain patterns. When one side in a long war shows sudden strength, it is usually for one of three reasons. The first is that it has formed some new alliance. Do the soldiers of these new armies differ in any way from those in the old?"

"Yes," I said. "I have heard that they are younger and on the whole less strong. And there are more women among them."

"No differences in tongue or dress?"

I shook my head.

"Then for the present at least we can dismiss an alliance. The second possibility would be the termination of another war, fought elsewhere. If that were so, the reinforcements would be veterans. You say they are not, thus only the third remains. For some reason your foes have need of an immediate victory and are straining every limb."

I had finished the bread, but I was truly curious by now. "Why should that be?"

"Without knowing more than I do, I cannot say. Perhaps their leaders fear their people, who have sickened of the war. Perhaps all the Ascians are only servants, and their masters now threaten to act for themselves."

"You extend hope at one moment and snatch it away at the next."

"Not I, but history. Have you yourself been at the front?"

I shook my head.

"That is well. In many respects, the more a man sees of war the less he knows of it. How stand the people of your Commonwealth? Are they united behind their Autarch? Or has the war so worn them that they shout for peace?"

I laughed at that, and all the old bitterness that had helped draw me to Vodalus came rushing back. "Unite? Shout? I know that you have isolated yourself, Master, to fix your mind on higher things, but I would not have thought any man could know so little of the land in which he lives. Careerists, mercenaries, and young would-be adventurers fight the war. A hundred leagues south it is less than a rumor, outside the House Absolute."

Master Ash pursed his lips. "Your Commonwealth is stronger than I would have believed, then. No wonder your foes are in despair."

"If that is strength, may the All Merciful preserve us from weakness. Master Ash, the front may collapse at any time. It would be wise for you to come with me to a safer place."

He appeared not to have heard. "If Erebus and Abaia and the rest enter the field themselves, it will be a new struggle. If and when. Interesting. But you are tired. Come with me. I will show you your bed and the high matters that, as you said a moment ago, I came here to study."

We ascended two flights and entered a room that must have been the one in which I had seen a light the evening before. It was a wide chamber of many windows, and it occupied the entire story. There were machines there, but they were smaller and fewer than those I had seen in Baldanders's castle, and there were tables too, and papers, and many books, and near the center a narrow bed.

"Here I nap," Master Ash explained, "when my work will not let me retire. It is not large for a man of your frame, but I think you will find it comfortable."

I had slept on stone the night before; it looked very appealing indeed.

After showing me where I could relieve myself and wash, he left. My last glimpse of him before he darkened the light caught the same perfect smile I had seen before.

An instant later, when my eyes had grown accustomed to the dark, I ceased to wonder about it, for outside all those many windows there shone an unbounded pearly radiance. "We are above the clouds," I said to myself (I, too, half smiling), "or rather, some low clouds have come to shroud this hilltop, unnoticed by me in the darkness but known in some fashion to him. Now I see the tops of those clouds, high matters surely, as I saw the tops of clouds from Typhon's eyes." And I laid myself down to sleep.

XVII

Ragnarok—The Final Winter

IT SEEMED STRANGE to wake without a weapon, though for some reason I cannot explain, that was the first morning on which I had felt so. After the destruction of *Terminus Est* I had slept at the sacking of Baldanders's castle without fear, and later journeyed north without fear. Only the night before, I had slept upon the bare rock of the cliff top weaponless and—perhaps only because I had been so tired—had not been afraid. I now think that during all those days, and indeed during all the days since I had left Thrax, I had been putting the guild behind me and coming to believe that I was what those who encountered me took me for—the sort of would-be adventurer I had mentioned the night before to Master Ash. As a torturer, I had not so much considered my sword a weapon as a tool and a badge of office. Now in retrospect it had become a weapon to me, and I had no weapon.

I thought about that as I lay upon my back on Master Ash's comfortable mattress, my hands behind my head. I would have to acquire another sword if I remained in the war-torn lands, and it would be wise to have one even if I turned south again. The question was whether to turn south or not. If I remained where I was, I risked being drawn into the fighting, where I might well be killed. But for me a return to the south would be even more dangerous. Abdiesus, the archon of Thrax, had no doubt posted a reward for my capture, and the guild would almost certainly procure my assassination if they learned I was anywhere near Nessus.

After vacillating over this decision for some time, as one does when only half-awake, I recalled Winnoc and what he had told me of the slaves of the Pelerines. Because it is a disgrace to us if our clients die after torment, we are taught a good deal of leech-craft in the guild; I thought I knew already at least as much as they. When I had cured the girl in the jacal, I had felt suddenly uplifted. The Chatelaine Mannea had a good opinion of me already and would have a better one when I returned with Master Ash.

A few moments before, I had been disturbed because I lacked a weapon. Now I felt I had one—resolution and a plan are better than a sword, because a man whets his own edges on them. I threw off the blankets, noticing then for the first time, I think, how soft they were. The big room was cold but filled with sunlight; it was almost as though there were suns on all four sides, as though all the walls were east walls. I walked naked to the nearest window and saw that undulating field of white I had vaguely noted the evening before.

It was not a mass of cloud but a plain of ice. The window would not open, or if it would, I could not solve the puzzle of its mechanism; but I put my face close to the glass and peered downward as well as I could. The Last House rose, as I had seen before, from a high hill of rock. Now this hilltop alone remained above the ice. I went from window to window, and the view from each was the same. Going back to the bed that had been mine, I pulled on my trousers and boots, and slung my cloak about my shoulders, hardly knowing what it was I did.

Master Ash appeared just as I finished dressing. "I hope I do not intrude," he said. "I heard you walking up here."

I shook my head.

"I did not want you to become disturbed."

Without my willing it, my hands had gone to my face. Now some foolish part of me became aware of my bristling beard. I said, "I meant to shave before putting on my cloak. That was stupid of me. I haven't shaved since I left the lazaret." It was as though my mind were trudging across the ice, leaving my tongue and lips to get along as best they might.

"There is hot water here, and soap."

"That's good," I said. And then, "If I go downstairs . . ."

That smile again. "Will it be the same? The ice? No. You are the first to have guessed. May I ask how you did it?"

"A long time ago—no, only a few months, actually, though it seems like such a long time now—I went to the Botanic Gardens in Nessus. There was a place called the Lake of Birds, where the bodies of the dead seemed to remain fresh forever. I was told it was some property of the water, but I wondered even then that there should be so much power in water. There was another place too, that they called the Jungle Garden, where the leaves were greener than I have ever known leaves to be—not a bright green but dark with greenness, as if the plants could never use all the energy the sun poured down. The people there seemed not of our time, though I could not say if they were of the past, or the future, or some third thing that is neither. They had a little house. It was much smaller than this, but this reminds me of it. I've thought often of the Botanic Gardens since I left them, and sometimes I've wondered if their secret were not that the time never changed in the Lake of Birds, and that one moved forward or backward—however it might be—when walking the path of the Jungle Garden. Am I perhaps speaking overmuch?"

Master Ash shook his head.

"Then when I was coming here, I saw your house at the top of this hill. But when I climbed to it, it was gone, and the valley below was not as I remembered it." I did not know what else to say, and fell silent.

"You are correct," Master Ash told me. "I have been put here to observe what you see about you now. The lower stories of my home, however, reach into older periods, of which yours is the oldest."

"That seems a great wonder."

He shook his head. "It is almost more wonderful that this spur of rock has been spared by the glaciers. The tops of peaks far higher are submerged. It is sheltered by a geographic pattern so subtle that it could only be achieved by accident."

"But it too will be covered at last?" I asked.

"Yes."

"And what then?"

"I shall leave. Or rather, I shall leave some time before it occurs."

I felt a surge of irrational anger, the same emotion I had sometimes known as a boy when I could not make Master Malrubius understand my questions. "I meant, what of Urth?"

He shrugged. "Nothing. What you see is the last glaciation. The surface of the sun is dull now; soon it will grow bright with heat, but the sun itself will shrink, giving less energy to its worlds. Eventually, should anyone come and stand upon the ice, he will see it only as a bright star. The ice he stands upon will not be that which you see but the atmosphere of this world. And so it will remain for a very long time. Perhaps until the close of the universal day."

I went to another window and looked out again on the expanse of ice. "Will this happen soon?"

"The scene you see is many thousands of years in your future."

"But before this, the ice must have come from the south."

Master Ash nodded. "And down from the mountaintops. Come with me."

We descended to the second level of the house, which I had scarcely noticed when I had come upstairs the night before. The windows were far fewer there, but Master Ash placed chairs before one and indicated that we would sit and look out. It was as he had said—ice, lovely in its purity, crept down the mountainsides to war with the pines. I asked if this too were far in the future, and he nodded once more. "You will not live to see it again."

"But so near that the life of a man will nearly reach it?"

He twitched his shoulders and smiled beneath his beard. "Let us say it is a thing of degree. You will not see this. Nor will your children, nor theirs. But the process has already begun. It began long before you were born."

I knew nothing of the south, but I found myself thinking of the island people of Hallvard's story, the precious little sheltered places with a growing season, the hunting of the seals. Those islands would not hold men and their families much longer. The boats would scrape over their stony beaches for the last time. *My wife, my children, my children, my wife.*

"At this time, many of your people are already gone," Master Ash continued. "Those you call the cacogens have mercifully carried them to fairer worlds. Many more will leave before the final victory of the ice. I am myself, you see, descended from those refugees."

I asked if everyone would escape.

He shook his head. "No, not everyone. Some would not go, some could not be found. No home could be found for others."

For some time I sat looking out at the beleaguered valley and trying to order my thoughts. At last I said, "I have always found that men of religion tell comforting things that are not true, while men of science recount hideous truths. The Chatelaine Mannea said you were a holy man, but you appear to be a man of science, and you said your people had sent you to our dead Urth to study the ice."

"The distinction you mention no longer holds. Religion and science have always been matters of faith in something.

It is the same something. You are yourself what you call a man of science, so I talk of science to you. If Mannea were here with her priestesses, I would talk differently."

I have so many memories that I often become lost among them. Now as I looked at the pines, waving in a wind I could not feel, I seemed to hear the beating of a drum. "I met another man who said he was from the future once," I said. "He was green—nearly as green as those trees—and he told me that his time was a time of brighter sun."

Master Ash nodded. "No doubt he spoke truly."

"But you tell me that what I see now is but a few lifetimes away, that it is part of a process already begun, and that this will be the last glaciation. Either you are a false prophet or he was."

"I am not a prophet," answered Master Ash, "nor was he. No one can know the future. We are speaking of the past."

I was angry again. "You told me this was only a few life-times away."

"I did. But you, and this scene, are past events for me."

"I am not a thing of the past! I belong to the present."

"From your own viewpoint you are correct. But you forget I cannot see you from your viewpoint. This is my house. It is through my windows that you have looked. My house strikes its roots into the past. Without that I should go mad here. As it is, I read these old centuries like books. I hear the voices of the long dead, yours among them. You think that time is a single thread. It is a weaving, a tapestry that extends forever in all directions. I follow a thread backward. You will trace a color forward, what color I cannot know. White may lead you to me, green to your green man."

Not knowing what to say, I could only mutter that I had conceived of time as a river.

"Yes—you came from Nessus, did you not? And that was a city built about a river. But it was once a city by the sea, and you would do better to think of time as a sea. The waves ebb and flow, and currents run beneath them."

"I would like to go downstairs," I said. "To return to my own time."

Master Ash said, "I understand."

"I wonder if you do. Your time, if I have heard you rightly, is that of this house's highest story, and you have a bed there, and other necessary things. Yet when you are not overwhelmed by your labors you sleep here, according to what you have told me. Yet you say this is nearer my time than your own."

He stood up. "I meant that I too flee the ice. Shall we go? You will want food before you begin the long trip back to Mannea."

"We both will," I said.

He turned to look at me before he started down the stair. "I told you I could not go with you. You have discovered for yourself how well hidden this house is. For all who do not walk the path correctly, even the lowest story stands in the future."

I caught both his arms behind him in a double lock and used my free hand to search him for weapons. There were none, and though he was strong, he was not as strong as I had feared he might be.

"You plan to carry me to Mannea. Is that correct?"

"Yes, Master, and we'll have a great deal less trouble if you will go willingly. Tell me where I can find some rope—I don't want to have to use the belt of your robe."

"There is none," he told me.

I bound his hands with his cincture, as I had first planned. "When we are some distance from here," I said, "I will loose you if you will give me your word to behave well."

"I made you welcome in my house. What harm have I done you?"

"Quite a bit, but that doesn't matter. I like you, Master Ash, and I respect you. I hope that you won't hold what I am doing to you against me any more than I hold what you have done to me against you. But the Pelerines sent me to fetch you, and I find I am a certain sort of man, if you understand what I mean. Now don't go down the steps too fast. If you fall, you won't be able to catch yourself."

I led him to the room to which he had first taken me and got some of the hard bread and a package of dried fruit. "I don't think of myself as one anymore," I continued, "but I was brought up as—" It was at my lips to say *torturer*, but I realized (then, I think, for the first time) that it was not quite the correct term for what the guild did and used the official one instead. "—as a Seeker for Truth and Penitence. We do what we have said we will do."

"I have duties to perform. In the upper level, where you slept."

"I am afraid they must go unperformed."

He was silent as we went out the door and onto the rocky hilltop. Then he said, "I will go with you, if I can. I have often wished to walk out of this door and never halt."

I told him that if he would swear upon his honor, I would untie him at once.

He shook his head. "You might think that I betrayed you."

I did not know what he meant.

"Perhaps somewhere there is the woman I have called Vine. But your world is your world. I can exist there only if the probability of my existence is high."

I said, "I existed in your house, didn't I?"

"Yes, but that was because your probability was complete. You are a part of the past from which my house and I have come. The question is whether I am the future to which you go."

I remembered the green man in Saltus, who had been solid enough. "Will you vanish like a soap bubble then?" I asked. "Or blow away like smoke?"

"I do not know," he said. "I do not know what will happen to me. Or where I will go when it does. I may cease to exist in any time. That was why I never left of my own will."

I took him by one arm, I suppose because I thought I could keep him with me in that way, and we walked on. I followed the route Mannea had drawn for me, and the Last House rose behind us as solidly as any other. My mind was busy with all the things he had told me and showed me, so that for a while, the space of twenty or thirty paces, perhaps, I did not look around at him. At last his remark about the tapestry suggested Valeria to me. The room where we had eaten cakes had been hung with them, and what he had said about tracing threads suggested the maze of tunnels through which I had run before encountering her. I started to tell him of it, but he was gone. My hand grasped empty air. For a moment I seemed to see the Last House afloat like a ship upon its ocean of ice. Then it merged into the dark hilltop on which it had stood; the ice was no more than what I had once taken it to be—a bank of cloud.

XVIII

Foila's Request

FOR ANOTHER HUNDRED paces or more, Master Ash was not entirely gone. I felt his presence, and sometimes even caught sight of him, walking beside me and half a step behind, when I did not try to look directly at him. How I saw him, how he could in some sense be present while in another absent, I do not know. Our eyes receive a rain of photons without mass or charge from swarming particles like a billion, billion suns—so Master Palaemon, who was nearly blind, had taught me. From the pattering of those photons we believe we see a man. Sometimes the man we believe we see may be as illusory as Master Ash, or more so.

His wisdom I felt with me too. It had been a melancholy wisdom, but a real one. I found myself wishing he had been able to accompany me, though I realized it would have meant the coming of the ice was certain. "I'm lonely, Master Ash," I said, not daring to look back. "How lonely I didn't realize until now. You were lonely also, I think. Who was the woman you called Vine?"

Perhaps I only imagined his voice. *"The first woman."*

"Meschiane? Yes, I know her, and she is very lovely. My Meschiane was Dorcas, and I am lonely for her, but for all the others too. When Thecla became a part of me, I thought I would never be lonely again. But now she is so much a part that we're only one person, and I can be lonely for others. For Dorcas, for Pia the island girl, for little Severian and Drotte and Roche. If Eata were here, I could hug him.

"Most of all, I'd like to see Valeria. Jolenta was the most beautiful woman I've ever seen, but there was something in Valeria's face that tore my heart out. I was only a boy, I suppose, though I didn't think so then. I crawled up out of the dark and found myself in a place they called the Atrium of Time. Towers—the towers of Valeria's family—rose on all sides of it. In the center was an obelisk covered with sundials, and though I remember its shadow on the snow, it couldn't have had sunlight there for more than two or three watches of each day; the towers must shade it most of the time. Your understanding is deeper than mine, Master Ash—can you tell me why they might have built it so?"

A wind that played among the rocks seized my cloak so that it billowed from my shoulders. I secured it again and pulled up my hood. "I was following a dog. I called him Triskele, and I said, even to myself, that he was mine, though I had no right to keep a dog. It was a winter day when I found him. We'd been doing laundry—washing the clients' bedclothes—and the drain plugged with rags and lint. I'd been shirking my work, and Drotte told me to go outside and ram a clothes prop up it. The wind was terribly cold. That was your ice coming, I suppose, though I didn't know it at the time—the winters getting a little worse each year. And of course when I got the drain open, a gush of filthy water would come out and wet my hands.

"I was angry because I was the oldest, except for Drotte and Roche, and I thought the younger apprentices ought to have to do the work. I was poking at the clog with my stick when I saw him across the Old Yard. The keepers in the Bear Tower had held a private fight, I suppose, the night before, and the dead beasts were lying outside their door waiting for the nacker. There was an arsinoither and a smilodon, and several dire wolves. The dog was lying on top. I suppose he had been the last to die, and from his wounds one of the dire wolves had killed him. Of course, he wasn't really dead, but he looked dead.

"I went over to see him—it was an excuse to stop what I was doing for a moment and blow on my fingers. He was as stiff and cold as . . . well, as anything I've ever seen. I killed a bull once with my sword, and when it was lying dead in its own blood it still looked quite a bit more living than Triskele did then. Anyway, I reached out and stroked his head. It was as big as a bear's, and they had cut off his ears, so that only two little points were left. When I touched him he opened his eyes. I dashed back across the Yard and rammed the stick up so hard it broke through at once, because I was afraid Drotte would send Roche down to see what I was doing.

"When I think back on it, it was as if I had the Claw already, more than a year before I got it. I can't describe how he looked when he rolled his eye up to see me. He touched my heart. I never revived an animal when I had the Claw, but then I never tried. When I was among them, I was usually wishing I could kill one, because I wanted something to eat. Now I'm no longer sure that killing animals to eat is something we are meant to do. I noticed that you had no meat in your supplies—only bread and cheese, and wine and dried fruit. Do your people, on whatever world it is where people live in your time, feel so too?"

I paused, hoping for an answer, but none came. All the mountaintops had dropped below the sun now; I was no longer certain whether some thin presence of Master Ash followed me or only my shadow.

I said, "When I had the Claw I found that it would not revive those dead by human acts, though it seemed to heal the man-ape whose hand I had struck off. Dorcas thought it was because I had done it myself. I can't say—I never thought the Claw knew who held it, but perhaps it did."

A voice—not Master Ash's but a voice I had never heard before—called out, "A fine new year to you!"

I looked up and and saw, perhaps forty paces off, just such an uhlan as Hethor's notules had killed on the green road to the House Absolute. Not knowing what else to do, I waved and shouted, "Is it New Year's Day, then?"

He touched spurs to his destrier and came galloping up. "Mid summer today, the beginning of the new year. A glorious one for our Autarch."

I tried to recall some of the phrases Jolenta had been so fond of. "Whose heart is the shrine of his subjects."

"Well said! I'm Ibar, of the Seventy-eighth Xenagie, patrolling the road until evening, worse luck."

"Surely it's lawful to use the road here."

"Entirely. Provided, of course, that you are prepared to identify yourself."

"Yes," I said. "Of course." I had almost forgotten the safe-conduct Mannea had written for me. Now I took it out and handed it to him.

When I had been stopped on my way to the Last House, I had by no means been sure that the soldiers who had questioned me could read. Each had stared wisely at the parchment, but it might well have been that they took in no more than the sigil of the order and Mannea's regular and vigorous, though slightly eccentric, penmanship. The uhlan unquestionably could. I could see his eyes traveling the lines of script, and even guess, I think, when they paused momentarily at "honorable interment."

He refolded the parchment carefully but retained it. "So you are a servant of the Pelerines."

"I have that honor, yes."

"You were praying, then. I thought you were talking to yourself when I saw you. I don't hold with any religious nonsense. We have the standard of the xenagie near at hand and the Autarch at a distance, and that's all I need of reverence and mystery; but I have heard that they were good women."

I nodded. "I believe—perhaps somewhat more than you. But they are indeed."

"And you were sent on a task for them. How many days ago?"

"Three."

"Are you returning to the lazaret at Media Pars now?"

I nodded again. "I hope to reach it before nightfall."

He shook his head. "You won't. Take it easy, that's my advice to you." He held out the parchment.

I took it and returned it to my sabretache. "I was traveling with a companion, but we were separated. I wonder if you've seen him." I described Master Ash.

The uhlan shook his head. "I'll keep an eye out for him and tell him which way you went if I see him. Now—will you answer a question for me? It's not official, so you can tell me it's none of my affair if you want."

"I will if I can."

"What will you do when you leave the Pelerines?"

I was somewhat taken aback. "Why, I hadn't planned to leave at all. Someday, perhaps."

"Well, keep the light cavalry in mind. You look like a man of your hands, and we can always use one. You'll live half as long as you would in the infantry, and have twice as much fun."

He urged his mount forward, and I was left to ponder what he had said. I did not doubt that he had been serious in telling me to sleep on the road; but that very seriousness made me hurry forward all the faster. I have been blessed with long legs, so that when I need to I can walk as fast as most men can trot. I used them then, dropping all thoughts of Master Ash and my own troubled past. Perhaps some thin presence of Master Ash still accompanied me; perhaps it does so yet. But if it did, I was and remain unaware of it.

Urth had not yet turned her face from the sun when I came to that narrow road the dead soldier and I had taken only a little over a week before. There was blood in its dust

still, much more than I had seen there previously. I had
feared from what the uhlan had said that the Pelerines had
been accused of some misdeed; now I felt sure that it was
only that a great influx of wounded had been brought to the
lazaret, and he had decided I deserved a night's rest before
being set to work on them. That thought was a vast relief to
me. A superabundance of the injured would give me an opportunity to show my skills and render it that much more
likely that Mannea would accept me when I offered to sell
myself to the order, if only I could contrive some tale to
account for my failure at the Last House.

When I turned the final bend in the road, however, what I
saw was entirely different.

Where the lazaret had stood, the ground seemed to have
been plowed by a host of madmen, plowed and dug—its bottom already a small lake of shallow water. Shattered trees
rimmed the circle.

Until darkness came, I walked back and forth across it. I
was looking for some sign of my friends, and also for some
trace of the altar that had held the Claw. I found a human
hand, a man's hand, blown off at the wrist. It might have
been Melito's, or Hallvard's, or the Ascian's, or Winnoc's. I
could not tell.

I slept beside the road that night. When morning came I
began my inquiries, and before evening I had located the
survivors, some half dozen leagues from the original site. I
went from cot to cot, but many were unconscious and so
bandaged about the head that I could not have known them.
It is possible that Ava, Mannea, and the Pelerine who had
carried a stool to my bedside were among them, though I did
not discover them there.

The only woman I recognized was Foila, and that only
because she recognized me, calling "Severian!" as I walked
among the wounded and dying. I went to her and tried to
question her, but she was very weak and could tell me little.
The attack had come without warning and shattered the

lazaret like a thunderbolt; her memories were all of the aftermath, of hearing the screams that for a long time had brought no rescuers, and at last being dragged forth by soldiers who knew little of medicine. I kissed her as well as I could, and promised to come and see her again—a promise, I think, that both of us knew I would not be able to keep. She said, "Do you recall the time when all of us told stories? I thought of that."

I said I knew she had.

"I mean while they were carrying us here. Melito and Hallvard and the rest are dead, I think. You will be the only one who remembers, Severian."

I told her I would remember always.

"I want you to tell other people. On winter days, or a night when there is nothing else to do. Do you remember the stories?"

" 'My land is the land of far horizons, of the wide sky.' "

"Yes," she said, and seemed to sleep.

My second promise I have kept, first copying all the stories onto the blank pages at the close of the brown book, then giving them here, just as I heard them in the long, warm noons.

Guasacht

THE NEXT TWO DAYS I spent in wandering. I will not say much of them here, for there is little to say. I might, I suppose, have enlisted in several units, but I was far from sure I wanted to enlist. I would have liked to return to the Last House, but I was too proud to cast myself on Master Ash's charity, assuming that Master Ash was again to be found there. I told myself I would gladly have returned to the post of Lictor of Thrax, yet if that had been possible, I am not certain I would have done so. I slept like an animal in wooded places and took what food I could, which was little.

On the third day I discovered a rusty falchion, dropped, as it appeared, in some campaign of the year before. I got out my little flask of oil and my broken whetstone (both of which I had retained, together with her hilt, when I had cast the wreck of *Terminus Est* into the water) and spent a happy watch in cleaning and sharpening it. When that was done, I trudged on, and soon struck a road.

With the protection of Mannea's safe-conduct effectively removed, I was more chary of showing myself than I had been on my way from Master Ash's. But it seemed probable that the dead soldier the Claw had raised, who now called himself Miles though I knew some part of him to be Jonas, had by now joined some unit. If so, he would be on a road or in camp near one, if he was not actually in battle; and I wished to speak to him. Like Dorcas, he had paused a time in the country of the dead. She had dwelt there longer, but I hoped that if I could question him before too much time had erased his memories of it, I might learn something that would—if not permit me to regain her—at least help reconcile me to her loss.

For I found I loved her now as I never had when we tramped cross-country to Thrax. Then my thoughts had been too much of Thecla; I had always been reaching inside myself to find her. Now it seemed, if only because she had been a part of me so long, that I had grasped her indeed, in an embrace more final than any coupling—or rather, that as the male's seed penetrates the female body to produce (if it be the will of Apeiron) a new human being, so she, entering my mouth, by my will had combined with the Severian that was to establish a new man: I who still call myself Severian but am conscious, as it were, of my double root.

Whether I could have learned what I sought from Miles-Jonas, I do not know. I have never found him, though I have persevered in the search from that day to this. By midafternoon I had entered a realm of broken trees, and from time to time I passed corpses in more or less advanced stages of decay. At first I tried to pillage them as I had the body of Miles-Jonas, but others had been there before me, and indeed the fennecs had come in the night with their sharp little teeth to loot the flesh.

Somewhat later, as my energies were beginning to flag, I paused at the smoldering remains of an empty supply wagon. The draft animals, which had not, it appeared, been dead long, lay in the road, with their driver pitched on his face between them; and it occurred to me that I might do worse than to cut as much meat as I wanted from their flanks and carry it to some isolated spot where I could kindle a fire. I

had fleshed the point of the falchion in the haunch of one of
these animals when I heard the drumming of hoofs, and sup-
posing them to belong to the destrier of an estafette, moved
to the edge of the road to let him pass.

It was instead a short, thick-bodied, energetic-looking man
on a tall, ill-used mount. He reined up at the sight of me, but
something in his expression told me there was no need for
fight or flight. (If there had been, it would have been *fight*.
His destrier would have done him little good among the
stumps and fallen logs, and despite his haubergeon and brass-
ringed buff cap, I thought I could best him.)

"Who are you?" he called. And when I told him, "Severian
of Nessus, eh? You're civilized then, or half-civilized, but you
don't look like you've been eating too well."

"On the contrary," I said. "Better than I've been accustomed to, recently." I did not want him to think me weak.

"But you could use some more—that's not Ascian blood on
your sword. You're a schiavoni? An irregular?"

"My life has been pretty irregular of late, certainly."

"But you're attached to no formation?" With startling
dexterity he vaulted from his saddle, threw the reins to the
ground, and came striding over. He was slightly bowlegged
and had one of those faces that appear to have been molded
in clay and flattened from the top and bottom before firing,
so that the forehead and chin are shallow but broad, the eyes
slits, the mouth wide. Still I liked him at once for his verve,
and because he took so little trouble to hide his dishonesty.

I said, "I'm attached to nothing and no one—memories
excepted."

"Ahh!" He sighed, and for an instant rolled his eyes upward. "I know—I know. We have all had our difficulties,
every one of us. What was it, a woman or the law?"

I had not previously viewed my troubles in that light, but
after thinking for a moment I admitted it had been a bit of
both.

"Well, you've come to the right place and you've met the

right man. How'd you like a good meal tonight, a whole crowd of new friends, and a handful of orichalks tomorrow? Sound good? Good!"

He returned to his mount, and his hand darted out as quickly as a fencer's blade to grasp her bridle before she could shy away. When he had the reins again, he leaped into the saddle as readily as he had left it. "Now you get up behind me," he called. "It's not far, and she'll carry two easily enough."

I did as he told me, though with considerably more diffi- culty since I had no stirrup to assist me. The instant I was seated, the destrier struck like a bushmaster at my leg; but her master, who had clearly been anticipating the maneuver, clubbed her so hard with the brass pommel of his poniard that she stumbled and nearly fell.

"Pay no mind," he said. The shortness of his neck did not permit him to look over his shoulder, so he spoke out of the left side of his mouth to make it clear he was addressing me. "She's a fine animal and a plucky fighter, and she just wants to make sure you understand her value. A sort of initiation, you know. You know what an initiation is?"

I told him I thought myself familiar with the term.

"Anything that's worth belonging to has one, you'll find— I've found that out myself. I've never seen one that a plucky lad couldn't handle and laugh about afterwards."

With that cryptic encouragement he set his enormous spurs to the sides of his fine animal as if he meant to eviscer- ate her on the spot, and we went flying down the road, trailed by a cloud of dust.

Since the time I had ridden Vodalus's charger out of Saltus, I had supposed in my innocence that all mounts might be divided into two sorts: the highbred and swift, and the cold-blooded and slow. The better, I thought, ran with the graceful ease, almost, of a coursing cat; the worse moved so tardily that it hardly mattered how they did it. It used to be a maxim of one of Thecla's tutors that all two-valued systems are false, and I discovered on that ride a new respect for him. My benefactor's mount belonged to that third class (which I have since discovered is fairly extensive) comprising those animals that outrace the birds but seem to run with legs of iron upon a road of stone. Men have numberless advantages over women and for that reason are rightly charged to protect them, yet there is one great one women may boast over men: No woman has ever had her organs of generation crushed between her own pelvis and the bony spine of one of these galloping brutes. That happened to me twenty or thirty times before we reined up, and when I slid over the crupper at last and leaped aside to dodge a kick, I was in no very good mood.

We had halted in one of those little, lost fields one sometimes finds among the hills, an area more or less level and a hundred strides or so across. A tent the size of a cottage had been erected in the center, with a faded flag of black and green flapping before it. Several score hobbled mounts grazed at will over the field, and an equal number of ragged men, with a sprinkling of unkempt women, lounged about cleaning armor, sleeping, and gambling.

"Look here!" my benefactor shouted, dismounting to stand beside me. "Here's a new recruit!" To me he announced, "Severian of Nessus, you're standing in the presence of the Eighteenth Bacele of the Irregular Contarii, every one of us a fighter of dauntless courage whenever there's a speck of money to be made."

The ragged men and women were standing and drifting toward us, many of them frankly grinning. A tall and very thin man led the way.

"Comrades, I give you Severian of Nessus!

"Severian," my benefactor continued, "I'm your condottiere. Call me Guasacht. This fishing pole here, taller even than you are, is my second, Erblon. The rest will introduce themselves, I'm sure.

"Erblon, I want to talk to you. There'll be patrols tomorrow." He took the tall man by the arm and led him into the tent, leaving me with the crowd of troopers who had by now surrounded me.

One of the largest, an ursine man almost my height and at least twice my weight, gestured toward the falchion. "Don't you have a scabbard for that? Let's see it."

I surrendered it without argument; whatever might happen next, I felt certain it would not be an occasion for killing.

"So, you're a rider, are you?"

"No," I said. "I've ridden a bit, but I don't consider myself an expert."

"But you know how to manage them?"

"I know men and women better."

Everyone laughed at that, and the big man said, "Well, that's just fine, because you probably won't do much riding, but a good understanding of women—and destriers—will be a help to you."

As he spoke, I heard the sound of hoofs. Two men were leading up a piebald, muscular and wild-eyed. His reins had been divided and lengthened, permitting the men to stand at either side of his head, about three paces away. A trollop with fox-colored hair and a laughing face sat the saddle with ease, and in lieu of the reins held a riding whip in each hand. The troopers and their women cheered and clapped, and at the sound the piebald reared like a whirlwind and pawed the air, showing the three horny growths on each forefoot that we call hoofs for what they were—talons adapted almost as well to combat as to gripping turf. Their feints outsped my eyes.

The big man slapped me on the back. "He's not the best I ever had, but he's good enough, and I trained him myself. Mesrop and Lactan there are going to pass you those reins, and all you have to do is get up on him. If you can do it without knocking Daria off, you can have her until we run you down." He raised his voice: *"All right, let him go!"*

I had expected the two men to give me the reins. Instead

they threw them at my face, and in snatching for them I missed them both. Someone goaded the piebald from behind, and the big man gave a peculiar, piercing whistle. The piebald had been taught to fight, like the destriers in the Bear Tower, and though his long teeth had not been augmented with metal, they had been left as nature made them and stood out from his mouth like knives.

I dodged a flashing forefoot and tried to grasp his halter; a blow from one of the whips caught me full across the face, and the piebald's rush knocked me sprawling.

The troopers must have held him back or I would have been trampled. Perhaps they also helped me to my feet—I cannot be sure. My throat was full of dust, and blood from my forehead trickled into my eyes.

I went for him again, circling to the right to keep clear of his hoofs, but he turned more quickly than I, and the girl called Daria snapped both lashes before my face to throw me off. More from anger than any plan I seized one. The thong of the whipstock was around her wrist; when I jerked the lash she came with it, falling into my arms. She bit my ear, but I got her by the back of the neck, spun her around, dug fingers into one firm buttock and lifted her. Kicking the air, her legs seemed to startle the piebald. I backed him through the crowd until one of his tormentors goaded him toward me, then stepped on his reins.

After that, it was easy. I dropped the girl, caught his halter, twisted his head, and kicked his forefeet from under him as we were taught to do with unruly clients. With a high-pitched, animal scream he came crashing down. I was in the saddle before he could get his legs beneath him, and from there I lashed his flanks with the long reins and sent him bolting through the crowd, then turned him and charged them again.

All my life I had heard of the excitement of this kind of fighting, though I had never experienced it. Now I found everything more than true. The troopers and their women were yelling and running, and a few flourished swords. They might have threatened a thunderstorm with more effect—I rode over half a dozen at a sweep. The girl's red hair flew like a banner as she fled, but no human legs could have outdistanced that steed. We flashed past her, and I caught her by that flaming banner and threw her over the arcione before me.

A twisting trail led to a dark ravine, and that ravine to another. Deer scattered ahead of us; in three bounds we overtook a buck in velvet and shouldered him out of the way. While I had been Lictor of Thrax, I had heard that the eclectics often raced game and leaped from their mounts to stab it. I believed those stories now—I could have cut the buck's throat with a butcher knife.

We left him behind, crested a new hill and dashed down into a silent, wooded valley. When the piebald had run himself out, I let him find his own path among the trees, which were the largest I had seen since leaving Saltus; and when he stopped to crop the sparse, tender grass that grew between their roots, I halted and threw the reins on the ground as I had seen Guasacht do, then dismounted and helped the red-haired girl off.

"Thanks," she said. And then, "You did it. I didn't think you could."

"Or you wouldn't have agreed to this? I had supposed they made you."

"I wouldn't have given you that cut with the whip. You'll want to repay me now, won't you? With the reins, I suppose."

"What makes you think that?" I was tired and sat down. Yellow flowers, each blossom no bigger than a drop of water, grew in the grass; I picked a few and found they smelled of calambac.

"You look the type. Besides, you carried me bottom up, and men who do that always want to hit it."

"I never knew that. It's an interesting thought."

"I have a lot of them—that kind." Quickly and gracefully she seated herself beside me and put a hand on my knee. "Listen, it was the initiation, that's all. We take turns, and it was my turn and I was supposed to hit you. Now it's over."

"I understand."

"Then you won't hurt me? That's wonderful. We can have a good time here, really. Whatever you want and as much as you want, and we won't go back until it's time to eat."

"I didn't say I wouldn't hurt you."

Her face, which had been wreathed with forced smiles, fell, and she looked at the ground. I suggested that she might run away.

"That would only make it more fun for you, and you'd hurt me more before we were through." Her hand crept up my thigh as she spoke. "You're nice looking, you know. And so tall." She made a sitting bow, pressing her face into my lap to give me a tingling kiss, then straightening up at once. "It could be nice. Really it could."

"Or you could kill yourself. Have you a knife?"

For an instant, her mouth formed a perfect little circle. "You're crazy, aren't you? I should have known." She leaped to her feet.

I caught her by one ankle and sent her sprawling to the soft forest floor. Her shift was rotten with wear—a pull and it fell away. "You said you wouldn't run."

She looked over her shoulder at me with large eyes.

I said, "You have no power over me, neither you nor they. I am not afraid of pain, or of death. There is only one living woman I desire, and no man but myself."

Patrol

WE HELD A PERIMETER no more than a couple of hundred paces across. For the most part, our enemies had only knives and axes—the axes and their ragged clothes recalled the volunteers I had helped Vodalus against in our necropolis—but there were hundreds of them already, and more coming.

The bacele had saddled up and left camp before dawn. The shadows were still long, somewhere along the shifting front, when a scout showed Guasacht the deep ruts of a coach traveling north. For three watches we tracked it.

The Ascian raiders who had captured it fought well, turning south to surprise us, then west, then north again like a writhing serpent; but always leaving a trail of dead, caught between our fire and that of the guards inside, who shot them through the loopholes. It was only toward the end, when the Ascians could no longer flee, that we grew aware of other hunters.

By noon, the little valley was surrounded. The gleaming steel coach with its dead and dying prisoners stood mired to the axles. Our Ascian prisoners squatted in front of it, guarded by our wounded. The Ascian officer spoke our tongue, and a watch earlier Guasacht had ordered him to free the coach and shot several Ascians when he had failed; thirty or more remained, nearly naked, listless and empty-eyed. Their weapons were piled some distance off, near our tethered mounts.

Now Guasacht was making the rounds, and I saw him pause at the stump that sheltered the trooper next to me. One of the enemy put her head from behind a clump of brush some way up the slope. My contus struck her with a bolt of flame; she leaped by reflex, then curled up as spiders do when someone tosses them among the coals of a campfire. She had been white-faced beneath her red bandana, and I suddenly understood that she had been made to look—that there were those behind that brush who had disliked her, or at least not valued her, and who had forced her to look out. I fired again, slashing the green growth with the bolt and bringing a puff of acrid smoke that drifted toward me like her ghost.

"Don't waste those charges," Guasacht said at my elbow. More from habit, I think, than from fear, he had thrown himself flat beside me.

I asked if the charges would be exhausted before night if I fired six times a watch.

He shrugged, then shook his head.

"That's how fast I've been shooting this thing, as well as I can judge by the sun. And when night comes . . ."

I looked at him, and he could only shrug again.

"When night comes," I continued, "we won't be able to see them until they're only a few steps away. We'll fire more or less at random and kill a few score, then draw swords and stand back to back, and they'll kill us."

He said, "Help will arrive before then," and when he saw I did not believe him, he spat. "I wish I'd never looked at the damned thing's track. I wish I'd never heard of it."

It was my turn to shrug. "Give it back to the Ascians, and we'll break out."

"It's coin, I tell you! Gold to pay our troops. It's too heavy to be anything else."

"The armor must weigh a good deal."

"Not that much. I've seen these coaches before, and it's gold from Nessus or the House Absolute. But those things inside—who's ever seen such creatures?"

"I have."

Guasacht stared at me.

"When I went out through the Piteous Gate in the Wall of Nessus. They are man-beasts, contrived by the same lost arts that made our destriers faster than the road engines of old." I tried to recall what else Jonas had told me of them, and finished rather weakly by saying, "The Autarch employs them in duties too laborious for men, or for which men cannot be trusted."

"I suppose that might be right enough. They can't very well steal the money. Where would they go? Listen, I've had my eye on you."

"I know," I said. "I've felt it."

"I've had my eye on you, I say. Particularly since you made that piebald of yours go for the man that trained him. Up here in Orithyia we see a lot of strong men and a lot of brave ones—mostly when we step over their bodies. We see a lot of smart ones too, and nineteen out of twenty are too smart to be of use to anybody, including themselves. What's valuable are men, and sometimes women, who've got a kind of power, the power that makes other people want to do what they say. I don't mean to brag, but I've got it. You've got it too."

"It hasn't been overwhelmingly apparent in my life before this."

"Sometimes it takes the war to bring it out. That's one of the benefits of the war, and since it hasn't got many we ought to appreciate the ones it does. Severian, I want you to go down to the coach and treat with these man-animals. You say you know something about them. Get them to come out and help us fight. We're both on the same side, after all."

THE CITADEL OF THE AUTARCH   158

I nodded. "And if I can get them to open the doors, we can divide the money among us. Some of us, at least, may escape."

Guasacht shook his head in disgust. "What did I tell you just a moment ago about being too smart? If you were really smart, you wouldn't have ignored it. No, you tell them that even if there's only three or four of them, every fighter counts. Besides, there's at least a chance the sight of them will frighten these damn freebooters away. Let me have your contus, and I'll hold your position for you until you come back."

I handed over the long weapon. "Who are these people, anyway?"

"These? Camp followers. Sutlers and whores—men as well as women. Deserters. Every so often the Autarch or one of his generals has them rounded up and put to work, but they slip away before long. Slipping away's their specialty. They ought to be wiped out."

"I have your authority to treat with our prisoners in the coach? You'll back me up?"

"They're not prisoners—well, yes, I suppose they are. You tell them what I said and make the best deal you can. I'll back you."

I looked at him for a moment, trying to decide whether he meant it. Like so many middle-aged men, he carried the old man he would become in his face, soured and obscene, already muttering the objections and complaints that would be his in the final skirmish.

"You've got my word. Go on."

"All right." I rose. The armored coach resembled the carriages that had been used to bring important clients to our tower in the Citadel. Its windows were narrow and barred, its rear wheels as high as a man. The smooth steel sides suggested those lost arts I had mentioned to Guasacht, and I knew the man-beasts inside had better weapons than ours. I extended my hands to show I was unarmed and walked as steadily as I could toward them until a face showed at one window grill.

When one hears of such creatures, one imagines something stable, midway between beast and human; but when one actually sees them—as I now saw this man-beast, and as I had seen the man-apes in the mine near Saltus—they are not like that at all. The best comparison I can make is to the flickering of a silver birch tossed by the wind. At one moment it seems a common tree, at the next, when the undersides of the leaves appear, a supernatural creation. So it is with the man-beasts. At first I thought a mastiff peered at me through the bars; then it seemed rather a man, nobly ugly, tawny-faced and amber-eyed. I raised my hands to the grill to give him my scent, thinking of Triskele.

"What do you want?" His voice was harsh but not unpleasant.

"I want to save your lives," I said. It was the wrong thing to say, and I knew it as soon as the words had left my mouth.

"We want to save our honor."

I nodded. "Honor is the higher life."

"If you can tell us how to save our honor, speak. We will listen. But we will never surrender our trust."

"You have already surrendered it," I said.

The wind died, and the mastiff was back in an instant, flashing teeth and blazing eyes.

"It was not to safeguard gold from the Ascians that you were put into this coach, but to safeguard it from those of our own Commonwealth who would steal it if they could. The Ascians are beaten—look at them. We are the Autarch's loyal humans. Those you were set to guard against will overwhelm us soon."

"They must kill me and my fellows before they can get the gold."

It *was* gold, then. I said, "They will do so. Come out and help us fight, while there is still a chance of victory."

He hesitated, and I was no longer sure that I had been

entirely wrong to speak first of saving his life. "No," he said. "We cannot. What you say may be reason, I do not know. Our law is not the law of reason. Our law is honor and obedience. We stay."

"But you know that we are not your enemies?"

"Anyone seeking what we guard is our enemy."

"We're guarding it too. If these camp followers and deserters came within range of your weapons, would you fire on them?"

"Yes, of course."

I walked over to the spiritless cluster of Ascians and asked to speak with their commander. The man who stood was only slightly taller than the rest; the intelligence in his face was the kind one sometimes sees in cunning madmen. I told him Guasacht had sent me to treat in his stead because I had often spoken with Ascian prisoners and knew their ways. This was, as I intended, overheard by his three wounded guards, who could see Guasacht manning my position on the perimeter.

"Greetings in the name of the Group of Seventeen," the Ascian said.

"In the name of the Group of Seventeen."

The Ascian looked startled but nodded.

"We are surrounded by the disloyal subjects of our Autarch, who are thus the enemies of both the Autarch and the Group of Seventeen. Our own commander, Guasacht, has devised a plan that will leave us all alive and free."

"The servants of the Group of Seventeen must not be expended without purpose."

"Precisely. Here is the plan. We will harness some of our destriers to the steel coach—as many as necessary to pull it free. You and your people must work to free it too. When it's free, we'll return your weapons and help you fight your way out of this cordon. Your soldiers and ours will go north, and you can keep the coach and the money inside to take to your superiors, just as you hoped when you captured it."

"The light of Correct Thought penetrates every darkness."

"No, we haven't gone over to the Group of Seventeen. You have to help us in return. In the first place, help get the coach out of the mud. In the second, help us fight our way out. In the third, provide us with an escort that will get us through your army and back to our own lines."

The Ascian officer glanced toward the gleaming coach. "No failure is permanent failure. But inevitable success may require new plans and greater strength."

"Then you approve of my new plan?" I had not been aware that I was perspiring, but now the sweat ran stinging into my eyes. I wiped my forehead with the edge of my cloak, just as Master Gurloes used to.

The Ascian officer nodded. "Study of Correct Thought eventually reveals the path of success."

"Yes," I said. "All right, I've studied it. Behind our efforts, let there be found our efforts."

When I returned to the coach, the same man-beast I had seen before came to the window again, not quite so hostile this time. I said, "The Ascians have agreed to try to push this thing out once more. We're going to have to unload it."

"That is impossible."

"If we don't, the gold will be lost with the sun. I'm not asking you to give it up—just take it out and mount guard over it. You'll have your weapons, and if any human bearing arms comes close to you, you can kill him. I'll be with you, unarmed. You can kill me too."

It took a great deal more talking, but eventually they did it. I got the wounded who had been watching the Ascians to lay down their conti and harness eight of our destriers to the coach, and got the Ascians positioned to pull on the harness and heave at the wheels. Then the door in the side of the steel coach swung open and the man-beasts carried out small metal chests, two working while the one I had spoken to stood guard. They were taller than I had expected and had fusils, with pistols in their belts to supplement them—the first pistols I had seen since I had watched the Hierodules use them to turn Baldanders's charges in the gardens of the House Absolute.

When all the chests were out and the three man-beasts were standing around them with their weapons at the ready, I shouted. The wounded troopers lashed every destrier in the new team, the Ascians heaved until their eyes started from their straining faces . . . and just when we all thought it would not, the steel coach lifted itself from the mud and lumbered half a chain before the wounded could bring it to a halt. Guasacht nearly got us both killed by running down from the perimeter waving my contus, but the man-beasts had just sense enough to see that he was merely excited and not dangerous.

He got a great deal more excited when he saw the man-beasts carry their gold inside again, and when he heard what I had promised the Ascians. I reminded him that he had given me leave to act in his name.

"When I act," he sputtered, "it's with the idea of winning."

I confessed I lacked his military experience, but told him I had found that in some situations winning consisted of disentangling oneself.

"Just the same, I had hoped you would work out something better."

Rising inexorably while we remained unaware of their motion, the mountain peaks to the west were already clawing for the lower edge of the sun; I pointed to it.

Suddenly, Guasacht smiled. "After all, these are the same Ascians we took it from before."

He called the Ascian officer over and told him our mounted troopers would lead the attack, and that his soldiers could follow the steel coach on foot. The Ascian agreed, but when his soldiers had rearmed themselves, he insisted on placing half a dozen on top of the coach and leading the attack himself with the rest. Guasacht agreed with an apparent bad grace that seemed to me entirely assumed. We put an armed trooper astride each of the eight destriers of the new team, and I saw Guasacht conversing earnestly with their cornet.

I had promised the Ascian we would break through the cordon of deserters to the north, but the ground in that direction proved to be unsuited to the steel coach, and in the end a route north by northwest was agreed upon. The Ascian infantry advanced at a pace not much short of a full run, firing as they came. The coach followed. The narrow, enduring bolts of the troopers' conti stabbed at the ragged mob who tried to close about it, and the Ascian arquebuses on its roof sent gouts of violet energy crashing among them. The man-beasts fired their fusils from the barred windows, slaughtering half a dozen with a single blast.

The remainder of our troops (I among them) followed the coach, having maintained our perimeter until it was gone. To save precious charges, many put their conti through the saddle rings, drew their swords, and rode down the straggling remnant the Ascians and the coach had left behind.

Then the enemy was past, and the ground clearer. At once the troopers whose mounts pulled the coach clapped spurs to them, and Guasacht, Erblon, and several others who were riding just behind it swept the Ascians from its top in a cloud of crimson flame and reeking smoke. Those on foot scattered, then turned to fire.

It was a fight I did not feel I could take part in. I reined up, and so saw—I believe, before any of the others—the first of the anpiels who dropped, like the angel in Melito's fable, from the sun-dyed clouds. They were fair to look upon, naked and having the slender bodies of young women; but their rainbow wings spread wider than any teratornis's, and each anpiel held a pistol in either hand.

· · ·

Late that night, when we were back in camp and the wounded had been cared for, I asked Guasacht if he would do as he had again.

He thought for a moment. "I hadn't any way of knowing those flying girls would come. Looking at it from this end, it's natural enough—there must have been enough in that coach to pay half the army, and they wouldn't hesitate to send elite troops looking for it. But before it happened, would you have guessed it?"

I shook my head.

"Listen, Severian, I shouldn't be talking to you like this. But you did what you could, and you're the best leech I ever saw. Anyway, it came out all right in the end, didn't it? You saw how friendly their seraph was. What did she see, after all? Plucky lads trying to save the coach from the Ascians. We'll get a commendation, I should think. Maybe a reward."

I said, "You could have killed the man-beasts, and the Ascians too, when the gold was out of the coach. You didn't because I would have died with them. I think you deserve a commendation. From me, at least."

He rubbed his drawn face with both hands. "Well, I'm just as happy. It would have been the end of the Eighteenth; in another watch we'd have been killing each other for the money."

Deployment

BEFORE THE BATTLE there were other patrols and days of idleness. Often enough we saw no Ascians, or saw only their dead. We were supposed to arrest deserters and drive from our area such peddlers and vagabonds as fatten on an army; but if they seemed to us such people as had surrounded the steel coach, we killed them, not executing them in any formal style but cutting them down from the saddle.

The moon waxed again nearly to the full, hanging like a green apple in the sky. Experienced troopers told me the worst fights always came at or near the full of the moon, which is said to breed madness. I suppose this is actually because its refulgence permits generals to bring up reinforcements by night.

On the day of the battle, the graisle's bray summoned us from our blankets at dawn. We formed a ragged double column in the mist, with Guasacht at our head and Erblon following him with our flag. I had supposed that the women would stay behind—as most had when we had gone on patrol—but more than half drew conti and came with us. Those who had helmets, I noticed, thrust their hair up into the bowl, and many wore corslets that flattened and concealed their breasts. I mentioned it to Mesrop, who rode opposite me.

"There might be trouble about the pay," he said. "Somebody with sharp eyes will be counting us, and the contracts usually call for men."

"Guasacht said there'd be more money today," I reminded him.

He cleared his throat and spat, the white phlegm vanishing into the clammy air as though Urth herself had swallowed it. "They won't pay until it's over. They never do."

Guasacht shouted and waved an arm; Erblon gestured with our flag, and we were off, the hoofbeats sounding like the thudding of a hundred muffled drums. I said, "I suppose that way they don't have to pay for those who are killed."

"They pay triple—once because he fought, once for blood money, and once for discharge money."

"Or she fought, I suppose."

Mesrop spat again.

We rode for some time, then halted at a spot that seemed no different from any other. As the column fell silent, I heard a humming or murmuring in the hills all around us. A scattered army, dispersed no doubt for sanitary reasons and to deprive the Ascian enemy of a concentrated target, was assembling now just as particles of dust in the stone town had come together in the bodies of its resuscitated dancers.

Not unnoticed. Even as birds of prey had once followed us before we reached that town, now five-armed shapes that spun like wheels pursued us above the scattered clouds that dimmed and melted in the level red light of dawn. At first, when they were highest, they seemed merely gray; but as we watched they dropped toward us, and I saw they were of a hue for which I can find no name but that stands to achroma as gold to yellow, or silver to white. The air groaned with their turning.

Another that we had not seen came leaping across our path, hardly higher than the treetops. Each spoke was the length of a tower, pierced with casements and ports. Though it lay flat upon the air, it seemed to stride along. Its wind whistled down upon us as if to blow away the trees. My piebald screamed and bolted, and so did many other destriers, often falling in that strange wind.

In the space of a heartbeat it was over. The leaves that had swirled about us like snow fell to earth. Guasacht shouted and Erblon sounded the graisle and brandished our flag. I got the piebald under control and cantered from one destrier to another, taking them by the nostrils until their riders could manage them again.

I rescued Daria, who I had not known was in the column, in this way. She looked very pretty and boyish dressed as a trooper, with a contus, and a slender sabre at either side of her saddle horn. I could not help thinking when I saw her of how other women I had known would appear in the same situation: Thea a theatrical warrior maid, beautiful and dramatic but essentially the figure of a figurehead; Thecla—now part of myself—a vengeful mimalone brandishing poisoned weapons; Agia astride a slender-legged sorrel, wearing a cuirass molded to her figure, while her hair, plaited with bowstrings, flew wild in the wind; Jolenta a floriate queen in armor spikey with thorns, her big breasts and fleshy thighs absurd at any gait faster than a walk, smiling dreamily at each halt and attempting to recline in the saddle; Dorcas a naiad riding, lifted momentarily like a fountain flashing with sunshine; Valeria, perhaps, an aristocratic Daria.

I had supposed, when I saw our people scatter, that it would be impossible to reassemble the column; but within a few moments of the time the pentadactyl air-strider had passed over us, we were together again. We galloped for a league or more—mostly, I suspect, to dissipate some of the nervous energy of our destriers—then halted by a brook and gave them just as much water as would wet their mouths without making them sluggish. When I had fought the piebald back from the bank, I rode to a clearing from which I could watch the sky. Soon Guasacht trotted over and asked me jocularly, "You looking for another one?"

I nodded and told him I had never seen such craft before.

"You wouldn't have, unless you've been close to the front. They'd never come back if they tried to go down south."

"Soldiers like us wouldn't stop them."

He grew suddenly serious, his tiny eyes mere slits in the sun-browned flesh. "No. But plucky lads can stop their raiding parties. The guns and air-galleys can't do that."

The piebald stirred and stamped with impatience. I said, "I come from a part of the city you've probably never heard of, the Citadel. There are guns there that look out over the whole quarter, but I've never known them to be fired except ceremonially." Still staring at the sky, I thought of the wheeling pentadactyls over Nessus, and a thousand blasts, issuing not just from the Barbican and the Great Keep, but from all the towers; and I wondered with what weapons the pentadactyls would reply.

"Come along," Guasacht said. "I know it's a temptation to keep a lookout for them, but it doesn't do any good."

I followed him back to the brook, where Erblon was lining up the column. "They didn't even fire at us. They must surely have guns in those fliers."

"We're pretty small fish." I could see that Guasacht wanted me to rejoin the column, though he hesitated to order me to do so directly.

For my part, I could feel fear grip me like a specter, strongest about my legs, but lifting cold tentacles into my bowels, touching my heart. I wanted to be silent, but I could not stop talking. "When we go onto the field of battle—" (I think I imagined this field like the shaven lawn of the Sanguinary Field, where I had fought Agilus.)

Guasacht laughed. "When we go into the fight, our gunners would be delighted to see them out after us." Before I
understood what he was about to do, he struck the piebald
with the flat of his blade and sent me cantering off.

Fear is like those diseases that disfigure the face with running sores. One becomes almost more afraid of their being
seen than of their source, and comes to feel not only disgraced but defiled. When the piebald began to slow, I dug
my heels into him and fell into line at the very end of the
column.

Only a short time before I had been on the point of replac-
ing Erblon; now I was demoted, not by Guasacht but by
myself, to the lowest position. And yet when I had helped
reassemble the scattered troopers, the thing I feared had already passed; so that the entire drama of my elevation had
been played out after it had ended in debasement. It was as
though one were to see a young man idling in a public garden
stabbed—then watch him, all unknowing, strike up an acquaintance with the voluptuous wife of his murderer, and at
last, having ascertained, as he thought, that her husband was
in another part of the city, clasp her to him until she cried
out from the pain of the dagger's hilt protruding from his
chest.

When the column lurched forward, Daria detached herself
from it and waited until she could fall in beside me. "You're
afraid," she said. It was not a question but a statement, and
not a reproach but almost a password, like the ridiculous
phrases I had learned at Vodalus's banquet.

"Yes. You're about to remind me of the boast I made to
you in the forest. I can only say that I did not know it to be
an empty one when I made it. A certain wise man once tried
to teach me that even after a client has mastered one excruciation, so that he can put it from his mind even while he
screams and writhes, another quite different excruciation
may be as effectual in breaking his will as in breaking a

child's. I learned to explain all this when he asked me but never until now to apply it, as I should, to my own life. But if I am the client here, who is the torturer?"

"We're all more or less afraid," she said. "That was why— yes, I saw it—Guasacht sent you away. It was to keep you from making his own feeling worse. If it were worse, he wouldn't be able to lead. When the time comes, you'll do what you have to, and that's all any of them do."

"Hadn't we better go?" I asked. The end of the column was moving off in that surging way the tail of a long line always does.

"If we go now, a lot of them will know we're at the rear because we're afraid. If we wait just a little while longer, many of those who saw you talking with Guasacht will think he sent you back here to speed up stragglers, and that I came back to be with you."

"All right," I said.

Her hand, damp with sweat and as thin as Dorcas's, came sliding into mine.

Until that moment, I had been certain she had fought before. Now I asked her, "Is this your first time too?"

"I can fight better than most of them," she declared, "and I'm sick of being called a whore."

Together, we trotted after the column.

XXII

Battle

.

I SAW THEM first as a scattering of colored dots on the farther side of the wide valley, skirmishers who seemed to move and mix, as bubbles do that dance upon the surface of a mug of cider. We were trotting through a grove of shattered trees whose white and naked wood was like the living bone of a compound fracture. Our column was much larger now, perhaps the whole of the irregular contarii. It had been under fire, in a more or less dilatory way, for about half a watch. Some troopers had been wounded (one, near me, quite badly) and several killed. The wounded cared for themselves and tried to help each other—if there were medical attendants for us they were too far behind us for me to be conscious of them.

From time to time we passed corpses among the trees; usually these were in little clusters of two or three, sometimes they were merely solitary individuals. I saw one who had contrived in dying to hook the collar of his brigandine jacket to a splinter protruding from one of the broken trunks, and I was struck by the horror of his situation, his being dead and yet unable to rest, and then by the thought that such was the plight of all those thousands of trees, trees that had been killed but could not fall.

At about the same time I became aware of the enemy, I realized that there were troops of our own army to either side. To our right a mixture, as it were, of mounted men and infantry, the riders helmetless and naked to the waist, with red and blue blanket rolls slung across their bronzed chests. They were better mounted, I thought, than most of us. They carried lancegays not much longer than the height of a man, many of them holding them aslant their saddle-bows. Each had a small copper shield bound to the upper part of his left arm. I had no idea from what part of the Commonwealth these men might come; but for some reason, perhaps only because of their long hair and bare chests, I felt sure they were savages.

If they were, the infantry that moved among them was something lower still, brown and stooped and shaggy-haired. I had only glimpses through the broken trees, but I thought they dropped to all fours at times. Occasionally one seemed to grasp the stirrup of some rider, as I had sometimes taken Jonas's when he rode his merychip; whenever that occurred, the rider struck at his companion's hand with the butt of his weapon.

A road ran through lower ground to our left; and down it, and to either side of it, there moved a force far more numerous than our column and the savage riders and their companions all combined: battalions of peltasts with blazing spears and big, transparent shields; hobilers on prancing mounts, with bows and arrow cases crossed over their backs; lightly armed cherkajis whose formations were seas of plumes and flags.

I could know nothing of the courage of all these strange soldiers who had suddenly become my comrades, but I unconsciously assumed it to be no greater than my own, and they seemed a slender defense indeed against the moving dots on the farther side. The fire to which we were subjected grew more intense, and so far as I could see, our enemies were under none at all.

Only a few weeks before (though it felt like at least a year now) I would have been terrified at the thought of being shot at with such a weapon as Vodalus had used on the foggy night in our necropolis with which I have begun this account. The bolts that struck all around us made that simple beam appear as childish as the shining slugs thrown from the hetman's archer's pellet bow.

I had no idea what sort of device was used to project these bolts, or even whether they were in fact pure energy or some type of missile; but as they landed among us, their nature was that of an explosion lengthened into something like a rod. And though they could not be seen until they struck, they whistled as they came, and by that whistled note, which endured no longer than the blink of an eye, I soon learned to tell how near they would hit and how powerful the extended detonation would be. If there was no change in the tone, so that it resembled the note a coryphaeus sounds on his pitch pipe, the strike would be some distance off. But if it rose quickly, as though a note first sounded for men had become one for women, its impact would be nearby; and though only the loudest of the monotonal bolts were dangerous, each that rose to a scream claimed at least one of us and often several.

It seemed madness to trot forward as we did. We should have scattered, or dismounted to take refuge among the trees; and if one of us had done it, I think all the rest would have followed him. With every bolt that fell, I was almost that one. But again and again, as if my mind were chained in some narrow circle, the memory of the fear I had shown earlier held me in my place. Let the rest run and I would run with them; but I would not run first.

Inevitably, a bolt struck parallel to our column. Six troopers flew apart as though they themselves had contained small bombs, the head of the first bursting in a gout of scarlet, the neck and shoulders of the second, the chest of the third, the bellies of the fourth and fifth, and the groin (or perhaps on the saddle and the back of his destrier) of the sixth, before the bolt struck the ground and sent up a geyser of dust and stones. The men and animals opposite those who were destroyed in this way were killed too, wracked by the force of the explosions and bombarded with the limbs and armor of the others.

Holding the piebald to a trot, and often to a walk, was the worst of it; if I could not run, I wanted to press forward, to get the fighting begun, to die if I was in fact to die. This hit gave me some opportunity to relieve my feelings. Waving to Daria to follow, I let the piebald lope past the little group of survivors who had been riding between us and the last trooper to die, and moved into the space in the column that had been the casualties'. Mesrop was there already, and he grinned at me. "Good thinking. Chances are there won't be another one here for quite a while." I forbore to disabuse him.

For a time it seemed he was correct anyway. Having hit us, the enemy gunners diverted their fire to the savages on our right. Their shambling infantry shrieked and gibbered as the bolts fell among them, but the riders reacted, so it appeared, by calling on magic to protect them. Often their chants sounded so clearly that I could make out the words, though they were in no language I had ever heard. Once one actually stood on his saddle like a performer in a riding exhibition, lifting a hand to the sun and extending the other toward the Ascians. Each rider seemed to have a personal spell; and it was easy to see, as I watched their numbers shrink under the bombardment, how such primitive minds come to believe in their charms, for the survivors could not but feel their thaumaturgy had saved them, and the rest could not complain of the failure of theirs.

Though we were advancing, for the most part, at the trot, we were not the first to engage the enemy. On the lower ground, the cherkajis had streaked across the valley, crashing against a square of foot soldiers like a wave of fire.

I had vaguely supposed that the enemy would be provided with weapons far superior to anything we had in the con-tarii—perhaps pistols and fusils, such as the man-beasts had carried—and that a hundred fighters so armed would easily destroy any quantity of cavalry. Nothing of the kind happened. Several rows of the square gave way, and I was close enough now to hear the riders' war cries, distant yet distinct, and see individual foot soldiers in flight. Some were casting aside immense shields, shields even larger than the glassy ones of the peltasts, though they shone with the luster of metal. Their offensive arms seemed to be splay-headed spears no more than three cubits long, weapons that could produce sheets of cleaving flame, but short in range.

A second infantry square emerged behind the first, then another and another, farther down the valley.

Just as I was sure we were about to ride to the assistance of the cherkajis, we received the order to halt. Looking to the right, I saw that the savages had already done so, stopping some distance behind us, and were now driving the hairy creatures that had accompanied them toward the side of their position farthest from us.

Guasacht called, "We're blocking! Sit easy, lads!"

I looked at Daria, who returned a look equally bewildered. Mesrop waved an arm toward the eastern end of the valley. "We're watching the flank. If nobody comes, we ought to have a good enough time of it today."

I said, "Except for the ones who've already died." The bombardment, which had been diminishing, now seemed to have stopped altogether. The silence of its absence lay all about us, almost more frightening than its screaming bolts had been.

"I suppose so." His shrug announced eloquently that we had lost a few dozen from a force of hundreds.

The cherkajis had recoiled, retreating behind a screen of hobilers who directed a shower of arrows at the leading edge of the Ascians' checkerboard battle line. Most seemed to glance off the shields, but a few must have buried their heads in the metal, which took fire from them and burned with a flame as bright as theirs and billowing white smoke.

When the arrows slackened, the squares of the checkerboard advanced again with a mechanical jerkiness. The cherkajis had continued to fall back and were now in the rear of a line of peltasts, very little in advance of us. I could see their dark faces clearly. They were all men and bearded, and numbered about two thousand; but they had among them a dozen or so bejeweled young women borne in gilded howdahs on the backs of caparisoned arsinoithers.

These women were dark-eyed and dark complexioned like the men, yet in their lush figures and languishing looks they reminded me of Jolenta. I pointed them out to Daria and asked if she knew how they were armed, since I could see no weapons.

"You'd like one, would you? Or two. I'll bet they look good to you even from here."

Mesrop winked and said, "I wouldn't mind a couple myself."

Daria laughed. "They'd fight like alraunes if either of you tried to have anything to do with them. They're sacred and forbidden, the Daughters of War. Have you ever been around those animals they're riding?"

I shook my head.

"They charge easy and nothing stops them, but they always go the same way—straight at whatever it is that bothers them and past it for a chain or two. Then they stop and go back."

I watched. Arsinoithers have two big horns—not spreading horns like the horns of bulls, but horns that diverge about as much as a man's first and second fingers can. As I soon saw, they charge head down, with those horns level with the ground, and these did just as Daria had said. The cherkajis rallied and attacked again with their slender lances and forked swords. Trailing far behind that lightning dash, the arsinoithers lumbered forward, gray-black heads down and tails up, with the deep-bosomed, dark-faced maidens standing erect under their canopies and gripping the gilded poles. One could see from the way these women held themselves that their thighs were as full as the udders of milch cows and round as the trunks of trees.

The charge carried them through the swirling fight and deep—but not too deep—into the checkerboard. The Ascian foot soldiers blasted the sides of their beasts, which must have been like burning horn or *cuir boli*; they tried to mount their heads and were tossed into the air; they struggled to climb the gray flanks. The cherkajis came crashing to the rescue, and the checkerboard flowed and ebbed and lost a square.

Watching it from such a distance, I recalled my own thoughts of battle as a game of chess, and I felt that somewhere someone else had entertained the same thoughts and unconsciously allowed them to shape his plan.

"They're lovely," Daria continued, teasing me. "Chosen at twelve and fed on honey and pure oils. I've heard their flesh is so tender they can't lie on the ground without being bruised. Bags of feathers are carried about for them to sleep on. If those are lost, the girls have to lie in mud that shapes itself to support their bodies. The eunuchs who care for them mix it with wine warmed over a fire, so they will sleep and not be cold."

"We should dismount," Mesrop said. "It'll spare the animals."

But I wanted to watch the battle and would not get down, though soon only Guasacht and I remained in the saddle out of our entire bacele.

The cherkajis had been driven back once again, and now came under a withering bombardment from unseen artillery.

The peltasts dropped to the ground, covering themselves with their shields. New squares of Ascian infantry emerged from the forest on the north side of the valley. There seemed to be no end to them; I felt we had been committed against an inexhaustible enemy.

The feeling grew stronger when the cherkajis charged a third time. A bolt struck an arsinoither, blowing it and the lovely woman it had carried to bloody ruin. The infantry was firing at those women now; one crumpled, and howdah and canopy vanished in a puff of flame. The infantry squares advanced over brightly clad corpses and dead destriers.

By each step in war the winner loses. The ground the checkerboard had won exposed the side of its leading square to us, and to my astonishment we were ordered to mount, spread into line, and wheeled against it, first trotting, then cantering, and at last, with the brass throats of all the graisles shouting, in a desperate rush that nearly blew the skin from our faces.

If the cherkajis were lightly armed, we were armed more lightly still. Yet there was a magic in the charge more powerful than the chants of our savage allies. The wildfire of our weapons played along the distant ranks as scythes attack a wheat field. I lashed the piebald with his reins to keep from being outdistanced by the roaring hoofs I heard behind me. Yet I was, and glimpsed Daria as she shot past, the flame of her hair flying free, her contus in one hand and a sabre in the other, her cheeks whiter than the foaming flanks of her destrier. I knew then how the custom of the cherkajis had begun, and I tried to charge faster still so that she should not die, though Thecla laughed through my lips at the thought.

Destriers do not run like common beasts—they skim the ground as arrows do air. For an instant, the fire of the Ascian infantry half a league away rose before us like a wall. A moment later we were among them, the legs of every mount bloody to the knee. The square that had seemed as solid as a building stone had become only a crowd of frantic soldiers with big shields and cropped heads, soldiers who often slew one another in their eagerness to slay us.

Fighting is a stupid business at best; but there are things to be learned about it, of which the first is that numbers tell only in time. The immediate struggle is always that of an individual against one or two others. In this our destriers gave us the upper hand—not only because of their height and weight, but because they bit and struck out with their fore-feet, and the blows of their hoofs were more powerful than any man save Baldanders could have delivered with a mace.

Fire cut through my contus. I dropped it but continued to kill, slashing left, then right, then left again with the falchion and hardly noticing that the blast had laid open my leg.

I think I must have cut down half a dozen Ascians before I saw that they all looked the same—not that they all had the same face (as the men in some units of our own army do, who are indeed closer than brothers), but that the differences among them seemed accidental and trivial. I had observed this among our prisoners when we had retrieved the steel coach, but it had not really impressed itself upon my mind. In the madness of battle it did so, for it seemed a part of that madness. The frenzied figures were male and female: the women had small but pendulous breasts and were half a head shorter, but there was no other distinction. All had large, brilliant, wild eyes, hair clipped nearly to the skull, starved faces, screaming mouths, and prominent teeth.

We fought free as the cherkajis had; the square had been dented but not destroyed. While we let our mounts catch breath it reformed, the light, polished shields to the front. A spearman broke ranks and came running toward us waving his weapon. At first I thought it mere bluster; then, as he came nearer (for a normal man runs much less swiftly than a des-trier), that he wished to surrender. At last, when he had al-most reached our line, he fired, and a trooper shot him down. In his convulsions he threw his blazing spear into the air; I remember how it twisted against the dark blue sky.

Guasacht came trotting over. "You're bleeding bad. Can you ride when we charge them again?"

I felt as strong as I ever had in my life and told him so.

"Still, you'd better get a bandage on that leg."

The seared flesh had cracked; blood was oozing out. Daria, who had not been hurt at all, bound it up.

The charge for which I had been prepared never took place. Quite unexpectedly (at least as far as I was concerned) the order came to turn about, and we went trotting off to the northeast over open, rolling country whisperous with coarse grass.

The savages seemed to have vanished. A new force appeared in their place, on the flank that had now become our front. At first I thought they were cavalry on centaurs, creatures whose pictures I had encountered in the brown book. I could see the heads and shoulders of the riders above the human heads of their mounts, and both appeared to bear arms. When they drew nearer, I saw they were nothing so romantic: merely small men—dwarfs, in fact—upon the shoulders of very tall ones.

Our directions of advance were nearly parallel but slowly converged. The dwarfs watched us with what seemed a sullen attention. The tall men did not look at us at all. At last, when our column was no more than a couple of chains from theirs, we halted and turned to face them. With a horror I had not felt before, I realized that these strange riders and strange steeds were Ascians; our maneuver had been intended to prevent them from taking the peltasts in the flank, and had now succeeded in that they would now have to make their attack, if they could, through us. There seemed to be about five thousand of them, however, and there were certainly many more than we had fit to fight.

Yet no attack came. We had halted and formed a tight line, stirrup to stirrup. Despite their numbers, they surged nervously up and down before it as though attracted first by the thought of passing it on the right, then on the left, then on the right again. It was clear, however, that they could not pass at all unless a part of their force engaged our front to prevent our striking the rest from behind. As if hoping to postpone the fight, we did not fire.

Now we saw repetitions of the behavior of the lone spearman who had left his square to attack us. One of the tall men dashed forward. In one hand he held a slender staff, hardly more than a switch; in the other, a sword of the kind called a *shotel*, which has a very long, double-edged blade whose forward half is curved into a semicircle. As he drew nearer he slowed, and I saw that his eyes were unfocused; that he was in fact blind. The dwarf on his shoulders had an arrow nocked to the string of a short, recurved bow.

When these two were within half a chain of us, Erblon detailed two men to drive them off. Before they could close with the blind man, he broke into a run as swift as any destrier's but eerily silent, and came flying toward us. Eight or ten troopers fired, but I saw then how difficult it is to hit a target moving at such speed. The arrow struck and burst in a blaze of orange light. A trooper tried to parry the blind man's wand—the shotel flashed down, and its hooked blade laid open the trooper's skull.

Then a group of three of the blind men with three riders detached itself from the mass of the enemy. Before they reached us, there were clusters of five or six coming. Far down the line, our hipparch raised his arm; Guasacht waved us forward and Erblon blew the charge, echoed to right and left—a bellowing note that seemed to have deep-mouthed bells in it.

Though I did not know it at the time, it is axiomatic that encounters purely between cavalry rapidly degenerate into mere skirmishes. So it was with ours. We rode at them, and though we lost twenty or thirty in doing so, we rode through them. At once we turned to engage them again, both to prevent their flanking the peltasts and to regain contact with our own army. They, of course, turned to face us; and in a short time neither we nor they had anything that could be called a front, or any tactics beyond those each fighter forged for himself.

My own were to veer away from any dwarf who looked ready to shoot and try to catch others from behind or from the side. They worked well enough when I could apply them, but I quickly found that though the dwarfs appeared almost helpless when the blind men they rode were killed under them, their tall steeds ran amok without their riders, attacking anything that stood in their path with frantic energy, so that they were more dangerous than ever.

Very soon the dwarfs' arrows and our conti had kindled scores of fires in the grass. The choking smoke rendered the confusion worse than ever. I had lost sight of Daria and Guasacht—of everyone I knew—sometime before. Through the acrid gray haze I could just make out a figure on a plunging destrier fighting off four Ascians. I went to him, and though one dwarf turned his blind steed and sent an arrow whizzing by my ear, I rode over them and heard the blind man's bones snap under the piebald's hoofs. A hairy figure rose from the smoldering grass behind the other pair and cut them down as a peon hews a tree—three or four strokes of his ax to the same spot until the blind man fell.

The mounted soldier I had come to rescue was not one of our troopers, but one of the savages who had been on our right earlier. He had been wounded, and when I saw the blood I recalled that I had been wounded too. My leg was stiff, my strength nearly gone. I would have ridden back toward the south crest of the valley and our own lines if I had known which way to go. As it was, I gave the piebald his head and a good slap from the reins, having heard that these animals will often return to the place where they last had water and rest. He broke into a canter that soon became a gallop. Once he jumped, nearly throwing me from the saddle, and I looked down to glimpse a dead destrier with Erblon dead beside him, and the brass graisle and the black and green flag lying on the burning turf. I would have turned the piebald and gone back for them, but by the time I pulled him up, I no longer knew the spot. To my right, a mounted line showed through the smoke, dark and almost formless, but serrated. Far behind it loomed a machine that flashed fire, a machine that was like a tower walking.

At one moment they were nearly invisible; at the next they were upon me like a torrent. I cannot say who the riders were or on what beasts they rode; not because I have forgotten (for I forget nothing) but because I saw nothing clearly. There was no question of fighting, only of seeking in some way to live. I parried a blow from a twisted weapon that was neither sword nor ax; the piebald reared, and I saw an arrow protruding from his chest like a horn of fire. A rider crashed against us, and we fell into the dark.

XXIII

The Pelagic Argosy Sights Land

WHEN I REGAINED consciousness, it was the pain in my leg that I felt first. It was pinned beneath the body of the piebald, and I struggled to free it almost before I knew who I was or how I found myself where I did. My hands and face, the very ground on which I lay, were crusted with blood.

And it was quiet—so quiet. I listened for the thudding of hoofs, the drum roll that makes Urth herself its drum. It was not there. The shouts of the cherkajis were no more, nor the shrill, mad cries that had come from the checkerboard of Ascian infantry. I tried to turn to push against the saddle, but I could not do so.

Somewhere far off, no doubt on one of the ridges that rimmed the valley, a dire wolf raised its maw to Lune. That inhuman howling, which Thecla had heard once or twice before when the court went to hunt near Silva, made me realize that the dimness of my sight was not due to the smoke of the grass fires that had burned earlier that day, or, as I had half feared, to some head injury. The land was twilit, though whether by dusk or dawn I could not say.

I rested and perhaps I slept, then roused again at the sound of footsteps. It was darker than I remembered. The footsteps were slow, soft, and heavy. Not the sound of cavalry on the move, nor yet the measured tread of marching infantry—a walk heavier than Baldanders's and more slow. I opened my mouth to cry for help, then closed it again, thinking I might call upon myself something more terrible than that I had once waked in the mine of the man-apes. I lunged away from the dead piebald until it seemed I would wrench my leg from its socket. Another dire wolf, as frightful as the first and much closer, howled to the green isle overhead.

As a boy, I was often told I lacked imagination. If it were ever true, Thecla must have brought it to our nexus, for I could see the dire wolves in my mind, black and silent shapes, each as large as an onyger, pouring down into the valley; and I could hear them cracking the ribs of the dead. I called, and called again, before I knew what it was I did.

It seemed to me that the heavy footsteps paused. Certainly they moved toward me, whether they had been coming toward me before or not. I heard a rustling in the grass, and a little phenocod, striped like a melon, bounded out, terrified by something I still could not see. It shied at the sight of me and in a moment was gone.

I have said that Erblon's graisle was silenced. Another blew now, a deeper, longer, wilder note than I had ever heard. The outline of a bent orphicleide showed against the dusky sky. When its music was ended it fell, and in a moment more I saw the head of the player blotting out the brightening moon at three times the height of a mounted trooper's helmet—a domed head shaggy with hair.

The orphicleide sounded once more, deep as a waterfall, and this time I saw it rise, and the white, curling tusks that guarded it on each side, and I knew I lay in the path of the very symbol of dominion, the beast called Mammoth.

Guasacht had said I held some mastery over animals, even without the Claw. I strove to use it now, whispering I know not what, concentrating my thought until it seemed my temples would burst. The mammoth's trunk came questing toward me, its tip nearly a cubit across. Lightly as a child's hand it touched my face, flooding me with moist, hot breath sweet with hay. The corpse of the piebald was lifted away; I tried to stand but somehow fell. The mammoth caught me up, winding its trunk about my waist, and lifted me higher than its own head.

The first thing I saw was the muzzle of a trilhoen with a dark, bulging lens the size of a dinner plate. It was fitted with a seat for the operator, but no one sat there. The gunner had come down and stood upon the mammoth's neck as a sailor might upon the deck of a ship, with one hand on the barrel for balance. For a moment a light shone in my face, blinding me.

"It's you. Miracles converge on us." The voice was not truly either a man's or a woman's; it might almost have been a boy's. I was laid at the speaker's feet, and he said, "You're hurt. Can you stand on that leg?"

I managed to say I did not think I could.

"This is a poor place to lie, but a good one to fall from. There's a gondola farther back, but I'm afraid Mamillian can't reach it with his trunk. You'll have to sit up here, with your back against the swivel."

I felt his hands, small, soft, and moist, beneath my arms. Perhaps it was their touch that told me who he was: The androgyne I had met in the snow-covered House Azure, and later in that artfully foreshortened room that posed as a painting hanging in a corridor of the House Absolute.

The Autarch.

In Thecla's memories I saw him robed in jewels. Although he had said he recognized me, I could not believe in my dazed state that it was so, and I gave him the code phrase he had once given me, saying, "The pelagic argosy sights land."

"It does. It does indeed. Yet if you fall overboard now, I'm afraid Mamillian's not quite quick enough to catch you . . . despite his undoubted wisdom. Give him as much help as you can. I'm not as strong as I look."

I got some part of the trilhoen's mount in one hand and was able to pull myself around on the musty-smelling mat that was the mammoth's hide. "To speak the truth," I said, "you've never looked strong to me."

"You have the professional eye and ought to know, but I'm not even as strong as that. You, on the other hand, have always seemed to me a construction of horn and boiled leather. And you must be, or you'd be dead by now. What happened to your leg?"

"Burned, I think."

"We'll have to get you something for it." He raised his voice slightly. "*Home! Back home, Mamillian!*"

"May I ask what you're doing here?"

"Having a look at the field of battle. You fought here today, I take it."

I nodded, though I felt my head would tumble from my shoulders.

"I didn't . . . or rather, I did, but not personally. I ordered certain bodies of light auxiliaries into action, with a legion of peltasts in support. I suppose you must have been one of the auxiliaries. Were any of your friends killed?"

"I only had one. She was all right the last time I saw her."

His teeth flashed in the moonlight. "You maintain your interest in women. Was it the Dorcas you told me of?"

"No. It doesn't matter." I did not quite know how to phrase what I was about to say. (It is the worst of bad manners to state openly that one has penetrated an incognito.) At last I managed, "I can see you hold high rank in our Commonwealth. If it won't get me pushed from the back of this animal, can you tell me what someone who commands legions was doing conducting that place in the Algedonic Quarter?"

While I spoke, the night had grown rapidly darker, the stars winking out one after another like the tapers in a hall when the ball is over and footmen walk among them with snuffers like mitres of gold dangling from spidery rods. At a great distance I heard the androgyne say, "You know who we are. We are the thing itself, the self-ruler, the Autarch. We know more. We know who you are."

Master Malrubius was, as I realize now, a very sick man before he died. At the time I did not know it, because the thought of sickness was foreign to me. At least half our apprentices, and perhaps more than half, died before they were raised to journeyman; but it never occurred to me that our tower might be an unhealthy place, or that the lower reaches of Gyoll, where we so often swam, were little purer than a cesspool. Apprentices had always died, and when we living apprentices dug their graves we turned up small pelvises and skulls, which we, the succeeding generation, reburied again and again until they were so much injured by the spade that their chalky particles were lost in the tarlike soil. I, however, never suffered more than a sore throat and a running nose, forms of sickness that serve only to deceive healthy people into the belief that they know in what disease consists. Master Malrubius suffered real illness, which is to see death in shadows.

As he stood at his little table, one felt that he was conscious of someone standing behind him. He looked straight to the front, never turning his head and hardly moving a shoulder, and he spoke as much for that unknown listener as for us.

"I have done my best to teach you boys the rudiments of learning. They are the seeds of trees that should grow and blossom in your minds. Severian, look to your Q. It should be round and full like the face of a happy boy, but one of its cheeks is as fallen-in as your own. You have all, all you boys, seen how the spinal cord, lifting itself toward its culmination, expands and at last blossoms in the myriad pathways of the brain. And this one, one cheek round, the other seared and shriveled."

His trembling hand reached for the slate pencil, but it

escaped his fingers and rolled over the edge of the table to clatter on the floor. He did not stoop to pick it up, fearful, I think, that in stooping he might glimpse the invisible presence.

"I have spent much of my life, boys, in trying to implant those seeds in the apprentices of our guild. I have had a few successes, but not many. There was a boy, but he—"

He went to the port and spat, and because I was sitting near it I saw the twisted shapes formed by the seeping blood and knew that the reason I could not see the dark figure (for death is of the color that is darker than fuligin) that accompanied him was that it stood within him.

Just as I had discovered that death in a new form, in the shape of war, could frighten me when it could no longer do so in its old ones, so I learned now that the weakness of my body could afflict me with the terror and despair my old teacher must have felt. Consciousness came and went.

Consciousness went and came like the errant winds of spring, and I, who so often have had difficulty in falling asleep among the besieging shades of memory, now fought to stay awake as a child struggles to lift a faltering kite by the string. At times I was oblivious to everything except my injured body. The wound in my leg, which I had hardly felt when I received it, and whose pain I had so effortlessly locked away when Daria had bandaged it, throbbed with an intensity that formed the background to all my thoughts, like the rumbling of the Drum Tower at the solstice. I turned from side to side, thinking always that I lay upon that leg.

I had hearing without sight and occasionally sight without hearing. I rolled my cheek from the matted hair of Mamillian and laid it on a pillow woven of the minute, downy feathers of hummingbirds.

Once I saw torches with dancing flames of scarlet and radiant gold held by solemn apes. A man with the horns and muzzled face of a bull bent over me, a constellation sprung to life. I spoke to him and found myself telling him that I was unsure of the precise date of my birth, that if his benign spirit of meadow and unfeigning force had governed my life I thanked him for it; then remembered that I knew the date, that my father had given a ball for me each year until his death, that it fell under the Swan. He listened intently, turning his head to watch me from one brown eye.

The Flier

SUNLIGHT IN MY FACE.

I tried to sit up, and in fact succeeded in getting one elbow beneath me. All about me shimmered an orb of color—purple and cyan, ruby and azure, with the orpiment of the sun piercing these enchanted tints like a sword to fall upon my eyes. Then it was blotted out, and its extinction revealed what its splendor had obscured: I lay in a domed pavilion of variegated silk, with an open door.

The rider of the mammoth was walking toward me. He was robed in saffron, as I had always seen him, and carried an ebony rod too light to be a weapon. "You have recovered," he said.

"I'd try and say yes, but I'm afraid the effort of speaking might kill me."

He smiled at that, though the smile was no more than a twitching of the mouth. "As you should know better than almost anyone, the sufferings we endure in this life make possible all the happy crimes and pleasant abominations we shall commit in the next . . . aren't you eager to collect?"

I shook my head and laid it on the pillow again. The softness smelled faintly of musk.

"That is just as well, because it will be some time before you do."

"Is that what your physician says?"

"I am my own, and I've been treating you myself. Shock was the principal problem. . . . It sounds like a disorder for old women, as you are no doubt thinking at this moment. But it kills a great many men with wounds. If all of mine who die of it would only live, I would readily consent to the death of those who take a thrust in the heart."

"While you were being your own physician—and mine— were you telling the truth?"

He smiled more broadly at that. "I always do. In my position, I have to talk too much to keep a skein of lies in order; of course, you must realize that the truth . . . the little, ordinary truths that farm wives talk of, not the ultimate and universal Truth, which I'm no more capable of uttering than you . . . that truth is more deceptive."

"Before I lost consciousness, I heard you say you are the Autarch."

He threw himself down beside me like a child, his body making a distinct sound as it struck the piled carpets. "I did. I am. Are you impressed?"

"I would be more impressed," I said, "if I did not recall you so vividly from our meeting in the House Azure."

(That porch, covered with snow, heaped with snow that deadened our footsteps, stood in the silken pavilion like a specter. When the Autarch's blue eyes met mine, I felt that Roche stood beside me in the snow, both of us dressed in unfamiliar and none-too-well-fitting clothes. Inside, a woman who was not Thecla was transforming herself into Thecla as I was later to make myself Meschia, the first man. Who can say to what degree an actor assumes the spirit of the person he portrays? When I played the Familiar, it was nothing, because it was so close to what I was—or had at least believed myself to be—in life; but as Meschia I had sometimes had thoughts that could never have occurred to me otherwise, thoughts alien equally to Severian and to Thecla, thoughts of the beginnings of things and the morning of the world.)

"I never told you, you will recall, that I was *only* the Autarch."

"When I met you in the House Absolute, you appeared to be a minor official of the court. I admit you never told me that, and in fact I knew then who you were. But it was you, wasn't it, who gave the money to Dr. Talos?"

"I would have told you that without a blush. It is completely true. In fact, I am several of the minor officials of my court. . . . Why shouldn't I be? I have the authority to appoint such officials, and I can just as well appoint myself. An order from the Autarch is often too heavy an instrument, you see. You would never have tried to slit a nose with that big headsman's sword you carried. There is a time for a decree from the Autarch, and a time for a letter from the third bursar, and I am both and more besides."

"And in that house in the Algedonic Quarter—"

"I am also a criminal . . . just as you are."

There is no limit to stupidity. Space itself is said to be bounded by its own curvature, but stupidity continues beyond infinity. I, who had always thought myself, though not truly intelligent, at least prudent and quick to learn simple things, who had always counted myself the practical and foreseeing one when I had traveled with Jonas or Dorcas, had never until that instant connected the Autarch's position at the very apex of the structure of legality with his certain knowledge that I had penetrated the House Absolute as an emissary of Vodalus. At that moment, I would have leaped up and fled from the pavilion if I could, but my legs were like water.

"All of us are—all of us must be who must enforce the law. Do you think your guild brothers would have been so severe with you—and my agent reports that many of them wished to kill you—if they had themselves been guilty of something of the same kind? You were a danger to them unless you were terribly punished because they might otherwise someday be tempted. A judge or a jailer who has no crime of his own is a monster, alternately purloining the forgiveness that belongs to the Increate alone and practicing a deathly rigor that belongs to no one and nothing.

"So I became a criminal. The violent crimes offended my love of humanity, and I lack the quickness of hand and thought required of a thief. After blundering about for some time . . . that would be in about the year you were born, I suppose . . . I found my true profession. It takes care of certain emotional needs I cannot now satisfy otherwise . . . and I have, I really do have, a knowledge of human nature. I know just when to offer a bribe and how much to give, and, the most important thing, when not to. I know how to keep the girls who work for me happy enough with their careers to continue, and discontented enough with their fates. . . . They're khaibits, of course, grown from the body cells of exultant women so an exchange of blood will prolong the exultants' youth. I know how to make my clients feel that the encounters I arrange are unique experiences instead of something midway between dewy-eyed romance and solitary vice. You felt that you had a unique experience, didn't you?"

"That's what we call them too," I said. "*Clients.*" I had been listening as much to the tone of his voice as to his words. He was happy, as I thought he had not been on either of the other occasions on which I had encountered him, and to hear him was like hearing a thrush speak. He almost seemed to know it himself, lifting his face and extending his throat, the Rs in *arrange* and *romance* trilled into the sunlight.

"It is useful too. It keeps me in touch with the underside of the population, so I know whether or not taxes are really being collected and whether they're thought fair, which elements are rising in society and which are going down."

I sensed that he was referring to me, though I had no idea what he meant. "Those women from the court," I said.

"Why didn't you get the real ones to help you? One of them was pretending to be Thecla when Thecla was locked under our tower."

He looked at me as though I had said something particularly stupid, as no doubt I had. "Because I can't trust them, of course. A thing like that has to remain a secret. . . . Think of the opportunities for assassination. Do you believe that because all those gilded personages from ancient families bow so low in my presence, and smile, and whisper discreet jokes and lewd little invitations, they feel some loyalty to me? You will learn differently, you may be sure. There are few at my court I can trust, and none among the exultants."

"You say I'll learn differently. Does that mean you don't intend to have me executed?" I could feel the pulse in my neck and see the scarlet gout of blood.

"Because you know my secret now? No. We have other uses for you, as I told you when we talked in the room behind the picture."

"Because I was sworn to Vodalus."

At that his amusement mastered him. He threw back his head and laughed, a plump and happy child who had just discovered the secret of some clever toy. When the laughter subsided at last into a merry gulping, he clapped his hands. Soft though they looked, the sound was remarkably loud.

Two creatures with the bodies of women and the heads of cats entered. Their eyes were a span apart and as large as plums; they strode on their toes as dancers sometimes do, but more gracefully than any dancers I have ever seen, with something in their motions that told me it was their normal gait. I have said they had the bodies of women, but that was not quite true, for I saw the tips of claws sheathed in the short, soft fingers that dressed me. In wonder, I took the hand of one and pressed it as I have sometimes pressed the paw of a friendly cat, and saw the claws barred. My eyes brimmed with tears at the sight of them, because they were shaped like that claw that is the Claw, that once lay concealed in the gem

THE CITADEL OF THE AUTARCH

that I, in my ignorance, called the Claw of the Conciliator. The Autarch saw I was weeping, and told the woman-cats they were hurting me and must put me down. I felt like an infant who has just learned he will never see his mother again.

"We do not harm him, Legion," one protested in such a voice as I had never heard before.

"Put him down, I said!"

"They have not so much as grazed my skin, Sieur," I told him.

With the woman-cats' support I was able to walk. It was morning, when all shadows flee the first sight of the sun; the light that had wakened me had been the earliest of the new day. Its freshness filled my lungs now, and the coarse grass over which we walked darkened my scuffed old boots with its dew; a breeze faint as the dim stars stirred my hair.

The Autarch's pavilion stood on the summit of a hill. All around lay the main bivouac of his army—tents of black and gray, and others like dead leaves; huts of turf and pits that led to shelters underground, from which streams of soldiers issued now like silver ants.

"We must be careful, you see," he said. "Though we are some distance behind the lines here, if this place were plainer it would invite attack from above."

"I used to wonder why your House Absolute lay beneath its own gardens, Sieur."

"The need has long passed now, but there was a time when they laid waste to Nessus."

Below us and all around us, the silver lips of trumpets sounded.

"Was it only the night?" I asked. "Or have I slept a whole day away?"

"No. Only the night. I gave you medicines to ease your pain and keep infection from your wound. I would not have roused you this morning, but I saw you were awake when I came in . . . and there is no more time."

I was not certain what he meant by that. Before I could ask, I caught sight of six nearly naked men hauling at a rope. My first impression was that they were bringing down some huge balloon, but it was a flier, and the sight of its black hull brought vivid memories of the Autarch's court.

"I was expecting—what was its name? Mamillian."

"No pets today. Mamillian is an excellent comrade, silent and wise and able to fight with a mind independent of my own, but when all is said and done, I ride him for pleasure. We will thieve a string from the Ascians' bow and use a mechanism today. They steal many from us."

"Is it true that it consumes their power to land? I think one of your aeronauts once told me that."

"When you were the Chatelaine Thecla, you mean. Thecla purely."

"Yes, of course. Would it be impolitic, Autarch, to ask why you had me killed? And how you know me now?"

"I know you because I see your face in the face of my young friend and hear your voice in his. Your nurses know you too. Look at them."

I did, and saw the woman-cats' faces twisted in snarls of fear and amazement.

"As to why you died, I will speak of that—to him—on board the flier . . . have we time. Now, go back. You find it easy to manifest yourself because he is weak and ill, but I must have him now, not you. If you will not go, there are means."

"Sieur—"

"Yes, Severian? Are you afraid? Have you entered such a contrivance before?"

"No," I said. "But I am not afraid."

"Do you recall your question about their power? It is true,

in a sense. Their lift is supplied by the antimaterial equivalent of iron, held in a penning trap by magnetic fields. Since
the anti-iron has a reversed magnetic structure, it is repelled
by promagnetism. The builders of this flier have surrounded
it with magnets, so that when it drifts from its position at the
center it enters a stronger field and is forced back. On an
antimaterial world, that iron would weigh as much as a boul-
der, but here on Urth it counters the weight of the promatter
used in the construction of the flier. Do you follow me?"

"I believe so, Sieur."

"The trouble is that it is beyond our technology to seal the
chamber hermetically. Some atmosphere—a few molecules—
is always creeping in through porosities in the welds, or by
penetrating the insulation of the magnetic wires. Each such
molecule neutralizes its equivalent in anti-iron and produces
heat, and each time one does so, the flier loses an infinitesimal amount of lift. The only solution anyone has found is to
keep fliers as high as possible, where there is effectively no air
pressure."

The flier was nosing down now, near enough for me to
appreciate the beautiful sleekness of its lines. It had precisely
the shape of a cherry leaf.

"I didn't understand all of that," I said. "But I would
think the ropes would have to be immensely long to allow
the fliers to float high enough to do any good, and that if the
Ascian pentadactyls came over by night they would cut them
and let the fliers drift away."

The woman-cats smiled at that with tiny, secretive twitch-
ings of their lips.

"The rope is only for landing. Without it, our flier would
require sufficient distance for its forward speed to drive it
down. Now, knowing we're below, it drops its cable just as a
man in a pond might extend his hand to someone who would
pull him out. It has a mind of its own, you see. Not like
Mamillian's—a mind we have made for it, but enough of a

mind to permit it to stay out of difficulties and come down when it receives our signal."

The lower half of the flier was of opaque black metal, the upper half a dome so clear as to be nearly invisible—the same substance, I suppose, as the roof of the Botanic Gardens. A gun like the one the mammoth had carried thrust out from the stern, and another twice as large protruded from the bow.

The Autarch lifted one hand to his mouth and seemed to whisper into his palm. An aperture appeared in the dome (it was as if a hole had opened in a soap bubble) and a flight of silver steps, as thin and insubstantial looking as the web ladder of a spider, descended to us. The bare-chested men had left off pulling. "Do you think you can climb those?" the Autarch asked.

"If I can use my hands," I said.

He went before me, and I crawled up ignominiously after him, dragging my wounded leg. The seats, long benches that followed the curve of the hull on either side, were upholstered in fur; but even this fur felt colder than any ice. Behind me, the aperture narrowed and vanished.

"We will have surface pressure in here no matter how high we go. You don't have to worry about suffocating."

"I am afraid I am too ignorant to feel the fear, Sieur."

"Would you like to see your old bacele? They're far to the right, but I'll try to locate them for you."

The Autarch had seated himself at the controls. Almost the only machinery I had seen before had been Typhon's and Baldanders's, and that which Master Gurloes controlled in the Matachin Tower. It was of the machines, not of suffocation, that I was afraid; but I fought the fear down.

"When you rescued me last night, you indicated that you had not known I was in your army."

"I made inquiries while you slept."

"And it was you who ordered us forward?"

"In a sense . . . I issued the order that resulted in your

movement, though I had nothing to do with your bacele directly. Do you resent what I did? When you joined, did you think you would never have to fight?"

We were soaring upward. Falling, as I had once feared to do, into the sky. But I remembered the smoke and the brassy shout of the graisle, the troopers blown to red paste by the whistling bolts, and all my terror turned to rage. "I knew nothing of war. How much do you know? Have you ever really been in a battle?"

He glanced over his shoulder at me, his blue eyes flashing. "I've been in a thousand. You are two, as people are usually counted. How many do you think I am?"

It was a long while before I answered him.

X X V

The Mercy of Agia

At first I thought there could be nothing stranger than to see the army stretch across the surface of Urth until it lay like a garland before us, coruscant with weapons and armor, many-hued; the winged anpiels soaring above it nearly as high as we, circling and rising on the dawn wind.

Then I beheld something stranger still. It was the army of the Ascians, an army of watery whites and grayish blacks, rigid as ours was fluid, deployed toward the northern horizon. I went forward to stare at it.

"I could show them to you more closely," the Autarch said. "Still, you would see only human faces."

I realized he was testing me, though I did not know how. "Let me see them," I said.

When I had ridden with the schiavoni and watched our troops go into action, I had been struck by their look of weakness in the mass, the cavalry all ebb and flow like a wave that crashes with great force—then drains away as mere water, too weak to bear the weight of a mouse, pale stuff a child might scoop up in his hands. Even the peltasts, with their serried ranks and crystal shields, had seemed hardly more formidable than toys on a tabletop. Now I saw how strong the rigid formations of our enemy appeared, rectangles that held machines as big as fortresses and a hundred thousand soldiers shoulder to shoulder.

But on a screen in the center of the control panel I looked under the visors of their helmets, and all that rigidity, all that strength, melted into a kind of horror. There were old people and children in the infantry files, and some who seemed idiots. Nearly all had the mad, famished faces I had observed the day before, and I recalled the man who had broken from his square and thrown his spear into the air as he died. I turned away.

The Autarch laughed. His laughter held no joy now; it was a flat sound, like the snapping of a flag in a high wind. "Did you see one kill himself?"

"No," I said.

"You were fortunate. I often do, when I look at them. They are not permitted arms until they are ready to engage us, and so many take advantage of the opportunity. The spearmen drive the butts of their weapons into soft ground, usually, then blast off their own heads. Once I saw two swordsmen—a man and a woman—who had made a compact. They stabbed each other in the belly, and I watched them counting first, moving their left hands . . . one . . . two . . . three, and dead."

"Who are they?" I asked.

He shot me a look I could not interpret. "What did you say?"

"I asked who they are, Sieur. I know they're our enemies, that they live to the north in the hot countries, and that they're said to be enslaved by Erebus. But who are they?"

"Up until now I doubt you knew you did not know. Did you?"

My throat felt parched, though I could not have told why. I said, "I suppose not. I'd never seen one until I came into the lazaret of the Pelerines. In the south, the war seems very remote."

He nodded. "We have driven them half as far to the north as they once drove us south, we autarchs. Who they are you will discover in due time. . . . What matters is that you wish to know." He paused. "Both could be ours. Both armies, not just the one to the south. . . . Would you advise me to take both?" As he spoke, he manipulated some control and the flier canted forward, its stern pointing at the sky and its bow to the green earth, as though he meant to pour us out upon the disputed ground.

"I don't understand what you mean," I told him.

"Half what you said of them was incorrect. They do not come from the hot countries of the north, but from the continent that lies across the equator. But you were right when you called them the slaves of Erebus. They think themselves the allies of those who wait in the deep. In truth, Erebus and his allies would give them to me if I would give our south to them. Give you and all the rest."

I had to grip the back of the seat to keep from falling toward him. "Why are you telling me this?"

The flier righted itself like a child's boat in a puddle, bobbing.

"Because it will soon be necessary for you to know that others have felt what you will feel."

I could not frame a question I dared to ask. At last I ventured, "You said you'd tell me here why you killed Thecla."

"Does she not live in Severian?"

A windowless wall in my mind fell to ruins. I shouted: "I *died!*" Not realizing what I had said until the words were past my lips.

The Autarch took a pistol from beneath the control panel, letting it lie across his thighs as he turned to face me.

"You won't need that, Sieur," I said. "I'm too weak."

"You have remarkable powers of recovery. . . . I have seen them already. Yes, the Chatelaine Thecla is gone, save as she endures in you, and though the two of you are always together, you are both lonely. Do you still seek for Dorcas? You told me of her, you remember, when we met in the Secret House."

"Why did you kill Thecla?"

"I did not. Your error lies in thinking I am at the bottom of everything. No one is. . . . Not I, or Erebus, or any other. As to the Chatelaine, you are she. Were you arrested openly?"

The memory came more vividly than I would have thought possible. I walked down a corridor whose walls were lined with sad masks of silver and entered one of the abandoned rooms, high-ceilinged and musty with ancient hangings. The courier I was to meet had not yet come. Because I knew the dusty divans would soil my gown, I took a chair, a spindly thing of gilt and ivory. The tapestry spilled from the wall behind me; I recalled looking up and seeing Destiny crowned in chains and Discontent with her staff and glass, all worked in colored wool, descending upon me.

The Autarch said, "You were taken by certain officers, who had learned that you were conveying information to your half sister's lover. Taken secretly, because your family has so much influence in the north, and conveyed to an almost forgotten prison. By the time I learned what had occurred, you were dead. Should I have punished those officers for acting in my absence? They are patriots, and you were a traitor."

"I, Severian, am a traitor too," I said, and I told him, then for the first time in detail, how I had once saved Vodalus, and of the banquet I had later shared with him.

When I had concluded, he nodded to himself. "Much of the loyalty you felt for Vodalus comes, surely, from the Chatelaine. Some she imparted to you while she was yet living, more after her death. Naive though you have been, I am certain you are not so naive as to think it a coincidence that it was she whose flesh was served to you by the corpse-eaters."

I protested, "Even if he had known of my connection with her, there was no time to bring her body from Nessus."

The Autarch smiled. "Have you forgotten that you told me a moment ago that when you had saved him, he fled in such a craft as this? From that forest, hardly a dozen leagues outside the City Wall, he could have flown to the center of Nessus, unearthed a corpse preserved by the chill soil of early spring, and returned in less than a watch. Actually, he need not have known so much or moved so swiftly. While you were imprisoned by your guild, he may have learned that the Chatelaine Thecla, who had been loyal to him even to death, was no more. By serving her flesh to his followers, he would strengthen them in his cause. He would require no additional motive to take her body, and no doubt he reinterred her in hoarded snow in some cellar, or in one of the abandoned mines with which that region abounds. You arrived, and wishing to bind you to him, he ordered her brought out."

Something passed too swiftly to be seen—an instant later the flier rocked with the violence of its motion. Sparks maneuvered on the screen.

Before the Autarch could take the controls again, we were scudding backward. There was a detonation so loud it seemed to paralyze me, and the reverberating sky opened in a blossom of yellow fire. I have seen a sparrow, struck by a stone from Eata's sling, reel in the air just as we did, and fall, like us, fluttering to one side.

I woke to darkness, pungent smoke, and the smell of fresh earth. For a moment or a watch I forgot my rescue and believed I lay on the field where Daria and I, with Guasacht, Erblon, and the rest, had fought the Ascians.

Someone lay near me—I heard the sigh of his breath, and the creakings and scrapings that betray movement—but at first I paid no heed to them, and later I came to believe that these sounds were made by foraging animals, and grew afraid; later still, I recalled what had happened and knew they were surely made by the Autarch, who must have survived the crash with me, and I called to him.

"So you still live, then." His voice was very weak. "I feared you would die . . . though I should have known better. I could not revive you, and your pulse was but faint."

"I have forgotten! Do you remember when we flew over the armies? For a time I forgot it! I know now what it is to forget."

There was pale laughter in his voice. "Which you will now remember always."

"I hope so, but it fades even as we speak. It vanishes like mist, which must itself be a forgetting. What was that weapon that brought us down?"

"I do not know. But listen. These are the most important words of my life. Listen. You have served Vodalus, and his dream of renewed empire. You still wish, do you not, that humankind should go again to the stars?"

I recalled something Vodalus had told me in the wood and said, "Men of Urth, sailing between the stars, leaping from galaxy to galaxy, the masters of the daughters of the sun."

"They were so once . . . and brought all the old wars of Urth with them, and in the young suns kindled new ones. Even they," (I could not see him, yet I knew by his tone that he had indicated the Ascians) "understand it must not be so again. They wish the race to become a single individual . . . the same, duplicated to the end of number. We wish each to carry all the race and its longings within himself. Have you noticed the phial I wear at my neck?"

"Yes, often."

"It contains a pharmacon like alzabo, already mixed and held in suspension. I am cold already below the waist. I will die soon. Before I die . . . you must use it."

"I cannot see you," I said. "And I can scarcely move."

"Nevertheless, you will find a way. You remember everything, and so you must recall the night you came to my House Azure. That night someone else came to me. I was a servant once, in the House Absolute. . . . That is why they hate me. As they will hate you, for what you once were. Paeon, who trained me, who was honey-steward fifty years gone by. I knew what he was in truth, for I had met him before. He told me you were the one . . . the next. I did not think it would be quite so soon. . . ."

His voice fell away, and I began to grope for him, pulling myself along. My hand found his, and he whispered, "Use the knife. We are behind the Ascian line, but I have called upon Vodalus to rescue you. . . . I hear the hoofs of his destriers."

The words were so faint I could hardly hear, though my ear was within a span of his mouth. "Rest," I said. Knowing that Vodalus hated him and sought to destroy him, I thought him delirious.

"I am his spy. That is another of my offices. He draws the traitors. . . . I learn who they are and what they do, what they think. That is one of his. Now I have told him the Autarch is trapped in this flier and given him our location. He has served me . . . as my bodyguard . . . before this."

Now even I could hear the sound of feet on the ground outside. I reached up, searching for some means by which to signal; my hand touched fur, and I knew the flier had over-turned, leaving us like hidden toads beneath it.

There was a snap and the scream of tearing metal. Moon-light, seeming bright as day but green as willow leaves, came flooding through a rent in the hull that gaped as I watched. I saw the Autarch, his thin white hair darkened with dried blood.

And above him silhouettes, green shades looking down upon us. Their faces were invisible; but I knew those gleam-ing eyes and narrow heads belonged to no followers of Vodalus. Frantically, I searched for the Autarch's pistol. My hands were seized. I was drawn up, and as I emerged I could not help thinking of the dead woman I had seen pulled from her grave in the necropolis, for the flier had fallen on soft ground and half buried itself. Where the Ascian bolt had struck it, its side was torn away, leaving a tangle of ruined wiring. The metal was twisted and burned.

I did not have much time to look at it. My captors turned me around and around as one after another took my face in his hands. My cloak was fingered as though they had never seen cloth. With their large eyes and hollow cheeks, these evzones seemed to me much like the infantry we had fought against, but though there were women among them, there were no old people and no children. They wore silvery caps and shirts in place of armor, and carried strangely shaped jezails, so long barreled that when their butt plates rested on the ground their muzzles were higher than their owners' heads. As I saw the Autarch lifted from the flier, I said, "Your message was intercepted, Sieur, I think."

"Nevertheless, it arrived." He was too weak to point, but I followed the direction of his eyes, and after a moment I saw flying shapes against the moon.

It almost seemed they slid down the beams to us, they came so quickly and so straight. Their heads were like the skulls of women, round and white, capped with miters of bone and stretched at the jaws into curved bills lined with pointed teeth. They were winged, the pinions so great they seemed to have no bodies at all. Twenty cubits at least these pinions stretched from tip to tip; when they beat they made no sound, but far below I felt the rush of air.

(Once I had imagined such creatures threshing the forests of Urth and beating flat her cities. Had my thought helped bring these?)

It seemed a long time before the Ascian evzones saw them. Then two or three fired at once, and the converging bolts caught one at their intersection and blew it to rags, then another and another. For an instant the light was blotted out, and something cold and flaccid struck my face, knocking me down.

When I could see again, half a dozen of the Ascians were

gone, and the rest were firing into the air at targets almost
imperceptible to me. Something whitish fell from them. I
thought it would explode and put my head down, but instead the hull of the wrecked flier rang like a cymbal. A
body—a human body broken like a doll's—had struck it, but
there was no blood.

One of the evzones jammed his weapon in my back and
pushed me forward. Two more were supporting the Autarch
much as the woman-cats had supported me. I discovered that
I had lost all sense of direction. Though the moon still shone,
masses of cloud veiled most of the stars. I looked in vain for
the cross and for those three stars that are, for reasons no one
understands, called *The Eight* and hang forever over the
southern ice. Several of the evzones were still firing when
there came blazing among us some arrow or spear that burst
in a mass of blinding white sparks.

"That will do it," the Autarch whispered.

I was rubbing my eyes as I stumbled along, but I managed
to ask what he meant.

"Can you see? No more can they. Our friends above . . .
Vodalus's, I think . . . did not know our captors were so well
armed. Now there will be no more good shooting, and as
soon as that cloud drifts across the disc of Lune . . ."

I felt cold, as though a chill mountain wind had cut the
tepid air around us. A few moments before I had been in
despair to find myself among these gaunt soldiers. Now I
would have given anything for some guarantee that I would
remain among them.

The Autarch was to my left, hanging limp between two
evzones who had slung their long-barreled jezails aslant their
backs. As I watched, his head lolled to one side, and I knew
he was unconscious or dead. "Legion" the woman-cats had
called him, and it did not take great intellect to combine
that name with what he had told me in the wrecked flier.
Just as Thecla and Severian had joined in me, many personalities were surely united in him. Ever since the night I

had first seen him, when Roche had brought me to the House Azure (whose odd name I was now, perhaps, beginning to grasp) I had sensed the complexity of his thought, as we sense, even in a bad light, the complexity of a mosaic, the myriad, infinitesimal chips that combine to produce the illuminated face and staring eyes of the New Sun.

He had said I was destined to succeed him, but for how long a reign? Preposterous as it was in a prisoner, and in a man so injured and so weak that a watch of rest on the coarse grass would have seemed like paradise, I was consumed with ambition. He had said I must eat his flesh and swallow the drug while he still lived; and, loving him, I would have torn my own from the grasp of my captors, if I had possessed the strength, to claim that luxury and pomp and power. I was Severian and Thecla united now, and perhaps the torturers' ragged apprentice had, without fully knowing it, longed for those things more than the young exultant held captive at court. I knew then what poor Cyriaca had felt in the gardens of the archon; yet if she had felt fully what I felt at that moment, it would have burst her heart.

An instant later I was unwilling. Some part of me treasured the privacy that not even Dorcas had entered. Deep inside the convolutions of my mind, in the embrace of the molecules, Thecla and I were twined together. For others—a dozen or a thousand, perhaps, if in absorbing the personality of the Autarch I was also to absorb those he had incorporated into himself—to come where we lay would be for the crowds of the bazaar to enter a bower. I clasped my heart's companion to me, and felt myself clasped. I felt myself clasped, and clasped my heart's companion to me.

The moon dimmed as a dark lantern does when one presses the lever that makes its plates iris closed until there remains no more than a point of light, then nothing. The Ascian evzones fired their jezails in a lattice of lilac and heliotrope, beams that diverged high in the atmosphere and at last pricked the clouds like colored pins; but without effect.

There was a wind, hot and sudden, and what I can only call a flash of black. Then the Autarch was gone, and something huge rushed toward me. I threw myself down.

Perhaps I struck the ground, but I do not remember it. In an instant, it seemed, I was swooping through the air, turning, climbing surely, the world below no more than a darker night. An emaciated hand, hard as stone and three times human size, clutched me about the waist.

We ducked, turned, lurched, slipped sidewise down a slope of air, then, catching a rising wind, climbed till the cold stung and stiffened my skin. When I craned my neck to look upward, I could see the white, inhuman jaws of the creature that bore me. It was the nightmare I had known months earlier when I had shared Baldanders's bed, though in my dream I had ridden the thing's back. Why that difference between dream and truth should be, I cannot say. I cried out (I do not know what) and above me the thing opened its scimitar beak to hiss.

From above, too, I heard a woman's voice call, "Now I have repaid you for the mine—you are still alive."

XXVI

Above the Jungle

WE LANDED BY STARLIGHT. It was like awakening; I felt that it was not the sky but the country of nightmare I was leaving behind. Like a falling leaf, the immense creature settled in narrowing circles through regions of progressively warmer air until I could smell the odor of the Jungle Garden: the mingling of green life and rotting wood with the perfume of wide, waxen, unnamed blossoms.

A ziggurat lifted its dark head above the trees—yet carried the trees with it, for they sprouted from its crumbling walls like fungi from a dead tree. We settled on it weightlessly, and at once there came torches and excited voices. I was still faint from the thin and icy air I had been breathing only moments before.

Human hands replaced the claws that had grasped me for so long. We wound down ledges and stairways of broken stone until at last I stood before a fire and saw across it the handsome, unsmiling face of Vodalus and the heart-shaped one of his consort, Thea, our half sister.

"Who is this?" Vodalus asked.

I tried to lift my arms, but they were held. "Liege," I said, "you must know me."

From behind me, the voice I had heard in the air answered, "This is the man of the price, the killer of my brother. For him, I—and Hethor, who serves me—have served you."

"Then why do you bring him to me?" Vodalus asked. "He is yours. Did you think that when I had seen him, I would repent of our agreement?"

Perhaps I was stronger than I felt myself to be. Perhaps I only caught the man on my right off-balance; however it was, I succeeded in twisting about, jerking him into the fire, where his feet sent the red brands flying.

Agia stood behind me, naked to the waist, and Hethor behind her, showing all his rotten teeth as he cupped her breasts. I fought to escape. She slapped me with an open hand—there was a pull at my cheek, tearing pain, then the warm rush of blood.

Since then, I have learned that the weapon is called a *lucivee*, and that Agia had it because Vodalus had forbidden any but his own bodyguard to carry arms in his presence. It is no more than a small bar with rings for the thumb and fourth finger, and four or five curved blades that can be concealed in the palm; but few have survived its blow.

I was one of those few, and rose after two days to find myself shut in a bare room. Perhaps in each life one room must become better known than any other: for prisoners, it is always a cell. I, who had worked outside so many, thrusting in trays of food to the disfigured and demented, now knew again a cell of my own. What the ziggurat had once been, I never guessed. Perhaps a prison indeed; perhaps a temple, or the atelier of some forgotten art. My cell was about twice the size of the one I had occupied beneath the tower of the torturers, six paces wide and ten long. A door of ancient, gleaming alloy stood against the wall, useless to Vodalus's jailers because they could not lock it; a new one, roughly made of the ironlike timbers of some jungle tree, closed the doorway. A window I believe had never been meant for one, a circular opening hardly bigger than my arm, pierced the discolored wall high up and gave light to the cell.

Three days more passed before I was strong enough to jump and, gripping its lower edge with one hand, pull myself up to look out. When that day came, I saw a rolling green country dotted with butterflies—a place so foreign to what I had expected that I felt I might be mad and lost my hold upon the window in my astonishment. It was, as I eventually realized, the country of treetops, where ten-chain hardwoods spread a lawn of leaves, seldom seen save by the birds.

An old man with a knowledgeable, evil face had bandaged my cheek and changed the dressings on my leg. Later he brought a lad of about thirteen whose bloodstream he linked with mine until the boy's lips turned the hue of lead. I asked the old leech where he came from, and he, apparently thinking me a native of these parts, said, "From the big city in the south, in the valley of the river that drains the cold lands. It is a longer river than yours, is the Gyoll, though its flood is not so fierce."

"You have great skill," I said. "I've never heard of a physician who did as much. I feel well already, and wish you would stop before this boy dies."

The old man pinched his cheek. "He'll recover quickly—in time to warm my bed tonight. At his age they always do. Nay, it's not what you think. I only sleep beside him because the night-breath of the young acts as a restorative to those of my years. Youth, you see, is a disease, and we may hope to catch a mild case. How stands your wound?"

There was nothing—not even an admission, which might have been rooted in some perverse desire to maintain an appearance of potency—that could have convinced me so completely as his denial. I told him the truth, that my right cheek was numb save for a vague burning as irritating as an itch, and wondered which of his duties the miserable boy minded most.

The old man stripped away my bandages and gave my wounds a second coating of the foul-smelling brown salve he had used previously. "I'll be back tomorrow," he told me. "Although I don't think you'll need Mamas here again. You're coming along nicely. Her exultancy" (with a jerk of the head to show this was an ironical reference to Agia's stature) "will be most pleased."

I said, in what I sought to make an offhand way, that I hoped all his patients were doing as well.

"You mean the delator who was brought in with you? He's as well as can be expected." He turned aside as he spoke, so that I would not see his frightened expression.

On the chance that I might gain influence with him that would enable me to aid the Autarch, I praised his understanding of his craft extravagantly and ended by saying that I failed to comprehend why a physician of his ability consorted with these wicked people.

He looked at me narrowly, and his face grew serious. "For knowledge. There is nowhere a man in my profession can learn as I learn here."

"You mean the eating of the dead? I have shared in that too, though they may not have told you so."

"No, no. Learned men—particularly those of my profession—practice that everywhere, and usually with better effect, since we are more selective of our subjects and confine ourselves to the most retentive tissues. The knowledge I seek cannot be learned in that way, since none of the recently dead possessed it, and perhaps no one has ever possessed it."

He was leaning against the wall now, and seemed to be speaking as much to some invisible presence as to me. "The past's sterile science led to nothing but the exhaustion of the planet and the destruction of its races. It was founded in the mere desire to exploit the gross energies and material substances of the universe, without regard to their attractions, antipathies, and eventual destinies. Look!" He thrust his hand into the beam of sunshine that was then issuing from my high, circular window. "Here is light. You will say that it is not a living entity, but you miss the point that it is more, not less. Without occupying space, it fills the universe. It nourishes everything, yet itself feeds upon destruction. We claim to control it, but does it not perhaps cultivate us as a source of food? May it not be that all wood grows so that it can be set ablaze, and that men and women are born to kindle fires? Is it not possible that our claim to master light is as absurd as wheat's claiming to master us because we prepare the soil for it and attend its intercourse with Urth?"

"All that is well said," I told him. "But nothing to the point. Why do you serve Vodalus?"

"Such knowledge is not gained without experiment." He smiled as he spoke, and touched the shoulder of the boy, and I had a vision of children in flames. I hope that I was wrong.

That had been two days before I pulled myself up to the window. The old leech did not come again; whether he had fallen from favor, or been dispatched to another place, or had merely decided no further attentions were necessary, I had no way of knowing.

Agia came once, and standing between two of Vodalus's armed women spat in my face as she described the torments she and Hethor had contrived for me when I was strong enough to endure them. When she finished, I told her quite truthfully that I had spent most of my life assisting at operations more terrible, and advised her to obtain trained assistance, at which she went away.

Thereafter for the better part of several days I was left alone. Each time I woke, I felt myself almost a different person, for in that solitude the isolation of my thoughts in the dark intervals of sleep was nearly sufficient to deprive me of my sense of personality. Yet all these Severians and Theclas sought freedom.

The retreat into memory was easy; we made it often, reliving those idyllic days when Dorcas and I had journeyed toward Thrax, the games played in the hedge-walled maze behind my father's villa and in the Old Yard, the long walk down the Adamnian Steps that Agia and I had taken before I knew her for my enemy.

But often too, I left memory and forced myself to think, sometimes limping up and down, sometimes only waiting for insects to enter the window so that I might for my amusement pluck them from the air. I planned escape, though until my circumstances altered there seemed no possibility of it; I pondered passages from the brown book and sought to match them to my own experiences in order to produce, insofar as possible, some general theory of human action that would be of benefit to me should I ever free myself.

For if the leech, who was an elderly man, could still pursue knowledge despite the certainty of imminent death, could not I whose death appeared more imminent still, take some comfort in the surety that it was less certain?

Thus I sifted the actions of the magicians, and of the man who had accosted me outside the jacal of the sick girl, and of many other men and women I had known, seeking for a key that would unlock all hearts.

I found none that could be expressed in few words: "Men and women do as they do because of thus and so. . . ." None of the ragged bits of metal fit—the desire for power, the lust of love, the need for reassurance, or the taste for seasoning life with romance. But I did find one principle, which I came to call that of Primitivity, that I believe is widely applicable, and which, if it does not initiate action, at least seems to influence the forms that action takes. I might state it this way: *Because the prehistoric cultures endured for so many chiliads, they have shaped our heritage in such a way as to cause us to behave as if their conditions obtained today.*

For example, the technology that once might have permitted Baldanders to observe all the actions of the hetman of the lakeside village has been dust now for thousands of years; but during the eons of its existence, it laid upon him a spell, as it were, by which it remained effective though no longer extant.

In the same way, we all have in us the ghosts of long-vanished things, of fallen cities and marvelous machines. The story I once read to Jonas when we were imprisoned (with how much less anxiety and how much more companionship) showed that clearly, and I read it over again in the ziggurat. The author, having need for some sea-born fiend like Erebus or Abaia, in a mythical setting, gave it a head like a ship—which was the whole of its visible body, the remainder being underwater—so that it was removed from protoplasmic reality and became the machine that the rhythms of his mind demanded.

While I amused myself with these speculations, I became increasingly aware of the impermanent nature of Vodalus's occupation of the ancient building. Though the leech came no more, as I have said, and Agia never visited me again, I frequently heard the sound of running feet in the corridor outside my door and occasionally a few shouted words.

Whenever such sounds came, I put my unbandaged ear to the planks; and in fact I often anticipated them, sitting that way for long periods in the hope of overhearing some snatch of conversation that would tell me something of Vodalus's plans. I could not help but think then, as I listened in vain, of the hundreds in our oubliette who must have listened to me when I carried their food to Drotte, and how they must have strained to overhear the fragments of conversation that drifted from Thecla's cell into the corridor, and thus into their own cells, when I visited her.

And what of the dead? I own that I thought of myself, at times, almost as dead. Are they not locked below ground in chambers smaller than mine was, in their millions of millions? There is no category of human activity in which the dead do not outnumber the living many times over. Most beautiful children are dead. Most soldiers, most cowards. The fairest women and the most learned men—all are dead.

Their bodies repose in caskets, in sarcophagi, beneath arches of rude stone, everywhere under the earth. Their spirits haunt our minds, ears pressed to the bones of our foreheads. Who can say how intently they listen as we speak, or for what word?

XXVII

Before Vodalus

ON THE MORNING of the sixth day, two women came for me. I had slept very little the night before. One of the blood bats common in those northern jungles had entered my room by the window, and though I had succeeded in driving it out and staunching the blood, it had returned again and again, attracted, I suppose, by the odor of my wounds. Even now I cannot see the vague green darkness that is diffused moonlight without imagining I see the bat crawling there like a big spider, then springing into the air.

The women were as surprised to find me awake as I was to see them; it was just dawn. They made me stand, and one bound my hands while the other held her dirk to my throat. She asked how my cheek was healing, however, and added that she had been told I was a handsome fellow when I was brought in.

"I was almost as near to death then as I am now," I said to her. The truth was that though the concussion I had suffered when the flier crashed had healed, my leg, as well as my face, was still giving me considerable pain.

The women brought me to Vodalus; not, as I had more or less expected, somewhere in the ziggurat or on the ledge where he had sat in state with Thea, but in a clearing embraced on three sides by slow green water. It was a moment or two—I had to stand waiting while some other business was conducted—before I realized that the course of this river was fundamentally to the north and east, and that I had never seen northeastward-flowing water before; all streams, in my previous experience, ran south or southwest to join south-western-flowing Gyoll.

At last Vodalus inclined his head toward me, and I was brought forward. When he saw that I could scarcely stand, he ordered my guards to seat me at his feet, then waved them back out of hearing distance. "Your entrance is somewhat less impressive than that you made in the forest beyond Nessus," he said.

I agreed. "But, Liege, I come now, as I did then, as your servant. Just as I was the first time you met me, when I saved your neck from the ax. If I appear before you in bloody rags and with bound hands, it is because you treat your servants so."

"Certainly I would agree that securing your wrists seems a trifle excessive in your condition." He smiled faintly. "Is it painful?"

"No. The feeling is gone."

"Still, the cords aren't needed." Vodalus stood and drew a slender blade, and leaning over me, flicked my bonds with the point.

I flexed my shoulders and the last strands parted. A thousand needles seemed to pierce my hands.

When he had taken his seat again, Vodalus asked if I were not going to thank him.

"You never thanked me, Liege. You gave me a coin instead. I think I have one here somewhere." I fumbled in my sabretache for the money I had been paid by Guasacht.

"You may keep your coin. I'm going to ask you for much more than that. Are you ready to tell me who you are?"

"I've always been ready to do that, Liege. I'm Severian, formerly a journeyman of the guild of torturers."

"But are you nothing else besides a former journeyman of that guild?"

"No."

Vodalus sighed and smiled, then leaned back in his chair and sighed again. "My servant Hildegrin always insisted you were important. When I asked him why, he had any number of speculations, none of which I found convincing. I thought he was trying to get silver from me for a little easy spying. Yet he was right."

"I have only been important once to you, Liege."

"Each time we meet, you remind me that you saved my life once. Did you know that Hildegrin once saved yours? It was he who shouted 'Run!' to your opponent when you dueled in the city. You had fallen, and he might have stabbed you."

"Is Agia here?" I asked. "She'll try to kill you if she hears that."

"No one can hear you but myself. You may tell her later, if you like. She will never believe you."

"You can't be sure of that."

He smiled more broadly. "Very well, I'll turn you over to her. You can then test your theory against mine."

"As you wish."

He brushed my acquiescence aside with an elegant motion of one hand. "You think you can stalemate me with your willingness to die. Actually you're offering me an easy exit from a dilemma. Your Agia came to me with a very valuable thaumaturgist in her train, and asked as the price of his service and her own only that you, Severian of the Order of the Seekers for Truth and Penitence, should be put into her hands. Now you say you are that Severian the Torturer and no one else, and it is with great embarrassment that I resist her demands."

"And whom do you wish me to be?" I asked.

"I have, or I should say I had, a most excellent servant in the House Absolute. You know him, of course, since it was to

him that you gave my message." Vodalus paused and smiled
again. "A week or so ago we received one from him. It was
not, to be sure, openly addressed to me, but I had seen to it
not long before that he was aware of our location, and we
were not far from him. Do you know what he said?"

I shook my head.

"That's odd, because you must have been with him at the
time. He said he was in a wrecked flier—and that the Autarch
was in the flier with him. He would have been an idiot to
have sent such a message in the ordinary course of things,
because he gave his location—and he was behind our lines, as
he must have known."

"You are a part of the Ascian army, then?"

"We serve them in certain scouting capacities, yes. I see
you are troubled by the knowledge that Agia and the thaumaturgist killed a few of their soldiers to take you. You need
not be. Their masters value them even less than I do, and it
was not a time for negotiation."

"But they did not capture the Autarch." I am not a good
liar, but I was too exhausted, I think, for Vodalus to read my
face easily.

He leaned forward, and for a moment his eyes glowed as
though candles burned in their depths. "He was there, then.
How wonderful. You have seen him. You have ridden in the
royal flier with him."

I nodded once more.

"You see, ridiculous though it sounds, I feared you were
he. One never knows. An Autarch dies and another takes his
place, and the new Autarch may be there for half a century
or a fortnight. There were three of you then? No more?"

"No."

"What did the Autarch look like? Let me have every detail."

I did as he asked, describing Dr. Talos as he had appeared
in the part.

"Did he escape both the thaumaturgist's creatures and the

Ascians? Or do the Ascians have him? Perhaps the woman and her paramour are holding him for themselves."

"I told you the Ascians did not take him."

Vodalus smiled again, but beneath his glowing eyes his twisted mouth suggested only pain. "You see," he repeated, "for a time I thought you might be the one. We have my servant, but he has suffered a head injury and is never conscious for more than a few moments. He will die very shortly, I'm afraid. But he has always told me the truth, and Agia says that you were the only one with him."

"You think that I am the Autarch? No."

"Yet you are changed from the man I met before."

"You yourself gave me the alzabo, and the life of the Chatelaine Thecla. I loved her. Did you think that to thus ingest her essence would leave me unaffected? She is with me always, so that I am two, in this single body. Yet I am not the Autarch, who in one body is a thousand."

Vodalus answered nothing, but half closed his eyes as though he were afraid I would see their fire. There was no sound but the lapping of the river water and the much-muted voices of the little knot of armed men and women, who talked among themselves a hundred paces off and glanced from time to time at us. A macaw shrieked, fluttering from one tree to another.

"I would still serve you," I told Vodalus, "if you would permit it." I was not certain it was a lie until the words had left my lips, and then I was bewildered in mind, seeking to understand how those words, which would have been true in the past for Thecla and for Severian too, were now false for me.

" 'The Autarch, who in one body is a thousand,' " Vodalus quoted me. "That is correct, but how few of us know it."

On the March

Today, this being the last before I am to leave the House Absolute, I participated in a solemn religious ceremony. Such rituals are divided into seven orders according to their importance, or as the heptarchs say, their "transcendence"—something I was quite ignorant of at the time of which I was writing a moment ago. At the lowest level, that of Aspiration, are the private pieties, including prayers pronounced privately, the casting of a stone upon a cairn, and so forth. The gatherings and public petitionings that I, as a boy, thought constituted the whole of organized religion, are actually at the second level, which is that of Integration. What we did today belonged to the seventh and highest, the level of Assimilation.

In accordance with the principle of circularity, most of the accretions gathered in the progression through the first six were now dispensed with. There was no music, and the rich vestments of Assurance were replaced by starched robes whose sculptural folds gave all of us something of the air of icons. It is no longer possible for us to carry out the ceremony, as once we did, wrapped in the shining belt of the galaxy; but to achieve the effect as nearly as possible, Urth's attractive field was excluded from the basilica. It was a novel sensation for me, and though I was unafraid, I was reminded again of that night I spent among the mountains when I felt myself on the point of falling off the world—something I will undergo in sober earnest tomorrow. At times the ceiling seemed a floor, or (what was to me far more disturbing) a wall became the ceiling, so that one looked upward through its open windows to see a mountainside of grass that lifted itself forever into the sky. Startling as it was, this vision was no less true than that we commonly see.

Each of us became a sun; the circling, ivory skulls were our planets. I said we had dispensed with music, yet that was not entirely true, for as they swung about us there came a faint, sweet humming and whistling, caused by the flow of air through their eye sockets and teeth; those in nearly circular orbits maintained an almost steady note, varying only slightly as they rotated on their axes; the songs of those in elliptical orbits waxed and waned, rising as they approached me, sinking to a moan as they receded.

How foolish we are to see in those hollow eyes and marble calottes only death. How many friends are among them! The brown book, which I carried so far, the only one of the possessions I took from the Matachin Tower that still remains with me, was sewn and printed and composed by men and women with those bony faces; and we, engulfed by their voices, now on behalf of those who are the past, offered ourselves and the present to the fulgurant light of the New Sun.

Yet at that moment, surrounded by the most meaningful and magnificent symbolism, I could not but think how different the actuality had been when we had left the ziggurat on the day after my interview with Vodalus and had marched (I under the guard of six women, who were sometimes forced to carry me) for what must have been a week or more through pestilential jungle. I did not know—and still do not know—

whether we were fleeing the armies of the Commonwealth or the Ascians who had been Vodalus's allies. Perhaps we were merely seeking to rejoin the major part of the insurgent force. My guards complained of the moisture that dripped from the trees to eat at their weapons and armor like acid, and of suffocating heat; I felt nothing of either. I remember looking down once at my thigh and noticing with surprise that the flesh had fallen away so that the muscles there stood out like cords and I could see the sliding parts of my knee as one sees the wheels and shafts of a mill.

The old leech was with us, and now visited me two or three times each day. At first he tried to keep dry bandages on my face; when he saw the effort was futile, he removed them all and contented himself with plastering the wounds there with his salve. After that, some of my women guards refused to look at me, and if they had reason to speak to me did so with downcast eyes. Others seemed to take pride in their ability to confront my torn face, standing straddle-legged (a pose they appeared to consider warlike) and resting their left hands upon the hilts of their weapons with studied casualness.

I talked with them as often as I could. Not because I desired them—the illness that had come with my wounds had taken all such desire from me—but because in the midst of the straggling column I was lonely in a way I had never been when I was alone in the war-torn north or even when I had been locked in my ancient, mold-streaked cell in the ziggurat, and because in some absurd corner of my mind I still hoped to escape. I questioned them about every subject of which they might conceivably have knowledge, and I was endlessly amazed to find how few were the points on which our minds coincided. Not one of the six had joined Vodalus because of an appreciation of the difference between the restoration of progress he sought to represent and the stagnation of the Commonwealth. Three had merely followed some man into the ranks; two had come in the hope of gaining revenge for

some personal injustice, and one because she had been fleeing from a detested stepfather. All but the last now wished
they had not joined. None knew with any precision where we
had been or had the slightest idea where we were going.

For guides our column had three savages: a pair of young
men who might have been brothers or even twins, and a
much older one, twisted, I thought, by deformities as well as
age, who perpetually wore a grotesque mask. Though the first
two were younger and the third much older, all three of them
recalled to me the naked man I had once seen in the Jungle
Garden. They were as naked as he and had the same dark,
metallic-looking skin and straight hair. The younger two carried cerbotanas longer than their outstretched arms and dart
bags hand-knotted of wild cotton and dyed a burnt umber,
doubtless with the juice of some plant. The old man had a
staff as crooked as himself, topped with the dried head of a
monkey.

A covered palanquin whose place in the column was considerably more advanced than my own bore the Autarch,
whom my leech gave me to understand was still alive; and
one night when my guards were chattering among themselves and I sat crouched over our little fire, I saw the old
guide (his bent figure and the impression of an immense head
conferred by his mask were unmistakable) approach this palanquin and slip beneath it. Some time passed before he scut-
tled away. This old man was said to be an *uturuncu*, a
shaman capable of assuming the form of a tiger.

Within a few days of our leaving the ziggurat, without
encountering anything that might be called a road or even a
path, we struck a trail of corpses. They were Ascians, and
they had been stripped of their clothing and equipment, so
that their starved bodies seemed to have dropped from the
air to the places where they lay. To me, they appeared to be
about a week dead; but no doubt decay had been accelerated

by the dampness and heat, and the actual time was much less. The cause of death was seldom apparent.

Until then we had seen few animals larger than the grotesque beetles that buzzed about our fires by night. Such birds as called from the treetops remained largely invisible, and if the blood-bats visited us, their inky wings were lost in the smothering dark. Now we moved, as it seemed, through an army of beasts drawn to the corpse trail as flies are to a dead sumpter. Hardly a watch passed without our hearing the sound of bones crushed by great jaws, and by night green and scarlet eyes, some of them two spans apart, shone outside our little circles of firelight. Though it was preposterous to suppose these carrion-gorged predators would molest us, my guards doubled their sentries; those who slept did so in their corslets, with curtelaxes in their hands.

With each new day the bodies were fresher, until at last not all were dead. A madwoman with cropped hair and staring eyes stumbled into the column just ahead of our party, shouted words no one could understand, and fled among the trees. We heard cries for help, screams, and ravings, but Vodalus permitted no one to turn aside, and on the afternoon of that day we plunged—much in the same sense we might earlier have been said to have plunged into the jungle—into the Ascian horde.

Our column consisted of the women and supplies, Vodalus himself and his household, and a few of his aides with their retinues. In all it surely amounted to no more than a fifth of his force; but if every insurgent he could have called to his banner had been there, and every fighter become a hundred, they would still have been among that multitude as a cupful of water in Gyoll.

Those we encountered first were infantry. I recalled that the Autarch had told me their weapons were kept from them until the time of battle; but if it were so, their officers must have thought that time to be at hand, or nearly. I saw thousands armed with the ransieur, so that at length I came to believe that all their infantry was equipped in that way; then, as night was falling, we overtook thousands more carrying demilunes.

Because we marched faster than they, we moved more deeply into their force; but we camped sooner than they (if they camped at all) and all that night, until at last I fell asleep, I heard their hoarse cries and the shuffling of their feet. In the morning we were again among their dead and dying, and it was a watch or more before we overtook the stumbling ranks.

These Ascian soldiers had a rigidity, a will-less attachment to order, that I have never seen elsewhere, and that appeared to me to have no roots in either spirit or discipline as I understand them. They seemed to obey because they could not conceive of any other course of action. Our soldiers nearly always carry several arms—at the very least an energy weapon and a long knife (among the schiavoni I was exceptional in not possessing such a knife in addition to my falchion). But I never saw an Ascian with more than one, and most of their officers bore no weapon at all, as if they regarded actual fighting with contempt.

Autarch of the Commonwealth

By THE MIDDLE of the day, we had again passed all those whom we had passed the afternoon before and came upon the baggage train. I think all of us were amazed to discover that the enormous force we had seen was no more than the rear guard of an army inconceivably greater.

The Ascians used uintathers and platybelodons as beasts of burden. Mixed with them were machines with six legs, machines apparently built to serve that purpose. So far as I could see, the drivers made no distinction between these devices and the animals; if a beast lay down and could not be made to rise again, or a machine fell and did not right itself, its load was distributed among those nearest to hand, and it was abandoned. There appeared to be no effort to slaughter the beasts for their meat or to repair or take parts from the machines.

Late in the afternoon some great excitement passed down our column, though neither I nor my guards could discover what it was. Vodalus himself and several of his lieutenants came hurrying by, and afterward there was much coming and going between the end of the column and its head. When dark came we did not camp, but continued to tramp through the night with the Ascians. Torches were passed back to us, and since I had no weapons to carry and was somewhat stronger than I had been, I carried them, feeling almost as though I commanded the six swords who surrounded me.

About midnight, as nearly as I could judge, we halted. My guards found sticks for a fire, which we kindled from a torch. Just as we were about to lie down, I saw a messenger rouse the palanquin bearers ahead of us and send them blundering forward in the dark. They were no sooner gone than he loped back to us and held a quick, whispered conversation with the sergeant of my guards. At once my hands were bound (as they had not been since Vodalus had cut them free) and we were hurrying after the palanquin. We passed the head of the column, marked by the Chatelaine Thea's little pavilion, without pausing, and were soon wandering among the myriad Ascian soldiers of the main body.

Their headquarters was a dome of metal. I suppose it must have folded or collapsed in some way as a tent does, but it appeared as permanent and solid as any building, black externally but glowing with a sourceless, pale light within when the side opened to admit us. Vodalus was there, stiff and deferential; beside him the palanquin stood with its curtains opened to show the immobile body of the Autarch. At the center of the dome, three women sat around a low table. Neither then nor later did they look at Vodalus, or the Autarch in his palanquin, or at me when I was brought forward, save for an occasional glance. There were stacks of papers before them, but they did not look at those at all—only at one another. In appearance they were much like the other Ascians I had seen, save that their eyes were saner and they were less starved looking.

"Here he is," Vodalus said. "Now you see them both before you."

One of the Ascians spoke to the other two in their own tongue. Both nodded and the one who had spoken said, "Only he who acts against the populace need hide his face."

There was a lengthy pause, then Vodalus hissed at me, "Answer her!"

"Answer what? There has been no question."

The Ascian said, "Who is the friend of the populace? He who aids the populace. Who is the enemy of the populace?"

Speaking very rapidly, Vodalus asked, "To the best of your knowledge are you, or is this unconscious man here, the leader of the peoples of the southern half of this hemisphere?"

"No," I said. It was an easy lie, since from what I had seen, the Autarch was the leader of very few in the Commonwealth. To Vodalus I added under my breath, "What kind of foolishness is this? Do they believe I would tell them if I were the Autarch?"

"All we say is being transmitted to the north."

One of the Ascians who had not spoken previously spoke now. Once she gestured in our direction. When she was finished, all three sat deathly still. I had the impression that they heard some voice inaudible to me, and that they did not dare move while it spoke; but that may have been mere imagination on my part. Vodalus fidgeted, I shifted my position to put a little less weight on my injured leg, and the Autarch's narrow chest heaved to the unsteady rhythm of his breathing, but the three of them remained as immobile as figures in a painting.

At last the one who had spoken first said, "All persons belong to the populace." At that the others seemed to relax.

"This man is ill," Vodalus said, looking toward the Autarch, "and he has been a useful servant to me, though I suppose his usefulness is now ended. The other I have promised to one of my followers."

"The merit of sacrifice falls on him who without thought to his own convenience offers what he has toward the service of the populace." The Ascian woman's tone made it clear that no further argument was possible.

Vodalus looked toward me and shrugged, then turned on

his heel and strode out of the dome. Almost at once a file of Ascian officers entered carrying lashes.

We were imprisoned in an Ascian tent perhaps twice the size of my cell in the ziggurat. There was a fire there but no bedding, and the officers who had carried in the Autarch had merely dropped him on the ground beside it. After working my hands free, I tried to make him comfortable, turning him over on his back as he had been in the palanquin and arranging his arms at his sides.

About us the army lay quiet, or at least as quiet as an Ascian army ever is. From time to time someone far off cried out—in sleep, it seemed—but for the most part there was no sound but the slow pacing of the sentries outside. I cannot express the horror that the thought of going north to Ascia evoked in me then. To see only the Ascians' wild, starved faces and to encounter myself, no doubt for the remainder of my life, whatever it was that had driven them mad, seemed to me a more horrible fate than any the clients in the Matachin Tower were ever forced to endure. I tried to lift the skirt of the tent, thinking that the sentries could do nothing worse than take my life; but the edges were welded to the ground by some means I did not understand. All four walls were of a slick, tough substance I could not tear, and Miles's razor had been taken from me by my six female guards. I was about to rush out the door when the Autarch's well-remembered voice whispered, "Wait." I dropped to my knees beside him, suddenly afraid we would be overheard.

"I thought you were—sleeping."

"I suppose I have been in a coma most of the time. But when I was not, I feigned, so Vodalus would not question me. Are you going to escape?"

"Not without you, Sieur. Not now. I had given you up for dead."

"You were not far wrong . . . certainly not by so much as a day. Yes, I think that is best, you must escape. Father Inire is with the insurgents. He was to bring you what is necessary, then help you get away. But we are no longer there . . . are we? He may not be able to aid you. Open my robe. What you first require is thrust into my waistband."

I did as he asked; the flesh my fingers brushed was as cold as a corpse's. Near his left hip I saw a hilt of silvery metal no thicker than a woman's finger. I drew the weapon forth; the blade was not half a span in length, but thick and strong, and of that deadly sharpness I had not felt since Baldanders's mace had shattered *Terminus Est*.

"You must not go yet," the Autarch whispered.

"I will not leave you while you live," I said. "Do you doubt me?"

"We will both live, and both go. You know the abomination . . ." His hand closed on mine. "The eating of the dead, to devour their dead lives. But there is another way you do not know, and another drug. You must take it, and swallow the living cells of my forebrain."

I must have drawn away, for his hand gripped my own harder.

"When you lie with a woman, you thrust your life into hers so that perhaps there will be new life. When you do as I have commanded you, my life and the lives of all those who live in me will be continued in you. The cells will enter your own nervous system and multiply there. The drug is in the vial I wear at my neck, and that blade will split the bones of my skull like pine. I have had occasion to use it, and I promise it. Do you recall how you swore to serve me when I shut the book? Use the knife now, and go as quickly as you can."

I nodded and promised I would.

"The drug will be stronger than any you have known, and though all but mine will be faint, there will be hundreds of personalities. . . . We are many lives."

"I understand," I said.

"The Ascians march at dawn. Can there be more than a single watch remaining of the night?"

"I hope that you will live it out, Sieur, and many more. That you'll recover."

"You must kill me now, before Urth turns to face the sun. Then I will live in you . . . never die. I live by mere volition now. I am relinquishing my life as I speak."

To my utter surprise, my eyes were streaming with tears. "I've hated you since I was a boy, Sieur. I've done you no harm, but I would have harmed you if I could, and now I'm sorry."

His voice had faded until it was softer than the chirping of a cricket. "You were right to hate me, Severian. I stand . . . as you will stand . . . for so much that is wrong."

"Why?" I asked. "*Why?*" I was on my knees beside him.

"Because all else is worse. Until the New Sun comes, we have but a choice of evils. All have been tried, and all have failed. Goods in common, the rule of the people . . . everything. You wish for progress? The Ascians have it. They are deafened by it, crazed by the death of Nature till they are ready to accept Erebus and the rest as gods. We hold humankind stationary . . . in barbarism. The Autarch protects the people from the exultants, and the exultants . . . shelter them from the Autarch. The religious comfort them. We have closed the roads to paralyze the social order. . . ."

His eyes fell shut. I put my hand upon his chest to feel the faint stirring of his heart.

"Until the New Sun . . ."

This was what I had sought to escape, not Agia or Vodalus or the Ascians. As gently as I could, I lifted the chain from his neck, unstoppered the vial and swallowed the drug. Then with that short, stiff blade I did what had to be done.

When it was over, I covered him from head to toe with his own saffron robe and hung the empty vial about my own neck. The effect of the drug was as violent as he had warned me it would be. You that read this, who have never, perhaps, possessed more than a single consciousness, cannot know what it is to have two or three, much less hundreds. They lived in me and were joyful, each in his own way, to find they had new life. The dead Autarch, whose face I had seen in scarlet ruin a few moments before, now lived again. My eyes and hands were his, I knew the work of the hives of the bees of the House Absolute and the sacredness of them, who steer by the sun and fetch gold of Urth's fertility. I knew his course to the Phoenix Throne, and to the stars, and back. His mind was mine and filled mine with lore whose existence I had never suspected and with the knowledge other minds had brought to his. The phenomenal world seemed dim and vague as a picture sketched in sand over which an errant wind veered and moaned. I could not have concentrated on it if I had wished to, and I had no such wish.

The black fabric of our prison tent faded to a pale dove-gray, and the angles of its top whirled like the prisms of a kaleidoscope. I had fallen without being aware of it and lay near the body of my predecessor, where my attempts to rise resulted in nothing more than the beating of my hands upon the ground.

How long I lay there I do not know. I had wiped the knife—now, still, *my* knife—and concealed it as he had. I could vividly picture a self of dozens of superposed images slitting the wall and slipping out into the night. Severian, Thecla, myriad others all escaping. So real was the thought that I often believed I had done it; but always, when I ought to have been running between the trees, avoiding the exhausted sleepers of the army of the Ascians, I found myself instead in the familiar tent, with the draped body not far from my own.

Hands clasped mine. I supposed that the officers had returned with their lashes, and tried to see and to rise so I would not be struck. But a hundred random memories intruded themselves like the pictures the owner holds up to us in rapid succession in a cheap gallery: a footrace, the towering pipes of an organ, a diagram with labeled angles, a woman riding in a cart.

Someone said, "Are you all right? What's happened to you?" I felt the spittle dribbling from my lips, but no words came.

The Corridors of Time

SOMETHING STRUCK MY FACE a tingling blow.

"What's happened? He's dead. Are you drugged?"

"*Yes. Drugged.*" Someone else was speaking, and after a moment I knew who it was: Severian, the young torturer.

But who was I?

"Get up. We've got to get out."

"*Sentry.*"

"Sentries," the voice corrected us. "There were three of them. We killed them."

I was walking down a stair white as salt, down to nenuphars and stagnant water. Beside me walked a suntanned girl with long and slanting eyes. Over her shoulder peered the sculptured face of one of the eponyms. The carver had worked in jade; the effect was that of a face of grass.

"Is he dying?"

"He sees us now. See his eyes."

I knew where I was. Soon the pitchman would thrust his head through the doorway of the tent to tell me to be gone. "Above ground," I said. "You told me I would see her above ground. But that was easy. She is here."

"We must go." The green man took my left arm and Agia my right, and they led me out.

We walked a long way, just as I had envisioned myself running, stepping sometimes over sleeping Ascians.

"They keep little guard," Agia whispered. "Vodalus told me their leaders are so well obeyed they can scarcely conceive of treacherous attack. In the war, our soldiers surprise them often."

I did not understand and repeated, " 'Our soldiers . . .'" like a child.

"Hethor and I will no longer fight for them. How could we, after we have seen them? My business is with you."

I was beginning to find myself again, the minds that made up *my* mind all falling into place. I had been told once that *autarch* meant "self-ruler," and I glimpsed the reason that title had come into being. I said, "You wanted to kill me. Now you are freeing me. You could have stabbed me." I saw a crooked dagger from Thrax quivering in Casdoe's shutter.

"I could have killed you more readily than that. Hethor's mirrors have given me a worm, no longer than your hand, that glows with white fire. I have only to fling it, and it kills and crawls back to me—one by one I slew the sentries so. But this green man would not permit it, and I would not wish it. Vodalus promised me your agony spread over weeks, and I will not have less."

"You're taking me back to him?"

She shook her head, and in the faint, gray dawn light that had crept through the leaves I saw her brown curls bounce on her shoulders as they had when I had watched her raise the gratings outside the rag shop. "Vodalus is dead. With the worm at my command, do you think I would let him cheat me and live? They would have taken you away. Now I will let you go free—because I have some inkling of where you will go—and in the end you will come into my hands again, as you did when our pteriopes took you from the evzones."

"You are rescuing me because you hate me then," I said, and she nodded. Vodalus, I suppose, had hated that part of me that had been the Autarch in the same way.

Or rather, he had hated his conception of the Autarch, for he had been loyal, in so far as he was capable of it, to the real Autarch, whom he supposed his servant. When I had been a boy in the kitchens of the House Absolute, there was a cook who so despised the armigers and exultants for whom he prepared food that, in order that he should never have to bear the indignity of their reproaches, he did everything with a feverish perfection. He was eventually made chief of the cooks of that wing. I thought of him, and while I did, Agia's touch on my arm, which had become almost imperceptible as we hastened along, vanished altogether. When I looked for her, she was gone; I was alone with the green man.

"How did you come to be here?" I asked him. "You nearly lost your life in these times, and I know you cannot thrive under our sun."

He smiled. Though his lips were green, his teeth were white; they gleamed in the faint light. "We are your children, and we are not less honest than you, though we do not kill to eat. You gave me half your stone, the stone that gnawed the iron and set me free. What did you think I would do when the chain no longer bound me?"

"I supposed you would return to your own day," I said. The spell of the drug had faded sufficiently for me to fear our talk would wake the Ascian soldiers. Yet I could see none—only the dark, towering boles of the jungle hardwoods.

"We requite our benefactors. I have been running up and down the corridors of Time, seeking for a moment in which you also were imprisoned, that I might free you."

When I heard that, I did not know what to say. At last I told him, "You cannot imagine how strange I feel now, knowing that someone has been searching my future, looking for an opportunity to do me good. But now, now that we are quits, surely you understand that I did not help you because I believed you could help me."

"You did—you desired my help in finding the woman who just left us, the woman whom since that occasion you have found several times. However, you ought to know that I was not alone: There are others questing there—I shall send two of them to you. And you and I are not yet at a balance, for although I found you captive here, the woman found you also and would have freed you without my help. So I shall see you again."

As he said these words, he let go of my arm and stepped in that direction I had never seen until I watched the ship vanish into it from the top of Baldanders's castle and could only see, it seemed, when there was something there. Immediately he turned and began to run, and despite the dimness of the dawn sky I could see his running figure for a long time, illuminated by intermittent but regular flashes. At last he faded to a point of darkness; but then, just when I expected that point to disappear utterly, it began to grow, so that I had the impression of something huge rushing toward me down that strangely angled tunnel.

It was not the ship I had seen but another and much smaller one. Still, it was so large that when it moved at last entirely into our field of consciousness, its gunwales touched several of the thick trunks at once. The hull dilated, and a pont, much shorter than the steps that had descended from the Autarch's flier, slid out to touch the ground.

Down it came Master Malrubius and my dog, Triskele.

At that moment I regained a command of my personality that I had not truly possessed since I had drunk alzabo with Vodalus and eaten Thecla's flesh. It was not that Thecla was gone (and indeed I could not wish her gone, though I knew that in many respects she had been a cruel and foolish woman) or that my predecessor and the hundred minds that had been enveloped in his had vanished. The old, simple structure of my single personality was no more; but the new, complex structure no longer dazzled and bewildered me. It was a maze, but I was the owner and even the builder of that maze, with the print of my thumb on every passageway. Malrubius touched me, and then taking my wondering hand in his laid it gently against his own cool cheek.

"You are real, then," I said.

"No. We are almost what you think us—powers from above the stage. Only not quite deities. You are an actor, I believe."

I shook my head. "Don't you know me, Master? You taught me when I was a boy, and I have become a journeyman of the guild."

"Yet you are an actor too. You have as much right to think of yourself in that way as the other. You had been performing when we spoke to you in the field near the Wall, and the next time we saw you, at the House Absolute, you were acting again. It was a good play; I should have liked to see the end."

"You were in our audience?"

Master Malrubius nodded. "As an actor, Severian, you surely know the phrase I hinted at a moment ago. It refers to some supernatural force, personified and brought onto the stage in the last act in order that the play may end well. None but poor playwrights do it, they say, but those who say so forget that it is better to have a power lowered on a rope, and a play that ends well, than to have nothing, and a play that ends badly. Here is our rope—many ropes, and a stout ship too. Will you come aboard?"

I said, "Is that why you are as you are? In order that I will trust you?"

"Yes, if you like." Master Malrubius nodded, and Triskele, who had been sitting at my feet and looking up into my face, ran with his bumping, three-legged gallop halfway up the pont and turned to look back at me, his stump tail wagging and his eyes pleading as a dog's eyes do.

"I know you can't be what you seem. Perhaps Triskele is, but I saw you buried, Master. Your face is no mask, but there's a mask somewhere, and under that mask you're what the common people call a cacogen, although Dr. Talos explained to me once that you prefer to be called Hierodules."

Again Malrubius laid his hand on mine. "We would not deceive you if we could. But I hope that you will deceive yourself, to your good and all Urth's. Some drug now dulls your mind—more than you realize—just as you were under the sway of sleep when we spoke to you in that meadow near the Wall. If you were undrugged now, perhaps you would lack the courage to come with us, even if you saw us, even if your reason convinced you that you should."

I said, "So far it hasn't convinced me of that, or of anything else. Where do you want to take me, and why do you want to take me there? Are you Master Malrubius or a Hierodule?" As I spoke I became more conscious of the trees, standing as soldiers stand while the officers of the staff discuss some point of strategy. Night was upon us still, but it had become a thinner darkness, even here.

"Do you know the meaning of that word *Hierodule* you use? I am Malrubius, and no Hierodule. Rather I serve those the Hierodules serve. *Hierodule* means *holy slave*. Do you think there can be slaves without masters?"

"And you take me—"

"To Ocean, to preserve your life." As if he had read my thought, he continued, "No, we do not take you to the paramours of Abaia, those who spared and succored you because you had been a torturer and would be Autarch. In any event, you have much worse to fear. Soon the slaves of Erebus, who held you captive here, will discover you have escaped; and Erebus would hurl that army, and many others like it, into the abyss to capture you. Come." He drew me onto the pont.

XXXI

The Sand Garden

THAT SHIP WAS worked by hands I could not see. I had supposed we would float up as the flier had or vanish like the green man down some corridor in time. Instead we rose so quickly I felt sick; alongside I heard the crashing of great limbs.

"You are the Autarch now," Malrubius told me. "Do you know it?" His voice seemed to blend with the whistle of the wind in the rigging.

"Yes. My predecessor, whose mind is now one of mine, came to office as I have. I know the secrets, the words of authority, though I haven't had time yet to think about them. Are you returning me to the House Absolute?"

He shook his head. "You are not ready. You believe that all the old Autarch knew is available to you now. You are correct—but it is not yet in your grasp, and when the tests come, you will encounter many who will slay you should you falter. You were nurtured in the Citadel of Nessus—what are the words for its castellan? How are the man-apes of the treasure mine to be commanded? What phrases unlock the vaults of the Secret House? You need not tell me, because these things are the arcana of your state, and I know them in any case. But do you yourself know them, without thinking long?"

The phrases I required were present in my mind, yet I failed when I sought to pronounce them to myself. Like little fish, they slipped aside, and in the end I could only lift my shoulders.

"And there is one thing more for you to do. One adventure more, beside the waters."

"What is it?"

"If I were to tell you, it would not come to pass. Do not be alarmed. It is a simple thing, over in a breath. But I must explain a great deal, and I have not much time in which to do it. Have you faith in the coming of the New Sun?"

As I had looked within myself for the words of command, so I looked within for my belief; and I could no more find it than I had found them. "I have been taught so all my life," I said. "But by teachers—the true Malrubius was one—who I think did not themselves believe. So I cannot now say whether I believe or not."

"Who is the New Sun? A man? If a man, how can it be that every green thing is to grow darkly green again at his coming, and the granaries full?"

It was unpleasant to be drawn back to things half heard in childhood now, when I was just beginning to understand that I had inherited the Commonwealth. I said, "He will be the Conciliator come again—his avatar, bringing justice and peace. In pictures he is shown with a shining face, like the sun. I was an apprentice of the torturers, not an acolyte, and that is all I can tell you." I drew my cloak about me for shelter from the cold wind. Triskele was huddled at my feet.

"And which does humanity need more? Justice and peace? Or a New Sun?"

At that I tried to smile. "It has occurred to me that though you cannot possibly be my old teacher, you may incorporate his personality as I do the Chatelaine Thecla's. If that is so, you already know my answer. When a client is driven to the utmost extremity, it is warmth and food and ease from pain he wants. Peace and justice come afterward. Rain symbolizes mercy and sunlight charity, but rain and sunlight are better than mercy and charity. Otherwise they would degrade the things they symbolize."

"To a large extent you are correct. The Master Malrubius you knew lives in me, and your old Triskele in this Triskele. But that is not important now. If there is time, you will understand before we go." Malrubius closed his eyes and scratched the gray hair on his chest, just as I remembered him doing when I was among the youngest of the apprentices. "You were afraid to board this little ship, even when I told you it would not carry you away from Urth, or even to a continent other than your own. Suppose I were to tell you—I do *not* tell you, but suppose I did—that it would in fact take you from Urth, past the orbit of Phaleg, which you call Verthandi, past Bethor and Aratron, and at last into the outer dark, and across the dark to another place. Would you be frightened, now that you have sailed with us?"

"No man enjoys saying he is afraid. But yes, I would."

"Afraid or not, would you go if it might bring the New Sun?"

It seemed then that some icy spirit from the gulf had already wrapped its hands about my heart. I was not deceived, nor, I think, did he mean I should be. To answer yes would be to undertake the journey. I hesitated, in silence except for the roar of my own blood in my ears.

"You need not answer now if you cannot. We will ask again. But I can tell you nothing more until you answer."

For a long time I stood on that strange deck, sometimes walking up and down, blowing on my fingers in the freezing wind while all my thoughts crowded around me. The stars watched us, and it seemed to me that Master Malrubius's eyes were two more such stars.

At last I returned to him and said, "I have long wanted . . . if it would bring the New Sun, I would go."

"I can give you no assurance. If it *might* bring the New Sun, would you then? Justice and peace, yes, but a New Sun—such an outpouring of warmth and energy upon Urth as she knew before the birth of the first man?"

Now came the strangest happening I have to tell in all this already overlong tale; yet there was no sound or sight associated with it, no speaking beast or gigantic woman. It was only that as I heard him I felt a pressure against my breastbone, as I had felt it in Thrax when I knew I should be going north with the Claw. I remembered the girl in the jacal. "Yes," I said. "If it might bring the New Sun, I would go."

"What if you were to stand trial there? You knew him who was autarch before you, and in the end you loved him. He lives in you. Was he a man?"

"He was a human being—as you, I think, are not, Master."

"That was not my question, as you know as well as I. Was he a man as you are a man? Half the dyad of man and woman?"

I shook my head.

"So you will become, should you fail the trial. Will you still go?"

Triskele laid his scarred head against my knee, the ambassador of all crippled things, of the Autarch who had carried a tray in the House Absolute and lain paralyzed in the palanquin waiting to pass to me the humming voices in his skull, of Thecla writhing under the Revolutionary, and of the woman even I, who had boasted I could forget nothing, had nearly forgotten, bleeding and dying beneath our tower. Perhaps after all it was my discovery of Triskele, which I have said changed nothing, that in the end changed everything. I did not have to answer this time; Master Malrubius saw my answer in my face.

"You know of the chasms of space, which some call the Black Pits, from which no speck of matter or gleam of light ever returns. But what you have not known until now is that these chasms have their counterparts in White Fountains, from which matter and energy rejected by a higher universe flow in endless cataract into this one. If you pass—if our race is judged ready to reenter the wide seas of space—such a white fountain will be created in the heart of our sun."

"But if I fail?"

"If you fail, your manhood will be taken from you, so that you cannot bequeath the Phoenix Throne to your descendants. Your predecessor also accepted the challenge."

"And failed. That is clear from what you said."

"Yes. Still, he was braver than many who are called heroes, the first to go in many reigns. Ymar, of whom you may have heard, was the last before him."

"Yet Ymar too must have been judged unfit. Are we going now? I can see only stars beyond the rail."

Master Malrubius shook his head. "You are not looking as carefully as you think. We are already near our destination."

Swaying, I walked to the railing. Some of my unsteadiness had its origin in the motion of the ship, I think; but some, too, came from the lingering effects of the drug.

Night still covered Urth, for we had flown swiftly to the west, and the faint dawn that had come to the Ascian army in the jungle had not yet appeared here. After a moment I saw that the stars over the side seemed to slip, and slide in their heaven, with an uneasy and wavering motion. Almost it seemed that something moved among the stars as the wind moves through wheat. Then I thought, *It is the sea . . .* and at that moment Master Malrubius said, "It is that great sea called Ocean."

"I have longed to visit it."

"In a short time you will be standing at its margin. You asked when you would leave this planet. Not until your rule here is secure. When the city and the House Absolute obey you and your armies have repelled the incursions of the slaves of Erebus. Within a few years, perhaps. But perhaps not for decades. We two will come for you."

"You are the second tonight to tell me I will see you

again," I said. Just as I spoke, there was a slight shock, like
the sensation one feels when a boat is brought skillfully to
the dock. I walked down the pont and out upon sand, and
Master Malrubius and Triskele followed me. I asked if they
would not stay with me for a time to counsel me.

"For a short time only. If you have further questions, you
must ask them now."

The silver tongue of the pont was already creeping back
into the hull. It seemed that it had hardly come home before
the ship lifted itself and scudded down the same aperture in
reality into which the green man had run.

"You spoke of the peace and justice that the New Sun is
to bring. Is there justice in his calling me so far? What is the
test I must pass?"

"It is not he who calls you. Those who call hope to summon the New Sun to them," Master Malrubius said, but I
did not understand him. Then he recounted to me in brief
words the secret history of Time, which is the greatest of all
secrets, and which I will set down here in the proper place.
When he had finished, my mind reeled and I feared I would
forget all he had said, because it seemed too great a thing for
any living man to know, and because I had learned at last
that the mists close for me as for other men.

"You will not forget, you above all. At Vodalus's banquet,
you said you felt sure you would forget the foolish passwords
he taught you in imitation of the words of authority. But you
did not. You will remember everything. Remember too, not
to be afraid. It may be that the epic penance of mankind is at
an end. The old Autarch told you the truth—we will not go
to the stars again until we go as a divinity, but that time may
not be far off now. In you all the divergent tendencies of our
race may have achieved synthesis."

Triskele stood on his hind legs for a moment as he used to,
then spun around and galloped down the starlit beach, three
paws scattering the little cat's-paw waves. When he was a

hundred strides off he turned and looked back at me, as though he wished me to follow.

I took a few steps toward him, but Master Malrubius said, "You cannot go where he is going, Severian. I know you think us cacogens of a kind, and for a time I felt it would not be wise to wholly undeceive you, but I must do so now. We are aquastors, beings created and sustained by the power of the imagination and the concentration of thought."

"I have heard of such things," I told him. "But I have touched you."

"That is no test. We are as solid as most truly false things are—a dance of particles in space. Only the things no one can touch are true, as you should know by now. Once you met a woman named Cyriaca, who told you tales of the great thinking machines of the past. There is such a machine on the ship in which we sailed. It has the power to look into your mind."

I asked, "Are you that machine, then?" A feeling of loneliness and vague fear grew in me.

"I am Master Malrubius, and Triskele is Triskele. The machine looked among your memories and found us. Our lives in your mind are not so complete as those of Thecla and the old Autarch, but we are there nevertheless, and live while you live. But we are maintained in the physical world by the energies of the machine, and its range is but a few thousand years."

As he spoke these final words, his flesh was already fading into bright dust. For a moment it glinted in the cold starlight. Then it was gone. Triskele remained with me a few breaths longer, and when his yellow coat was already silvered and blowing away in the gentle breeze, I heard his bark.

Then I stood alone at the edge of the sea I had longed for so often; but though I was alone, I found it cheering, and breathed the air that is like no other, and smiled to hear the soft song of the little waves. Land—Nessus, the House Absolute, and all the rest—lay to the east; west lay the sea; I walked north because I was reluctant to leave it too soon, and because Triskele had run in that direction, along the margin of the sea. There great Abaia might wallow with his women, yet the sea was older far, and wiser than he; we human beings, like all the life of the land, had come from the sea; and because we could not conquer it, it was ours always. The old, red sun rose on my right and touched the waves with his fading beauty, and I heard the calling of the sea birds, the innumerable birds.

By the time the shadows were short, I was tired. My face and my wounded leg pained me; I had not eaten since noon of the previous day and had not slept save for my trance in the Ascian tent. I would have rested if I could, but the sun was warm, and the line of cliffs beyond the beach offered no shade. At last I followed the tracks of a two-wheeled cart and came to a clump of wild roses growing from a dune. There I halted, and seated myself in their shadow to take off my boots and pour out the sand that had entered their splitting seams.

A thorn caught my forearm and broke from its branch, remaining embedded in my skin, with a scarlet drop of blood, no bigger than a grain of millet, at its tip. I plucked it out—then fell to my knees.

It was the Claw.

The Claw perfect, shining black, just as I had placed it under the altar stone of the Pelerines. All that bush and all the other bushes growing with it were covered with white blossoms and these perfect Claws. The one in my palm flamed with transplendent light as I looked at it.

I had surrendered the Claw, but I had retained the little leather sack Dorcas had sewn for it. I took it from my sabretache and hung it about my neck in the old way, with the Claw once more inside. It was only when I had thus put it away that I recalled seeing just such a bush in the Botanic Gardens at the beginning of my journey.

• • •

No one can explain such things. Since I have come to the House Absolute, I have talked with the heptarch and with various acaryas; but they have been able to tell me very little save that the Increate has chosen before this to manifest himself in these plants.

At that time I did not think of it, being filled with wonder—but may it not be that we were guided to the unfinished Sand Garden? I carried the Claw even then, though I did not know it; Agia had already slipped it under the closure of my sabretache. Might it not be that we came to the unfinished garden so that the Claw, flying as it were against the wind of Time, might make its farewell? The idea is absurd. But then, all ideas are absurd.

What struck me on the beach—and it struck me indeed, so that I staggered as at a blow—was that if the Eternal Principle had rested in that curved thorn I had carried about my neck across so many leagues, and if it now rested in the new thorn (perhaps the same thorn) I had only now put there, then it might rest in anything, and in fact probably did rest in everything, in every thorn on every bush, in every drop of water in the sea. The thorn was a sacred Claw because all thorns were sacred Claws; the sand in my boots was sacred sand because it came from a beach of sacred sand. The cenobites treasured up the relics of the sannyasins because the sannyasins had approached the Pancreator. But everything had approached and even touched the Pancreator, because everything had dropped from his hand. Everything was a relic. All the world was a relic. I drew off my boots, that had traveled with me so far, and threw them into the waves that I might not walk shod on holy ground.

XXXII

The *Samru*

AND I WALKED ON as a mighty army, for I felt myself in the company of all those who walked in me. I was surrounded by a numerous guard; and I was the guard about the person of the monarch. There were women in my ranks, smiling and grim, and children who ran and laughed and, daring Erebus and Abaia, hurled seashells into the sea.

In half a day I came to the mouth of Gyoll, so wide that the farther shore was lost in distance. Three-sided isles lay in it, and through them vessels with billowing sails picked their way like clouds among the peaks of the mountains. I hailed one passing the point on which I stood and asked for passage to Nessus. A wild figure I must have appeared, with my scarred face and tattered cloak and every rib showing.

Her captain sent a boat for me nonetheless, a kindness I have not forgotten. I saw fear and awe in the eyes of the rowers. Perhaps it was only at the sight of my half-healed wounds; but they were men who had seen many wounds, and I recalled how I had felt when I first saw the face of the Autarch in the House Azure, though he was not a tall man, or even a man, truly.

· · ·

Twenty days and nights the *Samru* made her way up
Gyoll. We sailed when we could, and rowed, a dozen sweeps
to a side, when we could not. It was a hard passage for the
sailors, for though the current is almost imperceptibly slow, it
runs day and night, and so long and so wide are the meanders
of the channel that an oarsman often sees at evening the spot
from which he labored when the beating of the drum first
roused the watch.

For me it was as pleasant as a yachting expedition. Although I offered to make sail and row with the rest, they
would not permit it. Then I told the captain, a sly-faced man
who looked as though he lived by bargaining as much as by
sailing, that I would pay him well when we reached Nessus;
but he would not hear of it, and insisted (pulling at his mustache, which he did whenever he wished to show the greatest
sincerity) that my presence was reward enough for him and
his crew. I do not believe they guessed I was their Autarch,
and for fear of such as Vodalus had been I was careful to
drop no hints to them; but from my eyes and manner they
seemed to feel I was an adept.

The incident of the captain's sword must have strength-
ened their superstition. It was a craquemarte, the heaviest of
the sea swords, with a blade as wide as my palm, sharply
curved and graven with stars and suns and other things the
captain did not understand. He wore it when we were close
enough to a riverbank village or another ship to make him
feel the occasion demanded dignity; but for the most part he
left it lying on the little quarterdeck. I found it there, and
having nothing else to do but watch sticks and fruit skins bob
in the green water, I took out my half stone and sharpened it.
After a time he saw me testing the edge with my thumb and
began to boast of his swordsmanship. Since the craquemarte
was at least two-thirds the weight of *Terminus Est,* with a
short grip, it was amusing to hear him; I listened with delight
for half a watch or so. As it happened there was a hempen
cable about the thickness of my wrist coiled nearby, and

when he began to lose interest in his own inventions, I had
him and the mate hold up three cubits or so between them.
The craquemarte severed it like a hair; then before either of
them could recover breath, I threw it flashing toward the sun
and caught it by the hilt.

As I fear that incident shows too well, I was beginning to
feel better. There is nothing to enthrall the reader in rest,
fresh air, and plain food; but they can work wonders against
wounds and exhaustion.

The captain would have given me his cabin if I had let
him, but I slept on deck rolled in my cloak, and on our one
night of rain found shelter under the boat, which was stowed
bottom-up amidships. As I learned on board, it is the nature
of breezes to die when Urth turns her back to the sun; so I
went to sleep, on most nights, with the chant of the rowers in
my ears. In the morning I woke to the rattle of the anchor
chain.

Sometimes, though, I woke before morning, when we lay
close to shore with only a sleepy lookout on deck. And sometimes the moonlight roused me to find us gliding forward
under reefed sails, with the mate steering and the watch
asleep beside the halyards. On one such night, shortly after
we had passed through the Wall, I went aft and saw the
phosphorescence of our wake like cold fire on the dark water
and thought for a moment that the man-apes of the mine
were coming to be cured by the Claw, or to gain an old
revenge. That, of course, was not truly strange—only the
foolish error of a mind still half in dream. What happened
the next morning was not truly strange either, but it affected
me deeply.

The oarsmen were rowing a slow beat to get us around a
leagues-long bend to a point where we could catch what little
wind there was. The sound of the drum and the hissing of
the water falling from the long blades of the sweeps are hyp-
notic, I think because they are so similar to the beating of

one's own heart in sleep and the sound the blood makes as it moves past the inner ear on its way to the brain.

I was standing by the rail looking at the shore, still marshy here where the plains of old have been flooded by silt-choked Gyoll; and it seemed to me that I saw forms in the hillocks and hummocks, as though all that vast, soft wilderness had a geometrical soul (as certain pictures do) that vanished when I stared at it, then reappeared when I took my eyes away. The captain came to stand beside me, and I told him I had heard that the ruins of the city extended far downriver and asked when we would sight them. He laughed and explained that we had been among them for the past two days, and loaned me his glass so I could see that what I had taken for a stump was in actuality a broken and tilted column covered with moss.

At once everything—walls, streets, monuments—seemed to spring from hiding, just as the stone town had reconstructed itself while we watched from the tomb roof with the two witches. No change had occurred outside my own mind, but I had been transported, far faster than Master Malrubius's ship could have taken me, from the desolate countryside to the midst of an ancient and immense ruin.

Even now I cannot help but wonder how much any of us see of what is before us. For weeks my friend Jonas had seemed to me only a man with a prosthetic hand, and when I was with Baldanders and Dr. Talos, I had overlooked a hundred clues that should have told me Baldanders was master. How impressed I was outside the Piteous Gate because Baldanders did not escape the doctor when he could.

As the day wore on, the ruins became plainer and plainer still. At each loop of the river, the green walls rose higher, from ever firmer ground. When I woke the next morning, some of the stronger buildings retained their upper stories.

Not long afterward, I saw a little boat, newly built, tied to an ancient pier. I pointed it out to the captain, who smiled at my naivety and said, "There are families who live, grandson following grandsire, by sifting these ruins."

"So I've been told, but that cannot be one of their boats. It's too small to take much loot away in."

"Jewelry or coins. No one else goes ashore here. There's no law—the pillagers murder each other, and anyone else who lands."

"I must go there. Will you wait for me?"

He stared at me as though I were mad. "How long?"

"Until noon. No later."

"Look," he said, and pointed. "Ahead is the last big bend. Leave us here and meet us there, where the channel bows around again. It will be afternoon before we get there."

I agreed, and he had the *Samru*'s boat put into the water for me, and told four men to row me ashore. As we were about to cast off, he unbelted his craquemarte and handed it to me, saying solemnly, "It has stood by me in many a grim fight. Go for their heads, but be careful not to knick the edge on their belt buckles."

I accepted his sword with thanks, and told him I had always favored the neck. "That's good," he said, "if you don't have shipmates by that might be hurt when you swing it flat," and he pulled his mustache.

Sitting in the stern, I had ample opportunity to observe the faces of my rowers, and it was plain they were nearly as frightened of the shore as they were of me. They laid us alongside the small boat, then nearly capsized their own in their haste to be away. After determining that what I had seen from the rail was in fact what I had taken it to be, a wilted scarlet poppy left lying on the single seat, I watched them row back to the *Samru* and saw that though a light wind now favored the billowing mains'l, the sweeps had been brought out and were beating a quick-stroke. Presumably the captain planned to round the long meander as swiftly as he could; if I were not at the spot he had pointed out, he could proceed without me, telling himself (and others, should others inquire) that it was I who had failed our appointment and not he. By parting with the craquemarte he had further salved his conscience.

Stone steps very like those I had swum from as a boy had been cut into the sides of the pier. Its top was empty, nearly as lush as a lawn with the grass that had rooted between its stones. The ruined city, my own city of Nessus though it was the Nessus of a time now long past, lay quiet before me. A few birds wheeled overhead, but they were as silent as the sun-dimmed stars. Gyoll, whispering to itself in midstream, already seemed detached from me and the empty hulks of buildings among which I limped. As soon as I was out of sight of its waters, it fell silent, like some uncertain visitor who ceases to speak when we step into another room.

It seemed that this could hardly be the quarter from which (as Dorcas had told me) furniture and utensils were taken. At first I looked in often at doors and windows, but nothing had been left within but wrack and a few yellow leaves, drifted already from the young trees that were overturning the paving blocks. Nor did I see any sign of human pillagers, although there were animal droppings and a few feathers and scattered bones.

I do not know how far inland I walked. It seemed a league, though it may have been much less. Losing the transportation of the *Samru* did not much bother me. I had walked from Nessus most of the way to the mountain war, and although my steps were uneven still, my bare feet had been toughened on the deck. Because I had never really become accustomed to carrying a sword at my waist, I drew the craquemarte and put it on my shoulder, as I had often borne *Terminus Est*. The summer sunshine held that special, luxurious warmth it gains when a suggestion of chill has crept into the morning air. I enjoyed it, and would have enjoyed it more, and the silence and solitude too, if I had not been thinking of what I would say to Dorcas, if I found her, and what she might say to me.

Had I only known, I might have saved myself that concern; I came upon her sooner than I could reasonably have expected, and I did not speak to her—nor did she speak to me, or so far as I could judge, even see me.

The buildings, which had been large and solid near the river, had long since given way to lesser, fallen-in structures that must once have been houses and shops. I do not know what guided me to hers. There was no sound of weeping, though there may have been some small, unconscious noise, the creaking of a hinge or the scrape of a shoe. Perhaps it was no more than the perfume of the blossom she wore, because when I saw her she had an arum, freckled white and sweet as Dorcas herself had always been, thrust into her hair. No doubt she had brought it there for that purpose, and had taken out the wilted poppy and cast it down when she had tied up her boat. (But I have gotten ahead of my story.)

I tried to enter the building from the front, but the rotting floor was falling into the foundation in places as the arches under it collapsed. The storeroom at the rear was less open; the silent, shadowed walk, green with ferns, had been a dangerous alley once, and shopkeepers had put small windows there or none. Still, I found a narrow door hidden under ivy, a door whose iron had been eaten like sugar by the rain, whose oak was falling into mould. Stairs nearly sound led to the floor above.

She was kneeling with her back to me. She had always been slender; now her shoulders made me think of a wooden chair with a woman's jupe hung over it. Her hair, like the palest gold, was the same—unchanged since I had seen her first in the Garden of Endless Sleep. The body of the old man who had poled the skiff there lay on a bier before her, his back so straight, his face, in death, so youthful, that I hardly knew him. On the floor near her was a basket—not small yet not large either, and a corked water jar.

I said nothing, and when I had watched her for a time I went away. If she had been there long, I would have called to her and embraced her. But she had just arrived, and I saw that it was impossible. All the time I had spent in journeying from Thrax to Lake Diuturna, and from the lake to the war, and all the time I had spent as a prisoner of Vodalus, and in sailing up Gyoll, she had spent in returning here to her place, where she had lived forty years ago or more though it had now fallen into decay.

As I had myself, an ancient buzzing with antiquity as a corpse with flies. Not that the minds of Thecla and the old Autarch, or the hundred contained in his, had made me old. It was not their memories but my own that aged me, as I thought of Dorcas shivering beside me on the brown track of floating sedge, both of us cold and dripping, drinking together from Hildegrin's flask like two infants, which in fact we had been.

I paid no heed to where I walked after that. I went straight down a long street alive with silence, and when it ended at last I turned at random. After a time I reached Gyoll, and looking downstream saw the *Samru* riding at anchor at the meeting place. A basilosaur swimming up from the open sea would not have astounded me more.

In a few moments I was mobbed by smiling sailors. The captain wrung my hand, saying, "I was afraid we'd come too late. In my mind's eye I could see you struggling for your life in sight of the river, and us still half a league off."

The mate, a man so abysmally stupid that he thought the captain a leader, clapped me on the back and shouted, "He'd have given 'em a good fight!"

XXXIII

The Citadel of the Autarch

THOUGH EVERY LEAGUE that separated me from Dorcas tore my heart, it was better than I can tell you to be back on the *Samru* again after seeing the empty, silent south.

Her decks were of the impure but lovely white of new-cut wood, scrubbed daily with a great mat called a *bear*—a sort of scouring pad woven from old cordage and weighed with the gross bodies of our two cooks, whom the crew had to drag over the last span of planking before breakfast. The crevices between the planks were sealed with pitch, so that the decks seemed terraces paved in a bold, fantastic design.

She was high in the bow, with a stem that curled back upon her. Eyes, each with a pupil as big as a plate and a sky-blue iris of the brightest obtainable paint, stared out across the green waters to help find her way; her left eye wept the anchor.

Forward of her stem, held there by a triangular wooden brace itself carved, pierced, gilded, and painted, was her figurehead, the bird of immortality. Its head was a woman's, the face long and aristocratic, the eyes tiny and black, its expressionlessness a magnificent commentary on the somber tranquillity of those who will never know death. Painted wooden feathers grew from its wooden scalp to clothe its shoulders and cup its hemispherical breasts; its arms were wings lifted up and back, their tips reaching higher than the termination of the stem and their gold and crimson primary feathers partially obscuring the triangular brace. I would have thought it a creature wholly fabulous—as no doubt the sailors did—had I not seen the Autarch's anpiels.

A long bowsprit passed to starboard of the stem, between the wings of the samru. The foremast, only slightly longer than this bowsprit, rose from the forecastle. It was raked forward to give the foresail room, as though it had been pulled out of true by the forestay and the laboring jib. The mainmast stood as straight as the pine it had once been, but the mizzenmast was raked back, so the mastheads of the three masts were considerably more separated than their bases. Each mast held a slanting yard made by lashing together two tapering spars that had once been entire saplings, and each of these yards carried a single, triangular, rust-colored sail.

The hull itself was painted white below the water and black above it, save for the figurehead and eyes I have already mentioned, and the quarterdeck rail, where scarlet had been used to symbolize both the captain's high state and his sanguinary background. This quarterdeck actually occupied no more than a sixth of the *Samru*'s length, but the wheel and the binnacle were there, and it was there that one had the finest view, short of that provided by the rigging. The ship's only real armament, a swivel gun not much larger than Mamillian's, was there, ready alike for freebooters and mutineers. Just aft of the sternrail, two iron posts as delicately curved as the horns of a cricket lifted many-faceted lanterns, one of palest red, the other viridescent as moonlight.

I was standing by these lanterns the next evening, listening to the thudding of the drum, the soft splashing of the sweep-blades, and the rowers' chant, when I saw the first lights

along the riverbank. Here was the dying edge of the city, the
home of the poorest of the poorest of the poor—which only
meant that the living edge of the city was here, that death's
dominion ended here. Human beings were preparing to sleep
here, perhaps still sharing the meal that marked the day's
end. I saw a thousand kindnesses in each of those lights, and
heard a thousand fireside stories. In some sense I was home
again; and the same song that had urged me forth in the
spring now bore me back:

> Row, brothers, row!
> The current is against us.
> Row, brothers, row!
> Yet God is for us.
> Row, brothers, row!
> The wind is against us.
> Row, brothers, row!
> Yet God is for us.

I could not help but wonder who was setting out that night.

Every long story, if it be told truly, will be found to contain all the elements that have contributed to the human
drama since the first rude ship reached the strand of Lune:
not only noble deeds and tender emotion, but grotesquerie,
bathos, and so on. I have striven to set down the unem-
bellished truth here, without the least worry that you, my
reader, would find some parts improbable and others insipid;
and if the mountain war was the scene of high deeds (belonging more to others than to me), and my imprisonment by
Vodalus and the Ascians a time of horror, and my passage on
the *Samru* an interlude of tranquillity, then we are come to
the interval of comedy.

We approached that part of the city where the Citadel
stands—which is southern but not the southernmost—under
sail and by day. I watched the sun-gilt eastern bank with

great care, and had the captain land me on those slimy steps where I had once swum and fought. I hoped to pass through the necropolis gate and so enter the Citadel through the breach in the curtain wall that was near the Matachin Tower; but the gate was closed and locked, and no convenient party of volunteers arrived to admit me. Thus I was forced instead to walk many chains along the margin of the necropolis, and several more along the curtain wall to the barbican.

There I encountered a numerous guard who carried me before their officer, who, when I told him I was a torturer, supposed me to be one of those wretches that, most often at the onset of winter, seek to gain admission to the guild. He decided (very properly, had he been correct) to have me whipped; and to prevent it I was forced to break the thumbs of two of his men, and then demand while I held him in the way called the *kitten and ball* that he take me to his superior, the castellan.

I admit I was somewhat awed at the thought of this official, whom I had seldom so much as seen in all the years I had been an apprentice in the fortress he commanded. I found him an old soldier, silver-haired and as lame as I. The officer stammered out his accusations while I stood by: I had assaulted and insulted (not true) his person, maimed two of his men, and so on. When he had finished, the castellan looked from me to him and back again, dismissed him, and offered me a seat.

"You are unarmed," he said. His voice was hoarse but soft, as though he had strained it shouting commands.

I admitted that I was.

"But you have seen fighting, and you have been in the jungle north of the mountains, where no battle has been since they turned our flank by crossing the Uroboros."

"That's true," I said. "But how can you know?"

"That wound in your thigh came from one of their spears. I've seen enough to recognize them. The beam flashed up through the muscle, reflected by the bone. You might have been up a tree and been stuck by a hastarus on the ground, I suppose, but the most likely thing is that you were mounted and charging infantry. Not a cataphract, or they wouldn't have got you so easily. The demilances?"

"Only the light irregulars."

"You'll have to tell me about that later, because you're a city man from your accent, and they're eclectics and suchlike for the most part. You have a double scar on your foot too, white and clean, with the marks half a span apart. That was a blood bat's bite, and they don't come that large except in the true jungle at the waist of the world. How did you get there?"

"Our flier crashed. I was taken prisoner."

"And escaped?"

In a moment more I would have been forced to talk of Agia and the green man, and of my journey from the jungle to the mouth of Gyoll, and those were high matters which I did not wish to disclose thus casually. Instead of an answer, I pronounced the words of authority applicable to the Citadel and its castellan.

Because he was lame, I would have had him remain seated if I could; but he sprang to his feet and saluted, then dropped to his knees to kiss my hand. He was thus, though he could not have known it, the first to pay me homage, a distinction that entitles him to a private audience once a year—an audience he has not yet requested and perhaps never will.

For me to proceed now, clothed as I was, was impossible. The old castellan would have died of a stroke had I demanded it, and he was so concerned for my safety that any incognito would have been accompanied by at least a platoon of lurking halberdiers. I soon found myself arrayed in lapis lazuli jazerant, cothurni, and a stephane, the whole set off by an ebony baculus and a voluminous damassin cape embroidered with rotting pearls. All these things were indescribably ancient, having been taken from a store preserved from the period when the Citadel was the residence of the autarchs.

Thus in place of entering our tower, as I had intended, in the same cloak in which I had left it, I returned as an unrecognizable being in ceremonial fancy dress, skeletally thin, lame, and hideously scarred. It was with this appearance that I entered Master Palaemon's study, and I am certain I must almost have frightened him to death, since he had been told only a few moments before that the Autarch was in the Citadel and wished to converse with him.

He seemed to me to have aged a great deal while I was gone. Perhaps it was simply that I recalled him not as he was when I was exiled, but as I had seen him in our little classroom when I was a boy. Still, I like to think he was concerned for me, and it is not really so unlikely that he was: I had always been his best pupil and his favorite; it was his vote, beyond doubt, that had countered Master Gurloes's and saved my life; he had given me his sword.

But whether he had worried much or little, his face seemed more deeply lined than it had been; and his scant hair, which I had thought gray, was now of that yellow hue seen in old ivory. He knelt and kissed my fingers, and was more than a little surprised when I helped him to rise and told him to seat himself behind his table again.

"You are too kind, Autarch," he said. Then, using an old formula, "Your mercy extends from sun to Sun."

"Do you not recall us?"

"Were you confined here?" He peered at me through the curious arrangement of lenses that alone permitted him to see at all, and I decided that his vision, exhausted long before I was born on the faded ink of the records of the guild, must have deteriorated further. "You have suffered torment, I see. But it is too crude, I hope, for our work."

"It was not your doing," I said, touching the scars on my cheek. "Nevertheless, we were confined for a time in the oubliette beneath this tower."

He sighed—an old man's shallow breath—and looked down at the gray litter of his papers. When he spoke I could not hear the words, and had to ask him to repeat them.

"It has come," he said. "I knew it would, but I hoped to be dead and forgotten. Will you dismiss us, Autarch? Or put us to some other task?"

"We have not yet decided what we will do with you and the guild you serve."

"It will not avail. If I offend you, Autarch, I ask your indulgence for my age . . . but still it will not avail. You will find in the end that you require men to do what we do. You may call it healing, if you wish. That has been done often. Or ritual, that has been done too. But you will find the thing itself grows more terrible in its disguise. Will you imprison those undeserving of death? You will find them a mighty army in chains. You will discover that you hold prisoners whose escape would be a catastrophe, and that you need servants who will wreak justice on those who have caused scores to die in agony. Who else will do that?"

"No one will wreak such justice as you. You say our mercy extends from sun to Sun, and we hope it is so. By our mercy we will grant even the foulest a quick death. Not because we pity them, but because it is intolerable that good men should spend a lifetime dispensing pain."

His head came up and the lenses flashed. For the only time in all the years I had known him, I was able to see the youth he had been. "It must be done by good men. You are badly advised, Autarch! What is intolerable is that it should be done by bad men."

I smiled. His face, as I had seen it then, had recalled something I had thrust from my mind months before. It was that this guild was my family, and all the home I should ever have. I would never find a friend in the world if I could not find friends here. "Between us, Master," I told him, "we have decided it should not be done at all."

He did not reply, and I saw from his expression that he had not even heard what I had said. He had been listening instead to my voice, and doubt and joy flickered over his worn, old face like shadow and firelight.

"Yes," I said. "It is Severian," and while he was struggling to regain possession of himself, I went to the door and got my sabretache, which I had ordered one of the officers of my guard to bring. I had wrapped it in what had been my fuligin guild cloak, now faded to mere rusty black. Spreading the cloak over Master Palaemon's table, I opened the sabretache and poured out its contents. "This is all we have brought back," I said.

He smiled as he used to in the schoolroom when he had caught me out in some minor matter. "That and the throne? Will you tell me about it?"

And so I did. It took a long while, and more than once my protectors rapped at the door to ascertain that I was unharmed, and at last I had a meal brought in to us; and when the pheasant was mere bones and the cakes were eaten and the wine drunk, we were still talking. It was then that I conceived the idea that has at last borne fruit in this record of my life. I had originally intended to begin it at the day I left our tower and to end it when I returned. But I soon saw that though such a construction would indeed supply the symmetry so valued by artists, it would be impossible for anyone to understand my adventures without knowing something of my adolescence. In the same way, some elements of my story would remain incomplete if I did not extend it (as I propose to do) a few days beyond my return. Perhaps I have contrived for someone *The Book of Gold.* Indeed, it may be that all my wanderings have been no more than a contrivance of the librarians to recruit their numbers; but perhaps even that is too much to hope.

XXXIV

The Key to the Universe

WHEN HE HAD HEARD everything, Master Palaemon went to my little heap of possessions and took up the grip, pommel, and silver guard that were all that remained of *Terminus Est*. "She was a good sword," he said. "Nearly I gave you your death, but she was a good sword."

"We were always proud to bear her, and never found reason to complain of her."

He sighed, and the breath seemed to catch in his throat. "She is gone. It is the blade that is the sword, not the sword furniture. The guild will preserve these somewhere, with your cloak and sabretache, because they have belonged to you. When you and I have been dead for centuries, old men like me will point them out to the apprentices. It's a pity we haven't the blade too. I used her for many years before you came to the guild, and never thought she would be destroyed fighting some diabolical weapon." He put down the opal pommel and frowned at me. "What's troubling you? I've seen men wince less when their eyes were torn out."

"There are many kinds of diabolical weapons, as you call them, that steel cannot withstand. We saw something of them when we were in Orithyia. And there are tens of thousands of our soldiers there holding them off with firework lances and javelins, and swords less well forged than *Terminus Est*. They succeed in so far as they do because the energy weapons of the Ascians are not numerous, and they are few because the Ascians lack the sources of power needed to produce them. What will happen if Urth is granted a New Sun? Won't the Ascians be better able to use its energy than we can?"

"Perhaps that may be," Master Palaemon acknowledged.

"We have been thinking with the autarchs who have gone before us—our guild brothers, as it were, in a new guild. Master Malrubius said that only our predecessor has dared the test in modern times. When we touch the minds of the others, we often find that they have refused it because they felt our enemies, who have retained so much more of the ancient sciences, would gain a greater advantage. Is it not possible they were right?"

Master Palaemon thought a long time before he answered. "I cannot say. You believe me wise because I taught you once, but I have not been north, as you have. You have seen armies of Ascians, and I have never seen one. You flatter me by asking my opinion. Still—from all you've said, they are rigid, cast hard in their ways. I would guess that very few among them think much."

I shrugged. "That is true in any aggregate, Master. But as you say, it is possibly more true among them. And what you call their rigidity is terrible—a deadness that surpasses belief. Individually they seem men and women, but together they are like a machine of wood and stone."

Master Palaemon rose and went to the port and looked out upon the thronging towers. "We are too rigid here," he said. "Too rigid in our guild, too rigid in the Citadel. It tells me a great deal that you, who were educated here, saw them as you did; they must be inflexible indeed. I think it may be that despite their science, which may amount to less than you suppose, the people of the Commonwealth will be better able to turn new circumstances to their benefit."

"We are not flexible or inflexible," I said. "Except for an unusually good memory, we are only an ordinary man."

"No, no!" Master Palaemon struck his table, and again the lenses flashed. "You are an extraordinary man in an ordinary time. When you were a little apprentice, I beat you once or twice—you will recall that, I know. But even when I beat you, I knew you would become an extraordinary personage, the greatest master our guild would ever have. And you will be a master. Even if you destroy our guild, we will elect you!"

"We have already told you we mean to reform the guild, not destroy it. We're not even sure we're competent to do that. You respect us because we've moved to the highest place. But we reached it by chance, and know it. Our predecessor reached it by chance too, and the minds he brought to us, which we touch only faintly even now, are not, with one or two exceptions, those of genius. Most are only common men and women, sailors and artisans, farmwives and wantons. Most of the rest are eccentric second-rate scholars of the sort Thecla used to laugh at."

"You have not just moved into the highest place," Master Palaemon said, "you have become it. You are the state."

"We are not. The state is everyone else—you, the castellan, those officers outside. We are the people, the Commonwealth." I had not known it myself until I spoke.

I picked up the brown book. "We are going to keep this. It was one of the good things, like your sword. The writing of books shall be encouraged again. There are no pockets in these clothes; but perhaps it will do good if we are seen to carry it when we leave."

"Carry it where?" Master Palaemon cocked his head like an old raven.

"To the House Absolute. We've been out of touch, or the Autarch has, if you wish to put it so, for over a month. We have to find out what's happening at the front, and perhaps dispatch reinforcements." I thought of Lomer and Nicarete, and the other prisoners in the antechamber. "We have other tasks there too," I said.

Master Palaemon stroked his chin. "Before you go, Severian—Autarch—would you like to tour the cells, for old times' sake? I doubt those fellows out there know of the door that opens to the western stair."

It is the least-used staircase in the tower, and perhaps the oldest. Certainly it is the one least altered from its original condition. The steps are narrow and steep, and wind down around a central column black with corrosion. The door to the room where I, as Thecla, had been subjected to the device called the Revolutionary stood half open, so that though we did not go inside, I nevertheless saw its ancient mechanisms: frightful, yet less hideous to me than the gleaming but far older things in Baldanders's castle.

Entering the oubliette meant returning to something I had, from the time I left for Thrax, assumed gone forever. Yet the metal corridors with their long rows of doors were unchanged, and when I peered through the tiny windows that pierced those doors I saw familiar faces, the faces of men and women I had fed and guarded as a journeyman.

"You are pale, Autarch," Master Palaemon said. "I feel your hand tremble." (I was supporting him a little with one hand on his arm.)

"You know that our memories never fade," I said. "For us the Chatelaine Thecla still sits in one of these cells, and the Journeyman Severian in another."

"I had forgotten. Yes, it must be terrible for you. I was going to take you to the Chatelaine's old one, but perhaps you would rather not see it."

I insisted that we visit it; but when we arrived, there was a new client inside, and the door was locked. I had Master Palaemon call the brother on duty to let us in, then stood for a moment looking at the cramped bed and the tiny table. At last I noticed the client, who sat upon the single chair, with wide eyes and an indescribable expression blended of hope and wonder. I asked him if he knew me.

"No, exultant."

"We are no exultant. We are your Autarch. Why are you here?"

He rose, then fell to his knees. "I am innocent! Believe me!"

"All right," I said. "We believe you. But we want you to tell us what you were accused of, and how you came to be convicted."

Shrilly, he began to pour forth one of the most complex and confused accounts I have ever heard. His sister-in-law had conspired with her mother against him. They said he had struck his wife, that he had neglected his ill wife, that he had stolen certain moneys from her that she had been entrusted with by her father, for purposes about which they disagreed. In explaining all this (and much more) he boasted of his own cleverness while decrying the frauds, tricks, and lies of the others that had sent him to the oubliette. He said that the gold in question had never existed, and also that his mother-in-law had used a part of it to bribe the judge. He said he had not known his wife was ill, and that he had procured the best physician he could afford for her.

When I left him, I went to the next call and heard the client there, and then to the next and the next, until I had visited fourteen. Eleven clients protested their innocence, some better than the first, some even worse; but I found none whose protestations convinced me. Three admitted that they were guilty (though one swore, I think sincerely, that though he had committed most of the crimes with which he had been charged, he had also been charged with several he had not committed). Two of these promised earnestly to do nothing that would return them to the oubliette if only I would release them; which I did. The third—a woman who had stolen children and forced them to serve as articles of furniture in a room she had set aside for the purpose, in one instance nailing the hands of a little girl to the underside of a small tabletop so that she became in effect its pedestal—told me with apparently equal frankness that she felt sure she would return to what she called her sport because it was the only activity that really interested her. She did not ask to be released, only to have her sentence commuted to simple imprisonment. I felt certain she was mad; yet nothing in her conversation or her clear blue eyes indicated it, and she told me she had been examined prior to her trial and pronounced sane. I touched her forehead with the New Claw, but it was as inert as the old Claw had been when I had attempted to use it to help Jolenta and Baldanders.

I cannot escape the thought that the power manifested in both Claws is drawn from myself, and that it is for this reason that their radiance, said by others to be warm, has always seemed cold to me. This thought is the psychological equivalent of that aching abyss in the sky into which I feared to fall when I slept in the mountains. I reject and fear it because I desire so fervently that it be true; and I feel that if there were the least echo of truth in it, I would detect it within myself. I do not.

Furthermore, there are profound objections to it besides this lack of internal resonance, the most important, convincing, and apparently inescapable being that the Claw unquestionably reanimated Dorcas after many decades of death—and did so before I knew I carried it.

That argument appears conclusive; and still I am not sure that it is so. Did I in fact know? What is meant by *know*, in an appropriate sense? I have assumed I was unconscious when Agia slipped the Claw into my sabretache; but I may have been merely dazed, and in any case, many have long believed that unconscious persons are aware of their surroundings and respond internally to speech and music. How else explain the dreams dictated by external sounds? What portion of the brain is unconscious, after all? Not the whole of it, or the heart would not beat and the lungs no longer breathe. Much of the memory is chemical. All that, in fact, I have from Thecla and the former Autarch is fundamentally so—the drugs serving only to permit the complex compounds of thought to enter my own brain as information. May it not be that certain information derived from external phenomena are chemically impressed on our brains even when the electrical activity on which we depend for conscious thought has temporarily ceased?

Besides, if the energy has its origins in me, why should it have been necessary for me to be aware of the presence of the Claw for them to operate, any more than it would be necessary if they had their origin in the Claw itself? A strong suggestion of another kind might be equally effective, and certainly our careening invasion of the sacred precincts of the Pelerines and the way in which Agia and I emerged unhurt from the accident that killed the animals might have furnished such a suggestion. From the cathedral we had gone to the Botanic Gardens, and there, before we entered the Garden of Endless Sleep, I had seen a bush covered with Claws. At that time I believed the Claw to be a gem, but may not they have suggested it nonetheless? Our minds often play such punning tricks. In the yellow house we had met three persons who believed us supernatural presences.

If the supernatural power is mine (and yet clearly it is not mine), how did I come to have it? I have devised two explanations, both wildly improbable. Dorcas and I talked once of the symbolic significance of real-world things, which by the teachings of the philosophers stand for things higher than themselves, and in a lower order are themselves symbolized. To take an absurdly simple example, suppose an artist in a garret limning a peach. If we put the poor artist in the place of the Increate, we may say that his picture symbolizes the peach, and thus the fruits of the soil, while the glowing curve of the peach itself symbolizes the ripe beauty of womanhood. Were such a woman to enter the artist's garret (an improbability we must entertain for the sake of the explanation), she would doubtless remain unaware that the fullness of her hip and the hardness of her heart found their echoes in a basket on the table by the window, though perhaps the artist might be able to think of nothing else.

But if the Increate is in actual fact in place of the artist, is it not possible that such connections as these, many of which must always be unguessable by human beings, may have profound effects on the structure of the world, just as the artist's obsession may color his picture? If I am he who is to renew the youth of the sun with the White Fountain of which I have been told, may it not be that I have been given, almost unconsciously (if that expression may be used), the attributes of life and light that will belong to the renewed sun?

The other explanation I mentioned is hardly more than a speculation. But if, as Master Malrubius told me, those who will judge me among the stars will take my manhood should I fail their judgment, is it not possible also that they will confirm me in some gift of equal worth should I, as Humanity's representative, conform to their desires? It seems to me that justice demands it. If that is the case, may it not be that their gift transcends time, as they do themselves? The Hierodules I met in Baldanders's castle said they interested themselves in me because I would gain the throne—but would their interest have been so great if I were to be no more than the embattled ruler of some part of this continent, one of many embattled rulers in the long history of Urth?

On the whole, I think the first explanation the most probable; but the second is not wholly unlikely. Either would seem to indicate that the mission I am about to set out on will succeed. I will go with good heart.

And yet there is a third explanation. No human being or near-human being can conceive of such minds as those of Abaia, Erebus, and the rest. Their power surpasses understanding, and I know now that they could crush us in a day if it were not that they count only enslavement, and not annihilation, as victory. The great undine I saw was their creature, and less than their slave: their toy. It is possible that the power of the Claw, the Claw taken from a growing thing so near their sea, comes ultimately from them. They knew my destiny as well as Ossipago, Barbatus, and Famulimus, and they saved me when I was a boy so that I might fulfill it. After I departed from the Citadel they found me again, and thereafter my course was twisted by the Claw. Perhaps they hope to triumph by raising a torturer to the Autarchy, or to that position that is higher than the Autarch's.

Now I think that it is time to record what Master Malrubius explained to me. I cannot vouch for its truth, but I believe it to be true. I know no more than I set down here.

Just as a flower blooms, throws down its seed, dies, and rises from its seed to bloom again, so the universe we know diffuses itself to nullity in the infinitude of space, gathers its fragments (which because of the curvature of that space meet at last where they began) and from that seed blooms again. Each such cycle of flowering and decay marks a divine year.

As the flower that comes is like the flower from which it came, so the universe that comes repeats the one whose ruin was its origin; and this is as true of its finer features as of its grosser ones: The worlds that arise are not unlike the worlds that perished, and are peopled by similar races, though just as the flower evolves from summer to summer, all things advance by some minute step.

In a certain divine year (a time truly inconceivable to us, though that cycle of the universes was but one in an endless succession), a race was born that was so like to ours that Master Malrubius did not scruple to call it human. It expanded among the galaxies of its universe even as we are said to have done in the remote past, when Urth was, for a time, the center, or at least the home and symbol, of an empire.

These men encountered many beings on other worlds who had intelligence to some degree, or at least the potential for intelligence, and from them—that they might have comrades in the loneliness between the galaxies and allies among their swarming worlds—they formed beings like themselves.

It was not done swiftly or easily. Uncountable billions suffered and died under their guiding hands, leaving ineradicable memories of pain and blood. When their universe was old, and galaxy so far separated from galaxy that the nearest could not be seen even as faint stars, and the ships were steered thence by ancient records alone, the thing was done. Completed, the work was greater than those who began it could have guessed. What had been made was not a new race like Humanity's, but a race such as Humanity wished its own to be: united, compassionate, just.

I was not told what became of the Humanity of that cycle. Perhaps it survived until the implosion of the universe, then perished with it. Perhaps it evolved beyond our recognition. But the beings Humanity had shaped into what men and women wished to be escaped, opening a passage to Yesod, the universe higher than our own, where they created worlds suited to what they had become.

From that vantage point they look both forward and back, and in so looking they have discovered us. Perhaps we are no more than a race like that who shaped them. Perhaps it was we who shaped them—or our sons—or our fathers. Malrubius said he did not know, and I believe he told the truth. However it may be, they shape us now as they themselves were shaped; it is at once their repayment and their revenge.

The Hierodules they have found too, and formed more quickly, to serve them in this universe. On their instructions, the Hierodules construct such ships as the one that bore me from the jungle to the sea, so that aquastors like Malrubius and Triskele may serve them also. With these tongs, we are held in the forge.

The hammer they wield is their ability to draw their servants back, down the corridors of time, and to send them hurtling forward to the future. (This power is in essence the same as that which permitted them to evade the death of their universe—to enter the corridors of time is to leave the universe.) On Urth at least, their anvil is the necessity of life: our need in this age to fight against an ever-more-hostile world with the resources of the depleted continents. Because it is as cruel as the means by which they themselves were shaped, there is a conservation of justice; but when the New Sun appears, it will be a signal that at least the earliest operations of the shaping are complete.

Father Inire's Letter

THE QUARTERS ASSIGNED to me were in the most ancient part of the Citadel. The rooms had been empty so long that the old castellan and the steward charged with maintaining them supposed the keys to have been lost, and offered, with many apologies and much reticence, to break the locks for me. I did not permit myself the luxury of watching their faces, but I heard their indrawn breath as I pronounced the simple words that controlled the doors.

It was fascinating, that evening, to see how much the fashions of the period in which those chambers were furnished differed from our own. They did without chairs as we know them, having for seats only complex cushions; and their tables lacked drawers and that symmetry we have come to consider essential. By our standards too, there was too much fabric and not enough wood, leather, stone, and bone; I found the effect at once sybaritic and uncomfortable.

Yet it was impossible that I should occupy a suite other than that anciently set aside for the autarchs; and impossible too that I should have it refurnished to a degree that would imply criticism of my predecessors. And if the furniture had more to recommend it to the mind than to the body, what a

delight it was to discover the treasures those same predecessors had left behind: There were papers relating to
matters now utterly forgotten and not always identifiable;
mechanical devices ingenious and enigmatic; a microcosm
that stirred to life at the warmth of my hands, and whose
minute inhabitants seemed to grow larger and more human
as I watched them; a laboratory containing the fabled "emer-
ald bench" and many other things, the most interesting of
which was a mandragora in spirits.

The cucurbit in which it floated was about seven spans in
height and half as wide; the homuncule itself no more than
two spans tall. When I tapped the glass, it turned eyes like
clouded beads toward me, eyes blinder far in appearance
than Master Palaemon's. I heard no sound when its lips
twitched, yet I knew at once what words they shaped—and in
some inexplicable sense I felt the pale fluid in which the
mandragora was immersed had become my own blood-tinged
urine.

*"Why have you called me, Autarch, from the contempla-
tion of your world?"*

I asked, "Is it truly mine? I know now that there are seven
continents, and none but a part of this are obedient to the
hallowed phrases."

"You are the heir," the wizened thing said and turned, I
could not tell if by accident or design, until it no longer faced
me.

I tapped the cucurbit again. "And who are you?"

*"A being without parents, whose life is passed immersed in
blood."*

"Why, such have I been! We should be friends then, you
and I, as two of similar background usually are."

"You jest."

"Not at all. I feel a real sympathy for you, and I think we
are more alike than you believe."

The tiny figure turned again until its little face looked up
into my own. *"I wish that I might credit you, Autarch."*

"I mean it. No one has ever accused me of being an honest man, and I've told lies enough when I thought they would serve my turn, but I'm quite sincere. If I can do anything for you, tell me what it is."

"Break the glass."

I hesitated. "Won't you die?"

"I have never lived. I will cease thinking. Break the glass."

"You do live."

"I neither grow, nor move, nor respond to any stimulus save thought, which is counted no response. I am incapable of propagating my kind, or any other. Break the glass."

"If you are indeed unliving, I would rather find some way to stir you to life."

"So much for brotherhood. When you were imprisoned here, Thecla, and that boy brought you the knife, why did not you look for more life then?"

The blood burned in my cheek, and I lifted the ebony baculus, but I did not strike. "Alive or dead, you have a penetrating intelligence. Thecla is that part of me most prone to anger."

"If you had inherited her glands with her memories, I would have succeeded."

"And you know that. How can you know so much, who are blind?"

"The acts of coarse minds create minute vibrations that stir the waters of this bottle. I hear your thoughts."

"I notice that I hear yours. How is it that I can hear them, and not others?"

Looking now directly into the pinched face, which was lit by the sun's last shaft penetrating a dusty port, I could not be sure the lips moved at all. *"You hear yourself, as ever. You cannot hear others because your mind shrieks always, like an infant crying in a basket. Ah, I see you remember that."*

"I remember a time very long ago when I was cold and hungry. I lay upon my back, encircled by brown walls, and heard the sound of my own screams. Yes, I must have been an infant. Not old enough to crawl, I think. You are very clever. What am I thinking now?"

"That I am but an unconscious exercise of your own power, as the Claw was. It is true, of course. I was deformed, and died before birth, and have been kept here since in white brandy. Break the glass."

"I would question you first," I said.

"Brother, there is an old man with a letter at your door."

I listened. It was strange, after having listened only to his words in my mind, to hear real noises again—the calling of the sleepy blackbirds among the towers and the tapping at the door.

The messenger was old Rudesind, who had guided me to the picture-room of the House Absolute. I motioned him in (to the surprise, I think, of the sentries) because I wanted to talk to him and knew that with him I had no need to stand upon my dignity.

"Never been in here in all my years," he said. "How can I help you, Autarch?"

"We're served already, just by the sight of you. You know who we are, don't you? You recognized us when we met before."

"If I didn't know your face, Autarch, I'd know a couple dozen times over anyhow. I've been told that often. Nobody here talks about anything else, seems like. How you was licked to shape right here. How they seen you this time and that time. How you looked, and what you said to them. There ain't one cook that didn't treat you to a pastry often. All them soldiers told you stories. Been a while now since I met a woman didn't kiss you and sew up a hole in your pants. You had a dog—"

"That's true enough," I said. "We did."

"And a cat and a bird and a coti that stole apples. And you climbed every wall in this place. And jumped off after, or else swung on a rope, or else hid and pretended you'd jumped. You're every boy that's ever been here, and I've heard stories put on you that belong to men that was old when I was just a boy, and I've heard about things I did myself, seventy years ago."

"We've already learned that the Autarch's face is always concealed behind the mask the people weave for him. No doubt it's a good thing; you can't become too proud once you understand how different you really are from the thing they bow to. But we want to hear about you. The old Autarch told us you were his sentinel in the House Absolute, and now we know you're a servant of Father Inire's."

"I am," the old man said. "I have that honor, and it's his letter I carry." He held up a small and somewhat smudged envelope.

"And we are Father Inire's master."

He made a countrified bow. "I know so, Autarch."

"Then we order you to sit down, and rest yourself. We've questions to ask you, and we don't want to keep a man your age standing. When we were that boy you say everyone's talking of, or at least not much older, you directed us to Master Ultan's stacks. Why did you do that?"

"Not because I knew something others didn't. Not because my master ordered it, either, if that's what you're thinking. Won't you read his letter?"

"In a moment. After an honest answer, in a few words."

The old man hung his head and pulled at his thin beard. I could see the dry skin of his face rise in hollow-sided, tiny cones as it sought to follow the white hairs. "Autarch, you think I guessed at something back then. Perhaps some did. Perhaps my master did, I don't know." His rheumy eyes rolled up under his brows to look at me, then fell again. "You were young, and seemed a likely-looking boy, so I wanted you to see."

"To see what?"

"I'm an old man. An old man then, and an old man now. You've grown up since. I see it in your face. I'm hardly any older, because that much time isn't anything to me. If you counted all the time I've spent just going up and down my ladder, it'd be longer than that. I wanted you to see there has been a lot come before you. That there was thousands and thousands that lived and died before you was ever thought of, some better than you. I mean, Autarch, the way you was then. You'd think anybody growing up here in the old Citadel would be born knowing all that, but I've found they're not. Being around it all the time, they don't see it. But going down there to Master Ultan brings it home to the cleverer ones."

"You are the advocate of the dead."

The old man nodded. "I am. People talk about being fair to this one and that one, but nobody I ever heard talks about doing right by them. We take everything they had, which is all right. And spit, most often, on their opinions, which I suppose is all right too. But we ought to remember now and then how much of what we have we got from them. I figure while I'm still here I ought to put a word in for them. And now, if you don't mind, Autarch, I'll just lay the letter here on this funny table—"

"Rudesind . . ."

"Yes, Autarch?"

"Are you going to clean your paintings?"

He nodded again. "That's one reason I'm eager to be gone, Autarch. I was at the House Absolute until my master—" here he paused and seemed to swallow, as men do when they feel they have perhaps said too much "—went away north. Got a Fechin to clean, and I'm behind."

"Rudesind, we already know the answers to the question you think we are going to ask. We know your master is what the people call a cacogen, and that for whatever reason, he is one of those few who have chosen to cast their lots entirely with humanity, remaining on Urth as a human being. The Cumaean is another such, though perhaps you did not know that. We even know that your master was with us in the jungles of the north, where he tried until it was too late to rescue my predecessor. We only want to say that if a young man with an errand comes past again while you are on your ladder, you are to send him to Master Ultan. That is our order."

When he had gone, I tore open the envelope. The sheet within was not large, but it was covered with tiny writing, as though a swarm of hatchling spiders had been pressed into its surface.

His servant Inire hails the bridegroom of the Urth, Master of Nessus and the House Absolute, Chief of his Race, Gold of his People, Messenger of Dawn, Helios, Hyperion, Surya, Savitar, and Autarch!

I hasten, and will reach you within two days.

It was a day and more ere I learned what had taken place. Much of my information came from the woman Agia, who at least by her own account was instrumental in freeing you. She told me also something of your past dealings with her, for I have, as you know, means of extracting information.

You will have learned from her that the Exultant Vodalus is dead by her act. His paramour, the Chatelaine Thea, at first attempted to gain control of those myrmidons who were about him at his death; but as she is by no means fitted to lead them, and still less to hold in check those in the south, I have contrived to set this woman Agia in her place. From your former mercy toward her, I trust that will meet with your approval. Certainly it is desirable to maintain in being a movement that has proved so useful in the past, and as long as the mirrors of the caller Hethor remain unbroken, she provides it with a plausible commander.

You will perhaps consider the ship I summoned to aid my master, the autarch of his day, inadequate—as for that matter do I—yet it was the best I could obtain, and I was hard pressed to get it. I myself have been forced to travel south otherwise, and much more slowly; the time may come soon when my cousins are ready to side not just with humankind but with *us*—but for the present they persist in viewing Urth as somewhat less significant than many of the colonized worlds, and ourselves on a par with the Ascians, and for that matter with the Xanthoderms and many others.

You will perhaps already have gained news both fresher and more precise than mine. On the chance that you have not: The war goes well and ill. Neither point of their envelopment penetrated far, and the southern thrust, particularly, suffered such losses that it may fairly be said to have been destroyed. I know the death of so many miserable slaves of Erebus will bring no joy to you, but at least our armies have a respite.

That they need badly. There is sedition among the Paralians, which must be rooted out. The Tarentines, your Antrustiones, and the city legions—the three groups that bore the brunt of the fighting—having suffered almost as badly as the enemy. There are cohorts among them that could not muster a hundred able soldiers.

I need not tell you we should obtain more small arms and, particularly, artillery, if my cousins can be persuaded to part with them at a price we can pay. In the meanwhile, what can be done to raise fresh troops must be done, and in time for the recruits to be trained by spring. Light units capable of skirmishing without scattering are the present need; but if the Ascians break out next year, we will require piquenaires and pilani by the hundreds of thousands, and it might be well to bring at least a part of them under arms now.

Any news you have of Abaia's incursions will be fresher than mine; I have had none since I left our lines. Hormisdas has gone into the South, I believe, but Olaguer may be able to inform you.

In haste and reverence,
INIRE

Of Bad Gold and Burning

NOT MUCH REMAINS to be told. I knew I would have to leave the city in a few days, so all I hoped to do here would have to be done quickly. I had no friends in the guild I could be sure of beyond Master Palaemon, and he would be of little use in what I planned. I summoned Roche, knowing that he could not deceive me to my face for long. (I expected to see a man older than myself, but the red-haired journeyman who came at my command was hardly more than a boy; when he had gone, I studied my own face in a mirror, something I had not done before.)

He told me that he and several others who had been friends of mine more or less close had argued against my execution when the will of most of the guild was to kill me, and I believed him. He also admitted quite freely that he had proposed that I be maimed and expelled, though he said he had only done so because he had felt it to be the only way to save my life. I think he expected to be punished in some way—his cheeks and forehead, normally so ruddy, were white enough to make his freckles stand out like splatters of paint. His voice was steady, however, and he said nothing that seemed intended to excuse himself by throwing blame on someone else.

The fact was, of course, that I did intend to punish him, together with the rest of the guild. Not because I bore him or them any ill will, but because I felt that being locked below the tower for a time would arouse in them a sensitivity to that principle of justice of which Master Palaemon had spoken, and because it would be the best way to assure that the order forbidding torture I intended to issue would be carried out. Those who spend a few months in dread of that art are not likely to resent its being discontinued.

However, I said nothing about that to Roche but only asked him to bring me a journeyman's habit that evening, and to be ready with Drotte and Eata to aid me the next morning.

He returned with the clothing just after vespers. It was an indescribable pleasure to take off the stiff costume I had been wearing and put on fuligin again. By night, its dark embrace is the nearest approach to invisibility I know, and after I had slipped out of my chambers by one of the secret exits, I moved between tower and tower like a shadow until I reached the fallen section of the curtain wall.

Day had been warm; but the night was cool, and the necropolis filled with mist, just as it had been when I had come from behind the monument to save Vodalus. The mausoleum where I had played as a boy stood as I had left it, its jammed door three-quarters shut.

I had brought a candle, and I lit it when I was inside. The funeral brasses I had once kept polished were green again; drifted leaves lay uncrushed everywhere. A tree had flung a slender limb through the little, barred window.

> Where I put you, there you lie,
> Never let a stranger spy,
> Like grass grow to any eye,
> Not of me.

Here be safe, never leave it,
Should a hand come, deceive it,
Let strange eyes not believe it,
Till I see.

The stone was smaller and lighter than I remembered. The coin beneath it had grown dull with damp; but it was still there, and in a moment I held it again and recalled the boy I had been, walking shaken back to the torn wall through the fog.

Now I must ask you, you that have pardoned so many deviations and digressions from me, to excuse one more. It is the last.

A few days ago (which is to say, a long time after the real termination of the events I have set myself to narrate) I was told that a vagabond had come here to the House Absolute saying that he owed me money, and that he refused to pay it to anyone else. I suspected that I was about to see some old acquaintance, and told the chamberlain to bring him to me.

It was Dr. Talos. He appeared to be in funds, and he had dressed himself for the occasion in a capot of red velvet and a chechia of the same material. His face was still that of a stuffed fox; but it seemed to me at times that some hint of life crept into it, that something or someone now peered through the glass eyes.

"You have bettered yourself," he said, making such a low bow that the tassel of his cap swept the carpet. "You may recall that I invariably affirmed you would. Honesty, integrity, and intelligence cannot be kept down."

"We both know that nothing is easier to keep down," I said. "By my old guild, they were kept down every day. But it is good to see you again, even if you come as the emissary of your master."

For a moment the doctor looked blank. "Oh, Baldanders, you mean. No, he has dismissed me, I'm afraid. After the fight. After he dived into the lake."

"You believe he survived, then."

"Oh, I'm quite sure he survived. You didn't know him as I did, Severian. Breathing water would be nothing to him. Nothing! He had a marvelous mind. He was a supreme genius of a unique sort: everything turned inward. He combined the objectivity of the scholar with the self-absorption of the mystic."

I said, "By which you mean he carried out experiments on himself."

"Oh, no, not at all. He reversed that! Others experiment upon themselves in order to derive some rule they can apply to the world. Baldanders experimented on the world and spent the proceeds, if I can put it so bluntly, upon his person. They say—" here he looked about nervously to make sure no one but myself was in earshot "—they say I'm a monster, and so I am. But Baldanders was more monster than I. In some sense he was my father, but he had built himself. It's the law of nature, and of what is higher than nature, that each creature must have a creator. But Baldanders was his own creation; he stood behind himself, and cut himself off from the line linking the rest of us with the Increate. However, I stray from my subject." The doctor had a wallet of scarlet leather at his belt; he loosened the strings and began to rummage in it. I heard the chink of metal.

"Do you carry money now?" I asked. "You used to give everything to him."

His voice sank until I could hardly hear it. "Wouldn't you, in my present position, do the same thing? Now I leave coins, little stacks of aes and orichalks, near water." He spoke more loudly: "It does no harm, and reminds me of the great days. But I am honest, you see! He always demanded that of me. And he was honest too, after his fashion. Anyway, do you recall the morning before we came out the gate? I was handing round the receipts from the night before, and we were interrupted. There was a coin left, and it was to go to you. I saved it and meant to give it to you later, but I forgot, and then when you came to the castle. . . ." He gave me a side-long glance. "But fair trade ends paid, as they say, and I have it here."

The coin was precisely like the one I had taken from under the stone.

"You see now why I couldn't give it to your man—I'm sure he thought me mad."

I flipped the coin and caught it. It felt as though it had been lightly greased. "To tell the truth, Doctor, we don't."

"Because it's false, of course. I told you so that morning. How could I have told him I had come to pay the Autarch, and then given him a bad coin? They're terrified of you, and they'd have disemboweled me looking for a good one! Is it true you've an explosive that takes days to go up, so you can blow people apart slowly?"

I was looking at the two coins. They had the same brassy shine and appeared to have been struck in the same die.

But that little interview, as I have said, took place a long time after the proper close of my narrative. I returned to my chambers in the Flag Tower by the way I had come, and when I reached them again, took off the dripping cloak and hung it up. Master Gurloes used to say that not wearing a shirt was the hardest thing about belonging to the guild. Though he meant it ironically, it was in some sense true. I, who had gone through the mountains with a naked chest, had been softened sufficiently by a few days in the stifling autarchial vestments to shiver at a foggy autumn night.

There were fireplaces in all the rooms, and each was piled with wood so old and dry that I suspected it would fall to dust should I strike it against an andiron. I had never lit any of these fires; but I decided to do so now, and warm myself, and spread the clothes Roche had brought over the back of a chair to dry. When I looked for my firebox, however, I discovered that in my excitement I had left it in the mausoleum with the candle. Thinking vaguely that the autarch who had inhabited these rooms before me (a ruler far beyond the reach of my memory) must surely have kept some means of kindling his numerous fires close to hand, I began searching the drawers of the cabinets.

These were largely filled with the papers that had so fascinated me before; but instead of stopping to read them, as I had when I had made my original survey of the rooms, I lifted them from each drawer to see if there was not a steel, igniter, or syringe of amadou beneath them.

I found none; but instead, in the largest drawer of the largest cabinet, concealed under a filigree pen case, I discovered a small pistol.

I had seen such weapons before—the first time having been when Vodalus had given me the false coin I had just reclaimed. Yet I had never held one in my own hands, and I found now that it was a very different thing from seeing them in the hands of others. Once when Dorcas and I were riding north toward Thrax we had fallen in with a caravan of tinkers and peddlers. We still had most of the money Dr. Talos had shared out when we met him in the forest north of the House Absolute; but we were uncertain how far it might carry us and how far we had to go, and so I was plying my trade with the rest, inquiring at each little town if there were not some malefactor to be mutilated or beheaded. The vagrants considered us two of themselves, and though some accorded us more or less exalted rank because I labored only for the authorities, others affected to despise us as the instruments of tyranny.

One evening, a grinder who had been friendlier than most and had done us several trifling favors offered to sharpen *Terminus Est* for me. I told him I kept her quite sharp enough for the work and invited him to test her edge with a finger. After he had cut himself slightly (as I had known he would) he grew quite taken with her, admiring not only her blade but her soft sheath, her carven guard, and so on. When I had answered innumerable questions regarding her making, history, and mode of use, he asked if I would permit him to hold her. I cautioned him about the weight of the blade and the danger of striking its fine edge against something that might injure it, then handed her over. He smiled and gripped the hilt as I had instructed him; but as he began to lift that long and shining instrument of death, his face went pale and his arms began to tremble so that I snatched her away from him before he dropped her. Afterward all he would say was *I've sharpened soldiers' swords often,* over and over.

Now I learned how he had felt. I laid the pistol on the table so quickly I nearly lost hold of it, then walked around and around it as though it had been a snake coiled to strike.

It was shorter than my hand, and so prettily made that it might have been a piece of jewelry; yet every line of it told of an origin beyond the nearer stars. Its silver had not yellowed with time, but might have come fresh from the buffing wheel. It was covered with decorations that were, perhaps, writing—I could not really tell which, and to eyes like mine, accustomed to patterns of straight lines and curves, they sometimes appeared to be no more than complex or shimmering reflections, save that they were reflections of something not present. The grips were encrusted with black stones whose name I did not know, gems like tourmalines but brighter. After a time I noticed that one, the smallest of all, seemed to vanish unless I looked at it straight on, when it sparkled with four-rayed brilliancy. Examining it more closely, I found it was not a gem at all, but a minute lens through which some inner fire shone. The pistol retained its charge then, after so many centuries.

Illogical though it might be, the knowledge reassured me. A weapon may be dangerous to its user in two ways: by wounding him by accident, or by failing him. The first remained; but when I saw the brightness of that point of light, I knew the second could be dismissed.

There was a sliding stud under the barrel that seemed likely to control the intensity of the discharge. My first thought was that whoever had last handled it would probably have set it to maximum intensity, and that by reversing the setting I would be able to experiment with some safety. But it was not so—the stud was positioned at the center of its range. At last I decided, by analogy with a bowstring, that the pistol was likely to be least dangerous when the stud was as far foward as possible. I put it there, pointed the weapon at the fireplace, and pulled the trigger.

The sound of a shot is the most horrible in the world. It is the scream of matter itself. Now the report was not loud, but threatening, like distant thunder. For an instant—so brief a time I might almost have believed I dreamed it—a narrow cone of violet flashed between the muzzle of the pistol and the heaped wood. Then it was gone, the wood was blazing, and slabs of burned and twisted metal fell with the noise of cracked bells from the back of the fireplace. A rivulet of silver ran out onto the hearth to scorth the mat and send up nauseous smoke.

I put the pistol into the sabretache of my new journeyman's habit.

Across the River Again

BEFORE DAWN, Roche was at my door, with Drotte and Eata. Drotte was the oldest of us, yet his face and flashing eyes made him seem younger than Roche. He was still the very picture of wiry strength, but I could not help but notice that I was now taller than he by the width of two fingers. I must surely have been so already when I left the Citadel, though I had not been conscious of it. Eata was still the smallest, and not yet even a journeyman—so I had only been away one summer, after all. He seemed a bit dazed when he greeted me, and I suppose he was having trouble believing I was now Autarch, particularly since he had not seen me again until now, when I was once more dressed in the habit of the guild.

I had told Roche that the three of them were to be armed; he and Drotte carried swords similar in form (though vastly inferior in workmanship) to *Terminus Est*, and Eata a clava I recalled having seen displayed at our Masking Day festivities. Before I had seen the fighting in the north, I would have thought them well-enough equipped; now all three, not only Eata, seemed like boys burdened with sticks and pinecones, ready to play at war.

For the last time we went out through the rent in the wall

and threaded the paths of bone that wound among the cypresses and tombs. The death roses I had hesitated to pick for Thecla still showed a few autumnal blooms, and I found myself thinking of Morwenna, the only woman whose life I have ever taken, and of her enemy, Eusebia.

When we had passed the gate of the necropolis and entered the squalid city streets, my companions seemed to become almost lighthearted. I think they must have been subconsciously afraid they would be seen by Master Gurloes and punished in some way for having obeyed the Autarch.

"I hope you're not planning on going for a swim," Drotte said. "These choppers would sink us."

Roche chuckled. "Eata can float with his."

"We're going far to the north. We'll need a boat, but I think we'll be able to hire one if we walk along the embankment."

"If anybody will rent to us. And if we're not arrested. You know, Autarch—"

"Severian," I reminded him. "For as long as I wear these clothes."

"—Severian, we're only supposed to carry these things to the block, and it will take a lot of talking to make the peltasts think three of us are necessary. Will they know who you are? I don't—"

This time it was Eata who interrupted him, pointing toward the river. "Look, there's a boat!"

Roche bellowed, all three waved, and I held up one of the chrisos I had borrowed from the castellan, turning it so it would flash in the sunlight that was then just beginning to show over the towers behind us. The man at the tiller waved his cap, and what appeared to be a slender lad sprang forward to put the dipping lugsails on the other tack.

She was two-masted, rather narrow of beam and low of freeboard—an ideal craft, no doubt, for running untaxed merchandise past the patrol cutters that had suddenly become mine. The grizzled old moonraker of a steersman looked capable of much worse, and the slender "lad" was a girl with laughing eyes and a facility for looking from them sidelong.

"Well, this 'pears to be a day," the steersman said when he saw our habits. "I thought you was in mournin', I did, till I got up close. Eyes? I never heard of 'um, no more than a crow in court."

"We are," I told him as I got on board. It gave me a ridiculous pleasure to find I had not lost the sea legs I had acquired on the *Samru*, and to watch Drotte and Roche grab for the sheets when the lugger rocked beneath their weight.

"Mind if I've a look at that yellow boy? Just to see if he's good. I'll send him right home."

I tossed him the coin, which he rubbed and bit and at last surrendered with a respectful look.

"We may need your boat all day."

"For the yellow boy, you can have her all night too. We'll both be glad of the company, like the undertaker remarked to the ghost. There was things in the river up till first light, which I suppose might have something to do with you optimates being out on the water this mornin'?"

"Cast off," I said. "You can tell me, if you will, what these strange things were while we are under way."

Although he had broached the subject himself, the steersman seemed reluctant to go into much detail—perhaps only because he had difficulty in finding words to express what he had felt and to describe what he had seen and heard. There was a light west wind, so that with the lugger's batten-stiffened sails drawn taut we were able to run upstream handily. The brown girl had little to do but sit in the bow and trade glances with Eata. (It is possible she thought him, in his dirty gray shirt and trousers, only a paid attendant of ours.) The steersman, who called himself her uncle, kept a steady pressure on the tiller as he talked, to keep the lugger from flying off the wind.

"I'll tell you what I saw myself, like the carpenter did when he had the shutter up. We was eight or nine leagues north of where you hailed us. Clams was our cargo, you see, and there's no stoppin' with them, not when there's a chance of a warm afternoon. We goes down to the lower river and buys them off the diggers, do you see, then runs them up the channel quick so's they can be et before they goes bad. If they goes off you lose all, but you make double or better if you can sell them good.

"I've spent more nights on the river in my life than anywhere else—it's my bedroom, you might say, and this boat's my cradle, though I don't usually get to sleep until mornin'. But last night—sometimes I felt like I wasn't on old Gyoll at all, but on some other river, one that run up into the sky, or under the ground.

"I doubt you noticed unless you was out late, but it was a still night with just little breaths of wind that would blow for about as long as it takes a man to swear, then die down, then blow again. There was mist too, thick as cotton. It hung over the water the way mists always does, with about so much clear space as you could roll a keg through between it and the river. Most of the time we couldn't see the lights on either shore, just the mist. I used to have a horn I blowed for those that couldn't see our lights, but it went over the side last year, and being copper it sunk. So I shouted last night, whenever I felt like there was another boat or anything close by us.

"About a watch after the mist came I let Maxellindis go to sleep. Both sails was set, and when each puff of air come we would go up river a bit, and then I'd set out the anchor again. You maybe don't know it, optimates, but the rule of the river is that them that's goin' up keeps to the sides and them that's goin' down takes the middle. We was goin' up and ought to have been over to the east bank, but with the mist I couldn't tell.

"Then I heard sweeps. I looked in the mist, but I couldn't see lights, and I hollered so they'd sheer off. I leaned over the gunnel and put my ear close to the water so's to hear better. A mist soaks up noises, but the best hearin' you can ever have

is when you gets your head under one, because the noise runs
right along the water. Anyway, I did that, and she was a big
one. You can't count how many sweeps there is with a good
crew pullin', because they all go in and come up together,
but when a big vessel goes fast you can hear water breakin'
under her bow, and this was a big one. I got up on top of the
deckhouse tryin' to see her, but there still wasn't any lights,
though I knew she had to be close.

"Just when I was climbin' down I caught the sight of her—
a galleass, four-masted and four-banked, no lights, comin'
right up the channel, as near as I could judge. Pray for them
that's comin' down, thinks I to myself, like the ox said when
he fell out of the riggin'.

"Of course I only saw her for a minute before she was gone
in the mist again, but I heard her a long while after. Seein'
her like that made me feel so queer I yelled every once in a
while even if no other craft was by. We had made another
half league, I suppose, or maybe a little less, when I heard
somebody yell back. Only it wasn't like answerin' my hail,
but like somebody'd laid a rope end to him. I called again,
and he called back regular, and it was a man I know named
Trason what has his own boat just like I do. 'Is it you?' he
called, and I said it was and asked if he was all right. 'Tie up!'
he says.

"I told him I couldn't. I had clams, and even if the night
was cool, I wanted to sell soon as I could. 'Tie up,' Trason
calls again, 'Tie up and go ashore.' So I call back, 'Why don't
you?' Just then he come in sight, and there was more on his
boat than I would've thought it would hold—pandours, I'd
have said, but every pandour ever I saw had a face brown as
mine or nearly, and these was white as the mist. They had
scorpions and voulges—I could see the heads of them stickin'
up over the crests of their helmets."

I interrupted him to ask if the soldiers he had seen were
starved looking and if they had large eyes.

He shook his head, one corner of his mouth twisting up.

"They was big men, bigger than you or me or anybody in this boat, a head taller than Trason. Anyway, they were gone in a moment, just like the galleass. That was the only other craft I saw till the mist lifted. But . . ."

I said, "But you saw something else. Or heard something."

He nodded. "I thought maybe you and your people here was out because of them. Yes, I saw and I heard things. There was things in this river I never saw before. Maxellindis, when she woke up and I told her about it, said it was the manatees. They're pale in moonlight and look human enough if you don't come too close. But I've seen 'em since I was a boy and never been fooled once. And there was women's voices, not loud but big. And something else. I couldn't understand what any of 'em was sayin', but I could hear the tone of it. You know how it is when you're listenin' to people over the water? They would say *so-and-so-and-so*. Then the deeper voice—I can't call it a man's because I don't think it was one—the deeper voice'd say *go-and-do-that-and-this-and-that*. I heard the women's voices three times and the other voice twice. You won't believe it, optimates, but sometimes it sounded like the voices was coming up out of the river."

With that he fell silent, looking out over the nenuphars. We were well above that part of Gyoll opposite the Citadel, but they were still packed more densely than wildflowers in any meadow this side of paradise.

The Citadel itself was visible now as a whole, and for all its vastness seemed a glittering flock fluttering upon the hill, its thousand metal towers ready to leap into the air at a word. Below them the necropolis spread an embroidery of mingled white and green. I know it is fashionable to speak in tones of faint disgust of the "unhealthy" growth of the lawns and trees in such places, but I have never observed that there is actually anything unhealthy about it. Green things die that men may live, and men die that green things may live, even that ignorant and innocent man I killed with his own ax there long ago. All our foliage is faded, so it is said, and no doubt it is so; and when the New Sun comes, his bride, the New Urth, will give glory to him with leaves like emeralds. But in the present day, the day of the old sun and old Urth, I have never seen any other green so deep as the great pines' in the necropolis when the wind swells their branches. They draw their strength from the departed generations of mankind, and the masts of argosies, that are built up of many trees, are not so high as they.

The Sanguinary Field stands far from the river. We four drew strange looks as we journeyed there, but no one halted us. The Inn of Lost Loves, which had ever seemed to me the least permanent of the houses of men, still stood as it had on the afternoon when I had come there with Agia and Dorcas. The fat innkeeper very nearly fainted when he saw us; I made him fetch Ouen, the waiter.

I had never really looked at him on that afternoon when he had carried in a tray for Dorcas, Agia, and me. I did so now. He was a balding man about as tall as Drotte, thin and somehow pinched looking; his eyes were deep blue, and there was a delicacy to the molding of his eyes and mouth that I recognized at once.

"Do you know who we are?" I asked him.

Slowly, he shook his head.

"Have you never had a torturer to serve?"

"Once this spring, sieur," he said. "And I know these two men in black are torturers. But you're no torturer, sieur, though you're dressed like one."

I let that pass. "You have never seen me?"

"No, sieur."

"Very well, perhaps you have not." (How strange it was to realize that I had changed so much.) "Ouen, since you do not know me, it might be well if I knew you. Tell me where you were born and who your parents were, and how you came to be employed at this inn."

"My father was a shopkeeper, sieur. We lived in Oldgate, on the west bank. When I was ten or so, I think, he sent me to an inn to be a potboy, and I've worked in one or another since."

"Your father was a shopkeeper. What of your mother?"

Ouen's face still held a waiter's deference, but his eyes were puzzled. "I never knew her, sieur. Cas they called her, but she died when I was young. In childbirth, my father said."

"But you know what she looked like."

He nodded. "My father had a locket with her likeness. Once when I was twenty or so I came to see him and found out he'd pledged it. I'd come into a bit of money then helping a certain optimate with his affairs—carrying messages to the ladies and standing watch outside doors and so on, and I went to the pawnbroker's and paid the pledge and took it. I still wear it, sieur. In a place like ours, where there's so many in 'n out all the time, it's best to keep your valuables about you."

He reached into his shirt and drew out a locket of cloisonné enamel. The pictures inside were of Dorcas in full face and profile, a Dorcas hardly younger than the Dorcas I had known.

"You say you became a potboy at ten, Ouen. But you can read and write."

"A bit, sieur." He looked embarrassed. "I've asked people, various times, what writing said. I don't forget much."

"You wrote something when the torturer was here this spring," I told him. "Do you recall what you wrote?"

Frightened, he shook his head. "Only a note to warn the girl."

"I do. It was, 'The woman with you has been here before. Do not trust her. Trudo says the man is a torturer. You are my mother come again.' "

Ouen tucked his locket under his shirt. "It was only that she was so much like her, sieur. When I was a younger man, I used to think that someday I'd find such a woman. I told myself, you know, that I was a better man than my father, and he had, after all. But I never did, and now I'm not so sure I'm a better man."

"At that time, you did not know what a torturer's habit looked like," I said. "But your friend Trudo, the ostler, knew. He knew a good deal more about torturers than you, and that was why he ran away."

"Yes, sieur. When he heard the torturer was asking for him, he did."

"But you saw the innocence of the girl and wanted to warn her against the torturer and the other woman. You were right about both of them, perhaps."

"If you say it, sieur."

"Do you know, Ouen, you look a bit like her."

The fat innkeeper had been listening more or less openly. Now he chuckled. "He looks more like you!"

I am afraid I turned to stare at him.

"No offense intended, sieur, but it's true. He's a bit older, but when you were talking I saw both your faces from the side, and there isn't a patch of difference."

I studied Ouen again. His hair and eyes were not dark like mine, but with that coloring aside, his face might almost have been my own.

"You said you never found a woman like Dorcas—like that one in your locket. Still you found a woman, I think."

His eyes would not meet mine. "Several, sieur."

"And fathered a child."

"No, sieur!" He was startled. "Never, sieur!"

"How interesting. Were you ever in difficulties with the law?"

"Several times, sieur."

"It is well to keep your voice low, but it need not be so low as that. And look at me when you speak to me. A woman you loved—or perhaps only one who loved you—a dark woman—was taken once?"

"Once, sieur," he said. "Yes, sieur. Catherine was her name. It's an old-fashioned name, they tell me." He paused and shrugged. "There was trouble, as you say, sieur. She'd run off from some order of monials. The law got her, and I never saw her again."

He did not want to come, but we brought him with us when we returned to the lugger.

When I had come upriver by night on the *Samru*, the line between the living and the dead city had been like that between the dark curve of the world and the celestial dome with its stars. Now, when there was so much more light, it had vanished. Half-ruinous structures lined the banks, but whether they were the homes of the most wretched of our citizens or mere deserted shells I could not determine until I saw a string on which three rags flapped.

"In the guild we have the ideal of poverty," I said to Drotte as we leaned on the gunnel. "But those people do not need the ideal; they have achieved it."

"I should think they'd need it most of all," he answered.

He was wrong. The Increate was there, a thing beyond the Hierodules and those they serve; even on the river, I could feel his presence as one feels that of the master of a great house, though he may be in an obscure room on another floor. When we went ashore, it seemed to me that if I were to step through any doorway there, I might surprise some shining figure; and that the commander of all such figures was everywhere invisible only because he was too large to be seen.

We found a man's sandal, worn but not old, lying in one of the grass-grown streets. I said, "I'm told there are looters wandering this place. That is one reason I asked you to come. If there were no one but myself involved, I would do it alone."

Roche nodded and drew his sword, but Drotte said, "There's no one here. You've become a great deal wiser than we are, Severian, but still, I think you've grown a little too accustomed to things that terrify ordinary people."

I asked what he meant.

"You knew what the boatman was talking about. I could see that in your face. You were afraid too, or at least concerned. But not frightened like he was in his boat last night, or like Roche or Ouen there or I would have been if we'd been close to the river and knew what was going on. The looters you're talking about were around last night, and they must keep a watch out for revenue boats. They won't be anywhere near water today, or for several days to come."

Eata touched my arm. "Do you think that girl—Maxellindis—is she in danger, back there on the boat?"

"She's not in as much danger as you are from her," I said. He did not know what I meant, but I did. His Maxellindis was not Thecla; his story could not be the same as my own. But I had seen the revolving corridors of Time behind the gamin face with the laughing brown eyes. Love is a long labor for torturers; and even if I were to dissolve the guild, Eata would become a torturer, as all men are, bound by the contempt for wealth without which a man is less than a man, inflicting pain by his nature, whether he willed it or not. I was sorry for him, and more sorry for Maxellindis the sailor girl.

Ouen and I went into the house, leaving Roche, Drotte, and Eata to keep watch from some distance away. As we stood at the door, I could hear the soft sound of Dorcas's steps inside.

"We will not tell you who you are," I said to Ouen. "And we cannot tell you what you may become. But we are your Autarch, and we tell you what you must do."

I had no words for him, but I discovered I did not need them. He knelt at once, as the castellan had.

"We brought the torturers with us so that you might know what was in store for you if you disobeyed us. But we do not wish you to disobey, and now, having met you, we doubt they were needed. There is a woman in this house. In a moment you will go in. You must tell her your story, as you told it to us, and you must remain with her and protect her, even if she tries to send you away."

"I will do my best, Autarch," Ouen said.

"When you can, you must persuade her to leave this city of death. Until then, we give you this." I took out the pistol and handed it to him. "It is worth a cartload of chrisos, but as long as you are here, it is far better for you to have than chrisos. When you and the woman are safe, we will buy it back from you, if you wish." I showed him how to operate the pistol and left him.

I was alone then, and I do not doubt that there are some who, reading this too-brief account of a summer more than normally turbulent, will say that I have usually been so. Jonas, my only real friend, was in his own eyes merely a machine; Dorcas, whom I yet love, is in her own eyes merely a kind of ghost.

I do not feel it is so. We choose—or choose not—to be alone when we decide whom we will accept as our fellows, and whom we will reject. Thus an eremite in a mountain cave is in company, because the birds and coneys, the initiates whose words live in his "forest books," and the winds— the messengers of the Increate—are his companions. Another man, living in the midst of millions, may be alone, because there are none but enemies and victims around him.

Agia, whom I might have loved, has chosen instead to become a female Vodalus, taking all that lives most fully in humanity as her opponent. I, who might have loved Agia, who loved Dorcas deeply but perhaps not deeply enough, was now alone because I had become a part of her past, which she loved better than she had ever (except, I think, at first) loved me.

XXXVIII

Resurrection

ALMOST NOTHING REMAINS to be told. Dawn has come, the red sun like a bloody eye. The wind blows cold through the window. In a few moments, a footman will carry in a steaming tray; with him, no doubt, will be old, twisted Father Inire, eager to confer during the last few moments that remain; old Father Inire, alive so long beyond the span of his short-lived kind; old Father Inire, who will not, I fear, long survive the red sun. How upset he will be to find I have been sitting up writing all night here in the clerestory.

Soon I must don robes of argent, the color that is more pure than white. Never mind.

There will be long, slow days on the ship. I will read. I still have so much to learn. I will sleep, dozing in my berth, listening to the centuries wash against the hull. This manuscript I shall send to Master Ultan; but while I am on the ship, when I cannot sleep and have tired of reading, I shall write it out again—I who forget nothing—every word, just as I have written it here. I shall call it *The Book of the New Sun*, for that book, lost now for so many ages, is said to have predicted his coming. And when it is finished again, I shall seal that second copy in a coffer of lead and set it adrift on the seas of space and time.

Have I told you all I promised? I am aware that at various places in my narrative I have pledged that this or that should be made clear in the knitting up of the story. I remember them all, I am sure, but then I remember so much else. Before you assume that I have cheated you, read again, as I will write again.

Two things are clear to me. The first is that I am not the first Severian. Those who walk the corridors of Time saw him gain the Phoenix Throne, and thus it was that the Autarch, having been told of me, smiled in the House Azure, and the undine thrust me up when it seemed I must drown. (Yet surely the first Severian did not; something had already begun to reshape my life.) Let me guess now, though it is only a guess, at the story of that first Severian.

He too was reared by the torturers, I think. He too was sent forth to Thrax. He too fled Thrax, and though he did not carry the Claw of the Conciliator, he must have been drawn to the fighting in the north—no doubt he hoped to escape the archon by hiding himself among the army. How he encountered the Autarch there I cannot say; but encounter him he did, and so, even as I, he (who in the final sense was and is myself) became Autarch in turn and sailed beyond the candles of night. Then those who walk the corridors walked back to the time when he was young, and my own story—as I have given it here in so many pages—began.

The second thing is this. He was not returned to his own time but became himself a walker of the corridors. I know now the identity of the man called the Head of Day, and why Hildegrin, who was too near, perished when we met, and why the witches fled. I know too in whose mausoleum I tarried as a child, that little building of stone with its rose, its fountain, and its flying ship all graven. I have disturbed my own tomb, and now I go to lie in it.

. . .

When Drotte, Roche, Eata, and I returned to the Citadel, I received urgent messages from Father Inire and from the House Absolute, and yet I lingered. I asked the castellan for a map. After much searching he produced one, large and old, cracked in many places. It showed the curtain wall whole, but the names of the towers were not the names I knew—or that the castellan knew, for that matter—and there were towers on that map that are not in the Citadel, and towers in the Citadel that were not on that map.

I ordered a flier then, and for half a day soared among the towers. No doubt I saw the place I sought many times, but if so I did not recognize it.

At last, with a bright and unfailing lamp, I went down into our oubliette once more, down flight after flight of steps until I had reached the lowest level. What is it, I wonder, that has given so great a power to preserve the past to underground places? One of the bowls in which I had carried soup to Triskele was there still. (Triskele, who had stirred back to life beneath my hand two years before I bore the Claw.) I followed Triskele's footprints once more, as I had when still an apprentice, to the forgotten opening, and from there my own into the dark maze of tunnels.

Now in the steady light of my lamp I saw where I had lost the track, running straight on when Triskele had turned aside. I was tempted then to follow him instead of myself, so that I might see where he had emerged, and in that way perhaps discover who it was who had befriended him and to whom he used to return after greeting me, sometimes, in the byways of the Citadel. Possibly when I come back to Urth I shall do so, if indeed I do come back.

But once again, I did not turn aside. I followed the boy-man I had been, down a straight corridor floored with mud and pierced at rare intervals with forbidding vents and doors. The Severian I pursued wore ill-fitting shoes with run-down heels and worn soles; when I turned and flashed my light behind me, I observed that though the Severian who pursued him had excellent boots, his steps were of unequal length and the toe of one foot dragged at each. I thought, One Severian had good boots, the other good legs. And I laughed to myself, wondering who should come here in afteryears, and whether he would guess that the same feet left both tracks.

To what use these tunnels were once put, I cannot say. Several times I saw stairs that had once descended farther still, but always they led to dark, calm water. I found a skeleton, its bones scattered by the running feet of Severian, but it was only a skeleton, and told me nothing. In places there was writing on the walls, writing in faded orange or sturdy black; but it was in a character I could not read, as unintelligible as the scrawlings of the rats in Master Ultan's library. A few of the rooms into which I looked held walls in which there had once ticked a thousand or more clocks of various kinds, and though all were dead now, their chimes silenced and their hands corroded at hours that would never come again, I thought them good omens for one who sought the Atrium of Time.

And at last I found it. The little spot of sunshine was just as I had remembered it. No doubt I acted foolishly, but I extinguished my lamp and stood for a moment in the dark, looking at it. All was silence, and its bright, uneven square seemed at least as mysterious as it had before.

I had feared I would have difficulty in squeezing through its narrow crevice, but if the present Severian was somewhat larger of bone, he was also leaner, so that when I had worked my shoulders through the rest followed easily enough.

The snow I recalled was gone, but a chill had come into the air to say that it would soon return. A few dead leaves, which must have been carried in some updraft very high indeed, had come to rest here among the dying roses. The tilted dials still cast their crazy shadows, useless as the dead clocks beneath them, though not so unmoving. The carven animals stared at them, unwinking still.

I crossed to the door and tapped on it. The timorous old

woman who had served us appeared, and I, stepping into that musty room in which I had warmed myself before, told her to bring Valeria to me. She hurried away, but before she was out of sight, something had wakened in the time-worn walls, its disembodied voices, hundred-tongued, demanding that Valeria report to some antiquely titled personage who I realized with a start must be myself.

Here my pen shall halt, reader, though I do not. I have carried you from gate to gate—from the locked and fog-shrouded gate of the necropolis of Nessus to that cloud-racked gate we call the sky, the gate that shall lead me, as I hope, beyond the nearer stars.

My pen halts, though I do not. Reader, you will walk no more with me. It is time we both take up our lives.

To this account, I, Severian the Lame, Autarch, do set my hand in what shall be called the last year of the old sun.

The Arms of the Autarch and the Ships of the Hierodules

NOWHERE ARE THE manuscripts of *The Book of the New Sun* more obscure than in their treatment of weapons and military organization.

The confusion concerning the equipment of Severian's allies and adversaries appears to derive from two sources, of which the first is his marked tendency to label every variation in design or purpose with a separate name. In translating these, I have endeavored to bear in mind the radical meaning of the words employed as well as what I take to be the appearance and function of the weapons themselves. Thus *falchion, fuscina,* and many others. At one point I have put the *athame,* the warlock's sword, into Agia's hands.

The second source of difficulty seems to be that three quite different gradations of technology are involved. The lowest of these could be termed the smith level. The arms produced by it appear to consist of swords, knives, axes, and pikes, such as might have been forged by any skilled metalworker of, say, the fifteenth century. These appear to be readily obtained by the average citizen and to represent the technological ability of the society as a whole.

The second gradation might be called the Urth level. The

long cavalry weapons I have chosen to call *lances, conti,* and
so on undoubtedly belong to this group, as do the "spears"
with which the hastarii menaced Severian outside the door of
the antechamber and other arms used by infantry. How
widely available such weapons were is not clear from the text,
which at one point speaks of "arrows" and "long-shafted
khetens" being offered for sale in Nessus. It seems certain
that Guasacht's irregulars were issued their conti before battle and that these were collected and stored somewhere (possibly in his tent) afterward. Perhaps it should be noted that
small arms were issued and collected in this way in the navies
of the eighteenth and nineteenth centuries, although cut-
lasses and firearms could be freely purchased ashore. The arbalests used by Agia's assassins outside the mine are surely
what I have called Urth weapons, but it is likely these men
were deserters.

The Urth weapons, then, appear to represent the highest
technology to be found on the planet, and perhaps in its
solar system. How efficient they would be in comparison with
our own arms is difficult to say. Armor appears to be not
wholly ineffective against them, but precisely this is true with
regard to our rifles, carbines, and submachine guns.

The third gradation I would call the stellar level. The
pistol given Thea by Vodalus and the one given Ouen by
Severian are unquestionably stellar weapons, but about many
other arms mentioned in the manuscript we cannot be so
sure. Some, or even all, of the artillery used in the mountain
war may be stellar. The *fusils* and *jezails* carried by special
troops on both sides may or may not belong to this gradation, though I am inclined to think they do.

It seems fairly clear that stellar weapons could not be produced on Urth and had to be obtained from the Hierodules
at great cost. An interesting question—to which I can offer no
certain answer—concerns the goods given in exchange. The
Urth of the old sun seems, by our standards, destitute of raw
materials; when Severian speaks of mining, he appears to

mean what we should call archaeological pillaging, and the
new continents said (in Dr. Talos's play) to be ready to rise
with the coming of the New Sun have among their attractions "gold, silver, *iron*, and *copper* . . ." (Italics added.)
Slaves—some slavery certainly exists in Severian's society—
furs, meat and other foodstuffs, and labor-intensive items
such as handmade jewelry would appear to be among the
possibilities.

We would like to know more about almost everything
mentioned in these manuscripts; but most of all, certainly,
we would like to know more about the ships that sail between the stars, commanded by the Hierodules but sometimes crewed by human beings. (Two of the most enigmatic
figures in the manuscripts, Jonas and Hethor, seem once to
have been such crewmen.) But here the translator is forced
against one of the most maddening of all his difficulties—
Severian's failure to distinguish clearly between space-going
and ocean-going craft.

Irritating though it is, it seems quite natural, given his
circumstances. If a distant continent is as remote as the
moon, then the moon is no more remote than a distant continent. Furthermore, the star-traveling ships appear to be pro-
pelled by light pressure on immense sails of metal foil, so
that an applied science of masts, cables, and spars is common
to ships of both kinds. Presumably, since many skills (and
perhaps most of all that of enduring long periods of isolation) would be required equally on both types of craft, crewmen from vessels that would only excite our contempt may
sign aboard others whose capabilities would astonish us. One
notes that the captain of Severian's lugger shares some of
Jonas's habits of speech.

And now, a final comment. In my translations and in these
appendixes I have attached to them, I have attempted to
eschew all speculations; it seems to me that now, near the
close of seven years' labor, I may be permitted one. It is that

the ability to traverse hours and aeons possessed by these ships may be no more than the natural consequence of their ability to penetrate interstellar and even intergalactic space, and to escape the death throes of the universe; and that to travel thus in time may not be so complex and difficult an affair as we are prone to suppose. It is possible that from the beginning Severian had some presentiment of his future.

G.W.

About the Author

GENE WOLFE was born in New York City and raised in Houston, Texas. He spent two and a half years at Texas A&M, then dropped out and was drafted. As a private in the Seventh Division during the Korean War, he was awarded the Combat Infantry Badge. The GI Bill permitted him to attend the University of Houston after the war, where he earned a degree in Mechanical Engineering. He is currently a senior editor on the staff of *Plant Engineering Magazine*.

Although he has written a "mainstream" novel, a young-adult novel, and many magazine articles, Wolfe is best known as a science-fiction writer, the author of over a hundred science-fiction short stories and of *The Fifth Head of Cerberus*. In 1973 his *The Death of Doctor Island* won the Nebula Award (given by the Science Fiction Writers of America) for the best science-fiction novella of the year. His novel *Peace* won the Chicago Foundation for Literature Award in 1977, and his "The Computer Iterates the Greater Trumps" has been awarded the Rhysling for science-fiction poetry.

The first volume of *The Book of the New Sun, The Shadow of the Torturer*, was nominated for the Nebula Award and has just received the award for Best Fantasy Novel of the Year from the World Fantasy Convention. Volume Two, *The Claw of the Conciliator*, has been nominated for the Nebula Award.

Mr. Wolfe lives with his wife and children in Barrington, Illinois. Although *The Citadel of the Autarch* completes this narrative of Severian's, Mr. Wolfe is at work on an independent book, *The Urth of the New Sun*, which further illuminates this future history.